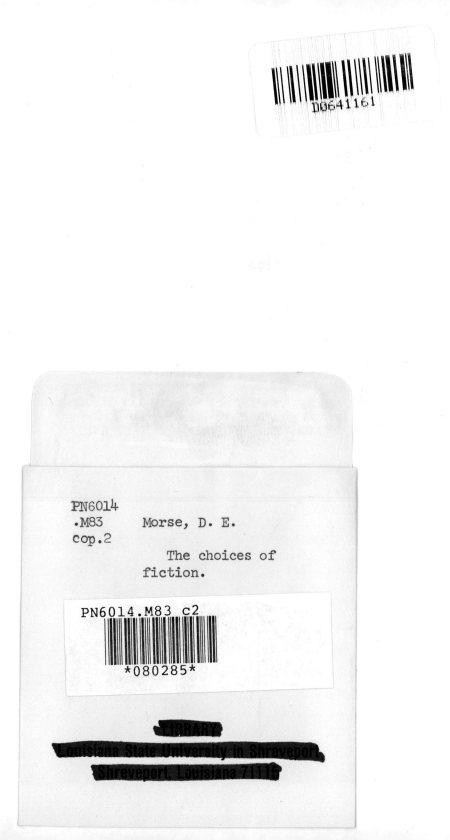

THE
CHOICES
OF FICTION

Donald E. Morse

Oakland University
Rochester, Michigan

Winthrop Publishers, Inc.
Cambridge, Massachusetts

Library of Congress Cataloging in Publication Data

Morse, Donald E   comp.
    The choices of fiction.

    1. Short stories. I. Title.
    PZ1.M8338Ch [PN6014]   808.83'1   73–13522
    ISBN 0–87626–126–8

*To Sean and Christopher
for sharing so many good stories*

Copyright © 1974 by Winthrop Publishers, Inc.
    17 Dunster Street, Cambridge, Massachusetts 02138

Contents

iii

Preface

The most important requirement for a reader of fiction is to be open to the new experience which a story offers. The writer faced with a blank piece of paper may choose to fill it with anything, but a reader confronting the printed page can only acknowledge what is there. A writer chooses his setting for a story; we react to that choice. A writer carefully selects his language; we listen to it until we are imaginatively drawn into the world he creates.

Besides recognizing the integrity of each story, a reader should also be aware of its unity. The introductions to the various sections of *The Choices of Fiction* emphasize this unity in fiction by presenting each facet, such as setting or point of view, using stories read previously from another perspective. The discussion of "Narrator, Point of View and Distance," for example, centers on stories encountered earlier in "Story, Plot and Character." Stories grouped under "Point of View" are then reexamined in "Setting," and so on through the book. Reading and rereading the stories from several angles enforces the idea that isolating an element for discussion is only an artificial means to a larger end. In medicine we dissect a corpse in order to understand the complete, living being; in literature we may examine a story's setting or analyze its language in order to enjoy more fully the complete tale. "Death of an Airman" by John Hawkes focuses on an unusual character and uses a special type of narrator; but the story also exploits the values in the setting, uses language economically but powerfully, and leaves us contemplating an intriguing theme. Hawkes' story cannot be identified with any one or two of its parts but must be read and experienced as a whole.

Another consideration underlying all of the introductory comments in *The Choices of Fiction* is the need for flexibility in organizing a textbook. This one may be read backwards, sideways or, more conveniently, forward. Readers who wish to build their knowledge of fiction piece by piece may begin with "Story, Plot and Character" and follow the text's outline. Those who would rather begin with the whole story, then proceed with its parts, may begin with "Artist, Theme and Story." Others may wish to organize their reading starting with the most important, complex element in fiction, "Point of View," while a few may prefer to skim all five introductions and then tackle the stories. Any of these approaches, or others of the readers' own devising, is valid as long as they recognize its artificiality.

The tales themselves range from the centuries-old "The Widow of Ephesus," "Cain and Abel" and "Tale of the Laughing Fish" to the recent "No Flies on Frank," "Upon the Sweeping Flood," and "Son in the Afternoon." There are folk and fairy tales, allegories, science fiction and satire, as well as realistic and symbolic, comic and pathetic stories. The collection begins and ends with comic tales of man's foibles and failings in "The Widow of Ephesus" and "Tale of the Laughing Fish." These, together with the other amusing stories, "The Background," "A Story," "The Drunkard," "Why I Live at the P.O." and "Final Request," should warn us against concluding that all fiction concentrates on the darkness, terror and pathos of what we sometimes pompously call "the human condition."

Included here are stories from the United States and Russia, especially from the nineteenth century when the modern short story came of age, and from Latin America, the source of many of the most original stories of the past hundred years. Also represented are Ireland by James Joyce, Tom Mac Intyre and Frank O'Connor; Italy by Giovanni Verga and Petronius; Great Britain by D. H. Lawrence, Aldous Huxley, Saki and Dylan Thomas; Austria by Franz Kafka; Poland by Isaac Bashevis Singer; and Armenia, by an anonymous storyteller. Included are the recognized modern American masters, Ernest Hemingway, Eudora Welty and William Faulkner and several of the best new writers of the past twenty-five years, Ralph Ellison, Tillie Olsen, John Hawkes, Joyce Carol Oates and John A. Williams. Many of the stories, such as "Final Request" by the amazingly productive Brazilian Machado de Assis, "Aura," "The Watchers" and "The She-Wolf," are rarely if ever anthologized, while others, such as "My Kinsman, Major Molineux" and "Bartleby, the Scrivener" may be quite familiar. All will be well worth reading and rereading.

Of the many people who directly or indirectly helped bring *The Choices of Fiction* into being, I would like to thank the students who constantly helped improve my reading of fiction; Marian Wilson, who typed the manuscript and whose several excellent suggestions are incorporated in it; Professor Robert Adolph of the Humanities Department, York University, Toronto, who discussed the early stages of the text and made invaluable suggestions for its improvement; Professor Robert W. Daniel, Kenyon College, who offered the kind of criticism of the early drafts which most writers dream of receiving but rarely experience; and my family, who often gave me the peace and occasion to think about fiction.

Acknowledgments

Machado de Assis, "Final Request," from *The Psychiatrist and Other Stories*. Originally published by the University of California Press; reprinted by permission of The Regents of the University of California.

Jorge Luis Borges, "Tlön, Uqbar, Orbis Tertius," from Jorge Luis Borges, *Labyrinths: Selected Stories & Other Writings*. Copyright © 1962 by New Directions Publishing Corporation. Reprinted by permission of New Directions Publishing Corporation.

Ray Bradbury, "There Will Come Soft Rains." Copyright 1950 by Ray Bradbury, reprinted by permission of the Harold Matson Company, Inc.

"Cain and Abel." From the Revised Standard Version of the Bible, copyrighted 1946 and 1952 by the Division of Christian Education of the National Council of the Churches of Christ in the U.S.A. and used by permission.

Willa Cather, "The Sculptor's Funeral," from *The Troll Garden* by Willa Cather, published by The New American Library, 1961.

Anton Chekhov, "A Trifling Occurrence," from *The Stories of Anton Tchekov*, edited by Robert N. Linscott. Copyright 1932 and renewed 1960 by The Modern Library, Inc. Reprinted by permission of Random House, Inc.

Fyodor Dostoevsky, "Akulka's Husband," from *The House of the Dead* by Fyodor Dostoevsky, translated by Constance Garnett. Reprinted with permission of the Macmillan Company and William Heinemann Ltd. Printed in Great Britain.

Ralph Ellison, "King of the Bingo Game." Reprinted by permission of William Morris Agency, Inc., on behalf of the author. Copyright 1944 by Ralph Ellison.

William Faulkner, "Wash." Copyright 1934 and renewed 1962 by William Faulkner. Reprinted from *The Collected Stories of William Faulkner* by permission of Random House, Inc.

E. M. Forster, excerpt from *Aspects of the Novel*. Published by Harcourt Brace Jovanovich, Inc., and Edward Arnold Ltd.

Carlos Fuentes, "Aura." Reprinted with the permission of Farrar, Straus & Giroux, Inc. Copyright © 1965 by Carlos Fuentes.

John Hawkes, "Death of an Airman," from *Lunar Landscapes* by John Hawkes. Copyright 1950 by John Hawkes. Reprinted with permission of New Directions Publishing Corporation.

Ernest Hemingway, "A Clean Well-Lighted Place." (Copyright 1933 Charles Scribner's Sons; renewal copyright © 1961 Ernest Hemingway) is reprinted by permission of Charles Scribner's Sons from *Winner Take Nothing* by Ernest Hemingway.

Aldous Huxley, "Nuns at Luncheon," from *Collected Short Stories* by Aldous Huxley. Copyright 1922, 1950 by Aldous Huxley. Reprinted by permission of Harper & Row, Publishers, Inc., and Chatto and Windus, Ltd.

Shirley Jackson, "After You, My Dear Alphonse." Reprinted with the permission of Farrar, Straus & Giroux, Inc. from *The Lottery* by Shirley Jackson, copyright 1943, 1949 by Shirley Jackson.

James Joyce, "Araby" from *Dubliners* by James Joyce. Originally published by B. W.

ONE
Story, Plot
and Character

The moment you grab somebody by the lapels and you've got something
to tell, that's a real story.
—Frank O'Connor

All stories have in common a sequence of events. Before there can be
a story to tell, something must happen. What happens may be as
significant as the creation of the earth or as trivial as losing a coin, as
unusual as the end of a war or as commonplace as birth and death. The
familiar rhyme "Solomon Grundy" contains a very simple story:

Solomon Grundy
Born on a Monday,
Christened on Tuesday,
Married on Wednesday,
Took ill on Thursday,
Worse on Friday,
Died on Saturday,
Buried on Sunday.
This is the end
Of Solomon Grundy.

Solomon Grundy is born, participates in religious and social ceremonies,
becomes ill, dies and is buried. The great events in his life pass as quickly
as a day in the week, and his life from beginning to end is as unremarkable
and brief as a week of the year. In the interest of simplicity the rhyme
neglects what readers often prize most in stories: *characterization,* which
is the stated or implied description of an actor and his role within the
story; and *plot,* which is the cause of events or the motivation of
character within the story.

Contrast this rhyme with the following, more complex nineteenth-century children's story which includes motivation and characterization in addition to the sequence of events. You've probably all heard or read a popular version of "The Three Bears," although only a few may know this sophisticated one which first appeared in Robert Southey's *The Doctor* (1848). Instead of the now-familiar yellow-haired Goldilocks, the original tale features a dirty-haired female intruder who trespasses upon the private property of those exemplars of virtue, trust and cleanliness, the three bears.

THE STORY OF THE THREE BEARS
Robert Southey

from The Doctor (*London, 1848*)

Once upon a time there were Three Bears, who lived together in a house of their own, in a wood. One of them was a Little, Small, Wee Bear; and one was a Middle-sized Bear, and the other was a Great, Huge Bear. They had each a pot for their porridge, a little pot for the Little, Small, Wee Bear; and a middle-sized pot for the Middle Bear; and a great pot for the Great, Huge Bear. And they had each a chair to sit in; a little chair for the Little, Small, Wee Bear; and a middle-sized chair for the Middle Bear; and a great chair for the Great, Huge Bear. And they had each a bed to sleep in; a little bed for the Little, Small, Wee Bear; and a middle-sized bed for the Middle Bear; and a great bed for the Great, Huge Bear.

One day, after they had made the porridge for their breakfast, and poured it into their porridge-pots, they walked out into the wood while their porridge was cooling, that they might not burn their mouths, by beginning too soon to eat it. And while they were walking, a little old Woman came to the house. She could not have been a good, honest old Woman; for first she looked in at that window, and then she peeped in at the keyhole; and seeing nobody in the house, she lifted the latch. The door was not fastened, because the Bears were good Bears, who did nobody any harm, and never suspected that any body would harm them. So the little old Woman opened the door, and went in; and well pleased she was when she saw the porridge on the table. If she had been a good little old Woman, she would have waited till the Bears came home, and then, perhaps, they would have asked her to breakfast; for they were good Bears,—a little rough or so, as the manner of Bears is, but for all that very good natured and hospitable. But she was an impudent, bad old Woman, and set about helping herself.

So first she tasted the porridge of the Great, Huge Bear, and that was too hot for her; and she said a bad word about that. And then she tasted the porridge of the Middle Bear, and that was too cold for her; and she said a bad word about that, too. And then she went to the porridge of the Little, Small, Wee Bear, and tasted that; and that was neither too hot, nor too cold, but just right; and she liked it so well, that she ate it all up: but the naughty old Woman said a bad word about the little porridge-pot, because it did not hold enough for her.

Then the little old Woman sat down in the chair of the Great, Huge Bear, and that was too hard for her. And then she sat down in the chair of the Middle Bear, and that was too soft for her. And then she sat down in the chair of the Little, Small, Wee Bear, and that was neither too hard, nor too soft, but just right. So she seated herself in it, and there she sat till the bottom of the chair came out, and down came hers, plump upon the ground. And the naughty old Woman said a wicked word about that too.

Then the little old Woman went up stairs into the bed-chamber in which the Three Bears slept. And first she lay down upon the bed of the Great, Huge Bear; but that was too high at the head for her. And she next lay down upon the bed of the Middle Bear; and that was too high at the foot for her. And then she lay down upon the bed of the Little, Small, Wee Bear; and that was neither too high at the head, nor at the foot, but just right. So she covered herself up comfortably, and lay there till she fell fast asleep.

By this time the Three Bears thought their porridge would be cool enough; so they came home to breakfast. Now the little old Woman had left the spoon of the Great, Huge Bear standing in his porridge.

"SOMEBODY HAS BEEN AT MY PORRIDGE!"

said the Great, Huge Bear, in his great, rough, gruff voice. And when the Middle Bear looked at his, he saw that the spoon was standing in it too. They were wooden spoons; if they had been silver ones, the naughty old Woman would have put them in her pocket.

"Somebody has been at my porridge!"

said the Middle Bear, in his middle voice.

Then the Little, Small, Wee Bear looked at his, and there was the spoon in the porridge-pot, but the porridge was all gone.

"Somebody has been at my porridge, and has eaten it all up!"

said the Little, Small, Wee Bear, in his little, small, wee voice.

Upon this the Three Bears, seeing that someone had entered their house, and eaten up the Little, Small, Wee Bear's breakfast, began to look about them. Now the little old Woman had not put the hard cushion straight when she rose from the chair of the Great, Huge Bear.

"SOMEBODY HAS BEEN SITTING IN MY CHAIR!"

said the Great, Huge Bear, in his great, rough, gruff voice.

And the little old Woman had squatted down the soft cushion of the Middle Bear.

"Somebody has been sitting in my chair!"

said the Middle Bear, in his middle voice.

And you know what the little old Woman had done to the third chair. "Somebody has been sitting in my chair, and has sat the bottom of it out!" said the Little, Small, Wee Bear, in his little, small, wee voice.

Then the Three Bears thought it necessary that they should make farther search; so they went up stairs into their bed-chamber. Now the little old Woman had pulled the pillow of the Great, Huge Bear out of its place.

"SOMEBODY HAS BEEN LYING IN MY BED!" said the Great, Huge Bear, in his great, rough, gruff voice.

And the little old Woman had pulled the bolster of the Middle Bear out of its place.

"Somebody has been lying in my bed!" said the Middle Bear, in his middle voice.

And when the Little, Small, Wee Bear came to look at his bed, there was the bolster in its place; and the pillow in its place upon the bolster; and upon the pillow was the little old Woman's ugly, dirty head,—which was not in its place, for she had no business there.

"Somebody has been lying in my bed,—and here she is!" said the Little, Small, Wee Bear, in his little, small, wee voice.

The little old Woman had heard in her sleep the great, rough, gruff voice of the Great, Huge Bear; but she was so fast asleep that it was no more to her than the roaring of wind, or the rumbling of thunder. And she had heard the middle voice of the Middle Bear, but it was only as if she had heard someone speaking in a dream. But when she heard the little, small, wee voice of the Little, Small, Wee Bear, it was so sharp, and so shrill, that it awakened her at once. Up she started; and when she saw the Three Bears on one side of the bed, she tumbled herself out at the other, and ran to the window. Now the window was open, because the Bears, like good, tidy Bears, as they were, always opened their bed-chamber window when they got up in the morning. Out the little old Woman jumped; and whether she broke her neck in the fall; or ran into the wood and was lost there; or found her way out of the wood, and was taken up by the constable and sent to the House of Correction for a vagrant as she was, I cannot tell. But the Three Bears never saw anything more of her.

Part of the fun in reading "The Three Bears" comes from encountering unexpected characters and events. The woman is not the innocent victim who goes for a Sunday stroll and becomes lost in the woods, but is an "impudent," "bad old Woman" guilty of breaking and entering. The bears are not vicious, aggressive marauders who raid larders and destroy furniture but are "good Bears—a little rough or so as the manner of Bears is, but for all that very good natured and hospitable."

As in most fables and fairy tales the characters lack depth of feeling or thought, have no real personality and fail to convince us they are genuine. The woman has only one side to her character, and it is pure ugliness. The bears, who lead virtuous lives, also remain static. The plot is equally uncomplicated: events occur and characters act because of what is obvious. For example, when the bears return from their walk and see the empty bowl and broken chair they reason together in a comically cumbersome, bear-like way until they reach the conclusion that someone must have broken into their house. They want to discover who, so they agree to "make farther search." In Southey's tale the sequence of events, character and plot are all equally important and equally simple.

An author may choose to place more or less emphasis on events, plot or character, depending upon the nature of the tale he tells. A story which concentrates on character will certainly be different from one which dwells on plot or action. In the stories which follow, "The Widow of Ephesus" subordinates character and motivation to event, whereas in "The She-Wolf" what happens may be crucial, but characterization is primary. The story line in "Cain and Abel" is spare, the characterization minimal—all attention focuses on the complexities of motivation. Some of the possible range for story, plot and character may be discovered in reading "The Drunkard," "Death of an Airman," and "After You, My Dear Alphonse." After examining these tales we will go on to consider one of storytelling's primary techniques, point of view, for there is clearly far more to short stories than a sequence of events, characterization and motivation—as fundamental and important as these are.

I borrowed the distinction between story and plot from E. M. Forster, who says in *Aspects of the Novel* (New York, 1927): "...a story [is]...a narrative of events arranged in their time-sequence. A plot is also a narrative of events, the emphasis falling on causality. 'The king died and the queen died' is a story. 'The king died, and the queen died of grief' is a plot. The time-sequence is preserved, but the sense of causality overshadows it" (p. 86).

THE WIDOW OF EPHESUS

Petronius

translated by william arrowsmith

Once upon a time there was a certain married woman in the city of
Ephesus whose fidelity to her husband was so famous that the women from
all the neighboring towns and villages used to troop into Ephesus merely
to stare at this prodigy. It happened, however, that her husband one day
died. Finding the normal custom of following the cortege with hair un-
bound and beating her breast in public quite inadequate to express her
grief, the lady insisted on following the corpse right into the tomb, an
underground vault of the Greek type, and there set herself to guard the
body, weeping and wailing night and day. Although in her extremes of
grief she was clearly courting death from starvation, her parents were
utterly unable to persuade her to leave, and even the magistrates, after
one last supreme attempt, were rebuffed and driven away. In short, all
Ephesus had gone into mourning for this extraordinary woman, all the
more since the lady was now passing her fifth consecutive day without
once tasting food. Beside the failing woman sat her devoted maid, sharing
her mistress' grief and relighting the lamp whenever it flickered out. The
whole city could speak, in fact, of nothing else: here at last, all classes
alike agreed, was the one true example of conjugal fidelity and love.

In the meantime, however, the governor of the province gave orders
that several thieves should be crucified in a spot close by the vault where
the lady was mourning her dead husband's corpse. So, on the following
night, the soldier who had been assigned to keep watch on the crosses so
that nobody could remove the thieves' bodies for burial suddenly noticed a
light blazing among the tombs and heard the sounds of groaning. And
prompted by a natural human curiosity to know who or what was making·
those sounds, he descended into the vault.

But at the sight of a strikingly beautiful woman, he stopped short in
terror, thinking he must be seeing some ghostly apparition out of hell.
Then, observing the corpse and seeing the tears on the lady's face and the
scratches her fingernails had gashed in her cheeks, he realized what it was:

a widow, in inconsolable grief. Promptly fetching his little supper back down to the tomb, he implored the lady not to persist in her sorrow or break her heart with useless mourning. All men alike, he reminded her, have the same end; the same resting place awaits us all. He used, in short, all those platitudes we use to comfort the suffering and bring them back to life. His consolations, being unwelcome, only exasperated the widow more; more violently than ever she beat her breast, and tearing out her hair by the roots, scattered it over the dead man's body. Undismayed, the soldier repeated his arguments and pressed her to take some food, until the little maid, quite overcome by the smell of the wine, succumbed and stretched out her hand to her tempter. Then, restored by the food and wine, she began herself to assail her mistress' obstinate refusal.

"How will it help you," she asked the lady, "if you faint from hunger? Why should you bury yourself alive, and go down to death before the Fates have called you? What does Vergil say?—

Do you suppose the shades and ashes of the dead are by such sorrow touched?

No, begin your life afresh. Shake off these woman's scruples; enjoy the light while you can. Look at that corpse of your poor husband: doesn't it tell you more eloquently than any words that you should live?"

None of us, of course, really dislikes being told that we must eat, that life is to be lived. And the lady was no exception. Weakened by her long days of fasting, her resistance crumbled at last, and she ate the food the soldier offered her as hungrily as the little maid had eaten earlier.

Well, you know what temptations are normally aroused in a man on a full stomach. So the soldier, mustering all those blandishments by means of which he had persuaded the lady to live, now laid determined siege to her virtue. And chaste though she was, the lady found him singularly attractive and his arguments persuasive. As for the maid, she did all she could to help the soldier's cause, repeating like a refrain the appropriate line of Vergil:

If love is pleasing, lady, yield yourself to love.

To make the matter short, the lady's body soon gave up the struggle; she yielded and our happy warrior enjoyed a total triumph on both counts. That very night their marriage was consummated, and they slept together the second and the third night too, carefully shutting the door of the tomb so that any passing friend or stranger would have thought the lady of famous chastity had at last expired over her dead husband's body.

As you can perhaps imagine, our soldier was a very happy man, utterly delighted with his lady's ample beauty and that special charm that a secret love confers. Every night, as soon as the sun had set, he bought what few provisions his slender pay permitted and smuggled them down to the tomb. One night, however, the parents of one of the crucified thieves, noticing that the watch was being badly kept, took advantage of our hero's absence to remove their son's body and bury it. The next morning, of course, the soldier was horror-struck to discover one of the bodies missing from its cross, and ran to tell his mistress of the horrible punishment which awaited him for neglecting his duty. In the circumstances, he told her, he would not wait to be tried and sentenced, but would punish himself then and there with his own sword. All he asked of her was that she make room for another corpse and allow the same gloomy tomb to enclose husband and lover together.

Our lady's heart, however, was no less tender than pure. "God forbid," she cried, "that I should have to see at one and the same time the dead bodies of the only two men I have ever loved. No, better far, I say, to hang the dead than kill the living." With these words, she gave orders that her husband's body should be taken from its bier and strung up on the empty cross. The soldier followed this good advice, and the next morning the whole city wondered by what miracle the dead man had climbed up on the cross.

THE SHE-WOLF
Giovanni Verga

translated by giovanni cecchetti

She was tall, thin; she had the firm and vigorous breasts of the olive-skinned—and yet she was no longer young; she was pale, as if always plagued by malaria, and in that pallor, two enormous eyes, and fresh red lips which devoured you.

In the village they called her the She-wolf, because she never had enough—of anything. The women made the sign of the cross when they saw her pass, alone as a wild bitch, prowling about suspiciously like a famished wolf; with her red lips she sucked the blood of their sons and husbands in a flash, and pulled them behind her skirt with a single glance of those devilish eyes, even if they were before the altar of Saint Agrippina. Fortunately, the She-wolf never went to church, not at Easter, not at Christmas, not to hear Mass, not for confession. —Father Angiolino of Saint Mary of Jesus, a true servant of God, had lost his soul on account of her.

Maricchia, a good girl, poor thing, cried in secret because she was the She-wolf's daughter, and no one would marry her, though, like every other girl in the village, she had her fine linen in a chest and her good land under the sun.

One day the She-wolf fell in love with a handsome young man who had just returned from the service and was mowing hay with her in the fields of the notary; and she fell in love in the strongest sense of the word, feeling the flesh afire beneath her clothes; and staring him in the eyes, she suffered the thirst one has in the hot hours of June, deep in the plain. But he went on mowing undisturbed, his nose bent over the swaths.

"What's wrong, Pina?" he would ask.

In the immense fields, where you heard only the crackling flight of the grasshoppers, as the sun hammered down overhead, the She-wolf gathered bundle after bundle, and sheaf after sheaf, never tiring, never straightening up for an instant, never raising the flask to her lips, just to remain at the heels of Nanni, who mowed and mowed and asked from time to time:

9

"What is it you want, Pina?"

One evening she told him, while the men were dozing on the threshing floor, tired after the long day, and the dogs were howling in the vast, dark countryside.

"It's you I want. You who're beautiful as the sun and sweet as honey. I want you!"

"And I want your daughter, instead, who's a maid," answered Nanni laughing.

The She-wolf thrust her hands into her hair, scratching her temples, without saying a word, and walked away. And she did not appear at the threshing floor any more. But she saw Nanni again in October, when they were making olive oil, for he was working near her house, and the creaking of the press kept her awake all night.

"Get the sack of olives," she said to her daughter, "and come with me."

Nanni was pushing olives under the millstone with a shovel, shouting "Ohee" to the mule, to keep it from stopping.

"You want my daughter Maricchia?" Pina asked him.

"What'll you give your daughter Maricchia?" answered Nanni.

"She has all her father's things, and I'll give her my house too; as for me, all I need is a little corner in the kitchen, enough for a straw mattress."

"If that's the way it is, we can talk about it at Christmas," said Nanni.

Nanni was all greasy and filthy, spattered with oil and fermented olives, and Maricchia didn't want him at any price. But her mother grabbed her by the hair before the fireplace, muttering between her teeth:

"If you don't take him, I'll kill you!"

The She-wolf was almost sick, and the people were saying that when the devil gets old he becomes a hermit. She no longer roamed here and there, no longer lingered at the doorway, with those bewitched eyes. Whenever she fixed them on his face, those eyes of hers, her son-in-law began to laugh and pulled out the scapular of the Virgin to cross himself. Maricchia stayed at home nursing the babies, and her mother went into the fields to work with the men, and just like a man too, weeding, hoeing, feeding the animals, pruning the vines, despite the northeast and levantine winds of January or the August sirocco, when the mules' heads drooped and the men slept face down along the wall, on the north side. "In those hours between nones and vespers when no good woman goes roving around,"* Pina was the only living soul to be seen wandering in the countryside, over the burning stones of the paths, through the scorched

* An old Sicilian proverb, which refers to the hours of the early afternoon, when the Sicilian countryside lies motionless under a scorching sun and no person would dare walk on the roads. Those hours are traditionally believed to be under the spell of malignant spirits. [Translator's note]

stubble of the immense fields that became lost in the suffocating heat, far, far away toward the foggy Etna, where the sky was heavy on the horizon.

"Wake up!" said the She-wolf to Nanni, who was sleeping in the ditch, along the dusty hedge, his head on his arms. "Wake up. I've brought you some wine to cool your throat."

Nanni opened his drowsy eyes wide, still half asleep, and finding her standing before him, pale, with her arrogant breasts and her coal-black eyes, he stretched out his hands gropingly.

"No! no good woman goes roving around in the hours between nones and vespers!" sobbed Nanni, throwing his face back into the dry grass of the ditch, deep, deep, his nails in his scalp. "Go away! go away! don't come to the threshing floor again!"

The She-wolf was going away, in fact, retying her superb tresses, her gaze bent fixedly before her as she moved through the hot stubble, her eyes as black as coal.

But she came to the threshing floor again, and more than once, and Nanni did not complain. On the contrary, when she was late, in the hours between nones and vespers, he would go and wait for her at the top of the white, deserted path, with his forehead bathed in sweat; and he would thrust his hands into his hair, and repeat every time:

"Go away! go away! don't come to the threshing floor again!"

Maricchia cried night and day, and glared at her mother, her eyes burning with tears and jealousy, like a young she-wolf herself, every time she saw her come, mute and pale, from the fields.

"Vile, vile mother!" she said to her. "Vile mother!"

"Shut up!"

"Thief! Thief!"

"Shut up!"

"I'll go to the Sergeant, I will!"

"Go ahead!"

And she really did go, with her babies in her arms, fearing nothing, and without shedding a tear, like a madwoman, because now she too loved that husband who had been forced on her, greasy and filthy, spattered with oil and fermented olives.

The Sergeant sent for Nanni; he threatened him even with jail and the gallows. Nanni began to sob and tear his hair; he didn't deny anything, he didn't try to clear himself.

"It's the temptation!" he said. "It's the temptation of hell!"

He threw himself at the Sergeant's feet begging to be sent to jail.

"For God's sake, Sergeant, take me out of this hell! Have me killed, put me in jail; don't let me see her again, never! never!"

"No!" answered the She-wolf instead, to the Sergeant. "I kept a little corner in the kitchen to sleep in, when I gave him my house as dowry. It's my house. I don't intend to leave it."

Shortly afterward, Nanni was kicked in the chest by a mule and was at the point of death, but the priest refused to bring him the Sacrament if the She-wolf did not go out of the house. The She-wolf left, and then her son-in-law could also prepare to leave like a good Christian; he confessed and received communion with such signs of repentance and contrition that all the neighbors and the curious wept before the dying man's bed. —And it would have been better for him to die that day, before the devil came back to tempt him again and creep into his body and soul, when he got well.

"Leave me alone!" he told the She-wolf. "For God's sake, leave me in peace! I've seen death with my own eyes! Poor Maricchia is desperate. Now the whole town knows about it! If I don't see you it's better for both of us..."

And he would have liked to gouge his eyes out not to see those of the She-wolf, for whenever they peered into his, they made him lose his body and soul. He did not know what to do to free himself from the spell. He paid for Masses for the souls in purgatory and asked the priest and the Sergeant for help. At Easter he went to confession, and in penance he publicly licked more than four feet of pavement, crawling on the pebbles in front of the church—and then, as the She-wolf came to tempt him again:

"Listen!" he said to her. "Don't come to the threshing floor again; if you do, I swear to God, I'll kill you!"

"Kill me," answered the She-wolf, "I don't care; I can't stand it without you."

As he saw her from the distance, in the green wheat fields, Nanni stopped hoeing the vineyard, and went to pull the ax from the elm. The She-wolf saw him come, pale and wild-eyed, with the ax glistening in the sun, but she did not fall back a single step, did not lower her eyes; she continued toward him, her hands laden with red poppies, her black eyes devouring him.

"Ah! damn your soul!" stammered Nanni.

CAIN AND ABEL

Now Adam knew Eve his wife, and she conceived and bore Cain, saying, "I have gotten a man with the help of the Lord." And again, she bore his brother Abel. Now Abel was a keeper of sheep, and Cain a tiller of the ground. In the course of time Cain brought to the Lord an offering of the fruit of the ground, and Abel brought of the firstlings of his flock and of their fat portions. And the Lord had regard for Abel and his offering, but for Cain and his offering he had no regard. So Cain was very angry, and his countenance fell. The Lord said to Cain, "Why are you angry, and why has your countenance fallen? If you do well, will you not be accepted? And if you do not do well, sin is couching at the door; its desire is for you, but you must master it."

Cain said to Abel his brother, "Let us go out to the field." And when they were in the field, Cain rose up against his brother Abel, and killed him. Then the Lord said to Cain, "Where is Abel your brother?" He said, "I do not know; am I my brother's keeper?" And the Lord said, "What have you done? The voice of your brother's blood is crying to me from the ground. And now you are cursed from the ground, which has opened its mouth to receive your brother's blood from your hand. When you till the ground, it shall no longer yield to you its strength; you shall be a fugitive and a wanderer on the earth." Cain said to the Lord, "My punishment is greater than I can bear. Behold, thou hast driven me this day away from the ground; and from thy face I shall be hidden; and I shall be a fugitive and a wanderer on the earth, and whoever finds me will slay me." Then the Lord said to him, "Not so! If any one slays Cain, vengeance shall be taken on him sevenfold." And the Lord put a mark on Cain, lest any who came upon him should kill him. Then Cain went away from the presence of the Lord, and dwelt in the land of Nod, east of Eden.

Nod: a Hebrew word meaning "wandering," which clearly implies that Cain became a nomad after being expelled from Eden.

THE DRUNKARD
Frank O'Connor

It was a terrible blow to Father when Mr. Dooley on the terrace died.
Mr. Dooley was a commercial traveller with two sons in the Dominicans
and a car of his own, so socially he was miles ahead of us, but he had no
false pride. Mr. Dooley was an intellectual, and, like all intellectuals the
thing he loved best was conversation, and in his own limited way Father
was a well-read man and could appreciate an intelligent talker. Mr. Dooley
was remarkably intelligent. Between business acquaintances and clerical
contacts, there was very little he didn't know about what went on in town,
and evening after evening he crossed the road to our gate to explain to
Father the news behind the news. He had a low, palavering voice and a
knowing smile, and Father would listen in astonishment, giving him a
conversational lead now and again, and then stump triumphantly in to
Mother with his face aglow and ask: "Do you know what Mr. Dooley
is after telling me?" Ever since, when somebody has given me some bit of
information off the record I have found myself on the point of asking:
"Was it Mr. Dooley told you that?"

Till I actually saw him laid out in his brown shroud with the rosary
beads entwined between his waxy fingers I did not take the report of his
death seriously. Even then I felt there must be a catch and that some
summer evening Mr. Dooley must reappear at our gate to give us the
lowdown on the next world. But Father was very upset, partly because
Mr. Dooley was about one age with himself, a thing that always gives a
distinctly personal turn to another man's demise; partly because now he
would have no one to tell him what dirty work was behind the latest scene
at the Corporation. You could count on your fingers the number of men
in Blarney Lane who read the papers as Mr. Dooley did, and none of these
would have overlooked the fact that Father was only a labouring man.
Even Sullivan, the carpenter, a mere nobody, thought he was a cut above
Father. It was certainly a solemn event.

"Half past two to the Curragh," Father said meditatively, putting down
the paper.

"But you're not thinking of going to the funeral?" Mother asked in alarm.

" 'Twould be expected," Father said, scenting opposition. "I wouldn't give it to say to them."

"I think," said Mother with suppressed emotion, "it will be as much as anyone will expect if you go to the chapel with him."

("Going to the chapel," of course, was one thing, because the body was removed after work, but going to a funeral meant the loss of a half-day's pay.)

"The people hardly know us," she added.

"God between us and all harm," Father replied with dignity, "we'd be glad if it was our own turn."

To give Father his due, he was always ready to lose a half day for the sake of an old neighbour. It wasn't so much that he liked funerals as that he was a conscientious man who did as he would be done by; and nothing could have consoled him so much for the prospect of his own death as the assurance of a worthy funeral. And, to give Mother her due, it wasn't the half-day's pay she begrudged, badly as we could afford it.

Drink, you see, was Father's great weakness. He could keep steady for months, even for years, at a stretch, and while he did he was as good as gold. He was first up in the morning and brought the mother a cup of tea in bed, stayed at home in the evenings and read the paper; saved money and bought himself a new blue serge suit and bowler hat. He laughed at the folly of men who, week in week out, left their hard-earned money with the publicans; and sometimes, to pass an idle hour, he took pencil and paper and calculated precisely how much he saved each week through being a teetotaller. Being a natural optimist he sometimes continued this calculation through the whole span of his prospective existence and the total was breathtaking. He would die worth hundreds.

If I had only known it, this was a bad sign; a sign he was becoming stuffed up with spiritual pride and imagining himself better than his neighbours. Sooner or later, the spiritual pride grew till it called for some form of celebration. Then he took a drink—not whisky, of course; nothing like that—just a glass of some harmless drink like lager beer. That was the end of Father. By the time he had taken the first he already realized that he had made a fool of himself, took a second to forget it and a third to forget that he couldn't forget, and at last came home reeling drunk. From this on it was "The Drunkard's Progress," as in the moral prints. Next day he stayed in from work with a sick head while Mother went off to make his excuses at the works, and inside a fortnight he was poor and savage and despondent again. Once he began he drank steadily through everything down to the kitchen clock. Mother and I knew all the phases and dreaded all the dangers. Funerals were one.

"I have to go to Dunphy's to do a half-day's work," said Mother in distress. "Who's to look after Larry?"

"I'll look after Larry," Father said graciously. "The little walk will do him good."

There was no more to be said, though we all knew I didn't need anyone to look after me, and that I could quite well have stayed at home and looked after Sonny, but I was being attached to the party to act as a brake on Father. As a brake I had never achieved anything, but Mother still had great faith in me.

Next day, when I got home from school, Father was there before me and made a cup of tea for both of us. He was very good at tea, but too heavy in the hand for anything else; the way he cut bread was shocking. Afterwards, we went down the hill to the church, Father wearing his best blue serge and a bowler cocked to one side of his head with the least suggestion of the masher. To his great joy he discovered Peter Crowley among the mourners. Peter was another danger signal, as I knew well from certain experiences after Mass on Sunday morning: a mean man, as Mother said, who only went to funerals for the free drinks he could get at them. It turned out that he hadn't even known Mr. Dooley! But Father had a sort of contemptuous regard for him as one of the foolish people who wasted their good money in public-houses when they could be saving it. Very little of his own money Peter Crowley wasted!

It was an excellent funeral from Father's point of view. He had it all well studied before we set off after the hearse in the afternoon sunlight.

"Five carriages!" he exclaimed. "Five carriages and sixteen covered cars!" There's one alderman, two councillors and 'tis unknown how many priests. I didn't see a funeral like this from the road since Willie Mack, the publican, died.

"Ah, he was well liked," said Crowley in his husky voice.

"My goodness, don't I know that?" snapped Father. "Wasn't the man my best friend? Two nights before he died—only two nights—he was over telling me the goings-on about the housing contract. Them fellows in the Corporation are night and day robbers. But even I never imagined he was as well connected as that."

Father was stepping out like a boy, pleased with everything: the other mourners, and the fine houses along Sunday's Well. I knew the danger signals were there in full force: a sunny day, a fine funeral, and a distinguished company of clerics and public men were bringing out all the natural vanity and flightiness of Father's character. It was with something like genuine pleasure that he saw his old friend lowered into the grave; with the sense of having performed a duty and the pleasant awareness that however much he would miss poor Mr. Dooley in the long summer evenings, it was he and not poor Mr. Dooley who would do the missing.

"We'll be making tracks before they break up," he whispered to Crowley as the gravediggers tossed in the first shovelfuls of clay, and away he went, hopping like a goat from grassy hump to hump. The drivers, who were probably in the same state as himself, though without months of abstinence to put an edge on it, looked up hopefully.

"Are they nearly finished, Mick?" bawled one.

"All over now bar the last prayers," trumpeted Father in the tone of one who brings news of great rejoicing.

The carriages passed us in a lather of dust several hundred yards from the public-house, and Father, whose feet gave him trouble in hot weather, quickened his pace, looking nervously over his shoulder for any sign of the main body of mourners crossing the hill. In a crowd like that a man might be kept waiting.

When we did reach the pub the carriages were drawn up outside, and solemn men in black ties were cautiously bringing out consolation to mysterious females whose hands reached out modestly from behind the drawn blinds of the coaches. Inside the pub there were only the drivers and a couple of shawly women. I felt if I was to act as a brake at all, this was the time, so I pulled Father by the coattails.

"Dadda, can't we go home now?" I asked.

"Two minutes now," he said, beaming affectionately. "Just a bottle of lemonade and we'll go home."

This was a bribe, and I knew it, but I was always a child of weak character. Father ordered lemonade and two pints. I was thirsty and swallowed my drink at once. But that wasn't Father's way. He had long months of abstinence behind him and an eternity of pleasure before. He took out his pipe, blew through it, filled it, and then lit it with loud pops, his eyes bulging above it. After that he deliberately turned his back on the pint, leaned one elbow on the counter in the attitude of a man who did not know there was a pint behind him, and deliberately brushed the tobacco from his palms. He had settled down for the evening. He was steadily working through all the important funerals he had ever attended. The carriages departed and the minor mourners drifted in till the pub was half full.

"Dadda," I said, pulling his coat again, "can't we go home now?"

"Ah, your mother won't be in for a long time yet," he said benevolently enough. "Run out in the road and play, can't you?"

It struck me as very cool, the way grown-ups assumed that you could play all by yourself on a strange road. I began to get bored as I had so often been bored before. I knew Father was quite capable of lingering there till nightfall. I knew I might have to bring him home, blind drunk, down Blarney Lane, with all the old women at their doors, saying: "Mick Delaney is on it again." I knew that my mother would be half crazy with anxiety; that next day Father wouldn't go out to work; and before the end of the week she would be running down to the pawn with the clock under her shawl. I could never get over the lonesomeness of the kitchen without a clock.

I was still thirsty. I found if I stood on tiptoe I could just reach Father's glass, and the idea occurred to me that it would be interesting to know what the contents were like. He had his back to it and wouldn't notice. I took down the glass and sipped cautiously. It was a terrible disappointment. I was astonished that he could even drink such stuff. It looked as if he had never tried lemonade.

I should have advised him about lemonade but he was holding forth himself in great style. I heard him say that bands were a great addition to a funeral. He put his arms in the position of someone holding a rifle in reverse and hummed a few bars of Chopin's Funeral March. Crowley nodded reverently. I took a longer drink and began to see that porter might have its advantages. I felt pleasantly elevated and philosophic. Father hummed a few bars of the Dead March in *Saul*. It was a nice pub and a very fine funeral, and I felt sure that poor Mr. Dooley in Heaven must be highly gratified. At the same time I thought they might have given him a band. As Father said, bands were a great addition.

But the wonderful thing about porter was the way it made you stand aside, or rather float aloft like a cherub rolling on a cloud, and watch yourself with your legs crossed, leaning against a bar counter, not worrying about trifles but thinking deep, serious, grown-up thoughts about life and death. Looking at yourself like that, you couldn't help thinking after a while how funny you looked, and suddenly you got embarrassed and wanted to giggle. But by the time I had finished the pint, that phase too had passed; I found it hard to put back the glass, the counter seemed to have grown so high. Melancholia was supervening again.

"Well," Father said reverently, reaching behind him for his drink, "God rest the poor man's soul, wherever he is!" He stopped, looked first at the glass, and then at the people round him. "Hello," he said in a fairly good-humoured tone, as if he were just prepared to consider it a joke, even if it was in bad taste, "who was at this?"

There was silence for a moment while the publican and the old women looked first at Father and then at his glass.

"There was no one at it, my good man," one of the women said with an offended air. "Is it robbers you think we are?"

"Ah, there's no one here would do a thing like that, Mick," said the publican in a shocked tone.

"Well, someone did it," said Father, his smile beginning to wear off.

"If they did, they were them that were nearer it," said the woman darkly, giving me a dirty look; and at the same moment the truth began to dawn on Father. I suppose I must have looked a bit starry-eyed. He bent and shook me.

"Are you all right, Larry?" he asked in alarm.

Peter Crowley looked down at me and grinned.

"Could you beat that?" he exclaimed in a husky voice.

I could, and without difficulty. I started to get sick. Father jumped back in holy terror that I might spoil his good suit, and hastily opened the back door.

"Run! run! run!" he shouted.

I saw the sunlit wall outside with the ivy overhanging it, and ran. The intention was good but the performance was exaggerated, because I lurched right into the wall, hurting it badly, as it seemed to me. Being always very polite, I said "Pardon" before the second bout came on me. Father, still concerned for his suit, came up behind and cautiously held me while I got sick.

"That's a good boy!" he said encouragingly. "You'll be grand when you get that up."

Begor, I was not grand! Grand was the last thing I was. I gave one unmerciful wail out of me as he steered me back to the pub and put me sitting on the bench near the shawlies. They drew themselves up with an offended air, still sore at the suggestion that they had drunk his pint.

"God help us!" moaned one, looking pityingly at me, "isn't it the likes of them would be fathers?"

"Mick," said the publican in alarm, spraying sawdust on my tracks, "that child isn't supposed to be in here at all. You'd better take him home quick in case a bobby would see him."

"Merciful God!" whimpered Father, raising his eyes to heaven and clapping his hands silently as he only did when distraught, "what misfortune was on me? Or what will his mother say?...If women might stop at home and look after their children themselves!" he added in a snarl for the benefit of the shawlies. "Are them carriages all gone, Bill?"

"The carriages are finished long ago, Mick," replied the publican.

"I'll take him home," Father said despairingly.... "I'll never bring you out again," he threatened me. "Here," he added, giving me the clean handkerchief from his breast pocket, "put that over your eye."

The blood on the handkerchief was the first indication I got that I was cut, and instantly my temple began to throb and I set up another howl.

"Whisht, whisht, whisht!" Father said testily, steering me out the door. "One'd think you were killed. That's nothing. We'll wash it when we get home."

"Steady now, old scout!" Crowley said, taking the other side of me. "You'll be all right in a minute."

I never met two men who knew less about the effects of drink. The first breath of fresh air and the warmth of the sun made me groggier than ever and I pitched and rolled between wind and tide till Father started to whimper again.

"God Almighty, and the whole road out! What misfortune was on me didn't stop at my work! Can't you walk straight?"

I couldn't. I saw plain enough that, coaxed by the sunlight, every woman old and young in Blarney Lane was leaning over her half-door or sitting on her doorstep. They all stopped gabbling to gape at the strange spectacle of two sober, middle-aged men bringing home a drunken small boy with a cut over his eye. Father, torn between the shamefast desire to get me home as quick as he could, and the neighbourly need to explain that it wasn't his fault, finally halted outside Mrs. Roche's. There was a gang of old women outside a door at the opposite side of the road. I didn't like the look of them from the first. They seemed altogether too interested in me. I leaned against the wall of Mrs. Roche's cottage with my hands in my trousers pockets, thinking mournfully of poor Mr. Dooley in his cold grave on the Curragh, who would never walk down the road again, and, with great feeling, I began to sing a favourite song of Father's.

> Though lost to Mononia and cold in the grave
> He returns to Kincora no more.

"Wisha, the poor child!" Mrs. Roche said. "Haven't he a lovely voice, God bless him!"

That was what I thought myself, so I was the more surprised when Father said "Whisht!" and raised a threatening finger at me. He didn't seem to realize the appropriateness of the song, so I sang louder than ever.

"Whisht, I tell you!" he snapped, and then tried to work up a smile for Mrs. Roche's benefit. "We're nearly home now. I'll carry you the rest of the way."

But, drunk and all as I was, I knew better than to be carried home ignominiously like that.

"Now," I said severely, "can't you leave me alone? I can walk all right. 'Tis only my head. All I want is a rest."

"But you can rest at home in bed," he said viciously, trying to pick me up, and I knew by the flush on his face that he was very vexed.

"Ah, Jasus," I said crossly, "what do I want to go home for? Why the hell can't you leave me alone?"

For some reason the gang of old women at the other side of the road thought this very funny. They nearly split their sides over it. A gassy fury began to expand in me at the thought that a fellow couldn't have a drop taken without the whole neighbourhood coming out to make game of him.

"Who are ye laughing at?" I shouted, clenching my fists at them. "I'll make ye laugh at the other side of yeer faces if ye don't let me pass."

They seemed to think this funnier still; I had never seen such ill-mannered people.

"Go away, ye bloody bitches!" I said.

"Whisht, whisht, whisht, I tell you!" snarled Father, abandoning all pretence of amusement and dragging me along behind him by the hand. I was maddened by the women's shrieks of laughter. I was maddened by Father's bullying. I tried to dig in my heels but he was too powerful for me, and I could only see the women by looking back over my shoulder.

"Take care or I'll come back and show ye!" I shouted. "I'll teach ye to let decent people pass. Fitter for ye to stop at home and wash yeer dirty faces."

" 'Twill be all over the road," whimpered Father. "Never again, never again, not if I lived to be a thousand!"

To this day I don't know whether he was forswearing me or the drink. By way of a song suitable to my heroic mood I bawled "The Boys of Wexford," as he dragged me in home. Crowley, knowing he was not safe, made off and Father undressed me and put me to bed. I couldn't sleep because of the whirling in my head. It was very unpleasant, and I got sick again. Father came in with a wet cloth and mopped up after me. I lay in a fever, listening to him chopping sticks to start a fire. After that I heard him lay the table.

Suddenly the front door banged open and Mother stormed in with Sonny in her arms, not her usual gentle, timid self, but a wild, raging woman. It was clear that she had heard it all from the neighbours.

"Mick Delaney," she cried hysterically, "what did you do to my son?"

"Whisht, woman, whisht, whisht!" he hissed, dancing from one foot to the other. "Do you want the whole road to hear?"

"Ah," she said with a horrifying laugh, "the road knows all about it by this time. The road knows the way you filled your unfortunate innocent child with drink to make sport for you and that other rotten, filthy brute."

"But I gave him no drink," he shouted, aghast at the horrifying interpretation the neighbours had chosen to give his misfortune. "He took it while my back was turned. What the hell do you think I am?"

"Ah," she replied bitterly, "everyone knows what you are now. God forgive you, wasting our hard-earned few ha'pence on drink, and bringing up your child to be a drunken corner-boy like yourself."

Then she swept into the bedroom and threw herself on her knees by the bed. She moaned when she saw the gash over my eye. In the kitchen Sonny set up a loud bawl on his own, and a moment later Father appeared in the bedroom door with his cap over his eyes, wearing an expression of the most intense self-pity.

"That's a nice way to talk to me after all I went through," he whined. "That's a nice accusation, that I was drinking. Not one drop of drink crossed my lips the whole day. How could it when he drank it all? I'm the one that ought to be pitied, with my day ruined on me, and I after being made a show for the whole road."

But next morning, when he got up and went out quietly to work with his dinner-basket, Mother threw herself on me in the bed and kissed me. It seemed it was all my doing, and I was being given a holiday till my eye got better.

"My brave little man!" she said with her eyes shining. "It was God did it you were there. You were his guardian angel."

DEATH OF AN AIRMAN
John Hawkes

On a white mile of fine sand breaking a foreign shore, Cecil Bodington
gently lay down his shovel and looked to sea. He squinted once at the
officer and carefully, as if reaching for the spade, stooped and sat down in
the sand. He gripped his thick hands across his knees and the single, loose
chevron hanging from his rolled sleeve never fluttered. The officer looked
up from his book: "Lance, this man's due to come up today. I'd keep
with it."

Even when he stopped digging in the shallow trench and concentrated
without moving on the dark wet sand—it was hot beneath the white top
layer—he could not hear any sound. Day and night, there was no breaking
of waves nor the slightest ripple of changing tide, no sound of wind across
the Air Force blue water. Since he did not know how to swim and since
swimming was prohibited, the sea was only something that hour on hour
changed color slightly to a man who, staked on the beach, grows parched
and blinded to the black of his own skin. He scraped again with the tip
of the shovel. If he stared long enough toward the narrow beach road he
could see their small, desert-painted lorry and beyond it, over the gray
sand, the salty branches of a few burned pines that marked the area collecting lot, an unguarded flat acre of clay. And to his left, the pink-tanned
officer sat on the flotsam barrel in shorts and dark glasses, read his book,
and borrowed matches from the corporal to light his pipe as the mosquito
swarms grew larger with the opening of the trench.

Bodington slipped a soiled khaki handkerchief over his mouth. He had
been assigned to a Graves Recording Post. It consisted of registrar, sometimes a clerk, a vehicle, several sets of spades and a non-commissioned
digger. These units, bad for morale, were segregated from the troops and
from each other; faces turned away when the trucks with the black flags
on the doors drove past, rattling, lurching, never sent to the fitters.

He worked in the open sun, moving a few feet up the beach each day,
opening the unmarked traps, driving to the collecting lot and digging
again. But the tide did change, though he could hear only the turning
pages. And occasionally he found bits of kelp on the sand, dried hard and

crisp by the time he unloaded his tools soon after sunrise. Some burials had occurred below the water mark. There the sand, once free of ocean and even before he turned it down, was cooler to his feet.

When he discovered where the head direction was, but before uncovering the man himself, he dug without care hoping only to hit the breast pocket, to find the pilot lying on his back. Once fallen into the ocean, they were not seen again along its surface until discovered rolled, dark and pierced, singly on the flat beach.

He felt a button. But there was no pocket, simply the bare outline of the papers he sought, somewhat the color of the body itself. He pulled them out. They tore, were quickly taken by the officer and he scraped again for throat and wrists, for rings and chain tags. Cecil paused and looked at a few bathers; they arrived, but as usual did not go into the still water, rather took turns under an old, faded umbrella. He sat on the edge of the trench and tried to loosen his heavy woolen trousers, brushing off the sharp grains of sand. The officer glanced at him from behind dark glasses and again he raised the shovel. As he emptied the sand—not into any one pile—he saw that all the bathers were crowding the umbrella together. One of their children carried a white cloth to the edge of the water, dipped it, and back at the umbrella was wrapped in it by his mother.

Later Cecil fried the officer some sardines over a small fire on the beach, strolled close to the bathers out of water and returned to work. The sun stayed at the same degree the whole day until it fell below the uncertain line of the sea. If squinted at, it burned the eyes a moment before hiding itself in its own sails, shadows and whitening aurora. He dropped the spade—its head was crusted and stopped at the strike of iron or bone—and tried to get a grip under the man's shoulders. The officer moved away and raised the book before his face. Disinterment Officer, his duty kept him on the beach—never in the collecting lot—and he saw their faces only as they came up, never as they went back down. This man was known as the most skillful D. O. in the entire sector.

Cecil raised the pilot's head to the level of the grave, held it with one hand and felt about with the other in the sand. He looked at the officer who thought: "He's forgotten it again. He's forgotten to bring down the blanket." Cecil breathed heavily through the handkerchief.

"Well," thought the D. O., "the odor's the same behind any army cook house." And he peered over the book. "Out of an old can or from the sand, the smell's still the same." He stared at the black figure in the soldier's arms. "They're coming out together." The D. O., seeing that he was unwatched, looked quickly at the still wet papers he had stuffed in the back of the book. "Number twelve, twenty-two, ten, sixty-six, coming up for the last time," he thought. "When you go down now, you'll stay." He wiped his face.

Cecil, needing the blanket, slid the body back into the pit. "Wait! You'll never get him out again!" The D. O. dropped the book and leaned forward, doing the work himself, perspiring at the hands of the novice. "I've just hauled my own body up from the pit," he thought, "and let it down again."

The child walked slowly toward the water, kicking up scoops of sand, to drench his sheet. It was hard for such a man as the D. O.—who had worked up from a shoveler himself, who had begun the trade as a boy carrying the sexton's pick and a candle-lit lantern, who had studied every feature of the dead and could gauge their position—it was hard for such a man, up from the flowered rows, to keep his eyes away from a trench that should be neatly opened with a precise three inches around the corpse. The dark glasses could not hide the old craftsman's look on his face.

Cecil wiped his hands on his battle jacket—he was used to the oil that preserved the dead—and started for the lorry.

"They should never be left open to the light of day." The D. O. shook his head. "Bodington," he called, "don't forget the decoration."

"Right, sir." The corporal walked toward the little car with the same slow pace as his old father. They used to walk the fields together, the old man first with his staff, Cecil next, glancing over his shoulder to see that the younger boys stayed in line. They walked through clumps of new forest, laid out by the owner of the land, and over pasturage, green and deep, that had not been touched since the first monk collected dues and sullen tillers thought they had a righteous cause. The only thing Cecil had ever buried—and that when a grown man—was a tough swan, wrenched from a poacher he labored on the head with a wooden fork.

He opened the back door of the wagon leaning on the slant of the road and felt about until he found the cutters in their leather thongs, a tangled coil of wire and one of the less stained blankets, all of which, requisitioned by the Graves Recording Group from the medical battalions, were too heavily darkened with iodine and stiff with salt solution to be used again on wounded men. From a dusty spark-plug box he picked one of the decoration ribbons and from the tool compartment, filled with bottles, he pulled the billing pad.

"This isn't a man's work," he thought. For a moment the heat inside the lorry—the wrinkled canvas top was hot to touch—made him think of the Graves Depot, where he had trained a fortnight and eaten his two meals a day by a practice pit. All diggers were drilled between rows of crosses, which though bearing names and numbers, marked no actual bodies. He pinned the decoration to his shirt front for safekeeping and left the truck.

"This is the real thing," thought the D. O., frowning at the trudging corporal, "and not for heavy peasants either." The D. O. had made mistakes himself when he started—a pick would get out of control and hit always the least likely arm or leg.

Cecil could handle the wire well from mending rakes and binding hay, but his folds in the blanket were loose and bulging, the flap over the flyer's feet came loose again and again. He put the spade across the ankles and stooped over and around the short body stretched on the sand. The officer wiped his brow and finally held the blanket himself: "All right now, string it up." And then, after Cecil had shipped the wire ends, the officer sat again on the barrel with the pad on his knee to fill in what he could. In section eight, he had no clerk and did such things himself, writing in the open sun, scratching his pen through the sand dust. He adjusted his broad, dark glasses and looked to the horizon away from the water where, silhouetted, stood a gray stone remnant of a Catholic tower, in which the bathers lived.

Cecil had learned to drive in the forces and never well. Hauling a dummy about the depot wasn't the same as carrying a pilot washed to shore across an ox track never as smooth and shaded as those over the sea. He heard the body rolling behind him, knocking into the tools, gear, and thudding against his bedding. The wheels shivered and caught as the path changed from sand to clay, the truck slipped down a slight shoulder and for a moment he lost sight of the sea, blue as an apothecary's flame. The lorry barely ground into the collecting lot. He left the body, sealed with a few mosquitos, in the back. He picked his spot and broke clay, the pick striking lost chips of a pink marble garden seat.

The saluters, with their rifles, black armbands and one with a standard, stood about waiting as he dug. It was an honored corps, but small, the last admission of an old custom, and its members mixed freely and went home on leave, were told to walk the streets, to impress saddened survivors with the honor, the excellence of military last rites.

The clay was hard, like packed fodder in his father's yard, and as he swung the pick he had no time to look at the cool tower behind him. Once he had seen the golden dome. He felt them at his back, perhaps impatient to get on to more important burials, and he pitched into the clay, rolling his sleeves higher. Though the sun spread itself immediately over a few dusty trees on the brick-like plain, the clay still smelled of the seashore, the undivided vacant place for the tide.

Beyond the old horse against the hill, below the thatch and poles turning black at dusk, among the soft birds in the valley, there, near his mother's hearth, was the only cemetery Cecil had ever known. He expected the shaded plot and deep grass. There was always moisture on the heavy leaves, the hedgerow was untrimmed and where a man lay beneath the earth that earth was undisturbed except for the careful shuffle of an old caretaker. He expected to see a darkened church by any resting place. He expected shadows and mementos on the stones, a stile, a gate rusted open and thick with foliage, a light burning far in the distance and, as he stooped in the damp weeds, he expected to find dates impressed on the leaning stones.

Cecil climbed from the hole and scanned the lot. They were hard to see, but luckily the turned-over clay did not reflect too highly the glare of the sun. The graves could be made out. He was expert, from long early days, at one thing: furrows. And up and down, from one spare bordering dune to the other the new pilots lay in even lines, straight, gray, with not a grapevine to scratch the dust between them. The saluters lined up and shot their volley. As he had learned at the Depot, he signed the chit. They left.

The D. O. knew the sun was about to set and that there was time for no more. He waved the corporal back to the lorry and wearily climbed in beside him. "To the base."

When night had come and the bathers left the beach, when the heat still drifted in from the sea and the D. O. was settled in his small tent, he was glad to take off the dark glasses, after securing the flap. He smelled the clay. Cecil tossed and turned in the back of his lorry, pushing the shovels out of the way, rearranging the blankets under his head. He had no idea how long these days would last, but he was just as tired at the end of each. He put his hand on his heart and felt the decoration. He had forgotten to pin it to the corpse.

AFTER YOU,
MY DEAR ALPHONSE
Shirley Jackson

Mrs. Wilson was just taking the gingerbread out of the oven when she heard Johnny outside talking to someone.

"Johnny," she called, "you're late. Come in and get your lunch."

"Just a minute, Mother," Johnny said. "After you, my dear Alphonse."

"After *you*, my dear Alphonse," another voice said.

"No, after *you*, my dear Alphonse," Johnny said.

Mrs. Wilson opened the door. "Johnny," she said, "you come in this minute and get your lunch. You can play after you've eaten."

Johnny came in after her, slowly. "Mother," he said, "I brought Boyd home for lunch with me."

"Boyd?" Mrs. Wilson thought for a moment. "I don't believe I've met Boyd. Bring him in, dear, since you've invited him. Lunch is ready."

"Boyd!" Johnny yelled. "Hey, Boyd, come on in!"

"I'm coming. Just got to unload this stuff."

"Well, hurry, or my mother'll be sore."

"Johnny, that's not very polite to either your friend or your mother," Mrs. Wilson said. "Come sit down, Boyd."

As she turned to show Boyd where to sit, she saw he was a Negro boy, smaller than Johnny but about the same age. His arms were loaded with split kindling wood. "Where'll I put this stuff, Johnny?" he asked.

Mrs. Wilson turned to Johnny. "Johnny," she said, "what did you make Boyd do? What is that wood?"

"Dead Japanese," Johnny said mildly. "We stand them in the ground and run over them with tanks."

"How do you do, Mrs. Wilson?" Boyd said.

"How do you do, Boyd? You shouldn't let Johnny make you carry all that wood. Sit down now and eat lunch, both of you."

"Why shouldn't he carry the wood, Mother? It's his wood. We got it at his place."

"Johnny," Mrs. Wilson said, "go on and eat your lunch."

"Sure," Johnny said. He held out the dish of scrambled eggs to Boyd.

"After you, my dear Alphonse."

"After *you,* my dear Alphonse," Boyd said.

"After *you,* my dear Alphonse," Johnny said. They began to giggle.

"Are you hungry, Boyd?" Mrs. Wilson asked.

"Yes, Mrs. Wilson."

"Well, don't you let Johnny stop you. He always fusses about eating, so you just see that you get a good lunch. There's plenty of food here for you to have all you want."

"Thank you, Mrs. Wilson."

"Come on, Alphonse," Johnny said. He pushed half the scrambled eggs on to Boyd's plate. Boyd watched while Mrs. Wilson put a dish of stewed tomatoes beside his plate.

"Boyd don't eat tomatoes, do you, Boyd?" Johnny said.

"*Doesn't* eat tomatoes, Johnny. And just because you don't like them, don't say that about Boyd. Boyd will eat *anything.*"

"Bet he won't," Johnny said, attacking his scrambled eggs.

"Boyd wants to grow up and be a big strong man so he can work hard," Mrs. Wilson said. "I'll bet Boyd's father eats stewed tomatoes."

"My father eats anything he wants to," Boyd said.

"So does mine," Johnny said. "Sometimes he doesn't eat hardly anything. He's a little guy, though. Wouldn't hurt a flea."

"Mine's a little guy, too," Boyd said.

"I'll bet he's strong, though," Mrs. Wilson said. She hesitated. "Does he...work?"

"Sure," Johnny said. "Boyd's father works in a factory."

"There, you see?" Mrs. Wilson said. "And he certainly has to be strong to do that—all that lifting and carrying at a factory."

"Boyd's father doesn't have to," Johnny said. "He's a foreman."

Mrs. Wilson felt defeated. "What does your mother do, Boyd?"

"My mother?" Boyd was surprised. "She takes care of us kids."

"Oh. She doesn't work, then?"

"Why should she?" Johnny said through a mouthful of eggs. "You don't work."

"You really don't want any stewed tomatoes, Boyd?"

"No, thank you, Mrs. Wilson," Boyd said.

"No, thank you, Mrs. Wilson, no, thank you, Mrs. Wilson, no thank you, Mrs. Wilson," Johnny said. "Boyd's sister's going to work, though. She's going to be a teacher."

"That's a very fine attitude for her to have, Boyd." Mrs. Wilson restrained an impulse to pat Boyd on the head. "I imagine you're all very proud of her?"

"I guess so," Boyd said.

"What about all your other brothers and sisters? I guess all of you want to make just as much of yourselves as you can."

"There's only me and Jean," Boyd said. "I don't know yet what I want to be when I grow up."

"We're going to be tank drivers, Boyd and me," Johnny said. "Zoom." Mrs. Wilson caught Boyd's glass of milk as Johnny's napkin ring, suddenly transformed into a tank, plowed heavily across the table.

"Look, Johnny," Boyd said. "Here's a foxhole. I'm shooting at you."

Mrs. Wilson, with the speed born of long experience, took the gingerbread off the shelf and placed it carefully between the tank and the foxhole.

"Now eat as much as you want to, Boyd," she said. "I want to see you get filled up."

"Boyd eats a lot, but not as much as I do," Johnny said. "I'm bigger than he is."

"You're not much bigger," Boyd said. "I can beat you running."

Mrs. Wilson took a deep breath. "Boyd," she said. Both boys turned to her. "Boyd, Johnny has some suits that are a little too small for him, and a winter coat. It's not new, of course, but there's lots of wear in it still. And I have a few dresses that your mother or sister could probably use. Your mother can make them over into lots of things for all of you, and I'd be very happy to give them to you. Suppose before you leave I make up a big bundle and then you and Johnny can take it over to your mother right away. . . ." Her voice trailed off as she saw Boyd's puzzled expression.

"But I have plenty of clothes, thank you," he said. "And I don't think my mother knows how to sew very well, and anyway I guess we buy about everything we need. Thank you very much, though."

"We don't have time to carry that old stuff around, Mother," Johnny said. "We got to play tanks with the kids today."

Mrs. Wilson lifted the plate of gingerbread off the table as Boyd was about to take another piece. "There are many little boys like you, Boyd, who would be very grateful for the clothes someone was kind enough to give them."

"Boyd will take them if you want him to, Mother," Johnny said.

"I didn't mean to make you mad, Mrs. Wilson," Boyd said.

"Don't think I'm angry, Boyd. I'm just disappointed in you, that's all. Now let's not say anything more about it."

She began clearing the plates off the table, and Johnny took Boyd's hand and pulled him to the door. " 'Bye, Mother," Johnny said. Boyd stood for a minute, staring at Mrs. Wilson's back.

"After you, my dear Alphonse," Johnny said, holding the door open.

"Is your mother still mad?" Mrs. Wilson heard Boyd ask in a low voice.

"I don't know," Johnny said. "She's screwy sometimes."

"So's mine," Boyd said. He hesitated. "After *you*, my dear Alphonse."

TWO
Narrator,
Point of View
and Distance

One of the pleasures in reading short stories lies in discovering the enormous variety possible within the form: variety not only in the choice of plot and character, but in the very way a story is told.

When an author begins to form his tale he must choose a narrator. The considerations involved in choosing the best narrator for a particular story may be summarized in three general questions: 1) From whose point of view will the story be told? 2) How much distance will there be between the narrator and the story's characters and events? 3) How closely will the author identify with his narrator? The possible answers to these questions range very wide until we begin to discuss individual stories.

To discover how vital the role of a narrator may be in determining point of view, compare the following versions of the second paragraph of "The Story of the Three Bears." The one on the left is edited to remove all comments by the narrator.

One day after they had made the porridge for their breakfast, and poured it into their porridge-pots, they walked out into the wood while their porridge was cooling. And while they were walking, a little old Woman came to the house. First she looked in at that window, then at the keyhole; she lifted the latch. The door was not fastened. The little old Woman

One day, after they had made the porridge for their breakfast, and poured it into their porridge-pots, they walked out into the wood while their porridge was cooling, that they might not burn their mouths, by beginning too soon to eat it. And while they were walking, a little old Woman came to the house. She could not have been a good, honest old Woman;

opened the door, went in, saw the porridge on the table and set about helping herself.

for first she looked in at that window, and then she peeped in at the keyhole; and seeing nobody in the house, she lifted the latch. The door was not fastened, because the Bears were good Bears, who did nobody any harm, and never suspected that anybody would harm them. So the little old Woman opened the door, and went in; and well pleased she was when she saw the porridge on the table. If she had been a good little old Woman, she would have waited till the Bears came home, and then, perhaps, they would have asked her to breakfast; for they were good Bears,—a little rough or so, as the manner of Bears is, but for all that very good natured and hospitable. But she was an impudent, bad old Woman, and set about helping herself.

By comparing the paragraphs we quickly perceive what holds true for the entire story: at every turn the voice of the narrator intrudes to tell us how to react to an event or a character. Notice how he introduces the old Woman: *"She could not have been a good, honest old Woman; for first she looked in that window. . . ."* If the first part of the italicized sentence were omitted, as in the edited version, other explanations might suggest themselves. The woman's curiosity might be so aroused at finding a house in the woods far from town that she could not resist peeking in the window. The narrator prevents such speculation by flatly asserting that the very act of looking in the window proves her dishonesty. The unlocked door, he maintains, shows conclusively that "the Bears were good Bears, who did nobody any harm, and never suspected that anybody would harm them." After listening to the narrator the worst a reader might think about the bears is that they are too naïve, too trusting or too ignorant of the ways of the world. Their failings arise from being too good and not—like the woman's—from following bad impulses. Readers of Southey's story have little or no choice in how to react either to the bears or to the woman: the bears are attractive, honest, trusting, careful of themselves and their possessions, while the old Woman is ugly, dishonest, suspicious, careless of her appearance and other people's possessions.

Throughout "The Three Bears" the narrator does not simply show what happens and let the reader draw his own conclusions; he also tells why. The bedroom window, so conveniently placed next to the Little, Small, Wee Bear's bed, is open when the old Woman needs it, not from negligence but "because the Bears, like good tidy Bears, as they were, always opened their bed-chamber window when they got up in the morning." In order to pass judgment on the bears' housekeeping habits, the narrator must know about events which occur before the story begins as well as know what truly motivates the characters. He is, therefore, an omniscient narrator—although not an impartial one. When the Middle Bear complains "Somebody has been at my porridge" because "the spoon was standing in it," the narrator gratuitously adds: "They were wooden spoons; if they had been silver ones, the naughty old Woman would have put them in her pocket." He tries to arouse our suspicions and, perhaps, our hostility not for something the woman does, but for something she would do *if* she had the opportunity.

In contrast, the narrator of "Death of an Airman" always remains discreetly in the background—giving the reader needed information, filling in details of character, but never commenting directly on the action. The incredible heat on the foreign shore, the never-ending, brutal job, the pleasant memories of home are all described, but the narrator gives no indication of what his own feelings, if any, might be about the two men, the burial or the war.

The narrator of "The Three Bears" concludes that he "cannot tell" where the old Woman goes after she leaps out the window. He is not being aloof or objective but implying that she holds no interest for anyone once she leaves the house. The reader, he assumes, will be indifferent whether she "broke her neck in the fall" or began an enforced stay in the House of Correction. What is important is that "the Three Bears never saw anything more of her." Indifference to the woman's fate is part of the narrator's point of view and, if his comments have their desired effect, it will be part of the reader's as well. Much of the enjoyment in reading this story comes from momentarily adopting its point of view—one we would probably never hold outside the tale—which says that there are wholly good characters such as the Bears and wholly bad characters such as the old Woman. In the world that exists "once upon a time," Good wins out over Evil so completely that the good characters "never saw anything more of her."

A very different kind of pleasure comes from identifying the point of view of the third person narrator in "After You, My Dear Alphonse." This narrator leaves the reader free to draw his own conclusions about the domestic drama taking place in Mrs. Wilson's kitchen and never intrudes with instructions on how to respond to a character or to evaluate an event. A reader is not free, however, to draw his conclusions at random, for the impartial narrator shows Mrs. Wilson's limitations through the carefully constructed dialogue and action. In the course of the story there emerges a narrow-minded woman who is angry because Boyd and his family refuse to fit her preconceptions. Behind all her conversation lies a patronizing attitude which the reader discovers by observing how she acts when her assumptions prove false. When Boyd refuses the used clothing, the narrator does not say—as the narrator in "The Three Bears" would—that Mrs. Wilson becomes angry and hurt by what she interprets as the little boy's gross ingratitude. Instead, her action mirrors her innermost thoughts: "Mrs. Wilson lifted the plate of gingerbread off the table as Boyd was about to take another piece." This petty act reveals, more clearly than words could, how piqued she feels, and the reader reacts against her small-minded, ungenerous point of view.

A similar reader reaction occurs after Johnny's mother learns that Boyd's sister is studying to be a teacher: "Mrs. Wilson restrained an impulse to pat Boyd on the head." Perhaps none of her gestures so succinctly conveys her condescension as this "impulse" to treat Boyd as she might a domestic animal who has just shown an aspiration to be human. The detail is a small one, but part of the reward in reading "After You, My Dear Alphonse" comes from discerning the implications in such details. Jackson's narrator does not present purely good or bad characters, but human beings—complex creatures who are sometimes good and sometimes bad. Mrs. Wilson may be a good mother to Johnny and have some generous impulses towards Boyd, but both facts are outweighed by her distasteful patronizing of those whom she mistakenly believes are so much less fortunate than she is. Her failings are implied in what she says, thinks and does as the point of view of the narrator helps make clear.

One way of closely defining a story's point of view is to ask, "How much distance is there between the narrator and the characters or events he describes?" In "The Three Bears" there is little distance between the point of view of the narrator and the point of view of the Bears, although there is considerable distance between that of the narrator and that of the old Woman. Distance is often achieved by using an omniscient narrator who remains above the action. But what if the narrator of the story is also its main character, as is Larry in O'Connor's "The Drunkard"? If we examine O'Connor's story carefully we discover that only in retrospect does Larry see clearly the disaster which his father's words, sentiments and actions will produce. When his father announces that he will attend the funeral of Mr. Dooley, Larry comments on what will happen: "If I had only known it, this was a bad sign. . . ." Like most fiction that uses a child narrator, "The Drunkard" is told in the past tense by an adult who is aware of the outcome of events before they happen (compare to Joyce's "Araby," in Chapter Four). As an adult, Larry recounts his hilarious misadventure and is properly bemused by this day's events. A good deal of the humor results from the distance between Larry, the boy who is the main character, and Larry, the adult who is the narrator. We may assume that the adult Larry shares our amusement at the young drunkard's exuberant performance on the road and at his father's keen embarrassment. The reeling boy, however, is far from amused by his father, the bystanders' reactions or his own actions, for he has the drunkard's exaggerated sense of his own dignity and self-importance. Only in later years, when sufficient distance intervenes between the participant and the events, will this story become wildly comic and ripe for telling. At the moment it happens, Larry is too serious, too dignified, too noisy and too sick to see its humor. That the main character in the story is also its narrator does not mean they must share the same point of view. The narrator of "The Drunkard" has what the boy could never have: a perspective gained through the passing of time.

The problem of the distance between the narrator of a story and its events becomes crucial when a reader has reason to believe that events did not happen exactly the way the narrator reports or when he believes the narrator fails to see their significance. In the stories so far discussed, there is no reason to question the truthfulness of any narrator: all are reliable. Nor do readers ask if the narrator left something out of his story of "The Widow of Ephesus" or if Verga's narrator neglected a crucial detail in "The She-Wolf," for both appear trustworthy. The ambiguity in "Cain and Abel" results from the inexplicable nature of the events described and not from the narrator's manipulation. If the many unanswered questions raised by the biblical tale of the first murderer disturb or puzzle readers, they will have to go outside the story—perhaps to theology, psychology or history—for possible answers.

A very different problem arises, however, when we encounter the narrators of some of the stories which follow. Compare, for example, the narrator of "A Trifling Occurrence" with that of "The Background." How does each arouse and hold our interest in his characters? Does it make any difference that the journalist tells his own tale, whereas an omniscient narrator tells Aliosha and Bieliayev's story? Are the narrators equally reliable in their reporting of events? The last question is even more crucial when asked about the narrator of "Bartleby, the Scrivener." Readers often disagree about the narrator's honesty. Might he not be shifting an occasional fact to put himself in the best possible light? Does the person telling the story of "Akulka's Husband" realize the implications of what he says? Does his listener? Does the prisoner who awakes to overhear their talk? In "Nuns at Luncheon" what attitude does the narrator have towards Miss Penny and her story? Who is the narrator of "Aura"? Does his telling the story using the second person, "you," increase your involvement in the strange events to the point where questions of distance appear irrelevant? Is the narrator reliable?

Unreliable? Or do you know? These questions about a narrator's truthfulness and knowledge are central in arriving at a clear understanding and valid interpretation of many stories. In a few instances, as in "Bartleby," the very nature of the story may depend upon whether or not a reader trusts the narrator. (Is "Bartleby" primarily about an enigmatic character faithfully described by an involved but objective narrator, or is it about a man who only partially understands the character of the "pallid Scrivener," and only half-acknowledges his own responsibility for and reaction to him?)

If a reader is troubled by the questionable veracity of a narrator, why not go directly to the author? The question of an author's relation to his story is most difficult, sometimes impossible to answer and often unprofitable to consider. We will probably never know what most authors thought about their stories, and perhaps that is just as well. As readers, when we are able to answer questions about the type of narrator—such as his reliability, the kind of distance he employs and the point of view he reflects—then we will greatly increase our enjoyment in the marvelously varied form that is the short story.

A TRIFLING OCCURRENCE
Anton Chekhov

translated by constance garnett

Nikolay Ilyich Bieliayev, a Petersburg landlord, very fond of the race-course, a well fed, pink young man of about thirty-two, once called to-wards evening on Madame Irnin—Olgo Ivanovna—with whom he had a liaison, or, to use his own phrase, spun out a long and tedious romance. And indeed the first pages of his romance, pages of interest and inspiration, had been read long ago; now they dragged on and on, and presented neither novelty nor interest.

Finding that Olga Ivanovna was not at home, my hero lay down a moment on the drawing-room sofa and began to wait.

"Good evening, Nikolay Ilyich," he suddenly heard a child's voice say. "Mother will be in in a moment. She's gone to the dressmaker's with Sonya."

In the same drawing-room on the sofa lay Olga Ivanovna's son, Aliosha, a boy about eight years old, well built, well looked after, dressed up like a picture in a velvet jacket and long black stockings. He lay on a satin pillow, and apparently imitating an acrobat whom he had lately seen in the circus, lifting up first one leg, then the other. When his elegant legs began to be tired, he moved his hands, or he jumped up impetuously and then went on all fours, trying to stand with his legs in the air. All this he did with a most serious face, breathing heavily, as if he himself found no happiness in God's gift of such a restless body.

"Ah, how do you do, my friend?" said Bieliayev. "Is it you? I didn't notice you. Is your mother well?"

At the moment Aliosha had just taken hold of the toe of his left foot in his right hand and got into a most awkward pose. He turned head over heels, jumped up, and glanced from under the big, fluffy lampshade at Bieliayev.

"How can I put it?" he said, shrugging his shoulders. "As a matter of plain fact Mother is never well. You see she's woman, and women, Nikolay Ilyich, have always some pain or another."

For something to do, Bieliayev began to examine Aliosha's face. All the time he had been acquainted with Olga Ivanovna he had never once turned his attention to the boy and had completely ignored his existence. A boy is stuck in front of your eyes, but what is he doing here, what is his rôle?—you don't want to give a single thought to the question.

In the evening dusk Aliosha's face with a pale forehead and steady black eyes unexpectedly reminded Bieliayev of Olga Ivanovna as she was in the first pages of the romance. He had the desire to be affectionate to the boy.

"Come here, whipper-snapper," he said. "Come and let me have a good look at you, quite close."

The boy jumped off the sofa and ran to Bieliayev.

"Well?" Nikolay Ilyich began, putting his hand on the thin shoulders. "And how are things with you?"

"How shall I put it?...They used to be much better before."

"How?"

"Quite simple. Before, Sonya and I only had to do music and reading, and now we're given French verses to learn. You've had your hair cut lately?"

"Yes, just lately."

"That's why I noticed it. Your beard's shorter. May I touch it... Doesn't it hurt?"

"No, not a bit."

"Why is it that it hurts if you pull one hair and when you pull a whole lot, it doesn't hurt a bit? Ah, ah! You know it's a pity you don't have side-whiskers. You should shave here, and at the sides...and leave the hair just here."

The boy pressed close to Bieliayev and began to play with his watch-chain.

"When I go to the gymnasium," he said, "Mother is going to buy me a watch. I'll ask her to buy me a chain just like this. What a fine locket! Father has one just the same, but yours has stripes, here, and his has got letters...Inside it's Mother's picture. Father has another chain now, not in links, but like a ribbon..."

"How do you know? Do you see your father?"

"I? Mm...no...I..."

Aliosha blushed and in the violent confusion of being detected in a lie began to scratch the locket busily with his finger-nail. Bieliayev looked steadily at his face and asked:

"Do you see your father?"

"No...No!"

"But, be honest—on your honour. By your face I can see you're not telling me the truth. If you made a slip of the tongue by mistake, what's the use of shuffling. Tell me, do you see him? As one friend to another."

Aliosha mused.

"And you won't tell Mother?" he asked.

"What next?"

"On your word of honour."

"My word of honour."

"Swear an oath."

"What a nuisance you are! What do you take me for?"

Aliosha looked round, made big eyes and began to whisper.

"Only for God's sake don't tell Mother! Never tell it to anyone at all, because it's a secret. God forbid that Mother should ever get to know; then I and Sonya and Pelagueya will pay for it...Listen. Sonya and I meet Father every Tuesday and Friday. When Pelagueya takes us for a walk before dinner, we go into Apfel's sweet-shop and Father's waiting for us. He always sits in a separate room, you know, where there's a splendid marble table and an ash-tray shaped like a goose without a back..."

"And what do you do there?"

"Nothing!—First, we welcome one another, then we sit down at a little table and Father begins to treat us to coffee and cakes. You know, Sonya eats meat-pies, and I can't bear pies with meat in them! I like them made of cabbage and eggs. We eat so much that afterwards at dinner we try to eat as much as we possibly can so that Mother shan't notice."

"What do you talk about there?"

"To Father? About anything. He kisses us and cuddles us, tells us all kinds of funny stories. You know, he says that he will take us to live with him when we are grown up. Sonya doesn't want to go, but I say 'Yes.' Of course, it'll be lonely without Mother; but I'll write letters to her. How funny: we could go to her for our holidays then—couldn't we? Besides, Father says that he'll buy me a horse. He's a splendid man. I can't understand why Mother doesn't invite him to live with her or why she says we mustn't meet him. He loves Mother very much indeed. He's always asking us how she is and what she's doing. When she was ill, he took hold of his head like this...and ran, ran, all the time. He is always telling us to obey and respect her. Tell me, is it true that we're unlucky?"

"H'm...how?"

"Father says so. He says: 'You are unlucky children.' It's quite strange to listen to him. He says: 'You are unhappy, I'm unhappy, and Mother's unhappy.' He says: 'Pray to God for yourselves and for her.'"

Aliosha's eyes rested upon the stuffed bird and he mused.

"Exactly..." snorted Bieliayev. "This is what you do. You arrange conferences in sweet-shops. And your mother doesn't know?"

"No—no...How could she know? Pelagueya won't tell for anything. The day before yesterday Father stood us pears. Sweet, like jam. I had two."

"H'm...well, now...tell me, doesn't your father speak about me?"

"About you? How shall I put it?"

Aliosha gave a searching glance to Bieliayev's face and shrugged his shoulders.

"He doesn't say anything in particular."

"What does he say, for instance?"

"You won't be offended?"

"What next? Why, does he abuse me?"

"He doesn't abuse you, but you know...he is cross with you. He says that it's through you that Mother's unhappy and that you...ruined Mother. But he is so queer! I explain to him that you are good and never shout at Mother, but he only shakes his head."

"Does he say those very words: that I ruined her?"

"Yes. Don't be offended, Nikolay Ilyich!"

Bieliayev got up, stood still a moment, and then began to walk about the drawing-room.

"This is strange, and...funny," he murmured, shrugging his shoulders and smiling ironically. "He is to blame all round, and now *I've* ruined her, eh? What an innocent lamb! Did he say those very words to you: that I ruined your mother?"

"Yes, but...you said that you wouldn't get offended."

"I'm not offended, and...and it's none of your business! No, it...it's quite funny though. I fell into the trap, yet I'm to be blamed as well."

The bell rang. The boy dashed from his place and ran out. In a minute a lady entered the room with a little girl. It was Olga Ivanovna, Aliosha's mother. After her, hopping, humming noisily, and waving his hands, followed Aliosha.

"Of course, who is there to accuse except me?" he murmured, sniffing. "He's right, he's the injured husband."

"What's the matter?" asked Olga Ivanovna.

"What's the matter! Listen to the kind of sermon your dear husband preaches. It appears I'm a scoundrel and a murderer, I've ruined you and the children. All of you are unhappy, and only I am awfully happy! Awfully, awfully happy!"

"I don't understand, Nikolay! What is it?"

"Just listen to this young gentleman," Bieliayev said, pointing to Aliosha.

Aliosha blushed, then became pale suddenly, and his whole face was twisted in fright.

"Nikolay Ilyich," he whispered loudly. "Shh!"

"Ask him, if you please," went on Bieliayev. "That stupid fool Pelagueya of yours, takes them to sweet-shops and arranges meetings with their dear father there. But that's not the point. The point is that the dear father is a martyr, and I'm a murderer, I'm a scoundrel, who broke the lives of both of you...."

"Nikolay Ilyich!" moaned Aliosha. "You gave your word of honour!"

"Ah, let me alone!" Bieliayev waved his hand. "This is something more important than any words of honour. The hypocrisy revolts me, the lie!"

"I don't understand," muttered Olga Ivanovna, and tears began to glimmer in her eyes. "Tell me, Liolka,"—she turned to her son, "Do you see your father?"

Aliosha did not hear and looked with horror at Bieliayev.

"It's impossible," said the mother. "I'll go and ask Pelagueya."

Olga Ivanovna went out.

"But, but you gave me your word of honour," Aliosha said, trembling all over.

Bieliayev waved his hand at him and went on walking up and down. He was absorbed in his insult, and now, as before, he did not notice the presence of the boy. He, a big serious man, had nothing to do with boys. And Aliosha sat down in a corner and in terror told Sonya how he had been deceived. He trembled, stammered, wept. This was the first time in his life that he had been set, roughly, face to face with a lie. He had never known before that in this world besides sweet pears and cakes and expensive watches, there exist many other things which have no name in children's language.

THE BACKGROUND
Saki (H. H. Munro)

"That woman's art-jargon tires me," said Clovis to his journalist friend. "She's so fond of talking of certain pictures as 'growing on one,' as though they were a sort of fungus."

"That reminds me," said the journalist, "of the story of Henri Deplis. Have I ever told it you?"

Clovis shook his head.

"Henri Deplis was by birth a native of the Grand Duchy of Luxemburg. On maturer reflection he became a commercial traveller. His business activities frequently took him beyond the limits of the Grand Duchy, and he was stopping in a small town of Northern Italy when news reached him from home that a legacy from a distant and deceased relative had fallen to his share.

"It was not a large legacy, even from the modest standpoint of Henri Deplis, but it impelled him towards some seemingly harmless extravagances. In particular it led him to patronize local art as represented by the tattoo-needles of Signor Andreas Pincini. Signor Pincini was, perhaps, the most brilliant master of tattoo craft that Italy had ever known, but his circumstances were decidedly impoverished, and for the sum of six hundred francs he gladly undertook to cover his client's back, from the collar-bone down to the waist-line, with a glowing representation of the Fall of Icarus. The design, when finally developed, was a slight disappointment to Monsieur Deplis, who had suspected Icarus of being a fortress taken by Wallenstein in the Thirty Years' War, but he was more than satisfied with the execution of the work, which was acclaimed by all who had the privilege of seeing it as Pincini's masterpiece.

"It was his greatest effort, and his last. Without even waiting to be paid, the illustrious craftsman departed this life, and was buried under an ornate tombstone, whose winged cherubs would have afforded singularly little scope for the exercise of his favourite art. There remained, however, the widow Pincini, to whom the six hundred francs were due. And thereupon arose the great crisis in the life of Henri Deplis, traveller of commerce. The legacy, under the stress of numerous little calls on its substance, had dwindled to very insignificant proportions, and when a pressing wine bill and sundry other current accounts had been paid, there remained little more than 430 francs to offer to the widow. The lady was properly indignant, not wholly, as she volubly explained, on account of the suggested writing-off of 170 francs, but also at the attempt to depreciate the value of her late husband's acknowledged masterpiece. In a week's time Deplis was obliged to reduce his offer to 405 francs, which circumstance fanned the widow's indignation into a fury. She cancelled the sale of the work of art, and a few days later Deplis learned with a sense of consternation that she had presented it to the municipality of Bergamo, which had gratefully accepted it. He left the neighbourhood as unobtrusively as possible, and was genuinely relieved when his business commands took him to Rome, where he hoped his identity and that of the famous picture might be lost sight of.

"But he bore on his back the burden of the dead man's genius. On presenting himself one day in the steaming corridor of a vapour bath, he was at once hustled back into his clothes by the proprietor, who was a North Italian, and who emphatically refused to allow the celebrated Fall of Icarus to be publicly on view without the permission of the municipality of Bergamo. Public interest and official vigilance increased as the matter became more widely known, and Deplis was unable to take a simple dip in the sea or river on the hottest afternoon unless clothed up to the collar-bone in a substantial bathing garment. Later on the authorities of Bergamo conceived the idea that salt water might be injurious to the masterpiece, and a perpetual injunction was obtained which debarred the muchly harassed commercial traveller from sea bathing under any circumstances. Altogether, he was fervently thankful when his firm of employers found him a new range of activities in the neighbourhood of Bordeaux. His thankfulness, however, ceased abruptly at the Franco-Italian frontier. An imposing array of official force barred his departure, and he was sternly reminded of the stringent law which forbids the exportation of Italian works of art.

"A diplomatic parley ensued between the Luxemburgian and Italian Governments, and at one time the European situation became overcast with the possibilities of trouble. But the Italian Government stood firm; it declined to concern itself in the least with the fortunes or even the existence of Henri Deplis, commercial traveller, but was immovable in its decision that the Fall of Icarus (by the late Pincini, Andreas) at present the property of the municipality of Bergamo, should not leave the country.

"The excitement died down in time, but the unfortunate Deplis, who was of a constitutionally retiring disposition, found himself a few months later once more the storm-centre of a furious controversy. A certain German art expert, who had obtained from the municipality of Bergamo permission to inspect the famous masterpiece, declared it to be a spurious

Pincini, probably the work of some pupil whom he had employed in his declining years. The evidence of Deplis on the subject was obviously worthless, as he had been under the influence of the customary narcotics during the long process of pricking in the design. The editor of an Italian art journal refuted the contentions of the German expert and undertook to prove that his private life did not conform to any modern standard of decency. The whole of Italy and Germany were drawn into the dispute, and the rest of Europe was soon involved in the quarrel. There were stormy scenes in the Spanish Parliament, and the University of Copenhagen bestowed a gold medal on the German expert (afterwards sending a commission to examine his proofs on the spot), while two Polish schoolboys in Paris committed suicide to show what *they* thought of the matter.

"Meanwhile, the unhappy human background fared no better than before, and it was not surprising that he drifted into the ranks of Italian anarchists. Four times at least he was escorted to the frontier as a dangerous and undesirable foreigner, but he was always brought back as the Fall of Icarus (attributed to Pincini, Andreas, early Twentieth Century). And then one day, at an anarchist congress at Genoa, a fellow-worker, in the heat of debate, broke a phial full of corrosive liquid over his back. The red shirt that he was wearing mitigated the effects, but the Icarus was ruined beyond recognition. His assailant was severely reprimanded for assaulting a fellow-anarchist and received seven years' imprisonment for defacing a national art treasure. As soon as he was able to leave the hospital Henri Deplis was put across the frontier as an undesirable alien.

"In the quieter streets of Paris, especially in the neighbourhood of the Ministry of Fine Arts, you may sometimes meet a depressed, anxious-looking man, who, if you pass him the time of day, will answer you with a slight Luxemburgian accent. He nurses the illusion that he is one of the lost arms of the Venus de Milo, and hopes that the French Government may be persuaded to buy him. On all other subjects I believe he is tolerably sane."

BARTLEBY, THE SCRIVENER
Herman Melville

I am a rather elderly man. The nature of my avocations, for the last thirty years, has brought me into more than ordinary contact with what would seem an interesting and somewhat singular set of men, of whom, as yet, nothing, that I know of, has ever been written—I mean, the law-copyists, or scriveners. I have known very many of them, professionally and privately, and, if I pleased, could relate divers histories, at which good-natured gentlemen might smile, and sentimental souls might weep. But I waive the biographies of all other scriveners, for a few passages in the life of Bartleby, who was a scrivener, the strangest I ever saw, or heard of. While, of other law-copyists, I might write the complete life, of Bartleby nothing of that sort can be done. I believe that no materials exist, for a full and satisfactory biography of this man. It is an irreparable loss to literature. Bartleby was one of those beings of whom nothing is ascertainable, except from the original sources, and, in his case, those are very small. What my own astonished eyes saw of Bartleby, *that* is all I know of him, except, indeed, one vague report, which will appear in the sequel.

Ere introducing the scrivener, as he first appeared to me, it is fit I make some mention of myself, my employés, my business, my chambers, and general surroundings; because some such description is indispensable to an adequate understanding of the chief character about to be presented. Imprimis: I am a man who, from his youth upward, has been filled with a profound conviction that the easiest way of life is the best. Hence, though I belong to a profession proverbially energetic and nervous, even to turbulence, at times, yet nothing of that sort have I ever suffered to invade my peace. I am one of those unambitious lawyers who never addresses a jury, or in any way draws down public applause; but, in the cool tranquillity of a snug retreat, do a snug business among rich men's bonds, and mortgages, and title-deeds. All who know me, consider me an eminently *safe* man. The late John Jacob Astor, a personage little given to poetic enthusiasm, had no hesitation in pronouncing my first grand point to be prudence; my next, method. I do not speak it in vanity, but simply record the fact, that I was not unemployed in my profession by the late John Jacob Astor; a name which, I admit, I love to repeat; for it hath a rounded and orbicular sound to it, and rings like unto bullion. I will freely add, that I was not insensible to the late John Jacob Astor's good opinion.

Some time prior to the period at which this little history begins, my avocations had been largely increased. The good old office, now extinct in the State of New York, of a Master in Chancery, had been conferred upon me. It was not a very arduous office, but very pleasantly remunerative. I seldom lose my temper; much more seldom indulge in dangerous indignation at wrongs and outrages; but, I must be permitted to be rash here, and declare, that I consider the sudden and violent abrogation of the office of Master in Chancery, by the new Constitution, as a—premature act; inasmuch as I had counted upon a life-lease of the profits, whereas I only received those of a few short years. But this is by the way.

My chambers were upstairs, at No. — Wall Street. At one end, they looked upon the white wall of the interior of a spacious skylight shaft, penetrating the building from top to bottom.

This view might have been considered rather tame than otherwise, deficient in what landscape painters call "life." But, if so, the view from the other end of my chambers offered, at least, a contrast, if nothing more. In that direction, my windows commanded an unobstructed view of a lofty brick wall, black by age and everlasting shade; which wall required no spy-glass to bring out its lurking beauties, but, for the benefit of all near-sighted spectators, was pushed up to within ten feet of my window panes. Owing to the great height of the surrounding buildings, and my chambers being on the second floor, the interval between this wall and mine not a little resembled a huge square cistern.

At the period just preceding the advent of Bartleby, I had two persons as copyists in my employment, and a promising lad as an office-boy. First, Turkey; second, Nippers; third, Ginger Nut. These may seem names, the like of which are not usually found in the Directory. In truth, they were nicknames, mutually conferred upon each other by my three clerks, and were deemed expressive of their respective persons or characters. Turkey was a short, pursy Englishman, of about my own age—that is, somewhere not far from sixty. In the morning, one might say, his face was of a fine florid hue, but after twelve o'clock, meridian—his dinner hour— it blazed like a grate full of Christmas coals; and continued blazing—but, as it were, with a gradual wane—till six o'clock, P.M., or thereabouts; after which, I saw no more of the proprietor of the face, which, gaining its meridian with the sun, seemed to set with it, to rise, culminate, and decline the following day, with the like regularity and undiminished glory. There are many singular coincidences I have known in the course of my life, not the least among which was the fact, that, exactly when Turkey displayed his fullest beams from his red and radiant countenance, just then, too, at that critical moment, began the daily period when I considered his business capacities as seriously disturbed for the remainder of the twenty-four hours. Not that he was absolutely idle, or averse to business, then; far from it. The difficulty was, he was apt to be altogether too energetic. There was a strange, inflamed, flurried, flighty recklessness of activity about him. He would be incautious in dipping his pen into his inkstand. All his blots upon my documents were dropped there after twelve o'clock, meridian. Indeed, not only would he be reckless, and sadly given to making blots in the afternoon, but, some days, he went further, and was rather noisy. At such times, too, his face flamed with augmented blazonry, as if cannel coal had been heaped on anthracite. He made an unpleasant racket with his chair; spilled his sand-box; in mending his pens, impatiently split them all to pieces, and threw them on the floor in a sudden passion; stood up, and leaned over his table, boxing his papers about in a most indecorous manner, very sad to behold in an elderly man like him. Nevertheless, as he was in many ways a most valuable person to me, and all the time before twelve o'clock, meridian, was the quickest, steadiest creature, too, accomplishing a great deal of work in a style not easily to be matched—for these reasons, I was willing to overlook his eccentricities, though, indeed, occasionally, I remonstrated with him. I did this very gently, however, because, though the civilest, nay, the blandest and most reverential of men in the morning, yet, in the afternoon, he was disposed, upon provocation, to be slightly rash with his tongue—in fact, insolent. Now, valuing his morning services as I did, and resolved not to lose them—yet, at the same time, made uncomfortable by his inflamed ways after twelve o'clock—and being a man of peace, unwilling by my admonitions to call forth unseemly retorts from him, I took upon me, one Saturday noon (he was always worse on Saturdays) to hint to him, very kindly, that, perhaps, now that he was growing old, it might be well to abridge his labours; in short, he need not come to my chambers after twelve o'clock, but, dinner over, had best go home to his lodgings, and rest himself till tea-time. But no; he insisted upon his afternoon devotions. His countenance became intolerably fervid, as he oratorically assured me—gesticulating with a long ruler at the other end of the room—that if his services in the morning were useful, how indispensable, then, in the afternoon?

"With submission, sir." said Turkey, on this occasion, "I consider myself your right-hand man. In the morning I but marshal and deploy my columns; but in the afternoon I put myself at their head, and gallantly charge the foe, thus"—and he made a violent thrust with the ruler.

"But the blots, Turkey," intimated I.

"True; but, with submission, sir, behold these hairs! I am getting old. Surely, sir, a blot or two of a warm afternoon is not to be severely urged against gray hairs. Old age—even if it blot the page—is honourable. With submission, sir, we *both* are getting old."

This appeal to my fellow-feeling was hardly to be resisted. At all events, I saw that go he would not. So, I made up my mind to let him stay, resolving, nevertheless, to see to it that, during the afternoon, he had to do with my less important papers.

Nippers, the second on my list, was a whiskered, sallow, and, upon the whole, rather piratical-looking young man, of about five-and-twenty. I always deemed him the victim of two evil powers—ambition and indigestion. The ambition was evinced by a certain impatience of the duties of a mere copyist, an unwarrantable usurpation of strictly professional affairs, such as the original drawing up of legal documents. The indigestion seemed betokened in an occasional nervous testiness and grinning irritability, causing the teeth to audibly grind together over mistakes committed in copying; unnecessary maledictions, hissed, rather than spoken, in the heat of business; and especially by a continual discontent with the height of the table where he worked. Though of a very ingenious mechanical turn, Nippers could never get this table to suit him. He put chips under it, blocks of various sorts, bits of pasteboard, and at last went so far as to attempt an exquisite adjustment, by final pieces of folded blotting-paper. But no invention would answer. If, for the sake of easing his back, he brought the table lid at a sharp angle well up toward his chin, and wrote there like a man using the steep roof of a Dutch house for his desk, then he declared that it stopped the circulation in his arms. If now he lowered the table to his waistbands, and stooped over it in writing, then there was a sore aching in his back. In short, the truth of the matter was, Nippers knew not what he wanted. Or, if he wanted anything, it was to be rid of a scrivener's table altogether. Among the manifestations of his diseased ambition was a fondness he had for receiving visits from certain ambiguous-looking fellows in seedy coats, whom he called his clients. Indeed, I was aware that not only was he, at times, considerable of a ward-politician, but he occasionally did a little business at the Justices' courts, and was not unknown on the steps of the Tombs. I have good reason to believe, however, that one individual who called upon him at my chambers, and who, with a grand air, he insisted was his client, was no other than a dun, and the alleged title-deed, a bill. But, with all his failings, and the annoyances he caused me, Nippers, like his compatriot Turkey, was a very useful man to me; wrote a neat, swift hand; and, when he chose, was not deficient in a gentlemanly sort of deportment. Added to this, he always dressed in a gentlemanly sort of way; and so, incidentally, reflected credit upon my chambers. Whereas, with respect to Turkey, I had much ado to keep him from being a reproach to me. His clothes were apt to look oily, and smell of eating-houses. He wore his pantaloons very loose and baggy in summer. His coats were execrable; his hat not to be handled. But while the hat was a thing of indifference to me, inasmuch as his natural civility and deference, as a dependent Englishman, always led him to doff it the moment he entered the room, yet his coat was another matter. Concerning his coats, I reasoned with him; but with no effect. The truth was, I suppose, that a man with so small an income could not afford to sport such a lustrous face and a lustrous coat at one and the same time. As Nippers once observed, Turkey's money went chiefly for red ink. One winter day, I presented Turkey with a highly respectable-looking coat of my own—a padded gray coat, of a most comfortable warmth, and which buttoned straight up from the knee to the neck. I thought Turkey would appreciate the favour, and abate his rashness and obstreperousness of afternoons. But no; I verily believe that buttoning himself up in so downy and blanket-like a coat had a pernicious effect upon him—upon the same principle that too much oats are bad for horses. In fact, precisely as a rash, restive horse is said to feel his oats, so Turkey felt his coat. It made him insolent. He was a man whom prosperity harmed.

Though, concerning the self-indulgent habits of Turkey, I had my own private surmises, yet, touching Nippers, I was well persuaded that, whatever might be his faults in other respects, he was, at least, a temperate young man. But, indeed, nature herself seemed to have been his vintner, and, at his birth, charged him so thoroughly with an irritable, brandy-like disposition, that all subsequent potations were needless. When I consider how, amid the stillness of my chambers, Nippers would sometimes impatiently rise from his seat, and stooping over his table, spread his arms wide apart, seize the whole desk, and move it, and jerk it, with a grim, grinding motion on the floor, as if the table were a perverse voluntary agent, intent on thwarting and vexing him, I plainly perceive that, for Nippers, brandy-and-water were altogether superfluous.

It was fortunate for me that, owing to its peculiar cause—indigestion—the irritability and consequent nervousness of Nippers were mainly observable in the morning, while in the afternoon he was comparatively mild. So that, Turkey's paroxysms only coming on about twelve o'clock, I never had to do with their eccentricities at one time. Their fits relieved each other, like guards. When Nippers's was on, Turkey's was off; and vice versa. This was a good natural arrangement, under the circumstances.

Ginger Nut, the third on my list, was a lad, some twelve years old. His father was a carman, ambitious of seeing his son on the bench instead of a cart, before he died. So he sent him to my office, as student at law, errand-boy, cleaner and sweeper, at the rate of one dollar a week. He had a little desk to himself, but he did not use it much. Upon inspection, the drawer exhibited a great array of the shells of various sorts of nuts. Indeed, to this quick-witted youth, the whole noble science of the law was contained in a nut-shell. Not the least among the employments of Ginger Nut, as well as one which he discharged with the most alacrity, was his duty as cake and apple purveyor for Turkey and Nippers. Copying law-papers being proverbially a dry, husky sort of business, my two scriveners were fain to moisten their mouths very often with Spitzenbergs, to be had at the numerous stalls nigh the Custom House and Post Office. Also, they sent Ginger Nut very frequently for that peculiar cake—small, flat, round, and very spicy—after which he had been named by them. Of a cold morning, when business was but dull, Turkey would gobble up scores of these cakes, as if they were mere wafers—indeed, they sell them at the rate of six or eight for a penny—the scrape of his pen blending with the crunching of the crisp particles in his mouth. Of all the fiery afternoon blunders and flurried rashnesses of Turkey, was his once moistening a ginger-cake between his lips, and clapping it on to a mortgage, for a seal. I came within an ace of dismissing him then. But he mollified me by making an oriental bow, and saying—"With submission, sir, it was generous of me to find you in stationery on my own account."

Now my original business—that of a conveyancer and title-hunter, and drawer-up of recondite documents of all sorts—was considerably increased by receiving the master's office. There was now great work for scriveners. Not only must I push the clerks already with me, but I must have additional help.

In answer to my advertisement, a motionless young man one morning stood upon my office threshold, the door being open, for it was summer. I can see that figure now—pallidly neat, pitiably respectable, incurably forlorn! It was Bartleby.

After a few words touching his qualifications, I engaged him, glad to have among my corps of copyists a man of so singularly sedate an aspect, which I thought might operate beneficially upon the flighty temper of Turkey, and the fiery one of Nippers.

I should have stated before that ground-glass folding-doors divided my premises into two parts, one of which was occupied by my scriveners, the other by myself. According to my humour, I threw open these doors, or closed them. I resolved to assign Bartleby a corner by the folding-doors, but on my side of them, so as to have this quiet man within easy call, in case any trifling thing was to be done. I placed his desk close up to a small side-window in that part of the room, a window which originally had afforded a lateral view of certain grimy back-yards and bricks, but which, owing to subsequent erections, commanded at present no view at all, though it gave some light. Within three feet of the panes was a wall, and the light came down from far above, between two lofty buildings, as from a very small opening in a dome. Still further to a satisfactory arrangement, I procured a high green folding-screen, which might entirely isolate Bartleby from my sight, though not remove him from my voice. And thus, in a manner, privacy and society were conjoined.

At first, Bartleby did an extraordinary quantity of writing. As if long famishing for something to copy, he seemed to gorge himself on my documents. There was no pause for digestion. He ran a day and night line, copying by sun-light and by candle-light. I should have been quite delighted with his application, had he been cheerfully industrious. But he wrote on silently, palely, mechanically.

It is, of course, an indispensable part of a scrivener's business to verify the accuracy of his copy, word by word. Where there are two or more scriveners in an office, they assist each other in this examination, one reading from the copy, the other holding the original. It is a very dull, wearisome, and lethargic affair. I can readily imagine that, to some sanguine temperaments, it would be altogether intolerable. For example, I cannot credit that the mettlesome poet, Byron, would have contentedly sat down with Bartleby to examine a law document of, say, five hundred pages, closely written in a crimpy hand.

Now and then, in the haste of business, it had been my habit to assist in comparing some brief document myself, calling Turkey or Nippers for this purpose. One object I had, in placing Bartleby so handy to me behind the screen, was, to avail myself of his services on such trivial occasions. It was on the third day, I think, of his being with me, and before any necessity had arisen for having his own writing examined, that, being much hurried to complete a small affair I had in hand, I abruptly called to Bartleby. In my haste and natural expectancy of instant compliance, I sat with my head bent over the original on my desk, and my right hand sideways, and somewhat nervously extended with the copy, so that, immediately upon emerging from his retreat, Bartleby might snatch it and proceed to business without the least delay.

In this very attitude did I sit when I called to him, rapidly stating what it was I wanted him to do—namely, to examine a small paper with me. Imagine my surprise, nay, my consternation, when, without moving from his privacy, Bartleby, in a singularly mild, firm voice, replied, "I would prefer not to."

I sat a while in perfect silence, rallying my stunned faculties. Immediately it occurred to me that my ears had deceived me, or Bartleby had entirely misunderstood my meaning. I repeated my request in the clearest tone I could assume; but in quite as clear a one came the previous reply, "I would prefer not to."

"Prefer not to," echoed I, rising in high excitement, and crossing the room with a stride. "What do you mean? Are you moon-struck? I want you to help me compare this sheet here—take it," and I thrust it toward him.

"I would prefer not to," said he.

I looked at him steadfastly. His face was leanly composed; his gray eye dimly calm. Not a wrinkle of agitation rippled him. Had there been the least uneasiness, anger, impatience, or impertinence in his manner; in other words, had there been anything ordinarily human about him, doubt-less I should have violently dismissed him from the premises. But as it was, I should have as soon thought of turning my pale plaster-of-paris bust of Cicero out of doors. I stood gazing at him a while, as he went on with his own writing, and then reseated myself at my desk. This is very strange, thought I. What had one best do? But my business hurried me. I concluded to forget the matter for the present, reserving it for my future leisure. So calling Nippers from the other room, the paper was speedily examined.

A few days after this, Bartleby concluded four lengthy documents, being quadruplicates of a week's testimony taken before me in my High Court of Chancery. It became necessary to examine them. It was an im-portant suit, and great accuracy was imperative. Having all things ar-ranged, I called Turkey, Nippers, and Ginger Nut, from the next room, meaning to place the four copies in the hands of my four clerks, while I should read from the original. Accordingly, Turkey, Nippers, and Ginger Nut had taken their seats in a row, each with his document in his hand, when I called to Bartleby to join this interesting group.

"Bartleby! quick, I am waiting."

I heard a slow scrape of his chair legs on the uncarpeted floor, and soon he appeared standing at the entrance of his hermitage.

"What is wanted?" said he mildly.

"The copies, the copies," said I hurriedly. "We are going to examine them. There"—and I held toward him the fourth quadruplicate.

"I would prefer not to," he said, and gently disappeared behind the screen.

For a few moments I was turned into a pillar of salt, standing at the head of my seated column of clerks. Recovering myself, I advanced toward the screen, and demanded the reason for such extraordinary conduct.

"*Why* do you refuse?"

"I would prefer not to."

With any other man I should have flown outright into a dreadful pas-sion, scorned all further words, and thrust him ignominiously from my presence. But there was something about Bartleby that not only strangely disarmed me, but, in a wonderful manner, touched and disconcerted me. I began to reason with him.

"These are your own copies we are about to examine. It is labour sav-ing to you, because one examination will answer for your papers. It is common usage. Every copyist is bound to help examine his copy. Is it not so? Will you not speak? Answer!"

"I prefer not to," he replied in a flute-like tone. It seemed to me that, while I had been addressing him, he carefully revolved every statement that I made; fully comprehended the meaning; could not gainsay the irresistible conclusion; but, at the same time, some paramount consideration prevailed with him to reply as he did.

"You are decided, then, not to comply with my request—a request made according to common usage and common sense?"

He briefly gave me to understand, that on that point my judgment was sound. Yes: his decision was irreversible.

It is not seldom the case that, when a man is brow-beaten in some unprecedented and violently unreasonable way, he begins to stagger in his own plainest faith. He begins, as it were, vaguely to surmise that, wonderful as it may be, all the justice and all the reason is on the other side. Accordingly, if any disinterested persons are present, he turns to them for some reinforcement for his own faltering mind.

"Turkey," said I, "what do you think of this? Am I not right?"

"With submission, sir," said Turkey, in his blandest tone, " I think that you are."

"Nippers," said I, "what do *you* think of it?"

"I think I should kick him out of the office."

(The reader, of nice perceptions, will here perceive that, it being morning, Turkey's answer is couched in polite and tranquil terms, but Nippers's replies in ill-tempered ones. Or, to repeat a previous sentence, Nippers's ugly mood was on duty, and Turkey's off.)

"Ginger Nut," said I, willing to enlist the smallest suffrage in my behalf, "what do *you* think of it?"

"I think, sir, he's a little *luny*," replied Ginger Nut, with a grin.

"You hear what they say," said I, turning toward the screen, "come forth and do your duty."

But he vouchsafed no reply. I pondered a moment in sore perplexity. But once more business hurried me. I determined again to postpone the consideration of this dilemma to my future leisure. With a little trouble we made out to examine the papers without Bartleby, though at every page or two Turkey deferentially dropped his opinion, that this proceeding was quite out of the common; while Nippers, twitching in his chair with a dyspeptic nervousness, ground out, between his set teeth, occasional hissing maledictions against the stubborn oaf behind the screen. And for his (Nippers's) part, this was the first and the last time he would do another man's business without pay.

Meanwhile Bartleby sat in his hermitage, oblivious to everything but his own peculiar business there.

Some days passed, the scrivener being employed upon another lengthy work. His late remarkable conduct led me to regard his ways narrowly. I observed that he never went to dinner; indeed, that he never went anywhere. As yet I had never, of my personal knowledge, known him to be outside of my office. He was a perpetual sentry in the corner. At about eleven o'clock though, in the morning, I noticed that Ginger Nut would advance toward the opening in Bartleby's screen, as if silently beckoned thither by a gesture invisible to me where I sat. The boy would then leave the office, jingling a few pence, and reappear with a handful of ginger-nuts, which he delivered in the hermitage, receiving two of the cakes for his trouble.

He lives, then, on ginger-nuts, thought I; never eats a dinner, properly speaking; he must be a vegetarian, then; but no; he never eats even vegetables, he eats nothing but ginger-nuts. My mind then ran on in reveries concerning the probable effects upon the human constitution of living entirely on ginger-nuts. Ginger-nuts are so called, because they contain ginger as one of their peculiar constituents, and the final flavouring one. Now, what was ginger? A hot, spicy thing. Was Bartleby hot and spicy? Not at all. Ginger, then, had no effect upon Bartleby. Probably he preferred it should have none.

Nothing so aggravates an earnest person as a passive resistance. If the individual so resisted be of a not inhumane temper, and the resisting one perfectly harmless in his passivity, then, in the better moods of the former, he will endeavour charitably to construe to his imagination what proves impossible to be solved by his judgment. Even so, for the most part, I regarded Bartleby and his ways. Poor fellow! thought I, he means no mischief; it is plain he intends no insolence; his aspect sufficiently evinces that his eccentricities are involuntary. He is useful to me. I can get along with him. If I turn him away, the chances are he will fall in with some less-indulgent employer, and then he will be rudely treated, and perhaps driven forth miserably to starve. Yes. Here I can cheaply purchase a delicious self-approval. To befriend Bartleby; to humour him in his strange wilfulness, will cost me little or nothing, while I lay up in my soul what will eventually prove a sweet morsel for my conscience. But this mood was not invariable with me. The passiveness of Bartleby sometimes irritated me. I felt strangely goaded on to encounter him in new opposition—to elicit some angry spark from him answerable to my own. But, indeed, I might as well have essayed to strike fire with my knuckles against a bit of Windsor soap. But one afternoon the evil impulse in me mastered me, and the following little scene ensued:—

"Bartleby," said I, "when those papers are all copied, I will compare them with you."

"I would prefer not to."

"How? Surely you do not mean to persist in that mulish vagary?"

No answer.

I threw open the folding-doors near by, and, turning upon Turkey and Nippers, exclaimed:

"Bartleby a second time says, he won't examine his papers. What do you think of it, Turkey?"

It was afternoon, be it remembered. Turkey sat glowing like a brass boiler; his bald head steaming; his hands reeling among his blotted papers.

"Think of it?" roared Turkey; "I think I'll just step behind his screen, and black his eyes for him!"

So saying, Turkey rose to his feet and threw his arms into a pugilistic position. He was hurrying away to make good his promise, when I detained him, alarmed at the effect of incautiously rousing Turkey's combativeness after dinner.

"Sit down, Turkey," said I, "and hear what Nippers has to say. What do you think of it, Nippers? Would I not be justified in immediately dismissing Bartleby?"

"Excuse me, that is for you to decide, sir. I think his conduct quite unusual, and, indeed, unjust, as regards Turkey and myself. But it may only be a passing whim."

"Ah," exclaimed I, "you have strangely changed your mind, then—you speak very gently of him now."

"All beer," cried Turkey; "gentleness is effects of beer—Nippers and I dined together to-day. You see how gentle *I* am, sir. Shall I go and black his eyes?"

"You refer to Bartleby, I suppose. No, not to-day, Turkey," I replied; "pray, put up your fists."

I closed the doors, and again advanced toward Bartleby. I felt additional incentives tempting me to my fate. I burned to be rebelled against again. I remembered that Bartleby never left the office.

"Bartleby," said I, "Ginger Nut is away; just step around to the Post Office, won't you? (it was but a three minutes' walk), and see if there is anything for me."

"I would prefer not to."

"You *will* not?"

"I *prefer* not."

I staggered to my desk, and sat there in a deep study. My blind inveteracy returned. Was there any other thing in which I could procure myself to be ignominiously repulsed by this lean, penniless wight?—my hired clerk? What added thing is there, perfectly reasonable, that he will be sure to refuse to do?

"Bartleby!"

No answer.

"Bartleby," in a louder tone.

No answer.

"Bartleby," I roared.

Like a very ghost, agreeably to the laws of magical invocation, at the third summons, he appeared at the entrance of his hermitage.

"Go to the next room, and tell Nippers to come to me."

"I prefer not to," he respectfully and slowly said, and mildly disappeared.

"Very good, Bartleby," said I, in a quiet sort of serenely-severe self-possessed tone, intimating the unalterable purpose of some terrible retribution very close at hand. At the moment I half intended something of the kind. But upon the whole, as it was drawing toward my dinner-hour, I thought it best to put on my hat and walk home for the day, suffering much from perplexity and distress of mind.

Shall I acknowledge it? The conclusion of this whole business was, that it soon became a fixed fact of my chambers, that a pale young scrivener, by the name of Bartleby, had a desk there; that he copied for me at the usual rate of four cents a folio (one hundred words); but he was permanently exempt from examining the work done by him, that duty being transferred to Turkey and Nippers, out of compliment, doubtless, to their superior acuteness; moreover, said Bartleby was never, on any account, to be dispatched on the most trivial errand of any sort; and that even if entreated to take upon him such a matter, it was generally understood that he would "prefer not to"—in other words, that he would refuse point-blank.

As days passed on, I became considerably reconciled to Bartleby. His steadiness, his freedom from all dissipation, his incessant industry (except when he chose to throw himself into a standing revery behind his screen), his great stillness, his unalterableness of demeanour under all circumstances, made him a valuable acquisition. One prime thing was this—*he was always there*—first in the morning, continually through the day, and the last at night. I had a singular confidence in his honesty. I felt my most precious papers perfectly safe in his hands. Sometimes, to be sure, I could not, for the very soul of me, avoid falling into sudden spasmodic passions with him. For it was exceeding difficult to bear in mind all the time those strange peculiarities, privileges, and unheard-of exemptions, forming the tacit stipulations on Bartleby's part under which he remained in my office. Now and then, in the eagerness of dispatching pressing business, I would inadvertently summon Bartleby, in a short, rapid tone, to put his finger, say, on the incipient tie of a bit of red tape with which I was about compressing some papers. Of course, from behind the screen the usual answer, "I prefer not to," was sure to come; and then, how could a human creature, with the common infirmities of our nature, refrain from bitterly exclaiming upon such perverseness — such unreasonableness. However, every added repulse of this sort which I received only tended to lessen the probability of my repeating the inadvertence.

Here it must be said, that according to the custom of most legal gentlemen occupying chambers in densely populated law-buildings, there were several keys to my door. One was kept by a woman residing in the attic, which person weekly scrubbed and daily swept and dusted my apartments. Another was kept by Turkey for convenience sake. The third I sometimes carried in my own pocket. The fourth I knew not who had.

Now, one Sunday morning I happened to go to Trinity Church, to hear a celebrated preacher, and finding myself rather early on the ground I thought I would walk round to my chambers for a while. Luckily I had my key with me; but upon applying it to the lock, I found it resisted by something inserted from the inside. Quite surprised, I called out; when to my consternation a key was turned from within; and thrusting his lean visage at me, and holding the door ajar, the apparition of Bartleby appeared, in his shirt-sleeves, and otherwise in a strangely tattered dishabille, saying quietly that he was sorry, but he was deeply engaged just then, and—preferred not admitting me at present. In a brief word or two, he moreover added, that perhaps I had better walk round the block two or three times, and by that time he would probably have concluded his affairs.

Now, the utterly unsurmised appearance of Bartleby, tenanting my law-chambers of a Sunday morning, with his cadaverously gentlemanly nonchalance, yet withal firm and self-possessed, had such a strange effect upon me, that incontinently I slunk away from my own door, and did as desired. But not without sundry twinges of impotent rebellion against the mild effrontery of this unaccountable scrivener. Indeed, it was his wonderful mildness chiefly, which not only disarmed me, but unmanned me as it were. For I consider that one, for the time, is a sort of unmanned when he tranquilly permits his hired clerk to dictate to him, and order him away from his own premises. Furthermore, I was full of uneasiness as to what Bartleby could possibly be doing in my office in his shirt-sleeves, and in an otherwise dismantled condition of a Sunday morning. Was anything amiss going on? Nay, that was out of the question. It was not to be thought of for a moment that Bartleby was an immoral person. But what could he be doing there?—copying? Nay again, whatever might be his eccentricities, Bartleby was an eminently decorous person. He would be the last man to sit down to his desk in any state approaching to nudity. Besides, it was Sunday; and there was something about Bartleby that forbade the supposition that he would by any secular occupation violate the proprieties of the day.

Nevertheless, my mind was not pacified; and full of a restless curiosity, at last I returned to the door. Without hindrance I inserted my key, opened it, and entered. Bartleby was not to be seen. I looked round anxiously, peeped behind his screen; but it was very plain that he was gone. Upon more closely examining the place, I surmised that for an indefinite period Bartleby must have ate, dressed, and slept in my office, and that, too, without plate, mirror, or bed. The cushioned seat of a rickety old sofa in one corner bore the faint impress of a lean, reclining form. Rolled away under his desk, I found a blanket; under the empty grate a blacking box and brush; on a chair, a tin basin, with soap and a ragged towel; in a newspaper a few crumbs of ginger-nuts and a morsel of cheese. Yes, thought I, it is evident enough that Bartleby has been making his home here, keeping bachelor's hall all by himself. Immediately then the thought came sweeping across me, what miserable friendlessness and loneliness are here revealed! His poverty is great; but his solitude, how horrible! Think of it. Of a Sunday, Wall Street is deserted as Petra; and every night of every day it is an emptiness. This building, too, which of week-days hums with industry and life, at nightfall echoes with sheer vacancy, and all through Sunday is forlorn. And here Bartleby makes his home; sole spectator of a solitude which he has seen all-populous—a sort of innocent and transformed Marius brooding among the ruins of Carthage!

For the first time in my life a feeling of overpowering stinging melancholy seized me. Before, I had never experienced aught but a not unpleasing sadness. The bond of a common humanity now drew me irresistibly to gloom. A fraternal melancholy! For both I and Bartleby were sons of Adam. I remembered the bright silks and sparkling faces I had seen that day, in gala trim, swan-like sailing down the Mississippi of Broadway; and I contrasted them with the pallid copyist, and thought to myself, Ah, happiness courts the light, so we deem the world is gay; but misery hides aloof, so we deem that misery there is none. These sad fancyings—chimeras, doubtless, of a sick and silly brain—led on to other and more special thoughts, concerning the eccentricities of Bartleby. Presentiments of strange discoveries hovered round me. The scrivener's pale form appeared to me laid out, among uncaring strangers, in its shivering winding-sheet.

Suddenly I was attracted by Bartleby's closed desk, the key in open sight left in the lock.

I mean no mischief, seek the gratification of no heartless curiosity, thought I; besides, the desk is mine, and its contents, too, so I will make bold to look within. Everything was methodically arranged, the papers smoothly placed. The pigeon-holes were deep, and removing the files of documents, I groped into their recesses. Presently I felt something there, and dragged it out. It was an old bandanna handkerchief, heavy and knotted. I opened it, and saw it was a savings-bank.

I now recalled all the quiet mysteries which I had noted in the man. I remembered that he never spoke but to answer; that, though at intervals he had considerable time to himself, yet I had never seen him reading—no, not even a newspaper; that for long periods he would stand looking out, at his pale window behind the screen, upon the dead brick wall; I was quite sure he never visited any refectory or eating-house; while his pale face clearly indicated that he never drank beer like Turkey, or tea and coffee even, like other men; that he never went anywhere in particular that I could learn; never went out for a walk, unless, indeed, that was the case at present; that he had declined telling who he was, or whence he came, or whether he had any relatives in the world; that though so thin and pale, he never complained of ill health. And more than all, I remembered a certain unconscious air of pallid—how shall I call it?—of pallid haughtiness, say, or rather an austere reserve about him, which had positively awed me into my tame compliance with his eccentricities, when I had feared to ask him to do the slightest incidental thing for me, even though I might know, from his long-continued motionlessness, that behind his screen he must be standing in one of those dead-wall reveries of his.

Revolving all these things, and coupling them with the recently discovered fact, that he made my office his constant abiding-place and home, and not forgetful of his morbid moodiness; revolving all these things, a prudential feeling began to steal over me. My first emotions had been those of pure melancholy and sincerest pity; but just in proportion as the forlornness of Bartleby grew and grew to my imagination, did that same melancholy merge into fear, that pity into repulsion. So true it is, and so terrible, too, that up to a certain point the thought or sight of misery enlists our best affections; but, in certain special cases, beyond that point it does not. They err who would assert that invariably this is owing to the inherent selfishness of the human heart. It rather proceeds from a certain hopelessness of remedying excessive and organic ill. To a sensitive being, pity is not seldom pain. And when at last it is perceived that such pity cannot lead to effectual succour, commonsense bids the soul be rid of it. What I saw that morning persuaded me that the scrivener was the victim of innate and incurable disorder. I might give alms to his body; but his body did not pain him; it was his soul that suffered, and his soul I could not reach.

I did not accomplish the purpose of going to Trinity Church that morning. Somehow, the things I had seen disqualified me for the time from church-going. I walked homeward, thinking what I would do with Bartleby. Finally, I resolved upon this—I would put certain calm questions to him the next morning, touching his history, etc., and if he declined to answer them openly and unreservedly (and I supposed he would prefer not), then to give him a twenty-dollar bill over and above whatever I might owe him, and tell him his services were no longer required; but that if in any other way I could assist him, I would be happy to do so, especially if he desired to return to his native place, wherever that might be, I would willingly help to defray the expenses. Moreover, if, after reaching home, he found himself at any time in want of aid, a letter from him would be sure of a reply.

The next morning came.

"Bartleby," said I, gently calling to him behind his screen.

No reply.

"Bartleby," said I, in a still gentler tone, "come here; I am not going to ask you to do anything you would prefer not to do—I simply wish to speak to you."

Upon this he noiselessly slid into view.

"Will you tell me, Bartleby, where you were born?"

"I would prefer not to."

"Will you tell me *anything* about yourself?"

"I would prefer not to."

"But what reasonable objection can you have to speak to me? I feel friendly toward you."

He did not look at me while I spoke, but kept his glance fixed upon my bust of Cicero, which, as I then sat, was directly behind me, some six inches above my head.

"What is your answer, Bartleby?" said I, after waiting a considerable time for a reply, during which his countenance remained immovable, only there was the faintest conceivable tremor of the white attenuated mouth.

"At present I prefer to give no answer," he said, and retired into his hermitage.

It was rather weak in me, I confess, but his manner, on this occasion, nettled me. Not only did there seem to lurk in it a certain calm disdain, but his perverseness seemed ungrateful, considering the undeniable good usage and indulgence he had received from me.

Again I sat ruminating what I should do. Mortified as I was at his behaviour, and resolved as I had been to dismiss him when I entered my office, nevertheless I strangely felt something superstitious knocking at my heart, and forbidding me to carry out my purpose, and denouncing me for a villain if I dared to breathe one bitter word against this forlornest of mankind. At last, familiarly drawing my chair behind his screen, I sat down and said: "Bartleby, never mind, then, about revealing your history; but let me entreat you, as a friend, to comply as far as may be with the usages of this office. Say now, you will help to examine papers to-morrow or next day: in short, say now, that in a day or two you will begin to be a little reasonable:—say so, Bartleby."

"At present I would prefer not to be a little reasonable," was his mildly cadaverous reply.

Just then the folding-doors opened, and Nippers approached. He seemed suffering from an unusually bad night's rest, induced by severer indigestion than common. He overheard those final words of Bartleby.

"*Prefer not*, eh?" gritted Nippers—"I'd *prefer* him, if I were you, sir," addressing me—"I'd *prefer* him; I'd give him preferences, the stubborn mule! What is it, sir, pray, that he *prefers* not to do now?"

Bartleby moved not a limb.

"Mr. Nippers," said I, "I'd prefer that you would withdraw for the present."

Somehow, of late, I had got into the way of involuntarily using this word "prefer" upon all sorts of not exactly suitable occasions. And I trembled to think that my contact with the scrivener had already and seriously affected me in a mental way. And what further and deeper aberration might it not yet produce? This apprehension had not been without efficacy in determining me to summary measures.

As Nippers, looking very sour and sulky, was departing, Turkey blandly and deferentially approached.

"With submission, sir," said he, "yesterday I was thinking about Bartleby here, and I think that if he would but prefer to take a quart of good ale every day, it would do much toward mending him, and enabling him to assist in examining his papers."

"So you have got the word too," said I, slightly excited.

"With submission, what word, sir," asked Turkey, respectfully crowding himself into the contracted space behind the screen, and by so doing, making me jostle the scrivener. "What word, sir?"

"I would prefer to be left alone here," said Bartleby, as if offended at being mobbed in his privacy.

"*That's* the word, Turkey," said I—"*that's* it."

"Oh, *prefer*? oh yes—queer word. I never use it myself. But, sir, as I was saying, if he would but prefer——"

"Turkey," interrupted I, "you will please withdraw."

"Oh certainly, sir, if you prefer that I should."

As he opened the folding-door to retire, Nippers at his desk caught a glimpse of me, and asked whether I would prefer to have a certain paper copied on blue paper or white. He did not in the least roguishly accent the word prefer. It was plain that it involuntarily rolled from his tongue. I thought to myself, surely I must get rid of a demented man, who already has in some degree turned the tongues, if not the heads of myself and clerks. But I thought it prudent not to break the dismission at once.

The next day I noticed that Bartleby did nothing but stand at his window in his dead-wall revery. Upon asking him why he did not write, he said that he had decided upon doing no more writing.

"Why, how now? what next?" exclaimed I, "do no more writing?"

"No more."

"And what is the reason?"

"Do you not see the reason for yourself?" he indifferently replied.

I looked steadfastly at him, and perceived that his eyes looked dull and glazed. Instantly it occurred to me, that his unexampled diligence in copying by his dim window for the first few weeks of his stay with me might have temporarily impaired his vision.

I was touched. I said something in condolence with him. I hinted that of course he did wisely in abstaining from writing for a while; and urged him to embrace that opportunity of taking wholesome exercise in the open air. This, however, he did not do. A few days after this, my other clerks being absent, and being in a great hurry to dispatch certain letters by the mail, I thought that having nothing else earthly to do, Bartleby would surely be less inflexible than usual, and carry these letters to the Post Office. But he blankly declined. So, much to my inconvenience, I went myself.

Still added days went by. Whether Bartleby's eyes improved or not, I could not say. To all appearance, I thought they did. But when I asked him if they did, he vouchsafed no answer. At all events, he would do no copying. At last, in reply to my urgings, he informed me that he had permanently given up copying.

"What!" exclaimed I; "suppose your eyes should get entirely well—better than ever before—would you not copy then?"

"I have given up copying," he answered, and slid aside.

He remained as ever, a fixture in my chamber. Nay—if that were possible—he became still more of a fixture than before. What was to be done? He would do nothing in the office; why should he stay there? In plain fact, he had now become a millstone to me, not only useless as a necklace, but afflictive to bear. Yet I was sorry for him. I speak less than truth when I say that, on his own account, he occasioned me uneasiness. If he would but have named a single relative or friend, I would instantly have written, and urged their taking the poor fellow away to some convenient retreat. But he seemed alone, absolutely alone in the universe. A bit of wreck in the mid-Atlantic. At length, necessities connected with my business tyrannised over all other considerations. Decently as I could, I told Bartleby that in six days' time he must unconditionally leave the office. I warned him to take measures, in the interval, for procuring some other abode. I offered to assist him in this endeavour, if he himself would but take the first step toward a removal. "And when you finally quit me, Bartleby," added I, "I shall see that you go not away entirely unprovided. Six days from this hour, remember."

At the expiration of that period, I peeped behind the screen, and lo! Bartleby was there.

I buttoned up my coat, balanced myself; advanced slowly toward him, touched his shoulder, and said, "The time has come; you must quit this place; I am sorry for you; here is money; but you must go."

"I would prefer not," he replied, with his back still toward me.

"You *must*."

He remained silent.

Now I had an unbounded confidence in this man's common honesty. He had frequently restored to me sixpences and shillings carelessly dropped upon the floor, for I am apt to be very reckless in such shirt-button affairs.

The proceeding, then, which followed will not be deemed extraordinary.

"Bartleby," said I, "I owe you twelve dollars on account; here are thirty-two; the odd twenty are yours—Will you take it?" and I handed the bills toward him.

But he made no motion.

"I will leave them here, then," putting them under a weight on the table. Then taking my hat and cane and going to the door, I tranquilly turned and added—"After you have removed your things from these offices, Bartleby, you will of course lock the door—since everyone is now gone for the day but you—and if you please, slip your key underneath the mat, so that I may have it in the morning. I shall not see you again; so good-bye to you. If, hereafter, in your new place of abode, I can be of any service to you, do not fail to advise me by letter. Good-bye, Bartleby, and fare you well."

But he answered not a word; like the last column of some ruined temple, he remained standing mute and solitary in the middle of the otherwise deserted room.

As I walked home in a pensive mood, my vanity got the better of my pity. I could not but highly plume myself on my masterly management in getting rid of Bartleby. Masterly I call it, and such it must appear to any dispassionate thinker. The beauty of my procedure seemed to consist in its perfect quietness. There was no vulgar bullying, no bravado of any sort, no choleric hectoring, and striding to and fro across the apartment, jerking out vehement commands for Bartleby to bundle himself off with his beggarly traps. Nothing of the kind. Without loudly bidding Bartleby depart—as an inferior genius might have done—I *assumed* the ground that depart he must; and upon that assumption built all I had to say. The more I thought over my procedure, the more I was charmed with it. Nevertheless, next morning, upon awakening, I had my doubts—I had somehow slept off the fumes of vanity. One of the coolest and wisest hours a man has, is just after he awakes in the morning. My procedure seemed as sagacious as ever—but only in theory. How it would prove in practice—there was the rub. It was truly a beautiful thought to have assumed Bartleby's departure; but, after all, that assumption was simply my own, and none of Bartleby's. The great point was, not whether I had assumed that he would quit me, but whether he would prefer so to do. He was more a man of preferences than assumptions.

After breakfast, I walked down town, arguing the probabilities *pro* and *con*. One moment I thought it would prove a miserable failure, and Bartleby would be found all alive at my office as usual; the next moment it seemed certain that I should find his chair empty. And so I kept veering about. At the corner of Broadway and Canal Street, I saw quite an excited group of people standing in earnest conversation.

"I'll take odds he doesn't," said a voice as I passed.

"Doesn't go?—done!" said I; "put up your money."

I was instinctively putting my hand in my pocket to produce my own, when I remembered that this was an election day. The words I had overheard bore no reference to Bartleby, but to the success or non-success of some candidate for the mayoralty. In my intent frame of mind, I had, as it were, imagined that all Broadway shared in my excitement, and were debating the same question with me. I passed on, very thankful that the uproar of the street screened my momentary absent-mindedness.

As I had intended, I was earlier than usual at my office door. I stood listening for a moment. All was still. He must be gone. I tried the knob. The door was locked. Yes, my procedure had worked to a charm; he indeed must be vanished. Yet a certain melancholy mixed with this: I was almost sorry for my brilliant success. I was fumbling under the door-mat for the key, which Bartleby was to have left there for me, when accidentally my knee knocked against a panel, producing a summoning sound, and in response a voice came to me from within—"Not yet; I am occupied."

It was Bartleby.

I was thunderstruck. For an instant I stood like the man who, pipe in mouth, was killed one cloudless afternoon long ago in Virginia, by summer lightning; at his own warm open window he was killed, and remained leaning out there upon the dreamy afternoon, till someone touched him, when he fell.

"Not gone!" I murmured at last. But again obeying that wondrous ascendency which the inscrutable scrivener had over me, and from which ascendency, for all my chafing, I could not completely escape, I slowly went downstairs and out into the street, and while walking round the block, considered what I should next do in this unheard-of perplexity. Turn the man out by an actual thrusting I could not; to drive him away by calling him hard names would not do; calling in the police was an unpleasant idea; and yet, permit him to enjoy his cadaverous triumph over me—this, too, I could not think of. What was to be done? or, if nothing could be done, was there anything further that I could *assume* in the matter? Yes, as before I had prospectively assumed that Bartleby would depart, so now I might retrospectively assume that departed he was. In the legitimate carrying out of this assumption, I might enter my office in a great hurry, and pretending not to see Bartleby at all, walk straight against him as if he were air. Such a proceeding would in a singular degree have the appearance of a home-thrust. It was hardly possible that Bartleby could withstand such an application of the doctrine of assumptions. But upon second thoughts the success of the plan seemed rather dubious. I resolved to argue the matter over with him again.

"Bartleby," said I, entering the office, with a quietly severe expression, "I am seriously displeased. I am pained, Bartleby. I had thought better of you. I had imagined you of such a gentlemanly organisation, that in any delicate dilemma a slight hint would suffice—in short, an assumption. But it appears I am deceived. Why," I added, unaffectedly starting, "you have not even touched that money yet," pointing to it, just where I had left it the evening previous.

He answered nothing.

"Will you, or will you not, quit me?" I now demanded in a sudden passion, advancing close to him.

"I would prefer *not* to quit you," he replied, gently emphasising the *not*.

"What earthly right have you to stay here? Do you pay any rent? Do you pay my taxes? Or is this property yours?"

He answered nothing.

"Are you ready to go on and write now? Are your eyes recovered? Could you copy a small paper for me this morning? or help examine a few lines? or step round to the Post Office? In a word, will you do any-thing at all, to give a colouring to your refusal to depart the premises?"

He silently retired into his hermitage.

I was now in such a state of nervous resentment that I thought it but prudent to check myself at present from further demonstrations. Bartleby and I were alone. I remembered the tragedy of the unfortunate Adams and the still more unfortunate Colt in the solitary office of the latter; and how poor Colt, being dreadfully incensed by Adams, and imprudently permitting himself to get wildly excited, was at unawares hurried into his fatal act—an act which certainly no man could possibly deplore more than the actor himself. Often it had occurred to me in my ponderings upon the subject, that had that altercation taken place in the public street, or at a private residence, it would not have terminated as it did. It was the circumstance of being alone in a solitary office, upstairs, of a building entirely unhallowed by humanising domestic associations—an uncarpeted office, doubtless, of a dusty, haggard sort of appearance—this it must have been, which greatly helped to enhance the irritable desperation of the hapless Colt.

But when this old Adam of resentment rose in me and tempted me con-cerning Bartleby, I grappled him and threw him. How? Why, simply by recalling the divine injunction: "A new commandment give I unto you, that ye love one another." Yes, this it was that saved me. Aside from higher considerations, charity often operates as a vastly wise and prudent principle—a great safeguard to its possessor. Men have committed murder for jealousy's sake, and anger's sake, and hatred's sake, and selfishness' sake, and spiritual pride's sake; but no man, that ever I heard of, ever committed a diabolical murder for sweet charity's sake. Mere self-interest, then, if no better motive can be enlisted, should, especially with high-tempered men, prompt all beings to charity and philanthropy. At any rate, upon the occasion in question, I strove to drown my exasperated feelings toward the scrivener by benevolently construing his conduct. Poor fellow, poor fellow! thought I, he don't mean anything; and besides, he has seen hard times, and ought to be indulged.

I endeavoured, also, immediately to occupy myself, and at the same time to comfort my despondency. I tried to fancy, that in the course of the morning, at such time as might prove agreeable to him, Bartleby, of his own free accord, would emerge from his heritage and take up some decided line of march in the direction of the door. But no. Half-past twelve o'clock came; Turkey began to glow in the face, overturn his ink-stand, and become generally obstreperous; Nippers abated down into quietude and courtesy; Ginger Nut munched his noon apple; and Bartleby remained standing at his window in one of his profoundest dead-wall reveries. Will it be credited? Ought I to acknowledge it? That afternoon I left the office without saying one further word to him.

Some days now passed, during which, at leisure intervals, I looked a little into "Edwards on the Will," and "Priestley on Necessity." Under the circumstances, those books induced a salutary feeling. Gradually I slid into the persuasion that these troubles of mine, touching the scrivener, had been all predestinated from eternity, and Bartleby was billeted upon me for some mysterious purpose of an all-wise Providence, which it was not for a mere mortal like me to fathom. Yes, Bartleby, stay there behind your screen, thought I; I shall persecute you no more; you are harmless and noiseless as any of these old chairs; in short, I never feel so private as when I know you are here. At last I see it, I feel it; I penetrate to the predestinated purpose of my life. I am content. Others may have loftier parts to enact; but my mission in this world, Bartleby, is to furnish you with office-room for such period as you may see fit to remain.

I believe that this wise and blessed frame of mind would have continued with me, had it not been for the unsolicited and uncharitable remarks obtruded upon me by my professional friends who visited the rooms. But thus it often is, that the constant friction of illiberal minds wears out at last the best resolves of the more generous. Though to be sure, when I reflected upon it, it was not strange that people entering my office should be struck by the peculiar aspect of the unaccountable Bartleby, and so be tempted to throw out some sinister observations concerning him. Sometimes an attorney, having business with me, and calling at my office, and finding no one but the scrivener there, would undertake to obtain some sort of precise information from him touching my whereabouts; but without heeding his idle talk, Bartleby would remain standing immovable in the middle of the room. So after contemplating him in that position for a time, the attorney would depart, no wiser than he came.

Also, when a reference was going on, and the room full of lawyers and witnesses, and business driving fast, some deeply occupied legal gentleman present, seeing Bartleby wholly unemployed, would request him to run round to his (the legal gentleman's) office and fetch some papers for him.

Thereupon, Bartleby would tranquilly decline, and yet remain idle as before. Then the lawyer would give a great stare, and turn to me. And what could I say? At last I was made aware that all through the circle of my professional acquaintance, a whisper of wonder was running round, having reference to the strange creature I kept at my office. This worried me very much. And as the idea came upon me of his possibly turning out a long-lived man, and keep occupying my chambers, and denying my authority; and perplexing my visitors; and scandalising my professional reputation; and casting a general gloom over the premises; keeping soul and body together to the last upon his savings (for doubtless he spent but half a dime a day), and in the end perhaps outlive me, and claim possession of my office by right of his perpetual occupancy: as all these dark anticipations crowded upon me more and more, and my friends continually intruded their relentless remarks upon the apparition in my room; a great change was wrought in me. I resolved to gather all my faculties together, and forever rid me of this intolerable incubus.

Ere revolving any complicated project, however, adapted to this end, I first simply suggested to Bartleby the propriety of his permanent departure. In a calm and serious tone, I commended the idea to his careful and mature consideration. But, having taken three days to meditate upon it, he apprised me, that his original determination remained the same; in short, that he still preferred to abide with me.

What shall I do? I now said to myself, buttoning up my coat to the last button. What shall I do? what ought I to do? what does conscience say I *should* do with this man, or, rather, ghost. Rid myself of him, I must; go, he shall. But how? You will not thrust him, the poor, pale, passive mortal—you will not thrust such a helpless creature out of your door? you will not dishonour yourself by such cruelty? No, I will not, I cannot do that. Rather would I let him live and die here, and then mason up his remains in the wall. What, then, will you do? For all your coaxing, he will not budge. Bribes he leaves under your own paperweight on your table; in short, it is quite plain that he prefers to cling to you.

Then something severe, something unusual must be done. What! surely you will not have him collared by a constable, and commit his innocent pallor to the common jail? And upon what ground could you procure such a thing to be done?—a vagrant, is he? What! he a vagrant, a wanderer, who refuses to budge? It is because he will *not* be a vagrant, then, that you seek to count him *as* a vagrant. That is too absurd. No visible means of support; there I have him. Wrong again: for indubitably he *does* support himself, and that is the only unanswerable proof that any man can show of his possessing the means so to do. No more, then. Since he will not quit me, I must quit him. I will change my offices; I will move elsewhere, and give him fair notice, that if I find him on my new premises I will then proceed against him as a common trespasser.

Acting accordingly, next day I thus addressed him: "I find these chambers too far from the City Hall; the air is unwholesome. In a word, I propose to remove my offices next week, and shall no longer require your services. I tell you this now, in order that you may seek another place."

He made no reply, and nothing more was said.

On the appointed day I engaged carts and men, proceeded to my chambers, and, having but little furniture, everything was removed in a few hours. Throughout, the scrivener remained standing behind the screen, which I directed to be removed the last thing. It was withdrawn; and, being folded up like a huge folio, left him the motionless occupant of a naked room. I stood in the entry watching him a moment, while something from within me upbraided me.

I re-entered, with my hand in my pocket—and—and my heart in my mouth.

"Good-bye, Bartleby; I am going—good-bye, and God some way bless you; and take that," slipping something in his hand. But it dropped upon the floor, and then—strange to say—I tore myself from him whom I had so longed to be rid of.

Established in my new quarters, for a day or two I kept the door locked, and started at every footfall in the passages. When I returned to my rooms, after any little absence, I would pause at the threshold for an instant, and attentively listen ere applying my key. But these fears were needless. Bartleby never came nigh me.

I thought all was going well, when a perturbed-looking stranger visited me, inquiring whether I was the person who had recently occupied rooms at No.—Wall Street.

Full of forebodings, I replied that I was.

"Then, sir," said the stranger, who proved a lawyer, "you are responsible for the man you left there. He refuses to do any copying; he refuses to do anything; he says he prefers not to; and he refuses to quit the premises."

"I am very sorry, sir," said I, with assumed tranquillity, but an inward tremor, "but, really, the man you allude to is nothing to me—he is no relation or apprentice of mine, that you should hold me responsible for him."

"In mercy's name, who is he?"

"I certainly cannot inform you. I know nothing about him. Formerly I employed him as a copyist; but he has done nothing for me now for some time past."

"I shall settle him, then—good morning, sir."

Several days passed, and I heard nothing more; and, though I often felt a charitable prompting to call at the place and see poor Bartleby, yet a certain squeamishness, of I know not what, withheld me.

All is over with him, by this time, thought I, at last, when, through another week, no further intelligence reached me. But, coming to my room the day after, I found several persons waiting at my door in a high state of nervous excitement.

"That's the man—here he comes," cried the foremost one, whom I recognised as the lawyer who had previously called upon me alone.

"You must take him away, sir, at once," cried a portly person among them, advancing upon me, and whom I knew to be the landlord of No.— Wall Street. "These gentlemen, my tenants, cannot stand it any longer; Mr. B——," pointing to the lawyer, "has turned him out of his room, and he now persists in haunting the building generally, sitting upon the banisters of the stairs by day, and sleeping in the entry by night. Everybody is concerned; clients are leaving the offices; some fears are entertained of a mob; something you must do, and that without delay."

Aghast at this torrent, I fell back before it, and would fain have locked myself in my new quarters. In vain I persisted that Bartleby was nothing to me—no more than to anyone else. In vain—I was the last person known to have anything to do with him, and they held me to the terrible account. Fearful, then, of being exposed in the papers (as one person present obscurely threatened), I considered the matter, and, at length, said, that if the lawyer would give me a confidential interview with the scrivener, in his (the lawyer's) own room, I would, that afternoon, strive my best to rid them of the nuisance they complained of.

Going upstairs to my old haunt, there was Bartleby silently sitting upon the banister at the landing.

"What are you doing here, Bartleby?" said I.

"Sitting upon the banister," he mildly replied.

I motioned him into the lawyer's room, who then left us.

"Bartleby," said I, "are you aware that you are the cause of great tribulation to me, by persisting in occupying the entry after being dismissed from the office?"

No answer.

"Now one of two things must take place. Either you must do something, or something must be done to you. Now what sort of business would you like to engage in? Would you like to re-engage in copying for someone?"

"No; I would prefer not to make any change."

"Would you like a clerkship in a dry-goods store?"

"There is too much confinement about that. No, I would not like a clerkship; but I am not particular."

"Too much confinement," I cried, "why, you keep yourself confined all the time!"

"I would prefer not to take a clerkship," he rejoined, as if to settle that little item at once.

"How would a bar-tender's business suit you? There is no trying of the eyesight in that."

"I would not like it at all; though, as I said before, I am not particular."

His unwonted wordiness inspirited me. I returned to the charge.

"Well, then, would you like to travel through the country collecting bills for the merchants? That would improve your health."

"No, I would prefer to be doing something else."

"How, then, would going as a companion to Europe, to entertain some young gentleman with your conversation—how would that suit you?"

"Not at all. It does not strike me that there is anything definite about that. I like to be stationary. But I am not particular."

"Stationary you shall be, then," I cried, now losing all patience, and, for the first time in all my exasperating connection with him, fairly flying into a passion. "If you do not go away from these premises before night, I shall feel bound—indeed, I *am* bound—to—to quit the premises myself!" I rather absurdly concluded, knowing not with what possible threat to try to frighten his immobility into compliance. Despairing of all further efforts, I was precipitately leaving him, when a final thought occurred to me—one which had not been wholly unindulged before.

"Bartleby," said I, in the kindest tone I could assume under such exciting circumstances, "will you go home with me now—not to my office, but my dwelling—and remain there till we can conclude upon some convenient arrangement for you at our leisure? Come, let us start now, right away."

"No; at present I would prefer not to make any change at all."

I answered nothing; but, effectually dodging everyone by the suddenness and rapidity of my flight, rushed from the building, ran up Wall Street toward Broadway, and, jumping into the first omnibus, was soon removed from pursuit. As soon as tranquillity returned, I distinctly perceived that I had now done all that I possibly could, both in respect to the demands of the landlord and his tenants, and with regard to my own desire and sense of duty, to benefit Bartleby, and shield him from rude persecution. I now strove to be entirely carefree and quiescent; and my conscience justified me in the attempt; though, indeed, it was not so successful as I could have wished. So fearful was I of being again hunted out by the incensed landlord and his exasperated tenants, that, surrendering my business to Nippers, for a few days, I drove about the upper part of the town and through the suburbs, in my rockaway; crossed over to Jersey City and Hoboken, and paid fugitive visits to Manhattanville and Astoria. In fact, I almost lived in my rockaway for the time.

When again I entered my office, lo, a note from the landlord lay upon the desk. I opened it with trembling hands. It informed me that the writer had sent to the police, and had Bartleby removed to the Tombs as a vagrant. Moreover, since I knew more about him than anyone else, he wished me to appear at that place, and make a suitable statement of the facts. These tidings had a conflicting effect upon me. At first I was indignant; but, at last, almost approved. The landlord's energetic, summary disposition had led him to adopt a procedure which I do not think I would have decided upon myself; and yet, as a last resort, under such peculiar circumstances, it seemed the only plan.

As I afterward learned, the poor scrivener, when told that he must be conducted to the Tombs, offered not the slightest obstacle, but, in his pale, unmoving way, silently acquiesced.

Some of the compassionate and curious bystanders joined the party; and headed by one of the constables arm in arm with Bartleby, the silent procession filed its way through all the noise, and heat, and joy of the roaring thoroughfares at noon.

The same day I received the note, I went to the Tombs, or, to speak more properly, the Halls of Justice. Seeking the right officer, I stated the purpose of my call, and was informed that the individual I described was, indeed, within. I then assured the functionary that Bartleby was a perfectly honest man, and greatly to be compassionated, however unaccountably eccentric. I narrated all I knew, and closed by suggesting the idea of letting him remain in as indulgent confinement as possible, till something less harsh might be done—though, indeed, I hardly knew what. At all events, if nothing else could be decided upon, the almshouse must receive him. I then begged to have an interview.

Being under no disgraceful charge, and quite serene and harmless in all his ways, they had permitted him freely to wander about the prison, and, especially, in the enclosed grass-platted yards thereof. And so I found him there, standing all alone in the quietest of the yards, his face toward a high wall, while all around, from the narrow slits of the jail windows, I thought I saw peering out upon him the eyes of murderers and thieves.

"Bartleby!"

"I know you," he said, without looking round—"and I want nothing to say to you."

"It was not I that brought you here, Bartleby," said I, keenly pained at his implied suspicion. "And to you, this should not be so vile a place. Nothing reproachful attaches to you by being here. And see, it is not so sad a place as one might think. Look, there is the sky, and here is the grass."

"I know where I am," he replied, but would say nothing more, and so I left him.

As I entered the corridor again, a broad meat-like man, in an apron, accosted me, and, jerking his thumb over his shoulder, said, "Is that your friend?"

"Yes."

"Does he want to starve? If he does, let him live on the prison fare, that's all."

"Who are you?" asked I, not knowing what to make of such an unofficially speaking person in such a place.

"I am the grub-man. Such gentlemen as have friends here, hire me to provide them with something good to eat."

"Is this so?" said I, turning to the turnkey.

He said it was.

"Well, then," said I, slipping some silver into the grub-man's hands (for so they called him), "I want you to give particular attention to my friend there; let him have the best dinner you can get. And you must be as polite to him as possible."

"Introduce me, will you?" said the grub-man, looking at me with an expression which seemed to say he was all impatience for an opportunity to give a specimen of his breeding.

Thinking it would prove of benefit to the scrivener, I acquiesced; and, asking the grub-man his name, went up with him to Bartleby.

"Bartleby, this is a friend; you will find him very useful to you."

"Your sarvant, sir, your sarvant," said the grub-man, making a low salutation behind his apron. "Hope you find it pleasant here, sir; nice grounds—cool apartments—hope you'll stay with us some time—try to make it agreeable. What will you have for dinner to-day?"

"I prefer not to dine to-day," said Bartleby, turning away. "It would disagree with me; I am unused to dinners." So saying, he slowly moved to the other side of the enclosure, and took up a position fronting the dead-wall.

"How's this?" said the grub-man, addressing me with a stare of astonishment. "He's odd, ain't he?"

"I think he is a little deranged," said I sadly.

"Deranged? deranged is it? Well, now, upon my word, I thought that friend of yourn was a gentleman forger; they are always pale and genteel-like, them forgers. I can't help pity 'em—can't help it, sir. Did you know Monroe Edwards?" he added touchingly, and paused. Then, laying his hand piteously on my shoulder, sighed, "he died of consumption at Sing-Sing. So you weren't acquainted with Monroe?"

"No, I was never socially acquainted with any forgers. But I cannot stop longer. Look to my friend yonder. You will not lose by it. I will see you again."

Some few days after this, I again obtained admission to the Tombs, and went through the corridors in quest of Bartleby; but without finding him.

"I saw him coming from his cell not long ago," said a turnkey, "maybe he's gone to loiter in the yards."

So I went in that direction.

"Are you looking for the silent man?" said another turnkey, passing me. "Yonder he lies—sleeping in the yard there. 'Tis not twenty minutes since I saw him lie down."

The yard was entirely quiet. It was not accessible to the common prisoners. The surrounding walls, of amazing thickness, kept off all sounds behind them. The Egyptian character of the masonry weighed upon me with its gloom. But a soft imprisoned turf grew under foot. The heart of the eternal pyramids, it seemed, wherein, by some strange magic, through the clefts, grass-seed, dropped by birds, had sprung.

Strangely huddled at the base of the wall, his knees drawn up, and lying on his side, his head touching the cold stones, I saw the wasted Bartleby. But nothing stirred. I paused; then went close up to him; stooped over, and saw that his dim eyes were open; otherwise he seemed profoundly sleeping. Something prompted me to touch him. I felt his hand, when a tingling shiver ran up my arm and down my spine to my feet.

The round face of the grub-man peered upon me now. "His dinner is ready. Won't he dine to-day, either? Or does he live without dining?"

"Lives without dining," said I, and closed the eyes.

"Eh!—He's asleep, ain't he?"

"With kings and counsellors," murmured I.

There would seem little need for proceeding further in this history. Imagination will readily supply the meagre recital of poor Bartleby's interment. But, ere parting with the reader, let me say, that if this little narrative has sufficiently interested him, to awaken curiosity as to who Bartleby was, and what manner of life he led prior to the present narrator's making his acquaintance, I can only reply, that in such curiosity I fully share, but am wholly unable to gratify it. Yet here I hardly know whether I should divulge one little item of rumour, which came to my ear a few months after the scrivener's decease. Upon what basis it rested I could never ascertain; and hence, how true it is I cannot now tell. But, inasmuch as this vague report has not been without a certain suggestive interest to me, however sad, it may prove the same with some others; and so I will briefly mention it. The report was this: that Bartleby had been a subordinate clerk in the Dead Letter Office at Washington, from which he had been suddenly removed by a change in the administration. When I think over this rumour, hardly can I express the emotions which seize me. Dead letters! does it not sound like dead men? Conceive a man by nature and misfortune prone to a pallid hopelessness, can any business seem more fitted to heighten it than that of continually handling these dead letters, and assorting them for the flames? For by the cartload they are annually burned. Sometimes from out the folded paper the pale clerk takes a ring—the finger it was meant for, perhaps, moulders in the grave; a bank-note sent in swiftest charity—he whom it would relieve, nor eats nor hungers any more; pardon for those who died despairing; hope for those who died unhoping; good tidings for those who died stifled by unrelieved calamities. On errands of life, these letters speed to death.

Ah, Bartleby! Ah, humanity!

"With kings and counsellors": Job 3:14.

AKULKA'S HUSBAND
Fyodor Dostoevsky

translated by constance garnett

It was rather late at night, about twelve o'clock. I had fallen asleep but soon woke up. The tiny dim light of the night-lamp glimmered faintly in the ward. . . . Almost all were asleep. Even Ustyantsev was asleep, and in the stillness one could hear how painfully he breathed and the husky wheezing in his throat at every gasp. Far away in the passage there suddenly sounded the heavy footsteps of the sentry coming to relieve the watch. There was a clang of a gun against the floor. The ward door was opened: the corporal, stepping in cautiously, counted over the patients. A minute later the ward was shut up, a new sentry was put on duty, the watchman moved away, and again the same stillness. Only then I noticed that on the left at a little distance from me there were two patients awake, who seemed to be whispering together. It used to happen in the ward sometimes that two men would lie side by side for days and months without speaking, and suddenly would begin talking, excited by the stillness of the night, and one would reveal his whole past to the other.

They had evidently been talking for a long time already. I missed the beginning and even now I could not make it all out; but by degrees I grew used to it and began to understand it all. I could not get to sleep; what could I do but listen? One was speaking with heat, half reclining on the bed, with his head raised, and craning his neck towards his companion. He was obviously roused and excited; he wanted to tell his story. His listener was sitting sullen and quite unconcerned in his bed, occasionally growling in answer or in token of sympathy with the speaker, more as it seemed out of politeness than from real feeling, and at every moment stuffing his nose with snuff. He was a soldier called Tcherevin from the disciplinary battalion, a man of fifty, a sullen pedant, a cold formalist and a conceited fool. The speaker, whose name was Shishkov, was a young fellow under thirty, a convict in the civil division in our prison, who worked in the tailor's workshop. So far, I had taken very little notice of him, and I was not drawn to see more of him during the remainder of my time in prison.

He was a shallow, whimsical fellow; sometimes he would be silent, sullen and rude and not say a word for weeks together. Sometimes he would suddenly get mixed up in some affair, would begin talking scandal, would get excited over trifles and flit from one ward to another repeating gossip, talking endlessly, frantic with excitement. He would be beaten and relapse into silence again. He was a cowardly, mawkish youth. Everyone seemed to treat him with contempt. He was short and thin, his eyes were restless and sometimes had a blank, dreamy look. At times he would tell a story; he would begin hotly, with excitement, gesticulating with his hands, and suddenly he would break off or pass to another subject, carried away by fresh ideas and forgetting what he had begun about. He was often quarrelling, and whenever he quarrelled would reproach his opponent for some wrong he had done him, would speak with feeling and almost with tears.
...He played fairly well on the balalaika and was fond of playing it. On holidays he even danced, and danced well when they made him. He could very easily be made to do anything. It was not that he was specially docile but he was fond of making friends and was ready to do anything to please.

For a long time I could not grasp what he was talking about. I fancy, too, that at first he was constantly straying away from his subject into other things. He noticed perhaps that Tcherevin took scarcely any interest in his story, but he seemed anxious to convince himself that his listener was all attention, and perhaps it would have hurt him very much if he had been convinced of the contrary.

"...He would go out into the market," he went on. "Everyone would bow to him. They felt he was a rich man; that's the only word for it."

"He had some trade, you say?"

"Yes, he had. They were poor folks there, regular beggars. The women used to carry water from the river ever so far up the steep bank to water their vegetables; they wore themselves out and did not get cabbage enough for soup in the autumn. It was poverty. Well, he rented a big piece of land, kept three labourers to work it; besides he had his own beehives and sold honey, and cattle too in our parts, you know; he was highly respected. He was pretty old, seventy if he was a day, his old bones were heavy, his hair was grey, he was a great big fellow. He would go into the market-place in a fox-skin coat and all did him honour. They felt what he was, you see! 'Good morning, Ankudim Trofimitch, sir.' 'Good day to you,' he'd say. He wasn't too proud to speak to anyone, you know. 'Long life to you, Ankudim Trofimitch!' 'And how's your luck?' he'd ask. 'Our luck's as right as soot is white; how are you doing, sir?' 'I am doing as well as my sins will let me, I am jogging along.' 'Good health to you, Ankudim Trofimitch!' He wasn't too proud for anyone, but if he spoke, every word he said was worth a rouble. He was a Bible reader, an educated man, always reading something religious. He'd set his old woman before him:

'Now wife, listen and mark!' and he'd begin expounding to her. And the old woman was not so very old, she was his second wife, he married her for the sake of children, you know, he had none from the first. But by the second, Marya Stepanovna, he had two sons not grown up. He was sixty when the youngest, Vasya, was born, and his daughter, Akulka, the eldest of the lot, was eighteen."

"Was that your wife?"

"Wait a bit. First there was the upset with Filka Morozov. 'You give me my share,' says Filka to Ankudim, 'give me my four hundred roubles— am I your servant? I won't be in business with you and I don't want your Akulka. I am going to have my fling. Now my father and mother are dead, so I shall drink up my money and then hire myself out, that is, go for a soldier, and in ten years I'll come back here as a field-marshal.' Ankudim gave him the money and settled up with him for good—for his father and the old man had set up business together. 'You are a lost man,' says he. 'Whether I am a lost man or not, you, greybeard, you'd teach one to sup milk with an awl. You'd save off every penny, you'd rake over rubbish to make porridge. I'd like to spit on it all. Save every pin and the devil you win. I've a will of my own,' says he. 'And I am not taking your Akulka, anyway. I've slept with her as it is,' says he. 'What!' says Ankudim, 'do you dare shame the honest daughter of an honest father? When have you slept with her, you adder's fat? You pike's blood!' And he was all of a tremble, so Filka told me.

" 'I'll take good care,' says he, 'that your Akulka won't get any husband now, let alone me; no one will have her, even Mikita Grigoritch won't take her, for now she is disgraced. I've been carrying on with her ever since autumn. I wouldn't consent for a hundred crabs now. You can try giving me a hundred crabs, I won't consent. . . .'

"And didn't he run a fine rig among us, the lad! He kept the country in an uproar and the town was ringing with his noise. He got together a crew of companions, heaps of money; he was carousing for three months, he spent everything. 'When I've got through all the money,' he used to say, 'I'll sell the house, sell everything, and then I'll either sell myself for a soldier or go on the tramp.' He'd be drunk from morning till night, he drove about with bells and a pair of horses. And the way the wenches ran after him was tremendous. He used to play the *torba* finely."

"Then he'd been carrying on with Akulka before?"

"Stop, wait a bit. I'd buried my father just then too, and my mother used to make cakes, she worked for Ankudim, and that was how we lived. We had a hard time of it. We used to rent a bit of ground beyond the wood and we sowed it with corn, but we lost everything after father died, for I went on the spree too, my lad. I used to get money out of my mother by beating her."

"That's not the right thing, to beat your mother. It's a great sin."

"I used to be drunk from morning till night, my lad. Our house was all right, though it was tumbledown, it was our own, but it was empty as a drum. We used to sit hungry, we had hardly a morsel from one week's end to another. My mother used to keep on nagging at me; but what did I care? I was always with Filka Morozov in those days. I never left him from morning till night. 'Play on the guitar and dance,' he'd say to me, 'and I'll lie down and fling money at you, for I'm an extremely wealthy man!' And what wouldn't he do! But he wouldn't take stolen goods. 'I'm not a thief,' he says, 'I'm an honest man. But let's go and smear Akulka's gate with pitch, for I don't want Akulka to marry Mikita Grigoritch. I care more for that than for jelly.' The old man had been meaning to marry Akulka to Mikita Grigoritch for some time past. Mikita, too, was an old fellow in spectacles and a widower with a business. When he heard the stories about Akulka he drew back: 'That would be a great disgrace to me, Ankudim Trofimitch,' says he, 'and I don't want to get married in my old age.' So we smeared Akulka's gate. And they thrashed her, thrashed her for it at home. . . . Marya Stepanovna cried, 'I'll wipe her off the face of the earth!' 'In ancient years,' says the old man, 'in the time of the worthy patriarchs, I should have chopped her to pieces at the stake, but nowadays it's all darkness and rottenness.' Sometimes the neighbours all along the street would hear Akulka howling—they beat her from morning till night. Filka would shout for the whole market-place to hear: 'Akulka's a fine wench to drink with,' says he, 'You walk in fine array, who's your lover, pray! I've made them feel it,' says he, 'they won't forget it.'

"About that time I met Akulka one day carrying the pails and I shouted at her, 'Good morning, Akulina Kudimovna. Greetings to your grace! You walk in fine array. Where do you get it, pray? Come, who's your lover, say!' That was all I said. But how she did look at me. She had such big eyes and she had grown as thin as a stick. And as she looked at me her mother thought she was laughing with me and shouted from the gateway, 'What are you gaping at, shameless hussy?' and she gave her another beating that day. Sometimes she'd beat her for an hour together. 'I'll do for her,' says she, 'for she is no daughter of mine now.'"

"Then she was a loose wench?"

"You listen, old man. While I was always drinking with Filka, my mother comes up to me one day—I was lying down. 'Why, are you lying there, you rascal?' says she. 'You are a blackguard,' says she. She swore at me in fact. 'You get married,' says she. 'You marry Akulka. They'll be glad to marry her now even to you, they'd give you three hundred roubles in money alone.' 'But she is disgraced in the eyes of all the world,' says I. 'You are a fool,' says she, 'the wedding ring covers all, it will be all the better for you if she feels her guilt all her life. And their money will set us on our feet again. I've talked it over with Marya Stepanovna already. She is very ready to listen.' 'Twenty roubles down on the table and I'll marry her,' says I. And would you believe it, right up to the day of the wedding I was drunk. And Filka Morozov was threatening me, too. 'I'll break all your ribs, Akulka's husband,' says he, 'and I'll sleep with your wife every night if I please. 'You lie, you dog's flesh,' says I. And then he put me to shame before all the street. I ran home: 'I won't be married,' says I, 'If they don't lay down another fifty roubles on the spot.' "

"But did they agree to her marrying you?"

"Me? Why not? We were respectable people. My father was only ruined at the end by a fire; till then we'd been better off than they. Ankudim says, 'You are as poor as a rat,' says he. 'There's been a lot of pitch smeared on your gate,' I answered. 'There's no need for you to cry us down,' says he. 'You don't know that she has disgraced herself, but there's no stopping people's mouths. Here's the ikon and here's the door,' says he. 'You needn't take her. Only pay back the money you've had.' Then I talked it over with Filka and I sent Mitri Bikov to tell him I'd dishonour him now over all the world; and right up to the wedding, lad, I was dead drunk. I was only just sober for the wedding. When we were driven home from the wedding and sat down, Mitrofan Stepanovitch, my uncle, said, 'Though it's done in dishonour, it's just as binding,' says he, 'the thing's done and finished.' Old Ankudim was drunk too and he cried, he sat there and the tears ran down his beard. And I tell you what I did, my lad: I'd put a whip in my pocket, I got it ready before the wedding. I'd made up my mind to have a bit of fun with Akulka, to teach her what it meant to get married by a dirty trick and that folks might know I wasn't being fooled over the marriage."

"Quite right too! To make her feel it for the future..."

"No, old chap, you hold your tongue. In our part of the country they take us straight after the wedding to a room apart while the others drink outside. So they left Akulka and me inside. She sits there so white, not a drop of blood in her face. She was scared, to be sure. Her hair, too, was as white as flax, her eyes were large and she was always quiet, you heard nothing of her, she was like a dumb thing in the house. A strange girl altogether. And can you believe it, brother, I got that whip ready and laid it beside me by the bed, but it turned out she had not wronged me at all, my lad!"

"You don't say so!"

"Not at all. She was quite innocent. And what had she had to go through all that torment for? Why had Filka Morozov put her to shame before all the world?"

"Yes..."

"I knelt down before her then, on the spot, and clasped my hands.

'Akulina Kudimovna,' says I, 'forgive me, fool as I am, for thinking ill of you too. Forgive a scoundrel like me,' says I. She sat before me on the bed looking at me, put both hands on my shoulders while her tears were flowing. She was crying and laughing. . . . Then I went out to all of them. 'Well,' says I, 'if I meet Filka Morozov now he is a dead man!' As for the old people, they did not know which saint to pray to. The mother almost fell at her feet, howling. And the old fellow said, 'Had we known this, we wouldn't have found a husband like this for you, our beloved daughter.'

"When we went to church the first Sunday, I in my astrakhan cap, coat of fine cloth and velveteen breeches, and she in her new hareskin coat with a silk kerchief on her head, we looked a well-matched pair: didn't we walk along! People were admiring us. I needn't speak for myself, and though I can't praise Akulina up above the rest, I can't say she was worse: and she'd have held her own with any dozen."

"That's all right, then."

"Come, listen. The day after the wedding, though I was drunk, I got away from my visitors and I escaped and ran away. 'Bring me that wretch Filka Morozov,' says I, 'bring him here, the scoundrel!' I shouted all over the market. Well, I was drunk too: I was beyond the Vlasovs' when they caught me, and three men brought me home by force. And the talk was all over the town. The wenches in the market-place were talking to each other: 'Girls, darlings, have you heard? Akulka is proved innocent.'

"Not long after, Filka says to me before folks, 'Sell your wife and you can drink. Yashka the soldier got married just for that,' says he. 'He didn't sleep with his wife, but he was drunk for three years.' I said to him, 'You are a scoundrel.' 'And you,' says he, 'a fool. Why, you weren't sober when you were married,' says he, 'how could you tell about it when you were drunk?' I came home and shouted, 'You married me when I was drunk,' said I. My mother began scolding me. 'Your ears are stopped with gold, mother. Give me Akulka.' Well, I began beating her. I beat her, my lad, beat her for two hours, till I couldn't stand up. She didn't get up from her bed for three weeks."

"To be sure," observed Tcherevin phlegmatically, "if you don't beat them, they'll. . . But did you catch her with a lover?"

"Catch her? No, I didn't," Shishkov observed, after a pause, and, as it were, with an effort. "But I felt awfully insulted. People teased me so and Filka led the way. 'You've a wife for show,' says he, 'for folks to look at.' Filka invited us with others, and this was the greeting he gave me: 'His wife is a tenderhearted soul,' says he, 'honourable and polite, who knows how to behave, nice in every way—that's what he thinks now. But you've forgotten, lad, how you smeared her gate with pitch yourself!' I sat drunk and then he seized me by the hair suddenly and holding me by the hair he shoved me down. 'Dance,' says he, 'Akulka's husband! I'll hold you by your hair and you dance to amuse me!' 'You are a scoundrel,' I shouted. And he says to me, 'I shall come to you with companions and thrash Akulka, your wife, before you, as much as I like.' Then I, would you believe it, was afraid to go out of the house for a whole month. I was afraid he'd come and disgrace me. And just for that I began beating her. . . ."

"But what did you beat her for? You can tie a man's hands but you can't stop his tongue. You shouldn't beat your wife too much. Show her, give her a lesson, and then be kind to her. That's what she is for."

Shishkov was silent for some time.

"It was insulting," he began again. "Besides, I got into the habit of it: some days I'd beat her from morning till night; everything she did was wrong. If I didn't beat her, I felt bored. She would sit without saying a word, looking out of the window and crying. . . . She was always crying, I'd feel sorry for her, but I'd beat her. My mother was always swearing at me about her: 'You are a scoundrel,' she'd say, 'you're a jail-bird!' 'I'll kill her,' I cried, 'and don't let anyone dare to speak to me; for they married me by a trick.' At first old Ankudim stood up for her; he'd come himself: 'You are no one of much account,' says he, 'I'll find a law for you.' But he gave it up. Marya Stepanovna humbled herself completely. One day she came and prayed me tearfully, 'I've come to entreat you, Ivan Semyonovitch, it's a small matter, but a great favour. Bid me hope again,' she bowed down, 'soften your heart, forgive her. Evil folk slandered our daughter. You know yourself she was innocent when you married her.' And she bowed down to my feet and cried. But I lorded it over her. 'I won't hear you now! I shall do just what I like to you all now, for I am no longer master of myself. Filka Morozov is my mate and my best friend. . . .'"

"So you were drinking together again then?"

"Nothing like it! There was no approaching him. He was quite mad with drink. He'd spent all he had and hired himself out to a storekeeper to replace his eldest son, and in our part of the country when a man sells himself for a soldier, up to the very day he is taken away everything in the house has to give way to him, and he is master over all. He gets the sum in full when he goes and till that time he lives in the house; he some-times stays there for six months and the way he'll go on, it's a disgrace to a decent house. 'I am going for a soldier in place of your son,' the fellow would say, 'so I am your benefactor, so you must all respect me, or I'll refuse.' So Filka was having a rare time at the shopkeeper's, sleeping with the daughter, pulling the father's beard every day after dinner, and doing just as he liked. He had a bath every day and insisted on using vodka for water, and the women carrying him to the bath-house in their arms. When he came back from a walk he would stand in the middle of the street and say, 'I won't go in at the gate, pull down the fence,' so they had to pull down the fence in another place beside the gate for him to go through. At last his time was up, they got him sober and took him off. The people came out in crowds into the street saying, 'Filka Morozov's being taken for a soldier!' He bowed in all directions. Just then Akulka came out of the kitchen garden. When Filka saw her just at our gate, 'Stop,' he cried, and leapt out of the cart and bowed down before her. 'You are my soul,' he said, 'my darling, I've loved you for two years, and now they are taking me for a soldier with music. Forgive me,' said he, 'honest daughter of an honest father, for I've been a scoundrel to you and it's all been my fault!' And he bowed down to the ground again. Akulka stood, seeming scared at first, then she made him a low bow and said, 'You forgive me too, good youth, I have no thought of any evil you have done.' I followed her into the hut. 'What did you say to him, dog's flesh?' And you may not believe me but she looked at me: 'Why, I love him now more than all the world,' said she."

"You don't say so!"

"I did not say one word to her all that day...only in the evening. 'Akulka, I shall kill you now,' says I. All night I could not sleep; I went into the passage to get some kvas to drink, and the sun was beginning to rise. I went back into the room. 'Akulka,' said I, 'get ready to go out to the field.' I had been meaning to go before and mother knew we were going. 'That's right,' said she. 'It's harvest-time now and I hear the labourer's been laid up with his stomach for the last three days.' I got the cart out without saying a word. As you go out of our town there's a pine forest that stretches for ten miles, and beyond the forest was the land we rented. When we had gone two miles I stopped the horse. 'Get out, Akulina,' said I, 'your end has come.' She looked at me, she was scared; she stood up before me, she did not speak. 'I am sick of you,' says I, 'say your prayers!' And then I snatched her by the hair; she had two thick long plaits. I twisted them round my hand and held her tight from behind between my knees. I drew out my knife, I pulled her head back and slid the knife along her throat. She screamed, the blood spurted out, I threw down the knife, flung my arms round her, lay down on the ground, embraced her and screamed over her, yelling; she screamed and I screamed; she was fluttering all over, struggling to get out of my arms, and the blood was simply streaming, simply streaming on to my face and on to my hands. I left her, a panic came over me, and I left the horse and set off running, and ran home along the backs of the houses and straight to the bath-house. We had an old bath-house we didn't use: I squeezed myself into a corner under the steps and there I sat. And there I sat till nightfall."

"And Akulka?"

"She must have got up, too, after I had gone and walked homewards too. They found her a hundred paces from the place."

"Then you hadn't killed her?"

"Yes. . . ." Shishkov paused for a moment.

"There's a vein, you know," observed Tcherevin, "if you don't cut through that vein straight-away a man will go on struggling and won't die, however much blood is lost."

"But she did die. They found her dead in the evening. They informed the police, began searching for me, and found me at nightfall in the bath-house! . . . And here I've been close upon four years," he added, after a pause.

"H'm. . .to be sure, if you don't beat them there will be trouble," Tcherevin observed coolly and methodically, pulling out his tobacco-pouch again. He began taking long sniffs at intervals. "Then again you seem to have been a regular fool, young fellow, too. I caught my wife with a lover once. So I called her into the barn; I folded the bridle in two. 'To whom do you swear to be true? To whom do you swear to be true?' says I. And I did give her a beating with that bridle, I beat her for an hour and a half. 'I'll wash your feet and drink the water,' she cried at last. Ovdotya was her name."

NUNS AT LUNCHEON
Aldous Huxley

"What have I been doing since you saw me last?" Miss Penny repeated my question in her loud, emphatic voice. "Well, when did you see me last?"

"It must have been June," I computed.

"Was that after I'd been proposed to by the Russian General?"

"Yes; I remember hearing about the Russian General."

Miss Penny threw back her head and laughed. Her long ear-rings swung and rattled—corpses hanging in chains: an agreeably literary simile. And her laughter was like brass, but that had been said before.

"That was an uproarious incident. It's sad you should have heard of it. I love my Russian General story. '*Vos yeux me rendent fou.*' " She laughed again.

Vos yeux—she had eyes like a hare's, flush with her head and very bright with a superficial and expressionless brightness. What a formidable woman. I felt sorry for the Russian General.

" '*Sans cœur et sans entrailles,*' " she went on, quoting the poor devil's words. "Such a delightful motto, don't you think? Like '*Sans peur et sans reproche.*' But let me think; what have I been doing since then?" Thoughtfully she bit into the crust of her bread with long, sharp, white teeth.

"Two mixed grills," I said parenthetically to the waiter.

"But of course," exclaimed Miss Penny suddenly. "I haven't seen you since my German trip. All sorts of adventures. My appendicitis; my nun."

"Your nun?"

"My marvellous nun. I must tell you all about her."

"Do." Miss Penny's anecdotes were always curious. I looked forward to an entertaining luncheon.

"You knew I'd been in Germany this autumn?"

"Well, I didn't, as a matter of fact. But still——"

"I was just wandering round." Miss Penny described a circle in the air with her gaudily jewelled hand. She always twinkled with massive and

Vos yeux me rendent fou: Your eyes drive me mad.
Sans coeur et sans entrailles: Heartless and ruthless.
Sans peur et sans reproche: Fearless and blameless.

improbable jewellery. "Wandering round, living on three pounds a week, partly amusing myself, partly collecting materials for a few little articles. 'What it Feels Like to be a Conquered Nation'—sob-stuff for the Liberal press, you know—and 'How the Hun is Trying to Wriggle out of the Indemnity,' for the other fellows. One has to make the best of all possible worlds, don't you find? But we mustn't talk shop. Well, I was wandering round, and very pleasant I found it. Berlin, Dresden, Leipzig. Then down to Munich and all over the place. One fine day I got to Grauburg. You know Grauburg? It's one of those picture-book German towns with a castle on a hill, hanging beer-gardens, a Gothic church, an old university, a river, a pretty bridge, and forests all round. Charming. But I hadn't much opportunity to appreciate the beauties of the place. The day after I arrived there—bang!—I went down with appendicitis—screaming, I may add."

"But how appalling!"

"They whisked me off to hospital, and cut me open before you could say knife. Excellent surgeon, highly efficient Sisters of Charity to nurse me —I couldn't have been in better hands. But it was a bore being tied there by the leg for four weeks—a great bore. Still, the thing had its compensations. There was my nun, for example. Ah, here's the food, thank Heaven!"

The mixed grill proved to be excellent. Miss Penny's description of the nun came to me in scraps and snatches. A round, pink, pretty face in a winged coif; blue eyes and regular features; teeth altogether too perfect —false, in fact; but the general effect extremely pleasing. A youthful Teutonic twenty-eight.

"She wasn't my nurse," Miss Penny explained. "But I used to see her quite often when she came in to have a look at the *tolle Engländerin*. Her name was Sister Agatha. During the war, they told me, she had converted any number of wounded soldiers to the true faith—which wasn't surprising, considering how pretty she was."

"Did she try and convert you?" I asked.

"She wasn't such a fool." Miss Penny laughed, and rattled the miniature gallows of her ears.

I amused myself for a moment with the thought of Miss Penny's conversion—Miss Penny confronting a vast assembly of Fathers of the Church, rattling her ear-rings at their discourses on the Trinity, laughing her appalling laugh at the doctrine of the Immaculate Conception, meeting the stern look of the Grand Inquisitor with a flash of her bright, emotionless hare's eyes. What was the secret of the woman's formidableness?

But I was missing the story. What had happened? Ah yes, the gist of

tolle Engländerin: the mad English woman.

it was that Sister Agatha had appeared one morning, after two or three days' absence, dressed, not as a nun, but in the overalls of a hospital charwoman, with a handkerchief instead of a winged coif on her shaven head.

"Dead," said Miss Penny; "she looked as though she were dead. A walking corpse, that's what she was. It was a shocking sight. I shouldn't have thought it possible for anyone to change so much in so short a time. She walked painfully, as though she had been ill for months, and she had great burnt rings round her eyes and deep lines in her face. And the general expression of unhappiness—that was something quite appalling."

She leaned out into the gangway between the two rows of tables, and caught the passing waiter by the end of one of his coat-tails. The little Italian looked round with an expression of surprise that deepened into terror on his face.

"Half a pint of Guinness," ordered Miss Penny. "And, after this, bring me some jam roll."

"No jam roll to-day, madam."

"Damn!" said Miss Penny. "Bring me what you like, then."

She let go of the waiter's tail, and resumed her narrative.

"Where was I? Yes, I remember. She came into my room, I was telling you, with a bucket of water and a brush, dressed like a charwoman. Naturally I was rather surprised. 'What on earth are you doing, Sister Agatha?' I asked. No answer. She just shook her head, and began to scrub the floor. When she'd finished, she left the room without so much as looking at me again. 'What's happened to Sister Agatha?' I asked my nurse when she next came in. 'Can't say.'—'Won't say,' I said. No answer. It took me nearly a week to find out what really had happened. Nobody dared tell me; it was *strengst verboten,* as they used to say in the good old days. But I wormed it out in the long run. My nurse, the doctor, the charwomen—I got something out of all of them. I always get what I want in the end." Miss Penny laughed like a horse.

"I'm sure you do," I said politely.

"Much obliged," acknowledged Miss Penny. "But to proceed. My information came to me in fragmentary whispers. 'Sister Agatha ran away with a man.'—Dear me!—'One of the patients.'—You don't say so.—'A criminal out of the jail.'—The plot thickens.—'He ran away from her.'—It seems to grow thinner again.—'They brought her back here; she's been disgraced. There's been a funeral service for her in the chapel—coffin and all. She had to be present at it—her own funeral. She isn't a nun any more. She has to do charwoman's work now, the roughest in the hospital.

strengst verboten: strictly forbidden.

She's not allowed to speak to anybody, and nobody's allowed to speak to her. She's regarded as dead.' " Miss Penny paused to signal to the harassed little Italian. "My small 'Guinness,' " she called out.

"Coming, coming," and the foreign voice cried "Guinness" down the lift, and from below another voice echoed, "Guinness."

"I filled in the details bit by bit. There was our hero, to begin with; I had to bring him into the picture, which was rather difficult, as I had never seen him. But I got a photograph of him. The police circulated one when he got away; I don't suppose they ever caught him." Miss Penny opened her bag. "Here it is," she said. "I always carry it about with me; it's become a superstition. For years, I remember, I used to carry a little bit of heather tied up with string. Beautiful, isn't it? There's a sort of Renaissance look about it, don't you think? He was half-Italian, you know."

Italian. Ah, that explained it. I had been wondering how Bavaria could have produced this thin-faced creature with the big dark eyes, the finely modelled nose and chin, and the fleshy lips so royally and sensually curved.

"He's certainly very superb," I said, handing back the picture.

Miss Penny put it carefully away in her bag. "Isn't he?" she said. "Quite marvellous. But his character and his mind were even better. I see him as one of those innocent, childlike monsters of iniquity who are simply unaware of the existence of right and wrong. And he had genius— the real Italian genius for engineering, for dominating and exploiting nature. A true son of the Roman aqueduct builders he was, and a brother of the electrical engineers. Only Kuno—that was his name—didn't work in water; he worked in women. He knew how to harness the natural energy of passion; he made devotion drive his mills. The commercial exploitation of love-power, that was his speciality. I sometimes wonder," Miss Penny added in a different tone, "whether I shall ever be exploited, when I get a little more middle-aged and celibate, by one of these young engineers of the passions. It would be humiliating, particularly as I've done so little exploiting from my side."

She frowned and was silent for a moment. No, decidedly, Miss Penny was not beautiful; you could not even honestly say that she had charm or was attractive. That high Scotch colouring, those hare's eyes, the voice, the terrifying laugh, and the size of her, the general formidableness of the woman. No, no, no.

"You said he had been in prison," I said. The silence, with all its implications, was becoming embarrassing.

Miss Penny sighed, looked up, and nodded. "He was fool enough," she said, "to leave the straight and certain road of female exploitation for the dangerous courses of burglary. We all have our occasional accesses of folly. They gave him a heavy sentence, but he succeeded in getting pneumonia, I think it was, a week after entering jail. He was transferred to the hospital. Sister Agatha, with her known talent for saving souls, was given him as his particular attendant. But it was he, I'm afraid, who did the converting."

Miss Penny finished off the last mouthful of the ginger pudding which the waiter had brought in lieu of jam roll.

"I suppose you don't smoke cheroots," I said, as I opened my cigar-case.

"Well, as a matter of fact, I do," Miss Penny replied. She looked sharply round the restaurant. "I must just see if there are any of those horrible little gossip paragraphers here to-day. One doesn't want to figure in the social and personal column to-morrow morning: 'A fact which is not so generally known as it ought to be, is that Miss Penny, the well-known woman journalist, always ends her luncheon with a six-inch Burma cheroot. I saw her yesterday in a restaurant—not a hundred miles from Carmelite Street—smoking like a house on fire.' You know the touch. But the coast seems to be clear, thank goodness."

She took a cheroot from the case, lit it at my proffered match, and went on talking.

"Yes, it was young Kuno who did the converting. Sister Agatha was converted back into the worldly Melpomene Fugger she had been before she became the bride of holiness."

"Melpomene Fugger?"

"That was her name. I had her history from my old doctor. He had seen all Grauburg, living and dying and propagating, for generations. Melpomene Fugger—why, he had brought little Melpel into the world, little Melpchen. Her father was Professor Fugger, the great Professor Fugger, the *berühmter Geolog*. Oh yes, of course, I know the name. So well...He was the man who wrote the standard work on Lemuria—you know, the hypothetical continent where the lemurs come from. I showed due respect. Liberal-minded he was, a disciple of Herder, a world-burgher, as they beautifully call it over there. Anglophile, too, and always ate porridge for breakfast—up till August 1914. Then, on the radiant morning of the fifth, he renounced it for ever, solemnly and with tears in his eyes. The national food of a people who had betrayed culture and civilisation—how could he go on eating it? It would stick in his throat. In future he would have a lightly boiled egg. He sounded, I thought, altogether charming. And his daughter, Melpomene—she sounded charming, too; and such thick, yellow pigtails when she was young! Her mother was dead, and a sister of the great Professor's ruled the house with an iron rod. Aunt Bertha was her name. Well, Melpomene grew up, very plump and appetising. When she was seventeen, something very odious and disagreeable happened to her. Even the doctor didn't know exactly what it was; but

berühmter Geolog: famous geologist.

he wouldn't have been surprised if it had had something to do with the then Professor of Latin, an old friend of the family's, who combined, it seems, great erudition with a horrid fondness for very young ladies."

Miss Penny knocked half an inch of cigar ash into her empty glass.

"If I wrote short stories," she went on reflectively "(but it's too much bother), I should make this anecdote into a sort of potted life history, beginning with a scene immediately after this disagreeable event in Melpomene's life. I see the scene so clearly. Poor little Melpel is leaning over the bastions of Grauburg Castle, weeping into the June night and the mulberry trees in the gardens thirty feet below. She is besieged by the memory of what happened this dreadful afternoon. Professor Engelmann, her father's old friend, with the magnificent red Assyrian beard...Too awful—too awful! But then, as I was saying, short stories are really too much bother; or perhaps I'm too stupid to write them. I bequeath it to you. You know how to tick these things off."

"You're generous."

"Not at all," said Miss Penny. "My terms are a ten per cent commission on the American sale. Incidentally there won't be an American sale. Poor Melpchen's history is not for the chaste public of Those States. But let me hear what you propose to do with Melpomene now you've got her on the castle bastions."

"That's simple," I said. "I know all about German university towns and castles on hills. I shall make her look into the June night, as you suggest; into the violet night with its points of golden flame. There will be the black silhouette of the castle, with its sharp roofs and hooded turrets, behind her. From the hanging beer-gardens in the town below the voices of the students, singing in perfect four-part harmony, will float up through the dark-blue spaces. 'Röslein, Röslein, Röslein rot' and "Das Ringlein sprang in zwei'— the heart-rendingly sweet old songs will make her cry all the more. Her tears will patter like rain among the leaves of the mulberry trees in the garden below. Does that seem to you adequate?"

"Very nice," said Miss Penny. "But how are you going to bring the sex problem and all its horrors into your landscape?"

"Well, let me think." I called to memory those distant foreign summers when I was completing my education. "I know. I shall suddenly bring a swarm of moving candles and Chinese lanterns under the mulberry trees. You imagine the rich lights and shadows, the jewel-bright leafage, the faces and moving limbs of men and women, seen for an instant and gone again. They are students and girls of the town come out to dance, this windless, blue June night, under the mulberry trees. And now they begin,

Röslein, Röslein, Röslein rot: Little Rose, Little Rose, Little Red Rose, a traditional poem adapted by Goethe.
Das Ringlein sprang in zwei: The Little Ring Broke in Two, a song written by Eichendorff.

thumping round and round in a ring, to the music of their own singing:

'Wir können spielen
Vio-vio-vio-lin,
Wir können spielen
Vi-o-lin.'

Now the rhythm changes, quickens:

'Und wir können tanzen Bumstarara,
Bumstarara, Bumstarara,
Und wir können tanzen Bumstarara,
Bumstarara-rara.'

The dance becomes a rush, an elephantine prancing on the dry lawn under the mulberry trees. And from the bastion Melpomene looks down and perceives, suddenly and apocalyptically, that everything in the world is sex, sex, sex. Men and women, male and female—always the same, and all, in the light of the horror of the afternoon, disgusting. That's how I should do it, Miss Penny."

"And very nice, too. But I wish you could find a place to bring in my conversation with the doctor. I shall never forget the way he cleared his throat and coughed before embarking on the delicate subject. 'You may know, ahem, gracious Miss,' he began—'you may know that religious phenomena are often, ahem, closely connected with sexual causes.' I replied that I had heard rumours which might justify me in believing this to be true among Roman Catholics, but that in the Church of England— and I for one was a practitioner of Anglicanismus—it was very different. That might be, said the doctor; he had had no opportunity in the course of his long medical career of personally studying Anglicanismus. But he could vouch for the fact that among his patients, here in Grauburg, mysticismus was very often mixed up with the *Geschlechtsleben*. Melpomene was a case in point. After that hateful afternoon she had become extremely religious; the Professor of Latin had diverted her emotions out of their normal channels. She rebelled against the placid Agnosticismus of her father, and at night, in secret, when Aunt Bertha's dragon eyes were closed, she would read such forbidden books as *The Life of St. Theresa, The Little Flowers of St. Francis, The Imitation of Christ*, and the horribly enthralling *Book of Martyrs*. Aunt Bertha confiscated these works whenever she came upon them; she considered them more pernicious than the novels of Marcel Prévost. The character of a good potential housewife

Wir können spielen / Vi-o-lin: We can play the violin, another student song.
Und wir können tanzen Bumstarara: We can dance and fall down.
Geschlechtsleben: sex life.

might be completely undermined by reading of this kind. It was rather a relief for Melpomene when Aunt Bertha shuffled off, in the summer of 1911, this mortal coil. She was one of those indispensables of whom one makes the discovery, when they are gone, that one can get on quite as well without them. Poor Aunt Bertha!"

"One can imagine Melpomene trying to believe she was sorry, and horribly ashamed to find that she was really, in secret, almost glad." The suggestion seemed to me ingenious, but Miss Penny accepted it as obvious.

"Precisely," she said; "and the emotion would only further confirm and give new force to the tendencies which her aunt's death left her free to indulge as much as she liked. Remorse, contrition—they would lead to the idea of doing penance. And for one who was now wallowing in the martyrology, penance was the mortification of the flesh. She used to kneel for hours, at night, in the cold; she ate too little, and when her teeth ached, which they often did,—for she had a set, the doctor told me, which had given trouble from the very first,—she would not go and see the dentist, but lay awake at night, savouring to the full her excruciations, and feeling triumphantly that they must, in some strange way, be pleasing to the Mysterious Powers. She went on like that for two or three years, till she was poisoned through and through. In the end she went down with gastric ulcer. It was three months before she came out of hospital, well for the first time in a long space of years, and with a brand new set of imperishable teeth, all gold and ivory. And in mind, too, she was changed—for the better, I suppose. The nuns who nursed her had made her see that in mortifying herself she had acted supererogatively and through spiritual pride; instead of doing right, she had sinned. The only road to salvation, they told her, lay in discipline, in the orderliness of established religion, in obedience to authority. Secretly, so as not to distress her poor father, whose Agnosticismus was extremely dogmatic, for all its unobtrusiveness, Melpomene became a Roman Catholic. She was twenty-two. Only a few months later came the war and Professor Fugger's eternal renunciation of porridge. He did not long survive the making of that patriotic gesture. In the autumn of 1914 he caught a fatal influenza. Melpomene was alone in the world. In the spring of 1915 there was a new and very conscientious Sister of Charity at work among the wounded in the hospital of Grauburg. Here," explained Miss Penny, jabbing the air with her forefinger, "you put a line of asterisks or dots to signify a six years' gulf in the narrative. And you begin again right in the middle of a dialogue between Sister Agatha and the newly convalescent Kuno."

"What's their dialogue to be about?" I asked.

"Oh, that's easy enough," said Miss Penny. "Almost anything would do. What about this, for example? You explain that the fever has just abated; for the first time for days the young man is fully conscious. He feels himself to be well, reborn, as it were, in a new world—a world so bright and novel and jolly that he can't help laughing at the sight of it. He looks about him; the flies on the ceiling strike him as being extremely comic. How do they manage to walk upside down? They have suckers on their feet, says Sister Agatha, and wonders if her natural history is quite sound. Suckers on their feet—ha, ha! What an uproarious notion! Suckers on their feet—that's good, that's damned good! You can say charming, pathetic, positively tender things about the irrelevant mirth of convalescents—the more so in this particular case, where the mirth is expressed by a young man who is to be taken back to jail as soon as he can stand firmly on his legs. Ha, ha! Laugh on, unhappy boy! It is the quacking of the Fates, the Parcæ, the Norns!"

Miss Penny gave an exaggerated imitation of her own brassy laughter. At the sound of it the few lunchers who still lingered at the other tables looked up, startled.

"You can write pages about Destiny and its ironic quacking. It's tremendously impressive, and there's money in every line."

"You may be sure I shall."

"Good! Then I can get on with my story. The days pass and the first hilarity of convalescence fades away. The young man remembers and grows sullen; his strength comes back to him, and with it a sense of despair. His mind broods incessantly on the hateful future. As for the consolations of religion, he won't listen to them. Sister Agatha perseveres— oh, with what anxious solicitude!—in the attempt to make him understand and believe and be comforted. It is all so tremendously important, and in this case, somehow, more important than in any other. And now you see the *Geschlechtsleben* working yeastily and obscurely, and once again the quacking of the Norns is audible. By the way," said Miss Penny, changing her tone and leaning confidentially across the table, "I wish you'd tell me something. Do you really—honestly, I mean—do you seriously believe in literature?"

"Believe in literature?"

"I was thinking," Miss Penny explained, "of Ironic Fate and the quacking of the Norns and all that."

" 'M yes."

"And then there's this psychology and introspection business; and construction and good narrative and word pictures and *le mot juste* and verbal magic and striking metaphors."

I remembered that I had compared Miss Penny's tinkling ear-rings to skeletons hanging in chains.

"And then, finally, and to begin with—Alpha and Omega—there's ourselves: two professionals gloating, with an absolute lack of sympathy, over a seduced nun, and speculating on the best method of turning her misfortunes into cash. It's all very curious, isn't it?—when one begins to think about it dispassionately."

le mot juste: the precise word.
Alpha and Omega: the first and last letters in the Greek alphabet.

"Very curious," I agreed. "But, then, so is everything else if you look at it like that."

"No, no," said Miss Penny. "Nothing's so curious as our business. But I shall never get to the end of my story if I get started on first principles."

Miss Penny continued her narrative. I was thinking of literature. Do you believe in it? Seriously? Ah! Luckily the question was quite meaningless. The story came to me rather vaguely, but it seemed that the young man was getting better; in a few more days, the doctor had said, he would be well—well enough to go back to jail. No, no. The question was meaningless. I would think about it no more. I concentrated my attention again.

"Sister Agatha," I heard Miss Penny saying, "prayed, exhorted, indoctrinated. Whenever she had half a minute to spare from her other duties she would come running into the young man's room. 'I wonder if you fully realise the importance of prayer?' she would ask, and, before he had time to answer, she would give him a breathless account of the uses and virtues of regular and patient supplication. Or else it was: 'May I tell you about St. Theresa?' or 'St. Stephen, the first martyr—you know about him, don't you?' Kuno simply wouldn't listen at first. It seemed so fantastically irrelevant, such an absurd interruption to his thoughts, his serious, despairing thoughts about the future. Prison was real, imminent, and this woman buzzed about him with her ridiculous fairy-tales. Then, suddenly, one day he began to listen, he showed signs of contrition and conversion. Sister Agatha announced her triumph to the other nuns, and there was rejoicing over the one lost sheep. Melpomene had never felt so happy in her life, and Kuno, looking at her radiant face, must have wondered how he could have been such a fool as not to see from the first what was now so obvious. The woman had lost her head about him. And he had only four days now—four days in which to tap the tumultuous love power, to canalise it, to set it working for his escape. Why hadn't he started a week ago? He could have made certain of it then. But now? There was no knowing. Four days was a horribly short time."

"How did he do it?" I asked, for Miss Penny had paused.

"That's for you to say," she replied, and shook her ear-rings at me. "I don't know. Nobody knows, I imagine, except the two parties concerned and perhaps Sister Agatha's confessor. But one can reconstruct the crime, as they say. How would you have done it? You're a man, you ought to be familiar with the processes of amorous engineering."

"You flatter me," I answered. "Do you seriously suppose——" I extended my arms. Miss Penny laughed like a horse. "No. But, seriously, it's a problem. The case is a very special one. The person, a nun; the place, a hospital; the opportunities, few. There could be no favourable circumstances—no moonlight, no distant music; and any form of direct attack would be sure to fail. That audacious confidence which is your amorist's best weapon would be useless here."

"Obviously," said Miss Penny. "But there are surely other methods. There is the approach through pity and the maternal instincts. And there's the approach through Higher Things, through the soul. Kuno must have worked on those lines, don't you think? One can imagine him letting himself be converted, praying with her, and at the same time appealing for her sympathy and even threatening—with a great air of seriousness—to kill himself rather than go back to jail. You can write that up easily and convincingly enough. But it's the sort of thing that bores me so frightfully to do. That's why I can never bring myself to write fiction. What is the point of it all? And the way you literary men think yourselves so important—particularly if you write tragedies. It's all very queer, very queer indeed."

I made no comment. Miss Penny changed her tone and went on with the narrative.

"Well," she said, "whatever the means employed, the engineering process was perfectly successful. Love was made to find out a way. On the afternoon before Kuno was to go back to prison, two Sisters of Charity walked out of the hospital gates, crossed the square in front of it, glided down the narrow streets towards the river, boarded a tram at the bridge, and did not descend till the car had reached its terminus in the farther suburbs. They began to walk briskly along the high road out into the country. 'Look!' said one of them, when they were clear of the houses; and with the gesture of a conjurer produced from nowhere a red leather purse. 'Where did it come from?' asked the other, opening her eyes. Memories of Elisha and the ravens, of the widow's cruse, of the loaves and fishes, must have floated through the radiant fog in poor Melpomene's mind. 'The old lady I was sitting next to in the tram left her bag open. Nothing could have been simpler.' 'Kuno! You don't mean to say you stole it?' Kuno swore horribly. He had opened the purse. 'Only sixty marks. Who'd have thought that an old camel, all dressed up in silk and furs, would only have sixty marks in her purse. And I must have a thousand at least to get away.' It's easy to reconstruct the rest of the conversation down to the inevitable, 'For God's sake, shut up,' with which Kuno put an end to Melpomene's dismayed moralising. They trudge on in silence. Kuno thinks desperately. Only sixty marks; he can do nothing with that. If only he had something to sell, a piece of jewellery, some gold or silver—anything, anything. He knows such a good place for selling things. Is he to be caught again for lack of a few marks? Melpomene is also thinking. Evil must often be done that good may follow. After all, had not she herself stolen Sister Mary of the Purification's clothes when she was asleep after night duty? Had not she run away from the convent, broken her vows? And yet how convinced she was that she was doing rightly! The mysterious Powers emphatically approved; she felt sure of it. And now there was the red purse. But what was a red purse in comparison with a saved soul—and, after all, what was she doing but saving Kuno's soul?" Miss Penny, who had adopted the voice and gestures of a debater asking rhetorical questions, brought her hand with a slap on to the table. "Lord, what a bore this sort of stuff is!" she exclaimed. "Let's get to the end of this dingy anecdote as quickly as possible. By this time, you must imagine, the shades of night were falling fast—the chill November twilight, and so on; but I leave the natural descriptions to you. Kuno gets into the ditch at the roadside and takes off his robes. One imagines that he would feel himself safer in trousers, more capable of acting with decision in a crisis. They tramp on for miles. Late in the evening they leave the high road and strike up through the fields towards the forest. At the fringe of the wood they find one of those wheeled huts where the shepherds sleep in the lambing season.

"The real 'Maison du Berger.' "

"Precisely," said Miss Penny, and she began to recite:

'Si ton coeur gémissant du poids de notre vie
 Se traine et se débat comme un aigle blessé. . . .'

How does it go on? I used to adore it all so much when I was a girl:

'Le seuil est perfumé, l'alcôve est large et sombre,
 Et là parmi les fleurs, nous trouverons dans l'ombre
 Pour nos cheveux unis un lit silencieux.'

I could go on like this indefinitely."

"Do," I said.

"No, no. No, no. I'm determined to finish this wretched story. Kuno broke the padlock of the door. They entered. What happened in that little hut?" Miss Penny leaned forward at me. Her large hare's eyes glittered, the long ear-rings swung and faintly tinkled. "Imagine the emotions of a virgin of thirty, and a nun at that, in the terrifying presence of desire. Imagine the easy, familiar brutalities of the young man. Oh, there's pages to be made out of this—the absolutely impenetrable darkness, the smell of straw, the voices, the strangled crying, the movements! And one likes to fancy that the emotions pulsing about in that confined space made palpable vibrations like a deep sound that shakes the air. Why, it's ready-made literature, this scene. In the morning," Miss Penny went on, after a pause, "two woodcutters on their way to work noticed that the door of

Si ton coeur...: If your heart, groaning under life's burdens, / drags itself along and struggles like a wounded eagle...
Le seuil est...: The threshold is perfumed, the alcove wide and dark, / And there among the flowers, we shall find in the shadows / A peaceful couch for our mingled hair.

the hut was ajar. They approached the hut cautiously, their axes raised and ready for a blow if there should be need of it. Peeping in, they saw a woman in a black dress lying face downwards in the straw. Dead? No; she moved, she moaned. 'What's the matter?' A blubbered face, smeared with streaks of tear-clotted grey dust, is lifted towards them. 'What's the matter?'—'He's gone!' What a queer, indistinct utterance. The wood-cutters regard one another. What does she say? She's a foreigner, perhaps. 'What's the matter?' they repeat once more. The woman bursts out violently crying. 'Gone, gone! He's gone,' she sobs out in her vague, inarticulate way. 'Oh, gone. That's what she says. Who's gone?'—'He's left me.'—'What?'—'Left me...'—'What the devil...? Speak a little more distinctly.'—'I can't,' she wails; 'he's taken my teeth.'—'Your what?'—'My teeth!'—and the shrill voice breaks into a scream, and she falls back sobbing into the straw. The woodcutters look significantly at one another. They nod. One of them applies a thick yellow-nailed forefinger to his forehead."

Miss Penny looked at her watch.

"Good heavens!" she said, "it's nearly half-past three. I must fly. Don't forget about the funeral service," she added, as she put on her coat. "The tapers, the black coffin in the middle of the aisle, the nuns in their white-winged coifs, the gloomy chanting, and the poor cowering creature without any teeth, her face all caved in like an old woman's, wondering whether she wasn't really and in fact dead—wondering whether she wasn't already in hell. Good-bye."

AURA
Carlos Fuentes

translated by lysander kemp

Man hunts and struggles. Woman intrigues and dreams; she is the mother
of fantasy, the mother of the gods. She has second sight, the wings that
enable her to fly to the infinite of desire and the imagination... The gods
are like men: they are born and they die on a woman's breast....

—Jules Michelet

I

You're reading the advertisement: an offer like this isn't made every day.
You read it and reread it. It seems to be addressed to you and nobody
else. You don't even notice when the ash from your cigarette falls into
the cup of tea you ordered in this cheap, dirty café. You read it again.
"Wanted, young historian, conscientious, neat. Perfect knowledge of col-
loquial French. Youth...knowledge of French, preferably after living in
France for a while...Four thousand pesos a month, all meals, comfortable
bedroom-study." All that's missing is your name. The advertisement should
have two more words, in bigger, blacker type: Felipe Montero. Wanted,
Felipe Montero, formerly on scholarship at the Sorbonne, historian full
of useless facts, accustomed to digging among yellowed documents, part-
time teacher in private schools, nine hundred pesos a month. But if you
read that, you'd be suspicious, and take it as a joke. "Address, Donceles
815." No telephone; come in person.

You leave a tip, reach for your briefcase, get up. You wonder if another
young historian, in the same situation you are, has seen this same advertisement, has got ahead of you and taken the job already. You walk down
to the corner, trying to forget this idea. As you wait for the bus, you
run over the dates you must have on the tip of your tongue so that your
sleepy pupils will respect you. The bus is coming now, and you're staring
at the tips of your black shoes. You've got to be prepared. You put your
hand in your pocket, search among the coins, and finally take out thirty
centavos. You've got to be prepared. You grab the hand-rail—the bus

slows down but doesn't stop—and jump aboard. Then you shove your way forward, pay the driver the thirty centavos, squeeze yourself in among the passengers already standing in the aisle, hang on to the overhead rail, press your briefcase tighter under your left arm, and automatically put your left hand over the back pocket where you keep your billfold.

This day is just like any other day, and you don't remember the advertisement until the next morning, when you sit down in the same café and order breakfast and open your newspaper. You come to the advertising section and there it is again: *young historian*. The job is still open. You reread the advertisement, lingering over the final words: four thousand pesos.

It's surprising to know that anyone lives on Donceles Street. You always thought that nobody lived in the old centre of the city. You walk slowly, trying to pick out the number 815 in that conglomeration of old colonial mansions, all of them converted into repair shops, jewellery shops, shoe stores, drugstores. The numbers have been changed, painted over, confused. A 13 next to a 200. And old plaque reading 47 over a scrawl in blurred charcoal: *Now* 924. You look up at the second storeys. Up there, everything is the same as it was. The jukeboxes don't disturb them. The mercury streetlights don't shine in. The cheap merchandise on sale along the street doesn't have any effect on that upper level...on the Baroque harmony of the carved stones; on the battered stone saints with pigeons clustering on their shoulders; on the latticed balconies, the copper gutters, the sandstone gargoyles; on the greenish curtains that darken the long windows; on that window from which someone draws back when you look at it. You gaze at the fanciful vines carved over the doorway, then lower your eyes to the peeling wall and discover 815, *formerly* 69.

You rap vainly with the knocker, that copper head of a dog, so worn and smooth that it resembles the head of a canine foetus in a museum of natural science. It seems as if the dog is grinning at you and you let go of the cold metal. The door opens at the first light push of your fingers, but before going in you give a last look over your shoulder, frowning at the long line of stalled cars that growl, honk, and belch out the unhealthy fumes of their impatience. You try to retain some single image of that indifferent outside world.

You close the door behind you and peer into the darkness of a roofed alleyway. It must be a patio of some sort, because you can smell the mould, the dampness of the plants, the rotting roots, the thick drowsy aroma. There isn't any light to guide you, and you're searching in·your coat pocket for the box of matches when a sharp, thin voice tells you, from a distance: "No, it isn't necessary. Please. Walk thirteen steps forward and you'll come to a stairway at your right. Come up, please. There are twenty-two steps. Count them."

Thirteen. To the right. Twenty-two.

The dank smell of the plants is all around you as you count out your steps, first on the paving-stones, then on the creaking wood, spongy from the dampness. You count to twenty-two in a low voice and then stop, with the matchbox in your hand, the briefcase under your arm. You knock on a door that smells of old pine. There isn't any knocker. Finally you push it open. Now you can feel a carpet under your feet, a thin carpet, badly laid. It makes you trip and almost fall. Then you notice the greyish, filtered light that reveals some of the humps.

"Señora," you say, because you seem to remember a woman's voice. "Señora..."

"Now turn to the left. The first door. Please be so kind."

You push the door open: you don't expect any of them to be latched, you know they all open at a push. The scattered lights are braided in your eyelashes, as if you were seeing them through a silken net. All you can make out are the dozens of flickering lights. At last you can see that they're votive-lights, all set on brackets or hung between unevenly-spaced panels. They cast a faint glow on the silver objects, the crystal flasks, the gilt-framed mirrors. Then you see the bed in the shadows beyond, and the feeble movement of a hand that seems to be beckoning to you.

But you can't see her face until you turn your back on that galaxy of religious lights. You stumble to the foot of the bed, and have to go around it in order to get to the head of it. A tiny figure is almost lost in its immensity. When you reach out your hand, you don't touch another hand, you touch the ears and thick fur of a creature that's chewing silently and steadily, looking up at you with its glowing red eyes. You smile and stroke the rabbit that's crouched beside her hand. Finally you shake hands, and her cold fingers remain for a long while in your sweating palm.

"I'm Felipe Montero. I read your advertisement."

"Yes, I know. I'm sorry, there aren't any chairs."

"That's all right. Don't worry about it."

"Good. Please let me see your profile. No, I can't see it well enough. Turn towards the light. That's right. Excellent."

"I read your advertisement..."

"Yes, of course. Do you think you're qualified? *Avez-vous fait des études?*"

"*A Paris, Madame.*"

"*Ah, oui, ça me fait plaisir, toujours, toujours, d'entendre...oui...vous savez...on était tellement habitué...et après...*"

You move aside so that the light from the candles and the reflections from the silver and crystal show you the silk coif that must cover a head

Avez-vous fait des études?: Have you finished your studies?

A Paris, Madame: In Paris, Madam.

Ah, oui, ça me fait...: Ah, yes, that pleases me, always, always, to hear...yes... you know...one was so accustomed...and afterwards...

of very white hair, and that frames a face so old it's almost childlike. Her whole body is covered by the sheets and the feather-pillows and the high, tightly-buttoned white collar, all except for her arms, which are wrapped in a shawl, and her pallid hands resting on her stomach. You can only stare at her face until a movement of the rabbit lets you glance furtively at the crusts and bits of bread scattered on the worn-out red silk of the pillows.

"I'll come directly to the point. I don't have many years ahead of me, Señor Montero, and therefore I decided to break a lifelong rule and place an advertisement in the newspaper..."

"Yes, that's why I'm here."

"Of course. So you accept."

"Well, I'd like to know a little more..."

"Yes. You're wondering."

She sees you glance at the night-table, the different-coloured bottles, the glasses, the aluminium spoons, the row of pillboxes, the other glasses—all stained with whitish liquids—on the floor within reach of her hand. Then you notice that the bed is hardly raised above the level of the floor. Suddenly the rabbit jumps down and disappears in the shadows.

"I can offer you four thousand pesos."

"Yes, that's what the advertisement said today."

"Ah, then it came out."

"Yes, it came out."

"It has to do with the memoirs of my husband, General Llorente. They must be put in order before I die. I want them to be published. I decided that a short time ago."

"But the General himself? Wouldn't he be able to..."

"He died sixty years ago, Señor. They're his unfinished memoirs. They have to be completed before I die."

"But..."

"I can tell you everything. You'll learn to write in my husband's own style. You'll only have to arrange and read his manuscripts to become fascinated by his style...his clarity...his..."

"Yes, I understand."

"Saga, Saga. Where are you? *Ici*, Saga..."

"Who?"

"My companion."

"The rabbit?"

"Yes. She'll come back."

When you raise your eyes, which you've been keeping lowered, her lips are closed but you can hear her words again—"She'll come back"—as if the old lady were pronouncing them at that instant. Her lips remain still.

Ici: here.

You look in back of you and you're almost blinded by the gleam from the religious objects. When you look at her again you see that her eyes have opened very wide, and that they're clear, liquid, enormous, almost the same colour as the yellowish whites around them, so that only the black dots of the pupils mar that clarity. It's lost a moment later in the heavy folds of her lowered eyelids, as if she wanted to protect that glance which is now hiding at the back of its dry cave.

"Then you'll stay here. Your room is upstairs. It's sunny there."

"It might be better if I didn't trouble you, Señora. I can go on living where I am and work on the manuscripts there."

"My conditions are that you have to live here. There isn't much time left."

"I don't know if..."

"Aura..."

The old woman moves for the first time since you entered her room. As she reaches out her hand again you sense that agitated breathing beside you, and another hand reaches out to touch the Señora's fingers. You look around and a girl is standing there, a girl whose whole body you can't see because she's standing so close to you and her arrival was so unexpected, without the slightest sound—not even those sounds that can't be heard but are real anyway because they're remembered immediately afterwards, because in spite of everything they're louder than the silence that accompanies them.

"I told you she'd come back."

"Who?"

"Aura. My companion. My niece."

"Good afternoon."

The girl nods and at the same instant the old lady imitates her gesture.

"This is Señor Montero. He's going to live with us."

You move a few steps so that the light from the candles won't blind you. The girl keeps her eyes closed, her hands folded at her side. She doesn't look at you at first, then little by little she opens her eyes as if she were afraid of the light. Finally you can see that those eyes are seagreen and that they surge, break to foam, grow calm again, then surge again like a wave. You look into them and tell yourself it isn't true, because they're beautiful green eyes just like all the beautiful green eyes you've ever known. But you can't deceive yourself: those eyes do surge, do change, as if offering you a landscape that only you can see and desire.

"Yes. I'm going to live with you."

II

The old woman laughs sharply and tells you that she is grateful for your kindness and that the girl will show you to your room. You're thinking about the salary of four thousand pesos, and how the work should be pleasant because you like these jobs of careful research that don't include physical effort or going from one place to another or meeting people you don't want to meet. You're thinking about this as you follow her out of the room, and you discover that you've got to follow her with your ears instead of your eyes: you follow the rustle of her skirt, the rustle of taffeta, and you're anxious now to look into her eyes again. You climb the stairs behind that sound in the darkness, and you're still unused to the obscurity. You remember it must be about six in the afternoon, and the flood of light surprises you when Aura opens the door to your bedroom—another door without a latch—and steps aside to tell you: "This is your room. We'll expect you for supper in an hour."

She moves away with that same faint rustle of taffeta, and you weren't able to see her face again.

You close the door and look up at the skylight that serves as a roof. You smile when you find that the evening light is blinding compared with the darkness in the rest of the house, and smile again when you try out the mattress on the gilded metal bed. Then you glance around the room: a red wool rug, olive and gold wall-paper, an easy-chair covered in red velvet, an old walnut desk with a green leather top, an old Argand lamp with its soft glow for your nights of research, and a bookshelf over the desk in reach of your hand. You walk over to the other door, and on pushing it open you discover an outmoded bathroom: a four-legged bath-tub with little flowers painted on the porcelain, a blue hand-basin, an old-fashioned toilet. You look at yourself in the large oval mirror on the door of the wardrobe—it's also walnut—in the bathroom hallway. You move your heavy eyebrows and wide thick lips, and your breath fogs the mirror. You close your black eyes, and when you open them again the mirror has cleared. You stop holding your breath and run your hand through your dark, limp hair; you touch your fine profile, your lean cheeks; and when your breath hides your face again you're repeating her name: "Aura."

After smoking two cigarettes while lying on the bed, you get up, put on your jacket, and comb your hair. You push the door open and try to remember the route you followed coming up. You'd like to leave the door open so that the lamplight could guide you, but that's impossible because the springs close it behind you. You could enjoy playing with that door, swinging it back and forth. You don't do it. You could take the lamp down with you. You don't do it. This house will always be in dark-ness, and you've got to learn it and relearn it by touch. You grope your way like a blind man, with your arms stretched out wide, feeling your way along the wall, and by accident you turn on the light-switch. You stop and blink in the bright middle of that long, empty hall. At the end of it you can see the banister and the spiral staircase.

You count the stairs as you go down: another custom you've got to learn in Señora Llorente's house. You take a step backward when you see the reddish eyes of the rabbit, which turns its back on you and goes hopping away.

You don't have time to stop in the lower hallway because Aura is waiting for you at a half-open stained-glass door, with a candelabra in her hand. You walk towards her, smiling, but you stop when you hear the painful yowling of a number of cats—yes, you stop to listen, next to Aura, to be sure that they're cats—and then follow her to the parlour.

"It's the cats," Aura tells you. "There's lots of rats in this part of the city."

You go through the parlour: furniture upholstered in faded silk; glass-fronted cabinets containing porcelain figurines, musical clocks, medals, glass balls; carpets with Persian designs; pictures of rustic scenes; green velvet curtains. Aura is dressed in green.

"Is your room comfortable?"

"Yes. But I have to get my things from the place where..."

"It won't be necessary. The servant has already gone for them."

"You shouldn't have bothered."

You follow her into the dining-room. She places the candelabra in the middle of the table. The room feels damp and cold. The four walls are panelled in dark wood, carved in Gothic style, with fretwork arches and large rosettes. The cats have stopped yowling. When you sit down, you notice that four places have been set. There are two large, covered plates and an old, grimy bottle.

Aura lifts the cover from one of the plates. You breath in the pungent odour of the liver and onions she serves you, then you pick up the old bottle and fill the cut-glass with that thick red liquid. Out of curiosity you try to read the label on the wine-bottle, but the grime has obscured it. Aura serves you some whole broiled tomatoes from the other plate.

"Excuse me," you say, looking at the two extra places, the two empty chairs, "but are you expecting someone else?"

Aura goes on serving the tomatoes. "No. Señora Consuelo feels a little ill tonight. She won't be joining us."

"Señora Consuelo? Your aunt?"

"Yes. She'd like you to go in and see her after supper."

You eat in silence. You drink that thick wine, occasionally shifting your glance so that Aura won't catch you in the hypnotized stare that you can't control. You'd like to fix the girl's features in your mind. Every time you glance away you forget them again, and an irresistible urge forces you to look at her once more. As usual, she has her eyes lowered. While you're searching for the pack of cigarettes in your coat pocket, you run across that big key, and remember, and say to Aura: "Ah! I forgot that one of the drawers in my desk is locked. I've got my papers in it."

And she murmurs: "Then you want to go out?" She says it as a reproach.

You feel confused, and reach out your hand to her with the key dangling from one finger.

"It isn't important. The servants can go for them tomorrow."

But she avoids touching your hand, keeping her own hands on her lap. Finally she looks up, and once again you question your senses, blaming the wine for your bewilderment, for the dizziness brought on by those shining, clear green eyes, and you stand up after Aura does, running your hand over the wooden back of the Gothic chair, without daring to touch her bare shoulder or her motionless head.

You make an effort to control yourself, diverting your attention away from her by listening to the imperceptible movement of a door behind you—it must lead to the kitchen—or by separating the two different elements that make up the room: the compact circle of light around the candelabra, illuminating the table and one carved wall, and the larger circle of darkness surrounding it. Finally you have the courage to go up to her, take her hand, open it, and place your key-ring in her smooth palm as a token.

She closes her hand, looks up at you, and murmurs, "Thank you." Then she rises and walks quickly out of the room.

You sit down in Aura's chair, stretch your legs, and light a cigarette, feeling a pleasure you've never felt before, one that you knew was part of you but that only now you're experiencing fully, setting it free, bringing it out because this time you know it'll be answered and won't be lost ...And Señora Consuelo is waiting for you, as Aura said. She's waiting for you after supper...

You leave the dining-room, and with the candelabra in your hand you walk through the parlour and the hallway. The first door you come to is the old lady's. You rap on it with your knuckles, but there isn't any answer. You knock again. Then you push the door open because she's waiting for you. You enter cautiously, murmuring: "Señora...Señora..."

She doesn't hear you, for she's kneeling in front of that wall of religious objects, with her head resting on her clenched fists. You see her from a distance: she's kneeling there in her coarse woollen nightgown, with her head sunk into her narrow shoulders; she's thin, even emaciated, like a medieval sculpture; her legs are like two sticks, and they're inflamed with erysipelas. While you're thinking of the continual rubbing of that rough wool against her skin, she suddenly raises her fists and strikes feebly at the air, as if she were doing battle against the images you can make out as you tiptoe closer: Christ, the Virgin, St Sebastian, St Lucia, the Archangel Michael, and the grinning demons in an old print, the only happy figures in that iconography of sorrow and wrath, happy because they're jabbing their pitchforks into the flesh of the damned, pouring cauldrons of boiling water on them, violating the women, getting drunk, enjoying all the liberties forbidden to the saints. You approach that central image, which is surrounded by the tears of Our Lady of Sorrows, the blood of Our Crucified Lord, the delight of Lucifer, the anger of the Archangel, the viscera preserved in bottles of alcohol, the silver heart: Señora Consuelo, kneeling, threatens them with her fists, stammering the words you can hear as you move even closer: "Come, City of God! Gabriel, sound your trumpet! Ah, how long the world takes to die!"

She beats her breast until she collapses in front of the images and candles in a spasm of coughing. You raise her by the elbow, and as you gently help her to the bed you're surprised at her smallness: she's almost a little girl, bent over almost double. You realize that without your assistance she'd have had to get back to bed on her hands and knees. You help her into that wide bed with its bread-crumbs and old feather-pillows, and cover her up, and wait till her breathing is back to normal, while the involuntary tears run down her parchment cheeks.

"Excuse me...excuse me, Señor Montero...Old ladies have nothing left but...the pleasures of devotion...Give me my handkerchief, please."

"Señorita Aura told me..."

"Yes, of course. I don't want to lose any time. We should...we should begin working as soon as possible...Thank you..."

"You should try to rest."

"Thank you...Here..."

The old lady raises her hand to her collar, unbuttons it, and lowers her head to remove the frayed purple ribbon that she hands to you. It's heavy because there's a copper key hanging from it.

"Over in that corner...Open that trunk and bring me the papers at the right, on top of the others...They're tied with a yellow ribbon..."

"I can't see very well..."

"Ah, yes...it's just that I'm so accustomed to the darkness. To my right...keep going till you come to the trunk...They've walled us in, Señor Montero. They've built up all around us and blocked off the light. They've tried to force me to sell, but I'll die first. This house is full of memories for us. They won't take us out of here till I'm dead...Yes, that's it. Thank you. You can begin reading this part. I'll give you the others later. Goodnight, Señor Montero. Thank you. Look, the candelabra has gone out. Light it outside the door, please. No, no, you can keep the key. I trust you."

"Señora, there's a rat's nest in that corner..."

"Rats? I never go over there..."

"You should bring the cats in here."

"The cats? What cats? Goodnight. I'm going to sleep. I'm very tired."

"Goodnight."

III

That same evening you read those yellow papers written in mustard-coloured ink, some of them with holes where a careless ash had fallen, others heavily fly-specked. General Llorente's French doesn't have the merits his wife attributed to it. You tell yourself you can make considerable improvements in the style, can tighten up his rambling account of past events: his childhood on an hacienda in Oaxaca, his military studies in France, his friendship with the Duke of Morny and the intimates of Napoleon III, his return to Mexico on the staff of Maximilian, the imperial ceremonies and gatherings, the battles, the defeat in 1867, his exile in France. Nothing that hasn't been described before. As you undress you think of the old lady's distorted notions, the value she attributes to these memoirs. You smile as you get into bed, thinking of the four thousand pesos.

You sleep soundly until a flood of light wakes you up at six in the morning; that glass roof doesn't have any curtain. You bury your head under the pillow and try to go back to sleep. Ten minutes later you give it up and walk into the bathroom, where you find all your things neatly arranged on a table and your few clothes hanging in the wardrobe. Just as you finish shaving the early morning silence is broken by that painful, desperate yowling.

You try to find out where it's coming from: you open the door to the hallway, but you can't hear anything from there: those cries are coming from up above, from the skylight. You jump up on the chair, from the chair on to the desk, and by supporting yourself on the bookshelf you can reach the skylight. You open one of the windows and pull yourself up to look out at that side garden, that square of yew-trees and brambles where five, six, seven cats—you can't count them, can't hold yourself up there for more than a second—are all twined together, all writhing in flames and giving off a dense smoke that reeks of burnt fur. As you get down again you wonder if you really saw it: perhaps you only imagined it from those dreadful cries that continue, grow less, and finally stop.

You put on your shirt, brush off your shoes with a piece of paper, and listen to the sound of a bell that seems to run through the passageways of the house until it arrives at your door. You look out into the hallway: Aura is walking along it with a bell in her hand. She turns her head to look at you and tells you that breakfast is ready. You try to detain her but she goes down the spiral staircase, still ringing that black-painted bell as if she were trying to wake up a whole asylum, a whole boarding-school.

You follow her in your shirt-sleeves, but when you reach the downstairs hallway you can't find her. The door of the old lady's bedroom opens behind you and you see a hand that reaches out from behind the partly-opened door, sets a chamberpot in the hallway and disappears again, closing the door.

In the dining-room your breakfast is already on the table, but this time only one place has been set. You eat quickly, return to the hallway, and knock at Señora Consuelo's door. Her sharp, weak voice tells you to come in. Nothing has changed: the perpetual shadows, the glow of the votive lights and the silver objects.

"Good morning, Señor Montero. Did you sleep well?"

"Yes. I read till quite late."

The old lady waves her hand as if in a gesture of dismissal. "No, no, no. Don't give me your opinion. Work on those pages and when you've finished I'll give you the others."

"Very well. Señora, would I be able to go into the garden?"

"What garden, Señor Montero?"

"The one that's outside my room."

"This house doesn't have any garden. We lost our garden when they built up all around us."

"I think I could work better outdoors."

"This house has only got that dark patio where you came in. My niece is growing some shade-plants there. But that's all."

"It's all right, Señora."

"I'd like to rest during the day. But come to see me tonight."

"Very well, Señora."

You spend all morning working on the papers, copying out the passages you intend to keep, rewriting the ones you think are especially bad, smoking one cigarette after another and reflecting that you ought to space your work so that the job lasts as long as possible. If you can manage to save at least twelve thousand pesos, you can spend a year on nothing but your own work, which you've postponed and almost forgotten. Your great, inclusive work on the Spanish discoveries and conquests in the New World. A work that sums up all the scattered chronicles, makes them intelligible, and discovers the resemblances among all the undertakings and adventures of Spain's Golden Age and all the human prototypes and major accomplishments of the Renaissance. You end up by putting aside the General's tedious pages and starting to compile the dates and summaries of your own work. Time passes and you don't look at your watch until you hear the bell again. Then you put on your coat and go down to the dining-room.

Aura is already seated. This time Señora Llorente is at the head of the table, wrapped in her shawl and nightgown and coif, hunching over her plate. But the fourth place has also been set. You note it in passing: it doesn't bother you any more. If the price of your future creative liberty is to put up with all the manias of this old woman, you can pay it easily. As you watch her eating her soup you try to figure out her age. There's a time after which it's impossible to detect the passing of the years, and Señora Consuelo crossed that frontier a long time ago. The General hasn't mentioned her in what you've already read of the memoirs. But if the General was 42 at the time of the French invasion, and died in 1901, forty years later, he must have died at the age of 82. He must have married the Señora after the defeat at Querétaro and his exile. But she would only have been a girl at that time...

The dates escape you because now the Señora is talking in that thin, sharp voice of hers, that bird-like chirping. She's talking to Aura and you listen to her as you eat, hearing her long list of complaints, pains, suspected illnesses, more complaints about the cost of medicines, the dampness of the house and so forth. You'd like to break in on this domestic conversation to ask about the servant who went for your things yesterday, the servant you've never even glimpsed and who never waits on table. You're about to ask about him but you're suddenly surprised to realize that up to this moment Aura hasn't said a word and is eating with a sort of mechanical fatality, as if she were waiting for some outside impulse before picking up her knife and fork, cutting a piece of liver—yes, it's liver again, apparently the favourite dish in this house—and carrying it to her mouth. You glance quickly from the aunt to the niece, but at that moment the Señora becomes motionless and at the same moment Aura puts her knife on her plate and also becomes motionless, and you remember that the Señora had put down her knife only a fraction of a second earlier.

There are several minutes of silence: you finish eating while they sit there rigid as statues, watching you. At last the Señora says, "I'm very tired. I ought not to eat at the table. Come, Aura, help me to my room."

The Señora tries to hold your attention: she looks directly at you so that you'll keep looking at her, although what she's saying is aimed at Aura. You have to make an effort in order to evade that look, which once again is wide, clear, and yellowish, free of the veils and wrinkles that usually obscure it. Then you glance at Aura, who is staring fixedly at nothing and silently moving her lips. She gets up with a motion like those you associate with dreaming, takes the arm of the bent old lady, and slowly helps her from the dining-room.

Alone now, you help yourself to the coffee that has been there since the beginning of the meal, the cold coffee you sip as you wrinkle your brow and ask yourself if the Señora doesn't have some secret power over her niece: if the girl, your beautiful Aura in her green dress, isn't kept in this dark old house against her will. But it would be so easy for her to escape while the Señora was asleep in her shadowy room. You tell yourself that her hold over the girl must be terrible. And you consider the way out that occurs to your imagination: perhaps Aura is waiting for you to release her from the chains in which the perverse, insane old lady, for some unknown reason, has bound her. You remember Aura as she was a few moments ago, spiritless, hypnotized by her terror, incapable of speaking in front of the tyrant, moving her lips in silence as if she were silently begging you to set her free; so enslaved that she imitated every gesture of the Señora, as if she were permitted to do only what the Señora did.

You rebel against this tyranny: you walk towards the other door, the one at the foot of the staircase, the one next to the old lady's room: that's where Aura must live, because there's no other room in the house. You push the door open and go in. This room is dark also, with whitewashed walls, and the only decoration is an enormous black Christ. At the left there's a door that must lead into the widow's bedroom. You go up to it on tiptoes, put your hands against it, then decide not to open it: you should talk with Aura alone.

And if Aura wants your help she'll come to your room. You go up there for a while, forgetting the yellowed manuscripts and your own notebooks, thinking only about the beauty of your Aura. And the more you think about her, the more you make her yours, not only because of her beauty and your desire, but also because you want to set her free: you've found a moral basis for your desire, and you feel innocent and self-satisfied. When you hear the bell again you don't go down to supper because you can't bear another scene like the one at the middle of the day. Perhaps Aura will realize it and come up to look for you after supper.

You force yourself to go on working on the papers. When you're bored with them you undress slowly, get into bed, and fall asleep at once, and for the first time in years you dream, dream of only one thing, of a fleshless hand that comes towards you with a bell, screaming that you should go away, everyone should go away; and when that face with its empty eye-sockets comes close to yours, you wake up with a muffled cry, sweating, and feel those gentle hands caressing your face, those lips murmuring in a low voice, consoling you and asking you for affection. You reach out your hands to find that other body, that naked body with a key dangling from its neck, and when you recognize the key you recognize the woman who is lying over you, kissing you, kissing your whole body. You can't see her in the black of the starless night, but you can smell the fragrance of the patio plants in her hair, can feel her smooth, eager body in your arms: you kiss her again and don't ask her to speak.

When you free yourself, exhausted, from her embrace, you hear her first whisper: 'You're my husband.' You agree. She tells you it's daybreak, then leaves you, saying that she'll wait for you that night in her room. You agree again and then fall asleep, relieved, unburdened, emptied of desire, still feeling the touch of Aura's body, her trembling, her surrender.

It's hard for you to wake up. There are several knocks on the door, and at last you get out of bed, groaning and still half-asleep. Aura, on the other side of the door, tells you not to open it: she says that Señora Consuelo wants to talk with you, is waiting for you in her room.

Ten minutes later you enter the widow's sanctuary. She's propped up against the pillows, motionless, her eyes hidden by those drooping, wrinkled, dead-white lids; you notice the puffy wrinkles under her eyes, the utter weariness of her skin.

Without opening her eyes she asks you, "Did you bring the key to the trunk?"

"Yes, I think so...Yes, here it is."

"You can read the second part. It's in the same place. It's tied with a blue ribbon."

You go over to the trunk, this time with a certain disgust: the rats are swarming around it, peering at you with their glittering eyes from the cracks in the rotted floorboards, galloping towards the holes in the rotted walls. You open the trunk and take out the second batch of papers, then return to the foot of the bed. Señora Consuelo is petting her white rabbit. A sort of croaking laugh emerges from her buttoned-up throat, and she asks you, "Do you like animals?"

"No, not especially. Perhaps because I've never had any."

"They're good friends. Good companions. Above all when you're old and lonely."

"Yes, they must be."

"They're always themselves, Señor Montero. They don't have any pretensions."

"What did you say his name is?"

"The rabbit? She's Saga. She's very intelligent. She follows her instincts. She's natural and free."

"I thought it was a male rabbit."

"Oh? Then you still can't tell the difference."

"Well, the important thing is that you don't feel all alone."

"They want us to be alone, Señor Montero, because they tell us that solitude is the only way to achieve saintliness. They forget that in solitude the temptation is even greater."

"I don't understand, Señora."

"Ah, it's better that you don't. Get back to work now, please."

You turn your back on her, walk to the door, leave her room. In the hallway you clench your teeth. Why don't you have courage enough to tell her that you love the girl? Why don't you go back and tell her, once and for all, that you're planning to take Aura away with you when you finish the job? You approach the door again and start pushing it open, still uncertain, and through the crack you see Señora Consuelo standing up, erect, transformed, with a military tunic in her arms: a blue tunic with gold buttons, red epaulettes, bright medals with crowned eagles—a tunic the old lady bites ferociously, kisses tenderly, drapes over her shoulders as she performs a few teetering dance-steps. You close the door.

Yes: "She was fifteen years old when I met her," you read in the second part of the memoirs. *"Elle avait quinze ans lorsque je l'ai connue et, si j'ose le dire, ce sont ses yeux verts qui ont fait ma perdition."* Consuelo's green eyes, Consuelo who was only fifteen in 1867, when General Llorente married her and took her with him into exile in Paris. *"Ma jeune poupée,"* he wrote in a moment of inspiration, *"ma jeune poupée aux yeux verts; je t'ai comblée d'amour."* He described the house they lived in, the outings, the dances, the carriages, the world of the Second Empire, but all in a dull enough way. *"J'ai même supporté ta haine des chats, moi qui aimais tellement les jolies bêtes..."* One day he found her torturing a cat: she had it clasped between her legs, with her crinoline skirt pulled up, and he didn't know how to attract her attention because it seemed to him that *"tu faisais ça d'une façon si innocente, par pur enfantillage,"* and in fact it excited him so much that if you can believe what he wrote, he made love to her that night with extraordinary passion, *"parce que tu m'avais dit que torturer les chats était ta manière à toi de rendre notre amour favorable, par un sacrifice symbolique..."* You've figured it up: Señora Consuelo must be 109. Her husband died fifty-nine years ago. *"Tu sais si bien t'habiller, ma douce Consuelo, toujours drappée dans de velours verts, verts comme tes yeux. Je pense que tu seras toujours belle, même dans cent ans..."* Always dressed in green. Always beautiful, even after a hundred years. *"Tu es si fière de ta beauté; que ne ferais tu pas pour rester toujours jeune?"*

IV

Now you know why Aura is living in this house: to perpetuate the illusion of youth and beauty in that poor, crazed old lady. Aura, kept here like a mirror, like one more icon on that votive wall with its clustered offerings, preserved hearts, imagined saints and demons.

You put the manuscript aside and go downstairs, suspecting there's only

Elle avait quinze ans...: She was fifteen years old when I first knew her and, if I dare say so, her green eyes were my undoing.
Ma jeune poupée: My little doll.
Ma jeune poupée aux...: My little doll with green eyes; I am deeply in love with you.
J'ai même supporté...: I endured your hatred for cats, I who so loved the pretty creatures.
tu faisais ça...: you did that so innocently out of pure childishness.
parce que tu m'avais...: because you told me that torturing cats was your way of rendering our love propitious by a symbolic sacrifice.
tu sais si bien...: How well you know how to dress, my sweet Consuelo, always draped in green velvet, green as your eyes. I think you will always be beautiful, even a hundred years from now.
Tu es si fière...: You are so proud of your beauty; what would you not do to remain young forever?

one place Aura could be in the morning: the place that greedy old woman has assigned to her.

Yes, you find her in the kitchen, at the moment she's beheading a kid: the vapour that rises from the open throat, the smell of spilt blood, the animal's glazed eyes, all give you nausea. Aura is wearing a ragged, blood-stained dress and her hair is dishevelled; she looks at you without recognition and goes on with her butchering.

You leave the kitchen: this time you'll really speak to the old lady, really throw her greed and tyranny in her face. When you push open the door she's standing behind the veil of lights, performing a ritual with the empty air: one hand stretched out and clenched, as if holding something up, and the other clasped around an invisible object, striking again and again at the same place. Then she wipes her hands against her breast, sighs, and starts cutting the air again, as if—yes, you can see it clearly—as if she were skinning an animal...

You run through the hallway, the parlour, the dining-room, to where Aura is slowly skinning the kid, absorbed in her work, heedless of your entrance or your words, looking at you as if you were made of air.

You climb up to your room, go in, and brace yourself against the door as if you were afraid someone would follow you: panting, sweating, victim of your horror, of your certainty. If something or someone should try to enter, you wouldn't be able to resist, you'd move away from the door, you'd let it happen. Frantically you drag the armchair over to that latch-less door, push the bed up against it, then fall on to the bed, exhausted, drained of your will-power, with your eyes closed and your arms wrapped around your pillow...the pillow that isn't yours...nothing is yours.

You fall into a stupor, into the depths of a dream that's your only escape, your only means of saying No to insanity. "She's crazy, she's crazy," you repeat again and again to make yourself sleepy, and you can see her again as she skins the imaginary kid with an imaginary knife. "She's crazy, she's crazy..."

in the depths of the dark abyss, in your silent dream with its mouths opening in silence, you see her coming towards you from the blackness of the abyss, you see her crawling towards you,

in silence,

moving her fleshless hand, coming towards you until her face touches yours and you see the old lady's bloody gums, her toothless gums, and you scream and she goes away again, moving her hand, sowing the abyss with the yellow teeth she carries in her bloodstained apron:

your scream is an echo of Aura's, she is standing in front of you in your dream, and she's screaming because someone's hands have ripped her green taffeta skirt in two, and then

she turns her head towards you

with the torn folds of the skirt in her hands, turns towards you and laughs silently, with the old lady's teeth superimposed on her own, while her legs, her naked legs, shatter into bits and fly towards the abyss...

There's a knock at the door, then the sound of the bell, the supper bell. Your head aches so much that you can't make out the hands on the clock, but you know it must be late: above your head you can see the night clouds beyond the skylight. You get up painfully, dazed and hungry. You hold the glass pitcher under the faucet, wait for the water to run, fill the pitcher, then pour it into the basin. You wash your face, brush your teeth with your worn toothbrush that's clogged with greenish paste, dampen hair—you don't notice you're doing all this in the wrong order—and comb it meticulously in front of the oval mirror on the walnut wardrobe. Then you tie your tie, put on your jacket and go down to the empty dining-room, where only one place has been set: yours.

Beside your plate, under your napkin, there's an object you start caressing with your fingers: a clumsy little rag doll, filled with a powder that trickles from its badly-sewn shoulder; its face is drawn with indian ink, and its body is naked, sketched with a few brushstrokes. You eat the cold supper—liver, tomatoes, wine—with your right hand while holding the doll in your left.

You eat mechanically, without noticing at first your own hypnotized attitude, but later you glimpse a reason for your oppressive sleep, your nightmare, and finally identify your sleep-walking movements with those of Aura and the old lady. You're suddenly disgusted by that horrible little doll, in which you begin to suspect a secret illness, a contagion. You let it fall to the floor. You wipe your lips with the napkin, look at your watch, and remember that Aura is waiting for you in her room.

You go cautiously up to Señora Consuelo's door, but there isn't a sound from within. You look at your watch again: it's barely nine o'clock. You decide to feel your way down to that dark, roofed patio you haven't been in since you came through it, without seeing anything, on the day you arrived here.

You touch the damp, mossy walls, breathe the perfumed air, and try to isolate the different elements you're breathing, to recognize the heavy, sumptuous aromas that surround you. The flicker of your match lights up the narrow, empty patio, where various plants are growing on each side in the loose, reddish earth. You can make out the tall, leafy forms that cast their shadows on the walls in the light of the match; but it burns down, singeing your fingers, and you have to light another one to finish seeing the flowers, fruits and plants you remember reading about in old chronicles, the forgotten herbs that are growing here so fragrantly and drowsily: the long, broad, downy leaves of the henbane; the twining stems with flowers that are yellow outside, red inside; the pointed, heart-shaped leaves of the nightshade; the ash-coloured down of the grape-mullein with its clustered flowers; the bushy gatheridge with its white blossoms; the belladonna. They come to life in the flare of your match, swaying gently with their shadows, while you recall the uses of these herbs that dilate the pupils, alleviate pain, reduce the pangs of childbirth, bring consolation, weaken the will, induce a voluptuous calm.

You're all alone with the perfumes when the third match burns out. You go up to the hallway slowly, listen again at Señora Consuelo's door, then tiptoe on to Aura's. You push it open without knocking and go into that bare room, where a circle of light reveals the bed, the huge Mexican crucifix, and the woman who comes towards you when the door is closed. Aura is dressed in green, in a green taffeta robe from which, as she approaches, her moon-pale thighs reveal themselves. The woman, you repeat as she comes close, the woman, not the girl of yesterday: the girl of yesterday—you touch Aura's fingers, her waist—couldn't have been more than 20; the woman of today—you caress her loose black hair, her pallid cheeks—seems to be 40. Between yesterday and today, something about her green eyes has turned hard; the red of her lips has strayed beyond their former outlines, as if she wanted to fix them in a happy grimace, a troubled smile: as if, like that plant in the patio, her smile combined the taste of honey and the taste of gall. You don't have time to think of anything more.

"Sit down on the bed, Felipe."

"Yes."

"We're going to play. You don't have to do anything. Let me do everything myself."

Sitting on the bed, you try to make out the source of that diffuse, opaline light that hardly lets you distinguish the objects in the room, and the presence of Aura, from the golden atmosphere that surrounds them. She sees you looking up, trying to find where it comes from. You can tell from her voice that she's kneeling down in front of you.

"The sky is neither high nor low. It's over us and under us at the same time."

She takes off your shoes and socks and caresses your bare feet.

You feel the warm water that bathes the soles of your feet, while she washes them with a heavy cloth, now and then casting furtive glances at that Christ carved from black wood. Then she dries your feet, takes you by the hand, fastens a few violets in her loose hair, and begins to hum a melody, a waltz, to which you dance with her, held by the murmur of her voice, gliding around to the slow, solemn rhythm she's setting, very different from the light movements of her hands, which unbutton your shirt, caress your chest, reach around to your back and grasp it. You also murmur that wordless song, that melody rising naturally from your throat: you glide around together, each time closer to the bed, until you muffle the song with your hungry kisses on Aura's mouth, until you stop the dance with your crushing kisses on her shoulders and breasts.

You're holding the empty robe in your hands. Aura, squatting on the bed, places an object against her closed thighs, caressing it, summoning you with her hand. She caresses that thin wafer, breaks it against her thighs, oblivious of the crumbs that roll down her hips: she offers you half of the wafer and you take it, place it in your mouth at the same time she does, and swallow it with difficulty. Then you fall on Aura's naked body, you fall on her naked arms, which are stretched out from one side of the bed to the other like the arms of the crucifix hanging on the wall, the black Christ with that scarlet silk wrapped around his thighs, his spread knees, his wounded side, his crown of thorns set on a tangled black wig with silver spangles. Aura opens like an altar.

You murmur her name in her ear. You feel the woman's full arms against your back. You hear her warm voice in your ear: "Will you love me for ever?"

"For ever, Aura. I'll love you for ever."

"For ever? Do you swear it?"

"I swear it."

"Even though I grow old? Even though I lose my beauty? Even though my hair turns white?"

"For ever, my love, for ever."

"Even if I die, Felipe? Will you love me for ever, even if I die?"

"For ever, for ever. I swear it. Nothing can separate us."

"Come, Felipe, come..."

When you wake up, you reach out to touch Aura's shoulder, but you only touch the still-warm pillow and the white sheet that covers you.

You murmur her name.

You open your eyes and see her standing at the foot of the bed, smiling but not looking at you. She walks slowly towards the corner of the room, sits down on the floor, places her arms on the knees that emerge from the darkness you can't peer into, and strokes the wrinkled hand that comes forward from the lessening darkness: she's sitting at the feet of the old lady, of Señora Consuelo, who is seated in an armchair you hadn't noticed earlier: Señora Consuelo smiles at you, nodding her head, smiling at you along with Aura, who moves her head in rythm with the old lady's; they both smile at you, thinking you. You lie back, without any will, thinking that the old lady has been in the room all the time;

you remember her movements, her voice, her dance,
though you keep telling yourself she wasn't there.

The two of them get up at the same moment, Consuelo from the chair, Aura from the floor. Turning their backs on you, they walk slowly towards the door that leads to the widow's bedroom, enter that room where the lights are for ever trembling in front of the images, close the door behind them, and leave you to sleep in Aura's bed.

V

Your sleep is heavy and unsatisfying. In your dreams you had already felt the same vague melancholy, the weight on your diaphragm, the sadness that won't stop oppressing your imagination. Although you're sleeping in Aura's room, you're sleeping all alone, far from the body you believe you've possessed.

When you wake up, you look for another presence in the room, and realize it's not Aura who disturbs you but rather the double presence of something that was engendered during the night. You put your hands on your forehead, trying to calm your disordered senses: that dull melancholy is hinting to you in a low voice, the voice of memory and premonition, that you're seeking your other half, that the sterile conception last night engendered your own double.

And you stop thinking, because there are things even stronger than the imagination: the habits that force you to get up, look for a bathroom off this room without finding one, go out into the hallway rubbing your eyelids, climb the stairs tasting the thick bitterness of your tongue, enter your own room feeling the rough bristles on your chin, turn on the bathroom faucets and then slide into the warm water, letting yourself relax into forgetfulness.

But while you're drying yourself, you remember the old lady and the girl as they smiled at you before leaving the room arm in arm; you recall that whenever they're together they always do the same things: they embrace, smile, eat, speak, enter, leave, at the same time, as if one were imitating the other, as if the will of one depended on the existence of the other...You cut yourself lightly on one cheek as you think of these things while you shave; you make an effort to get control of yourself. When you finish shaving you count the objects in your travelling-case, the bottles and tubes which the servant you've never seen brought over from your boarding-house: you murmur the names of these objects, touch them, read the contents and instructions, pronounce the names of the manufacturers, keeping to those objects in order to forget that other one, the one without a name, without a label, without any rational consistency. What is Aura expecting of you? you ask yourself, closing the travelling-case. What does she want, what does she want?

In answer you hear the dull rhythm of her bell in the corridor telling you breakfast is ready. You walk to the door without your shirt on. When you open it you find Aura there: it must be Aura because you see the green taffeta she always wears, though her face is covered with a green veil. You take her by the wrist, that slender wrist which trembles at your touch...

"Breakfast is ready," she says, in the faintest voice you've ever heard.

"Aura. Let's stop pretending."

"Pretending?"

"Tell me if Señora Consuelo keeps you from leaving, from living your own life. Why did she have to be there when you and I...Please tell me you'll go with me when..."

"Go away? Where?"

"Out of this house. Out into the world, to live together. You shouldn't feel bound to your aunt for ever...Why all this devotion? Do you love her that much?"

"Love her?"

"Yes. Why do you have to sacrifice yourself this way?"

"Love her? She loves me. She sacrifices herself for me."

"But she's an old woman, almost a corpse. You can't..."

"She has more life than I do. Yes, she's old and repulsive...Felipe, I don't want to become...to be like her...another..."

"She's trying to bury you alive. You've got to be reborn, Aura."

"You have to die before you can be reborn...No, you don't understand. Forget about it, Felipe. Just have faith in me."

"If you'd only explain."

"Just have faith in me. She's going to be out today for the whole day..."

"She?"

"Yes, the other."

"She's going out? But she never..."

"Yes, sometimes she does. She makes a great effort and goes out. She's going out today. For all day...You and I could..."

"Go away?"

"If you want to."

"Well...perhaps not yet. I'm under contract. But as soon as I can finish the work, then..."

"Ah, yes. But she's going to be out all day. We could do something."

"What?"

"I'll wait for you this evening in my aunt's bedroom. I'll wait for you as always."

She turns away, ringing her bell like the lepers who use a bell to announce their approach, telling the unwary: "Out of the way, out of the way." You put on your shirt and coat and follow the sound of the bell calling you to the dining-room. In the parlour the widow Llorente comes towards you, bent over, leaning on a knobby cane; she's dressed in an old white gown with a stained and tattered gauze veil. She goes by without looking at you, blowing her nose into a handkerchief, blowing her nose and spitting. She murmurs, "I won't be at home today, Señor Montero. I have complete confidence in your work. Please keep at it. My husband's memoirs must be published."

She goes away, stepping across the carpets with her tiny feet, which are like those of an antique doll, and supporting herself with her cane, and spitting and sneezing as if she wanted to clear something from her congested lungs. It's only by an effort of the will that you keep yourself from following her with your eyes, despite the curiosity you feel at seeing the yellowed bridal gown she's taken from the bottom of that old trunk in her bedroom...

You scarcely touch the cold coffee that's waiting for you in the dining-room. You sit for an hour in the tall arch-back chair, smoking, waiting for the sounds you never hear, until finally you're sure the old lady has left the house and can't catch you at what you're going to do. For the last hour you've had the key to the trunk clutched in your hand, and now you get up and silently walk through the parlour into the hallway, where you wait for another fifteen minutes—your watch tells you how long— with your ear against Señora Consuelo's door. Then you slowly push it open until you can make out, beyond the spider's web of candles, the empty bed on which her rabbit is gnawing at a carrot: the bed that's always littered with scraps of bread, and that you touch gingerly as if you thought the old lady might be hidden among the rumples of the sheets. You walk over to the corner where the trunk is, stepping on the tail of one of those rats; it squeals, escapes from your feet, and scampers off to warn the others. You fit the copper key into the rusted padlock, remove the padlock, and then raise the lid, hearing the creak of the old, stiff hinges. You take out the third portion of the memoirs—it's tied with a red ribbon —and under it you discover those photographs, those old, brittle, dog-eared photographs. You pick them up without looking at them, clutch the whole treasure to your breast, and hurry out of the room without closing the trunk, forgetting the hunger of the rats. You close the door, lean against the wall in the hallway until you catch your breath, then climb the stairs to your room.

Up there you read the new pages, the continuation, the events of an agonized century. In his florid language General Llorente describes the personality of Eugenia de Montijo, pays his respects to Napoleon the Small, summons up his most martial rhetoric to declare the Franco-Prussian War, fills whole pages with his sorrow at the defeat, harangues all men of honour about the Republican monster, sees a ray of hope in General Boulanger, sighs for Mexico, believes that in the Dreyfus affair the honour —always that word "honour"!—of the army has asserted itself again...

The brittle pages crumble at your touch: you don't respect them now, you're only looking for a reappearance of the woman with green eyes. "I know why you weep at times, Consuelo. I have not been able to give you children, although you are so radiant with life..." And later: "Consuelo, you should not tempt God. We must reconcile ourselves. Is not my affection enough? I know that you love me; I feel it. I am not asking you for resignation, because that would offend you. I am only asking you to

AURA   **117**

see, in the great love which you say you have for me, something sufficient, something that can fill both of us, without the need of turning to sick imaginings..."

On another page: "I told Consuelo that those medicines were utterly useless. She insists on growing her own herbs in the garden. She says she is not deceiving herself. The herbs are not to strengthen the body, but rather the soul..." Later: "I found her in a delirium, embracing the pillow. She cried, 'Yes, yes, yes, I've done it, I've recreated her! I can invoke her, I can give her life with my own life!' It was necessary to call the doctor. He told me he could not quiet her, because the truth was that she was under the effects of narcotics, not of stimulants..." And finally: "Early this morning I found her walking barefooted through the hallways. I wanted to stop her. She went by without looking at me, but her words were directed to me. 'Don't stop me,' she said. 'I'm going towards my youth, and my youth is coming towards me. It's coming in, it's in the garden, it's come back...' Consuelo, my poor Consuelo, even the devil was an angel at one time..."

There isn't any more. The memoirs of General Llorente end with that sentence: *"Consuelo, le démon aussi était un ange, avant..."*

And after the last page, the portraits. The portrait of an elderly gentleman in a military uniform, an old photograph with these words in one corner: *"Moulin, Photographe, 35 Boulevard Haussmann"* and the date "1894." Then the photograph of Aura, of Aura with her green eyes, her black hair gathered in ringlets, leaning against a Doric column with a painted landscape in the background: the landscape of a Lorelei in the Rhine. Her dress is buttoned up to the collar, there's a handkerchief in her hand, she's wearing a bustle: Aura, and the date "1876" in white ink, and on the back of the daguerrotype, in spidery handwriting: *"Fait pour notre dixième anniversaire de mariage,"* and a signature in the same hand, "Consuelo Llorente." In the third photograph you see both Aura and the old gentleman, but this time they're dressed in outing-clothes, sitting on a bench in a garden. The photograph has become a little blurred: Aura doesn't look as young as she did in the other picture, but it's she, it's he, it's...it's you. You stare and stare at the photographs, then hold them up to the skylight. You cover General Llorente's beard with your finger, and imagine him with black hair, and you only discover yourself: blurred, lost, forgotten, but you, you, you.

Your head is spinning, overcome by the rhythm of that distant waltz, by the odour of damp, fragrant plants; you fall exhausted on the bed, touching your cheeks, your eyes, your nose, as if you were afraid that some invisible hand had ripped off the mask you've been wearing for

Consuelo, le démon...: Consuelo, the devil too was an angel, before...
Fait pour notre...: Made for our tenth wedding anniversary.

twenty-seven years, the cardboard features that hid your true face, your real appearance, the appearance you once had but then forgot. You bury your face in the pillow, trying to keep the wind of the past from tearing away your own features, because you don't want to lose them. You lie there with your face in the pillow, waiting for what has to come, for what you can't prevent. You don't look at your watch again, that useless object tediously measuring time in accordance with human vanity, those little hands marking out the long hours that were invented to disguise the real passage of time, which races with a mortal and insolent swiftness no clock could ever measure. A life, a century, fifty years: you can't imagine these lying measurements any longer, you can't hold that bodiless dust within your hands.

When you look up from the pillow, you find you're in darkness. Night has fallen.

Night has fallen. Beyond the skylight the swift black clouds are hiding the moon, which tries to free itself, to reveal its pale, round, smiling face. It escapes for only a moment, then the clouds hide it again. You haven't got any hope left. You don't even look at your watch. You hurry down the stairs, out of that prison cell with its old papers and faded daguerrotypes, and stop at the door of Señora Consuelo's room, and listen to your own voice, muted and transformed after all those hours of silence: "Aura..."

Again: "Aura..."

You enter the room. The votive-lights have gone out. You remember that the old lady has been away all day, without her faithful attention the candles have all burned up. You grope forward in the darkness to the bed.

And again: "Aura."

You hear a faint rustle of taffeta, and the breathing that keeps time with your own. You reach out your hand to touch Aura's green robe.

"No...Don't touch me...Lie down at my side."

You find the edge of the bed, swing up your legs, and remain there stretched out and motionless. You can't help feeling a shiver of fear: "She might come back any minute."

"She won't come back."

"Never?"

"I'm exhausted. She's already exhausted. I've never been able to keep her with me for more than three days."

"Aura..."

You want to put your hand on Aura's breasts. She turns her back: you can tell by the difference in her voice.

"No...Don't touch me..."

"Aura...I love you."

"Yes. You love me. You told me yesterday that you'd always love me."

"I'll always love you, always. I need your kisses, your body..."

"Kiss my face. Only my face."

You bring your lips close to the head that's lying next to yours. You stroke Aura's long black hair. You grasp that fragile woman by the shoulders, ignoring her sharp complaint. You tear off her taffeta robe, embrace her, feel her small and lost and naked in your arms, despite her moaning resistance, her feeble protests, kissing her face without thinking, without distinguishing, and you're touching her withered breasts when a ray of moonlight shines in and surprises you, shines in through a chink in the wall that the rats have chewed open, an eye that lets in a beam of silvery moonlight. It falls on Aura's eroded face, as brittle and yellowed as the memoirs, as creased with wrinkles as the photographs. You stop kissing those fleshless lips, those toothless gums: the ray of moonlight shows you the naked body of the old lady, of Señora Consuelo, limp, spent, tiny, ancient, trembling because you touch her, you love her, you too have come back...

You plunge your face, your open eyes, into Consuelo's silver-white hair, and you'll embrace her again when the clouds cover the moon, when you're both hidden again, when the memory of youth, of youth re-embodied, rules the darkness.

"She'll come back, Felipe. We'll bring her back together. Let me recover my strength and I'll bring her back..."

THREE
Setting

Setting, the place where a story occurs and the time when it happens, must be judged by how appropriate it is for an individual story. The nature and value of a setting will vary greatly from tale to tale: it may be as commonplace as the restaurant in "Nuns at Luncheon" or as unusual as the house in "Aura"; it may be an elaborately described office in "Bartleby" or a briefly noted drawing room in "A Trifling Occurrence"; it may go unmentioned in "The Background" or dominate in "The Fall of the House of Usher"; it may help create a mood in "A Story" or establish an atmosphere in "The Sculptor's Funeral." Both "The Widow of Ephesus" and "Death of an Airman" are set in a graveyard; yet the first is a light, comic tale while the second is a serious, bleak vignette. By focusing in such detail on the barren grave site, Hawkes accentuates the lonely, mechanical, inhuman job the airman must perform; Petronius, by avoiding any mention of the morbidity inherent in tombs, crypts or crucifixions, enhances rather than detracts from his comic situation. Both writers, using similar settings, achieve remarkably different results. Compare their use of setting with that in two of the following stories: "The Fall of the House of Usher," by Edgar Allan Poe, and "There Will Come Soft Rains," by Ray Bradbury. Poe engages then increases our curiosity about what will happen in the strange house by infusing the setting with a sense of foreboding: the day is "dull, dark and soundless," and the countryside "singularly dreary." Seeing the melancholy house for the first time, the narrator says he instinctively reacted so that " a sense of insufferable gloom pervaded my spirit." An equally ominous house provides the setting for Bradbury's science fiction tale, where the narrator arouses our curiosity by creating an uneasy feeling:

In the living room the voice-clock sang, *Tick-tock, seven o'clock, time to get up, time to get up, seven o'clock!* as if it were afraid that nobody would. The morning house lay empty. The clock ticked on, repeating and repeating its sounds into the emptiness. *Seven-nine, breakfast time, seven-nine!*

The personified clock, which is "afraid," accentuates the house's emptiness. We expect something unusual—and perhaps unpleasant—to happen. The presentation of the setting leads us to believe that the empty house, like Poe's melancholy one, holds a secret which only the teller of the tale can reveal.

Such expectations created by the setting will obviously change if the terms of the description change. If the house in the wood which the little old woman discovers in "The Three Bears" were more realistically described we would anticipate quite a different story. Suppose the tale began not "once upon a time" but:

The neglected, tumbledown shack on the edge of the forest having long ago lost its last human inhabitant now housed three bears. The door sagged a bit on its hinges and the bedroom window needed repair, but still the bears found it quite comfortable.

Such a naturalistic setting leads us to assume that real bears will appear, and not those fairy-tale creatures who cook porridge for breakfast. We could shift the story again by changing the shack to a vine-covered cottage and, ignoring the possible state of disrepair, focus on a beautiful lush natural world:

The day dawned bright and cool as the sun rose behind the cosy, vine-covered cottage in which three bears lived. There were only a few golden and pink clouds in the sky as a gentle breeze stirred the trees in the beautiful lush green forest next the house.

We expect a different series of events to occur and different inhabitants to live in the "cosy cottage" than in the "tumbledown shack." Setting is not an isolated but an integral part of any story and must, therefore, be seen in relation to characters, events, plot and point of view.

When adroitly used, setting may help refine our view of character, define the point of view or clarify meaning. Melville uses the Wall Street setting, for example, to emphasize Bartleby's isolation as well as the narrator's complacency. Walled in his little cubicle, the pallid scrivener has only a blank screen or wall of bricks at which to stare. The lawyer-narrator remarks that the scene is "deficient in...'life,'" but we might observe that it is abundant in death. Moving outside the office onto the city streets at high noon only increases the poignancy of Bartleby's plight as "arm-in-arm with the constable" he leads a "silent procession through the financial district." Even the grass in the prison yard provides an opportunity for commenting on Bartleby's predicament. The grass does not symbolize the tenacity with which nature clings to life, but points to futility, hopelessness and death. This grass is "imprisoned" like that growing at "the heart of the eternal pyramids," and the difference between the Egyptian pyramids—those fantastic monuments to death—and the New York City jail so aptly named "the Tombs" is slight. Instead of housing the lifelike mummified dead, the jail holds those entombed while alive. No matter where he moves—Wall Street, the Tombs or the Dead Letter Office—Bartleby always encounters in his setting the same sad truth that "errands of life speed to death."

Authors sometimes refurbish an old story simply by moving it into a new setting. One of the world's oldest, most often repeated tales is that of the person who becomes an example of virtue for others but who quickly yields when tempted himself. By placing this well-worn plot in a new tomb setting, Petronius gives it new life. Not even the sight of the dear, departed husband's corpse stops the widow from doing what comes naturally. Instead, the corpse becomes a splendid illustration of the cliché that now is the time for love, life and laughter, not hatred, death and tears; for "all men alike...have the same end; the same resting place awaits us all." The setting also makes possible the anticlimactic, comic ending where the dead husband becomes a stand-in for the missing corpse on the cross—much to the amazement and amusement of the townspeople.

Not all such shifts are as successful as Petronius'. The following rewriting of "The Three Bears" as a murder mystery replete with appropriately brooding setting, sounds more like a parody than the real thing:

The wind howled about the lonely house on Bear Heights. "Beware," it seemed to wail, while whirling the abandoned leaves into lonely corners. Flakes of snow swirled out of the leaden sky, flinging dead leaves about the frozen earth. In the darkening forest the swaying trees held their branches aloft as if to ward off intruders.

Because the ominous and the mysterious are so exaggerated, this description may amuse rather than frighten a reader. Compare it with the beginning of "Aura," where Carlos Fuentes skillfully uses setting to create an atmosphere which makes us aware of a strange, perhaps supernatural, force at work. When the young man, Felipe, enters the house at number 815 Donceles, a sense of the unknown enters with him. The dog's-head doorknocker appears to be alive—or is his imagination overactive and playing tricks on him? The doors seem to open too easily, almost of their own accord. As he walks down the passageway the atmosphere becomes more oppressive, suggesting death and decay: "It must have been a patio of some sort, because you can smell the mould, the dampness of the plants, the rotting roots, the thick drowsy aroma." The all-pervasive dreamlike, mysterious atmosphere is charged with an almost demonic power that leads us to believe anything can happen—and it does.

Fuentes' use of setting may be compared with Willa Cather's in "The Sculptor's Funeral," where she dwells on the approaching train and the Merrick house before introducing each group of characters. Unlike the waiting, undifferentiated men, the speeding train hurtles out of the darkness with life, purpose and energy. The "naked, weather-beaten" Merrick home, with its gate hanging on one hinge and its makeshift board footbridge across the yard, provides a good physical counterpart to the emotional starvation it holds inside and from which the young artist fled in life and to which he now returns in death.

Sometimes the setting for a story or group of stories is so exact or vivid that readers become convinced of its reality outside the tale. People make pilgrimages to the little town in Wales where Dylan Thomas' stories are set. Others keep track of Faulkner's characters by locating their homes or activities on a scale map of the mythical county where his novels and stories take place. Some readers even argue about the historical identification and architectural features of the "large, square mansion, distinguished from its neighbors by a balcony" across from which Robin waits to see his kinsman, Major Molineux. All are so persuaded of the setting's existence that they want to touch, see or at least locate it in time or space as well as in their imagination.

If used well, setting—whether realistic or fantastic—helps lead us from our everyday world into the imaginative one where stories happen.

THE SCULPTOR'S FUNERAL
Willa Cather

A group of the townspeople stood on the station siding of a little Kansas town, awaiting the coming of the night train, which was already twenty minutes overdue. The snow had fallen thick over everything; in the pale starlight the line of bluffs across the wide, white meadows south of the town made soft, smoke-colored curves against the clear sky. The men on the siding stood first on one foot and then on the other, their hands thrust deep into their trousers pockets, their overcoats open, their shoulders screwed up with the cold; and they glanced from time to time toward the southeast, where the railroad track wound along the river shore. They conversed in low tones and moved about restlessly, seeming uncertain as to what was expected of them. There was but one of the company who looked as though he knew exactly why he was there, and he kept conspicuously apart, walking to the far end of the platform, returning to the station door, then pacing up the track again, his chin sunk in the high collar of his overcoat, his burly shoulders drooping forward, his gait heavy and dogged. Presently he was approached by a tall, spare, grizzled man clad in a faded Grand Army suit, who shuffled out from the group and advanced with a certain deference, craning his neck forward until his back made the angle of a jack-knife three-quarters open.

"I reckon she's a-goin' to be pretty late agin to-night, Jim," he remarked in a squeaky falsetto. "S'pose it's the snow?"

"I don't know," responded the other man with a shade of annoyance, speaking from out an astonishing cataract of red beard which grew fiercely and thickly in all directions.

The spare man shifted the quill toothpick he was chewing to the other side of his mouth. "It ain't likely that anybody from the East, will come with the corpse, I s'pose?" he went on reflectively.

"I don't know," responded the other, more curtly than before.

"It's too bad he didn't belong to some lodge or other. I like an order funeral myself. They seem more appropriate for people of some repytation," the spare man continued, with an ingratiating concession in his shrill voice, as he carefully placed his toothpick in his vest pocket. He always carried the flag at the G. A. R. funerals in the town.

The heavy man turned on his heel without replying, and walked up the siding. The spare man shuffled back to the uneasy group. "Jim's ez full ez a tick, ez ushel," he commented commiseratingly.

Just then a distant whistle sounded, and there was a shuffling of feet on the platform. A number of lanky boys of all ages appeared as suddenly and slimily as eels wakened by the crack of thunder; some came from the waiting-room, where they had been warming themselves by the red stove, or half asleep on the slat benches; others uncoiled themselves from baggage trucks or slid out of express wagons. Two clambered down from the driver's seat of a hearse that stood backed up against the siding. They straightened their stooping shoulders and lifted their heads, and a flash of momentary animation kindled their dull eyes at that cold, vibrant scream, the world-wide call for men. It stirred them like the note of a trumpet, just as it had often stirred in his boyhood the man who was coming home to-night.

The night express shot, red as a rocket, out of the eastward marsh lands, and wound along the river shore under the long lines of shivering poplars that sentineled the meadows, the escaping steam hanging in gray masses against the still, pale sky and blotting out the Milky Way. In a moment the red glare from the headlight streamed up the snow-covered track before the siding and glittered on the wet, black rails. The burly man with the disheveled red beard walked swiftly up the platform toward the approaching train, uncovering his head as he went. The group of men behind him hesitated, glanced questioningly at one another, and awkwardly followed his example. The train stopped, and the crowd shuffled up to the express car just as the door was thrown open, the spare man in the G. A. R. suit thrusting his head forward with curiosity. The express messenger appeared in the doorway, accompanied by a young man in a long ulster and traveling-cap.

"Are Mr. Merrick's friends here?" inquired the young man.

The group on the platform swayed and shuffled uneasily. Philip Phelps, the banker, responded with dignity: "We have come to take charge of the body. Mr. Merrick's father is very feeble and can't be about."

"Send the agent out here," growled the express messenger, "and tell the operator to lend a hand."

The coffin was got out of its rough box and down on the snowy platform. The townspeople drew back enough to make room for it and then formed a close semicircle about it, looking curiously at the palm-leaf which lay across the black cover. No one said anything. The baggageman stood by his truck, waiting to get at the trunks. The engine panted heavily, and the fireman dodged in and out among the wheels with his yellow torch and long oil-can, snapping the spindle boxes. The young Bostonian, one of the dead sculptor's pupils, who had come with the body, looked about him helplessly. He turned to the banker, the only one of that black, uneasy, stoop-shouldered group who seemed enough of an individual to be addressed.

"None of Mr. Merrick's brothers are here?" he asked uncertainly.

The man with the red beard for the first time stepped up and joined the group. "No, they have not come yet; the family is scattered. The body will be taken directly to the house." He stooped and took hold of one of the handles of the coffin.

"Take the long hill road up, Thompson; it will be easier on the horses," called the liveryman, as the undertaker snapped the door of the hearse and prepared to mount to the driver's seat.

Laird, the red-bearded lawyer, turned again to the stranger: "We didn't know whether there would be any one with him or not," he explained. "It's a long walk, so you'd better go up in the hack." He pointed to a single battered conveyance, but the young man replied stiffly: "Thank you, but I think I will go up with the hearse. If you don't object," turning to the undertaker, "I'll ride with you."

They clambered up over the wheels and drove off in the starlight up the long, white hill toward the town. The lamps in the still village were shining from under the low, snow-burdened roofs; and beyond, on every side, the plains reached out into emptiness, peaceful and wide as the soft sky itself, and wrapped in a tangible, white silence.

When the hearse backed up to a wooden sidewalk before a naked, weather-beaten frame house, the same composite, ill-defined group that had stood upon the station siding was huddled about the gate. The front yard was an icy swamp, and a couple of warped planks, extending from the sidewalk to the door, made a sort of rickety footbridge. The gate hung on one hinge, and was opened wide with difficulty. Steavens, the young stranger, noticed that something black was tied to the knob of the front door.

The grating sound made by the casket, as it was drawn from the hearse, was answered by a scream from the house; the front door was wrenched open, and a tall, corpulent woman rushed out bareheaded into the snow and flung herself upon the coffin, shrieking: "My boy, my boy! And this is how you've come home to me!"

As Steavens turned away and closed his eyes with a shudder of unutterable repulsion, another woman, also tall, but flat and angular, dressed entirely in black, darted out of the house and caught Mrs. Merrick by the shoulders, crying sharply: "Come come, mother; you mustn't go on like this!" Her tone changed to one of obsequious solemnity as she turned to the banker: "The parlor is ready, Mr. Phelps."

The bearers carried the coffin along the narrow boards, while the undertaker ran ahead with the coffin-rests. They bore it into a large, unheated room that smelled of dampness and disuse and furniture polish, and set it down under a hanging lamp ornamented with jingling glass prisms and before a "Rogers group" of John Alden and Priscilla, wreathed with smilax. Henry Steavens stared around him with the sickening conviction that there had been some horrible mistake, and that he had somehow arrived at the wrong destination. He looked painfully about over the clover-green Brussels, the fat plush upholstery; among the hand-painted china plaques and panels and vases, for some mark of identification, for something that might once have conceivably belonged to Harvey Merrick. It was not until he recognized his friend in the crayon portrait of a little boy in kilts and curls, hanging over the piano, that he felt willing to let any of these people approach the coffin.

"Take the lid off, Mr. Thompson; let me see my boy's face," wailed the elder woman between her sobs. This time Steavens looked fearfully, almost beseechingly, into her face, red and swollen under its masses of strong, black, shiny hair. He flushed, dropped his eyes, and then, almost incredulously, looked again. There was a kind of power about her face—a kind of brutal handsomeness, even; but it was scarred and furrowed by violence, and so colored and coarsened by fiercer passions that grief seemed never to have laid a gentle finger there. The long nose was distended and knobbed at the end, and there were deep lines on either side of it; her heavy, black brows almost met across her forehead, her teeth were large and square, and set far apart—teeth that could tear. She filled the room; the men were obliterated, seemed tossed about like twigs in an angry water, and even Steavens felt himself being drawn into the whirlpool.

The daughter—the tall, raw-boned woman in crêpe, with a mourning-comb in her hair which curiously lengthened her long face—sat stiffly upon the sofa, her hands, conspicuous for their large knuckles, folded in her lap, her mouth and eyes drawn down, solemnly awaiting the opening of the coffin. Near the door stood a mulatto woman, evidently a servant in the house, with a timid bearing and an emaciated face pitifully sad and gentle. She was weeping silently, the corner of her calico apron lifted to her eyes, occasionally suppressing a long, quivering sob. Steavens walked over and stood beside her.

Feeble steps were heard on the stairs, and an old man, tall and frail, odorous of pipe smoke, with shaggy, unkempt gray hair and a dingy beard, tobacco-stained about the mouth, entered uncertainly. He went slowly up to the coffin and stood rolling a blue cotton handkerchief between his hands, seeming so pained and embarrassed by his wife's orgy of grief that he had no consciousness of anything else.

"There, there, Annie, dear, don't take on," he quavered timidly, putting out a shaking hand and awkwardly patting her elbow. She turned with a cry, and sank upon his shoulder with such violence that he tottered a little. He did not even glance toward the coffin, but continued to look at her with a dull, frightened, appealing expression, as a spaniel looks at the whip. His sunken cheeks slowly reddened and burned with miserable shame. When his wife rushed from the room, her daughter strode after her with set lips. The servant stole up to the coffin, bent over it for a moment, and then slipped away to the kitchen, leaving Steavens, the lawyer, and the father to themselves. The old man stood trembling and looking down at his dead son's face. The sculptor's splendid head seemed even more noble in its rigid stillness than in life. The dark hair had crept down upon the wide forehead; the face seemed strangely long, but in it there was not that beautiful and chaste repose which we expect to find in the faces of the dead. The brows were so drawn that there were two deep lines above the beaked nose, and the chin was thrust forward defiantly. It was as though the strain of life had been so sharp and bitter that death could not at once wholly relax the tension and smooth the countenance into perfect peace—as though he were still guarding something precious and holy which might even yet be wrested from him.

The old man's lips were working under his stained beard. He turned to the lawyer with timid deference: "Phelps and the rest are comin' back to set up with Harve, ain't they?" he asked. "Thank 'ee, Jim, thank 'ee." He brushed the hair back gently from his son's forehead. "He was a good boy, Jim; always a good boy. He was ez gentle ez a child and the kindest of 'em all—only we didn't none of us ever onderstand him." The tears trickled slowly down his beard and dropped upon the sculptor's coat.

"Martin, Martin—Oh, Martin! come here," his wife wailed from the top of the stairs. The old man started timorously: "Yes, Annie, I'm coming." He turned away, hesitated, stood for a moment in miserable indecision; then reached back and patted the dead man's hair softly, and stumbled from the room.

"Poor old man, I didn't think he had any tears left. Seems as if his eyes would have gone dry long ago. At his age nothing cuts very deep," remarked the lawyer.

Something in his tone made Steavens glance up. While the mother had been in the room the young man had scarcely seen any one else; but now, from the moment he first glanced into Jim Laird's florid face and blood-shot eyes, he knew that he had found what he had been heart-sick at not finding before—the feeling, the understanding, that must exist in some one, even here.

The man was red as his beard, with features swollen and blurred by dissipation, and a hot, blazing blue eye. His face was strained—that of a man who is controlling himself with difficulty—and he kept plucking at his beard with a sort of fierce resentment. Steavens, sitting by the window, watched him turn down the glaring lamp, still its jangling pendants with an angry gesture, and then stand with his hands locked behind him, staring down into the master's face. He could not help wondering what link there could have been between the porcelain vessel and so sooty a lump of potter's clay.

From the kitchen an uproar was sounding; when the dining-room door opened, the import of it was clear. The mother was abusing the maid for having forgotten to make the dressing for the chicken salad which had been prepared for the watchers. Steavens had never heard anything in the least like it; it was injured, emotional, dramatic abuse, unique and masterly in its excruciating cruelty, as violent and unrestrained as had been her grief of twenty minutes before. With a shudder of disgust, the lawyer went into the dining-room and closed the door into the kitchen.

"Poor Roxy's getting it now," he remarked when he came back. "The Merricks took her out of the poor-house years ago; and if her loyalty would let her, I guess the poor old thing could tell tales that would curdle your blood. She's the mulatto woman who was standing in here a while ago, with her apron to her eyes. The old woman is a fury; there never was anybody like her for demonstrative piety and ingenious cruelty. She made Harvey's life a hell for him when he lived at home; he was so sick ashamed of it. I never could see how he kept himself so sweet."

"He was wonderful," said Steavens slowly, "wonderful; but until to-night I have never known how wonderful."

"That is the true and eternal wonder of it, anyway; that it can come even from such a dung-heap as this," the lawyer cried, with a sweeping gesture which seemed to indicate much more than the four walls within which they stood.

"I think I'll see whether I can get a little air. The room is so close I am beginning to feel rather faint," murmured Steavens, struggling with one of the windows. The sash was stuck, however, and would not yield, so he sat down dejectedly and began pulling at his collar. The lawyer came over, loosened the sash with one blow of his red fist, and sent the window up a few inches. Steavens thanked him, but the nausea which had been gradually climbing into his throat for the last half hour left with but one desire—a desperate feeling that he must get away from this place with what was left of Harvey Merrick. Oh, he comprehended well enough now the gentle bitterness of the smile that he had seen so often on his master's lips!

He remembered that once, when Merrick returned from a visit home, he brought with him a singularly feeling and suggestive bas-relief of a thin, faded old woman, sitting and sewing something pinned to her knee; while a full-lipped, full-blooded little urchin, his trousers sustained by a single gallows, stood beside her impatiently twitching her gown to call her attention to a butterfly he had caught. Steavens, impressed by the tender and delicate modeling of the thin, tired face, had asked him if it were his mother. He remembered the dull flush that had burned up in the sculptor's face.

The lawyer was sitting in a rocking-chair beside the coffin, his head thrown back and his eyes closed. Steavens looked at him earnestly, puzzled at the line of the chin, and wondering why a man should conceal a feature of such distinction under that disfiguring shock of red beard. Suddenly, as though he felt the young sculptor's keen glance, he opened his eyes.

"Was he always a good deal of an oyster?" he asked abruptly. "He was terribly shy as a boy."

"Yes, he was an oyster, since you put it so," rejoined Steavens. "Although he could be very fond of people, he always gave one the impression of being detached. He disliked violent emotion; he was reflective, and rather distrustful of himself—except, of course, as regarded his work. He was surefooted enough there. He distrusted men pretty thoroughly, and women even more, yet somehow without believing ill of them. He was determined, indeed, to believe the best, but he seemed afraid to investigate."

"A burnt dog dreads the fire," said the lawyer grimly, and closed his eyes.

Steavens went on and on, reconstructing that whole miserable boyhood. All this raw, biting ugliness had been the portion of the man whose tastes were refined beyond the limits of the reasonable—whose mind was an exhaustless gallery of beautiful impressions, so sensitive that the mere shadow of a poplar leaf flickering against a sunny wall would be etched and held there forever. Surely, if ever a man had the magic wand in his finger-tips, it was Merrick. Whatever he touched, he revealed its holiest secret; liberated it from enchantment and restored it to its pristine loveliness, like the Arabian prince who fought the enchantress, spell for spell. Upon whatever he had come in contact with, he had left a beautiful record of the experience—a sort of ethereal signature; a scent, a sound, a color that was his own.

Steavens understood now the real tragedy of his master's life; neither love nor wine, as many had conjectured, but a blow which had fallen earlier and cut deeper than these could have done—a shame not his, and yet so unescapably his, to hide in his heart from his very boyhood. And without, the frontier warfare; the yearning of a boy, cast ashore upon a desert of newness and ugliness and sordidness, for all that is chastened and old, and noble with traditions.

At eleven o'clock the tall, flat woman in black crêpe entered and announced that the watchers were arriving, and asked them "to step into the dining-room." As Steavens rose, the lawyer said dryly: "You go on —it'll be a good experience for you, doubtless; as for me, I'm not equal to that crowd to-night; I've had twenty years of them."

As Steavens closed the door after him, he glanced back at the lawyer, sitting by the coffin in the dim light, with his chin resting on his hand.

The same misty group that had stood before the door of the express-car shuffled into the room. In the light of the kerosene lamp they separated and became individuals. The minister, a pale, feeble-looking man with white hair and blond chin-whiskers, took his seat beside a small table, and placed his Bible upon it. The Grand Army man took a seat behind the stove and tilted his chair back comfortably against the wall, fishing his quill toothpick from his waistcoat pocket. The two bankers, Phelps and Elder, sat off in a corner behind the dinner-table, where they could finish their discussion of the new usury law and its effect on chattel security loans. The real estate agent, an old man with a smiling, hypocritical face, soon joined them. The coal and lumber dealer and the cattle shipper sat on opposite sides of the hard coal burner, their feet on the nickel-work. Steavens took a book from his pocket and began to read. The talk around him ranged through various topics of local interest while the house was quieting down. When it was clear that the members of the family were in bed, the Grand Army man hitched his shoulders, and untangling his long legs, caught his heels on the rounds of his chair.

"S'pose there'll be a will, Phelps?" he queried in his weak falsetto.

The banker laughed disagreeably, and began trimming his nails with a pearl-handled pocket-knife.

"There'll scarcely be any need for one, will there?" he queried in his turn.

The restless Grand Army man shifted his position again, getting his knees still nearer his chin. "Why, the ole man says Harve's done right well lately," he chirped.

The other banker spoke up. "I reckon he means by that Harve ain't asked him to mortgage any more farms lately so as he could go on with his education."

"Seems like my mind don't reach back to a time when Harve wasn't bein' edycated," tittered the Grand Army man.

There was a general chuckle. The minister took out his handkerchief and blew his nose sonorously. Banker Phelps closed his knife with a snap. "It's too bad the old man's sons didn't turn out better," he remarked, with reflective authority. "They never hung together. He spent money enough on Harve to stock a dozen cattle-farms, and he might as well have poured it into Sand Creek. If Harve had stayed at home and helped nurse what little they had, and gone into stock on the old man's bottom farm, they might all have been well fixed. But the old man had to trust everything to tenants and was cheated right and left."

"Harve never could have handled stock none," interposed the cattleman. "He hadn't it in him to be sharp. Do you remember when he bought Sander's mules for eight-year olds, when everybody in town knew that Sander's father-in-law give 'em to his wife for a wedding present eighteen years before, an' they was full-grown mules then?"

Every one chuckled, and the Grand Army man rubbed his knees with a spasm of childish delight.

"Harve never was much account for anything practical, and he shore was never fond of work," began the coal and lumber dealer. "I mind the last time he was home; the day he left, when the old man was out to the barn helpin' his hand hitch up to take Harve to the train, and Cal. Moots was patchin' up the fence, Harve, he come out on the step and sings out, in his ladylike voice: 'Cal. Moots, Cal. Moots! please come cord my trunk.' "

"That's Harve for you," approved the Grand Army man gleefully. "I kin hear him howlin' yet, when he was a big feller in long pants, and his mother used to whale him with a rawhide in the barn for lettin' the cows git foundered in the cornfield when he was drivin' 'em home from pasture. He killed a cow of mine that-a-way onct—a pure Jersey and the best milker I had, an' the ole man had to put up for her. Harve, he was watchin' the sun set acrost the marshes when the anamile got away; he argued that sunset was oncommon fine."

"Where the old man made his mistake was in sending the boy East to school," said Phelps, stroking his goatee and speaking in a deliberate, judicial tone. "There was where he got his head full of traipsing to Paris and all such folly. What Harve needed, of all people, was a course in some first-class Kansas City business college."

The letters were swimming before Steavens's eyes. Was it possible that these men did not understand, that the palm on the coffin meant nothing to them? The very name of their town would have remained forever buried in the postal guide, had it not been now and again mentioned in the world in connection with Harvey Merrick's. He remembered what his master had said to him on the day of his death, after the congestion of both lungs had shut off any probability of recovery, and the sculptor had asked his pupil to send his body home. "It's not a pleasant place to be lying while the world is moving and doing and bettering," he had said, with a feeble smile: "but it rather seems as though we ought to go back to the place we came from in the end. The townspeople will come in for a look at me; and after they have had their say, I shan't have much to fear from the judgment of God. The wings of the Victory, in there"—with a weak gesture toward his studio—"will not shelter me."

The cattleman took up the comment. "Forty's young for a Merrick to cash in; they usually hang on pretty well. Probably he helped it along with whisky."

"His mother's people were not long-lived, and Harvey never had a robust constitution," said the minister mildly. He would have liked to say more. He had been the boy's Sunday-school teacher, and had been fond of him; but he felt that he was not in a position to speak. His own sons had turned out badly, and it was not a year since one of them had made his last trip home in the express-car, shot in a gambling-house in the Black Hills.

"Nevertheless, there is no disputin' that Harve frequently looked upon the wine when it was red, also variegated, and it shore made an oncommon fool of him," moralized the cattleman.

Just then the door leading into the parlor rattled loudly, and everyone started involuntarily, looking relieved when only Jim Laird came out. His red face was convulsed with anger, and the Grand Army man ducked his head when he saw the spark in his blue, blood-shot eye. They were all afraid of Jim; he was a drunkard, but he could twist the law to suit his client's needs as no other man in all Western Kansas could do; and there were many who tried. The lawyer closed the door gently behind him, leaned back against it, and folded his arms, cocking his head a little to one side. When he assumed this attitude in the court-room, ears were always pricked up, as it usually foretold a flood of withering sarcasm.

"I've been with you gentlemen before," he began in a dry, even tone, "when you've sat by the coffins of boys born and raised in this town; and, if I remember rightly, you were never any too well satisfied when you checked them up. What's the matter, anyhow? Why is it that reputable young men are as scarce as millionaires in Sand City? It might almost seem to a stranger that there was some way something the matter with your progressive town. Why did Reuben Sayer, the brightest young lawyer you ever turned out, after he had come home from the university as straight as a die, take to drinking, and forge a check and shoot himself? Why did Bill Merrit's son die of the shakes in a saloon in Omaha? Why was Mr. Thomas's son, here, shot in a gambling-house? Why did young Adams burn his mill to beat the insurance companies, and go to the pen?"

The lawyer paused and unfolded his arms, laying one clenched fist quietly on the table. "I'll tell you why: because you drummed nothing but money and knavery into their ears from the time they wore knicker-bockers; because you carped away at them as you've been carping here to-night, holding our friends Phelps and Elder up to them for their models, as our grandfathers held up George Washington and John Adams. But the boys, worse luck, were young, and raw at the business you put them to; and how could they match coppers with such artists as Phelps and Elder? You wanted them to be successful rascals; they were only unsuccessful ones—that's all the difference. There was only one boy ever raised in this borderland between ruffianism and civilization who didn't come to grief, and you hated Harvey Merrick more for winning out than you hated all the other boys who got under the wheels. Lord, Lord, how you did hate him! Phelps, here, is fond of saying that he could buy and sell us all out any time he's a mind to; but he knew Harve wouldn't have given a tinker's damn for his bank and all his cattle-farms put together; and a lack of appreciation, that way, goes hard with Phelps.

"Old Nimrod, here, thinks Harve drank too much; and this from such as Nimrod and me!

"Brother Elder says Harve was too free with the old man's money—fell short in filial consideration, maybe. Well, we can all remember the very tone in which Brother Elder swore his own father was a liar, in the county court; and we all know that the old man came out of that partnership with his son as bare as a sheared lamb. But maybe I'm getting personal, and I'd better be driving ahead at what I want to say."

The lawyer paused a moment, squared his heavy shoulders, and went on: "Harvey Merrick and I went to school together, back East. We were in dead earnest, and we wanted you all to be proud of us some day. We meant to be great men. Even I, and I haven't lost my sense of humor, gentlemen, I meant to be a great man. I came back here to practise, and I found you didn't in the least want me to be a great man. You wanted me to be a shrewd lawyer—oh, yes! Our veteran here wanted me to get him an increase of pension, because he had dyspepsia; Phelps wanted a new county survey that would put the widow Wilson's little bottom farm inside his south line; Elder wanted to lend money at 5 per cent a month and get it collected; old Stark here wanted to wheedle old women up in Vermont into investing their annuities in real-estate mortgages that are not worth the paper they are written on. Oh, you needed me hard enough, and you'll go on needing me; and that's why I'm not afraid to plug the truth home to you this once.

"Well, I came back here and became the damned shyster you wanted me to be. You pretend to have some sort of respect for me; and yet you'll stand up and throw mud at Harvey Merrick, whose soul you couldn't dirty, and whose hands you couldn't tie. Oh, you're a discriminating lot of Christians! There have been times when the sight of Harvey's name in some Eastern paper has made me hang my head like a whipped dog; and, again, times when I liked to think of him off there in the world, away from all this hog-wallow, doing his great work, and climbing the big, clean up-grade he'd set for himself.

"And we? Now that we've fought and lied and sweated and stolen and hated, as only the disappointed strugglers in a bitter, dead little Western town know how to do, what have we got to show for it? Harvey Merrick wouldn't have given one sunset over your marshes for all you've got put together, and you know it. It's not for me to say why, in the inscrutable wisdom of God, a genius should ever have been called from this place of hatred and bitter waters; but I want this Boston man to know that the drivel he's been hearing here to-night is the only tribute any truly great man could ever have from such a lot of sick, side-tracked, burnt-dog, land-poor sharks as the here-present financiers of Sand City—upon which town may God have mercy!"

The lawyer thrust out his hand to Steavens as he passed him, caught up his overcoat in the hall, and had left the house before the Grand Army man had found time to lift his ducked head and crane his long neck about at his fellows.

Next day Jim Laird was drunk and unable to attend the funeral services. Steavens called twice at his office, but was compelled to start East without seeing him. He had a presentiment that he would hear from him again, and left his address on the lawyer's table; but if Laird found it, he never acknowledged it. The thing in him that Harvey Merrick had loved must have gone under ground with Harvey Merrick's coffin; for it never spoke again, and Jim got the cold he died of driving across the Colorado mountains to defend one of Phelps's sons, who had got into trouble out there by cutting government timber.

THE FALL OF THE HOUSE OF USHER
Edgar Allan Poe

Son cœur est un luth suspendu;
Sitôt qu'on le touche il rèsonne.

—De Béranger

During the whole of a dull, dark, and soundless day in the autumn of the year, when the clouds hung oppressively low in the heavens, I had been passing alone, on horseback, through a singularly dreary tract of country; and at length found myself, as the shades of the evening drew on, within view of the melancholy House of Usher. I know not how it was—but, with the first glimpse of the building, a sense of insufferable gloom pervaded my spirit. I say insufferable; for the feeling was unrelieved by any of that half-pleasurable, because poetic, sentiment, with which the mind usually receives even the sternest natural images of the desolate or terrible. I looked upon the scene before me—upon the mere house, and the simple landscape features of the domain—upon the bleak walls—upon the vacant eye-like windows—upon a few rank sedges—and upon a few white trunks of decayed trees—with an utter depression of soul which I can compare to no earthly sensation more properly than to the after-dream of the reveller upon opium—the bitter lapse into everyday life—the hideous dropping off of the veil. There was an iciness, a sinking, a sickening of the heart—an unredeemed dreariness of thought which no goading of the imagination could torture into aught of the sublime. What was it—I paused to think—what was it that so unnerved me in the contemplation of the House of Usher? It was a mystery all insoluble; nor could I grapple with the shadowy fancies that crowded upon me as I pondered. I was forced to fall back upon the unsatisfactory conclusion, that while, beyond doubt, there *are* combinations of very simple natural objects which have the power of thus affecting us, still the analysis of this power lies among considerations beyond our depth. It was possible, I reflected, that a mere

Son coeur est...: His heart is a hanging lute; / Only touch it and it resounds.

different arrangement of the particulars of the scene, of the details of the picture, would be sufficient to modify, or perhaps to annihilate its capacity for sorrowful impression; and, acting upon this idea, I reined my horse to the precipitous brink of a black and lurid tarn that lay in unruffled lustre by the dwelling, and gazed down—but with a shudder even more thrilling than before—upon the remodelled and inverted images of the gray sedge, and the ghastly tree-stems, and the vacant and eye-like windows.

Nevertheless, in this mansion of gloom I now proposed to myself a sojourn of some weeks. Its proprietor, Roderick Usher, had been one of my boon companions in boyhood; but many years had elapsed since our last meeting. A letter, however, had lately reached me in a distant part of the country—a letter from him—which, in its wildly importunate nature, had admitted of no other than a personal reply. The MS. gave evidence of nervous agitation. The writer spoke of acute bodily illness—of a mental disorder which oppressed him—and of an earnest desire to see me, as his best, and indeed his only personal friend, with a view of attempting, by the cheerfulness of my society, some alleviation of his malady. It was the manner in which all this, and much more, was said—it was the apparent *heart* that went with his request—which allowed me no room for hesitation; and I accordingly obeyed forthwith what I still considered a very singular summons.

Although, as boys, we had been even intimate associates, yet I really knew little of my friend. His reserve had been always excessive and habitual. I was aware, however, that his very ancient family had been noted, time out of mind, for a peculiar sensibility of temperament, displaying itself, through long ages, in many works of exalted art, and manifested, of late, in repeated deeds of munificent yet unobtrusive charity, as well as in a passionate devotion to the intricacies, perhaps even more than to the orthodox and easily recognisable beauties, of musical science. I had learned, too, the very remarkable fact, that the stem of the Usher race, all time-honored as it was, had put forth, at no period, any enduring branch; in other words, that the entire family lay in the direct line of descent, and had always, with very trifling and very temporary variation, so lain. It was this deficiency, I considered, while running over in thought the perfect keeping of the character of the premises with the accredited character of the people, and while speculating upon the possible influence which the one, in the long lapse of centuries, might have exercised upon the other—it was this deficiency, perhaps, of collateral issue, and the consequent undeviating transmission, from sire to son, of the patrimony with the name, which had, at length, so identified the two as to merge the original title of the estate in the quaint and equivocal appellation of the "House of Usher"—an appellation which seemed to include, in the minds of the peasantry who used it, both the family and the family mansion.

I have said that the sole effect of my somewhat childish experiment—that of looking down within the tarn—had been to deepen the first singular impression. There can be no doubt that the consciousness of the rapid increase of my superstition—for why should I not so term it?—served mainly to accelerate the increase itself. Such, I have long known, is the paradoxical law of all sentiments having terror as a basis. And it might have been for this reason only, that, when I again uplifted my eyes to the house itself, from its image in the pool, there grew in my mind a strange fancy—a fancy so ridiculous, indeed, that I but mention it to show the vivid force of the sensations which oppressed me. I had so worked upon my imagination as really to believe that about the whole mansion and domain there hung an atmosphere peculiar to themselves and their immediate vicinity—an atmosphere which had no affinity with the air of heaven, but which had reeked up from the decayed trees, and the gray wall, and the silent tarn—a pestilent and mystic vapor, dull, sluggish, faintly discernible, and leaden-hued.

Shaking off from my spirit what *must* have been a dream, I scanned more narrowly the real aspect of the building. Its principal feature seemed to be that of an excessive antiquity. The discoloration of ages had been great. Minute fungi overspread the whole exterior hanging in a fine tangled webwork from the eaves. Yet all this was apart from any extraordinary dilapidation. No portion of the masonry had fallen; and there appeared to be a wild inconsistency between its still perfect adaptation of parts, and the crumbling condition of the individual stones. In this there was much that reminded me of the specious totality of old wood-work which has rotted for long years in some neglected vault, with no disturbance from the breath of the external air. Beyond this indication of extensive decay, however, the fabric gave little token of instability. Perhaps the eye of a scrutinizing observer might have discovered a barely perceptible fissure, which, extending from the roof of the building in front, made its way down the wall in a zigzag direction, until it became lost in the sullen waters of the tarn.

Noticing these things, I rode over a short causeway to the house. A servant in waiting took my horse, and I entered the Gothic archway of the hall. A valet, of stealthy step, thence conducted me, in silence, through many dark and intricate passages in my progress to the studio of his master. Much that I encountered on the way contributed, I know not how, to heighten the vague sentiments of which I have already spoken. While the objects around me—while the carvings of the ceilings, the sombre tapestries of the walls, the ebon blackness of the floors, and the phantasmagoric armorial trophies which rattled as I strode, were but matters to which, or to such as which, I had been accustomed from my infancy—while I hesitated not to acknowledge how familiar was all this—I still wondered to find how unfamiliar were the fancies which ordinary images were stirring up. On one of the staircases, I met the physician of the family. His countenance, I thought, wore a mingled expression of low cunning and perplexity. He accosted me with trepidation and passed on. The valet now threw open a door and ushered me into the presence of his master.

The room in which I found myself was very large and lofty. The windows were long, narrow, and pointed, and at so vast a distance from the black oaken floor as to be altogether inaccessible from within. Feeble gleams of encrimsoned light made their way through the trellissed panes, and served to render sufficiently distinct the more prominent objects around; the eye, however, struggled in vain to reach the remoter angles of the chamber, or the recesses of the vaulted and fretted ceiling. Dark draperies hung upon the walls. The general furniture was profuse, comfortless, antique, and tattered. Many books and musical instruments lay scattered about, but failed to give any vitality to the scene. I felt that I breathed an atmosphere of sorrow. An air of stern, deep, and irredeemable gloom hung over and pervaded all.

Upon my entrance, Usher arose from a sofa on which he had been lying at full length, and greeted me with a vivacious warmth which had much in it, I at first thought, of an overdone cordiality—of the constrained effort of the *ennuyé* man of the world. A glance, however, at his countenance, convinced me of his perfect sincerity. We sat down; and for some moments, while he spoke not, I gazed upon him with a feeling half of pity, half of awe. Surely, man had never before so terribly altered, in so brief a period, as had Roderick Usher! It was with difficulty that I could bring myself to admit the identity of the wan being before me with the companion of my early boyhood. Yet the character of his face had been at all times remarkable. A cadaverousness of complexion; an eye large, liquid, and luminous beyond comparison; lips somewhat thin and very pallid, but of a surpassingly beautiful curve; a nose of a delicate Hebrew model, but with a breadth of nostril unusual in similar formations; a finely moulded chin, speaking, in its want of prominence, of a want of moral energy; hair of a more than web-like softness and tenuity; these features, with an inordinate expansion above the regions of the temple, made up altogether a countenance not easily to be forgotten. And now in the mere exaggeration of the prevailing character of these features, and of the expression they were wont to convey, lay so much of change that I doubted to whom I spoke. The now ghastly pallor of the skin, and the now miraculous lustre of the eye, above all things startled and even awed me. The silken hair, too, had been suffered to grow all unheeded, and as, in its wild gossamer texture, it floated rather than fell about the face, I

ennuyé: bored.

could not, even with effort, connect its Arabesque expression with any idea of simple humanity.

In the manner of my friend I was at once struck with an incoherence—an inconsistency; and I soon found this to arise from a series of feeble and futile struggles to overcome an habitual trepidancy—an excessive nervous agitation. For something of this nature I had indeed been prepared, no less by his letter, than by reminiscences of certain boyish traits, and by conclusions deduced from his peculiar physical conformation and temperament. His action was alternately vivacious and sullen. His voice varied rapidly from a tremulous indecision (when the animal spirits seemed utterly in abeyance) to that species of energetic concision—that abrupt, weighty, unhurried, and hollow-sounding enunciation—that leaden, self-balanced and perfectly modulated guttural utterance, which may be observed in the lost drunkard, or the irreclaimable eater of opium, during the periods of his most intense excitement.

It was thus that he spoke of the object of my visit, of his earnest desire to see me, and of the solace he expected me to afford him. He entered, at some length, into what he conceived to be the nature of his malady. It was, he said, a constitutional and a family evil, and one for which he despaired to find a remedy—a mere nervous affection, he immediately added, which would undoubtedly soon pass off. It displayed itself in a host of unnatural sensations. Some of these, as he detailed them, interested and bewildered me; although, perhaps, the terms, and the general manner of the narration had their weight. He suffered much from a morbid acuteness of the senses; the most insipid food was alone endurable; he could wear only garments of certain texture; the odors of all flowers were oppressive; his eyes were tortured by even a faint light; and there were but peculiar sounds, and these from stringed instruments, which did not inspire him with horror.

To an anomalous species of terror I found him a bounden slave. "I shall perish," said he, "I *must* perish in this deplorable folly. Thus, thus, and not otherwise, shall I be lost. I dread the events of the future, not in themselves, but in their results. I shudder at the thought of any, even the most trivial incident, which may operate upon this intolerable agitation of soul. I have, indeed, no abhorrence of danger, except in its absolute effect—in terror. In this unnerved—in this pitiable condition—I feel that the period will sooner or later arrive when I must abandon life and reason together, in some struggle with the grim phantasm, FEAR."

I learned, moreover, at intervals, and through broken and equivocal hints, another singular feature of his mental condition. He was enchained by certain superstitious impressions in regard to the dwelling which he tenanted, and whence, for many years, he had never ventured forth—in regard to an influence whose supposititious force was conveyed in terms too shadowy here to be re-stated—an influence which some peculiarities in the mere form and substance of his family mansion, had, by dint of long sufferance, he said, obtained over his spirit—an effect which the physique of the gray walls and turrets, and of the dim tarn into which they all looked down, had, at length, brought about upon the morale of his existence.

He admitted, however, although with hesitation, that much of the peculiar gloom which thus afflicted him could be traced to a more natural and far more palpable origin—to the severe and long-continued illness—indeed to the evidently approaching dissolution—of a tenderly beloved sister—his sole companion for long years—his last and only relative on earth. "Her decease," he said, with a bitterness which I can never forget, "would leave him (him the hopeless and the frail) the last of the ancient race of the Ushers." While he spoke, the lady Madeline (for so was she called) passed slowly through a remote portion of the apartment, and, without having noticed my presence, disappeared. I regarded her with an utter astonishment not unmingled with dread—and yet I found it impossible to account for such feelings. A sensation of stupor oppressed me, as my eyes followed her retreating steps. When a door, at length, closed upon her, my glance sought instinctively and eagerly the countenance of the brother—but he had buried his face in his hands, and I could only perceive that a far more than ordinary wanness had overspread the emaciated fingers through which trickled many passionate tears.

The disease of the lady Madeline had long baffled the skill of her physicians. A settled apathy, a gradual wasting away of the person, and frequent although transient affections of a partially cataleptical character, were the unusual diagnosis. Hitherto she had steadily borne up against the pressure of her malady, and had not betaken herself finally to bed; but, on the closing in of the evening of my arrival at the house, she succumbed (as her brother told me at night with inexpressible agitation) to the prostrating power of the destroyer; and I learned that the glimpse I had obtained of her person would thus probably be the last I should obtain—that the lady, at least while living, would be seen by me no more.

For several days ensuing her name was unmentioned by either Usher or myself: and during this period I was busied in earnest endeavors to alleviate the melancholy of my friend. We painted and read together; or I listened, as if in a dream, to the wild improvisations of his speaking guitar. And thus, as a closer and still closer intimacy admitted me more unreservedly into the recesses of his spirit, the more bitterly did I perceive the futility of all attempt at cheering a mind from which darkness, as if an inherent positive quality, poured forth upon all objects of the moral and physical universe, in one unceasing radiation of gloom.

I shall ever bear about me a memory of the many solemn hours I thus spent alone with the master of the House of Usher. Yet I should fail in any attempt to convey an idea of the exact character of the studies, or of the occupations, in which he involved me, or led me the way. An excited and highly distempered ideality threw a sulphureous lustre over all. His long improvised dirges will ring forever in my ears. Among other things, I hold painfully in mind a certain singular perversion and amplification of the wild air of the last waltz of Von Weber. From the paintings over which his elaborate fancy brooded, and which grew, touch by touch, into vaguenesses at which I shuddered the more thrillingly, because I shuddered knowing not why;—from these paintings (vivid as their images now are before me) I would in vain endeavor to educe more than a small portion which should lie within the compass of merely written words. By the utter simplicity, by the nakedness of his designs, he arrested and overawed attention. If ever mortal painted an idea, that mortal was Roderick Usher. For me at least—in the circumstances then surrounding me—there arose out of the pure abstractions which the hypochondriac contrived to throw upon his canvass, an intensity of intolerable awe, no shadow of which felt I ever yet in the contemplation of the certainly glowing yet too concrete reveries of Fuseli.

One of the phantasmagoric conceptions of my friend, partaking not so rigidly of the spirit of abstraction, may be shadowed forth, although feebly, in words. A small picture presented the interior of an immensely long and rectangular vault or tunnel, with low walls, smooth, white, and without interruption or device. Certain accessory points of the design served well to convey the idea that this excavation lay at an exceeding depth below the surface of the earth. No outlet was observed in any portion of its vast extent, and no torch, or other artificial source of light was discernible; yet a flood of intense rays rolled throughout, and bathed the whole in a ghastly and inappropriate splendor.

I have just spoken of that morbid condition of the auditory nerve which rendered all music intolerable to the sufferer, with the exception of certain effects of stringed instruments. It was, perhaps, the narrow limits to which he thus confined himself upon the guitar, which gave birth, in great measure, to the fantastic character of his performances. But the fervid facility of his impromptus could not be so accounted for. They must have been, and were, in the notes, as well as in the words of his wild fantasias (for he not unfrequently accompanied himself with rhymed verbal improvisations), the result of that intense mental collectedness and concentration to which I have previously alluded as observable only in particular moments of the highest artificial excitement. The words of one of these rhapsodies I have easily remembered. I was, perhaps, the more forcibly impressed with it, as he gave it, because, in the under or mystic current of its meaning, I fancied that I perceived, and for the first time, a full consciousness on the part of Usher, of the tottering of his lofty reason upon her throne. The verses, which were entitled "The Haunted Palace," ran very nearly, if not accurately, thus:

I.

In the greenest of our valleys,
By good angels tenanted,
Once a fair and stately palace—
Radiant palace—reared its head.
In the monarch Thought's dominion—
It stood there!
Never seraph spread a pinion
Over fabric half so fair.

II.

Banners yellow, glorious, golden,
On its roof did float and flow;
(This—all this—was in the olden
Time long ago)
And every gentle air that dallied,
In that sweet day,
Along the ramparts plumed and pallid,
A winged odor went away.

III.

Wanderers in that happy valley
Through two luminous windows saw
Spirits moving musically
To a lute's well-tuned law,
Round about a throne, where sitting
(Porphyrogene!)
In state his glory well befitting,
The ruler of the realm was seen.

IV.

And all with pearl and ruby glowing
Was the fair palace door,
Through which came flowing, flowing, flowing
And sparkling evermore,

A troop of Echoes whose sweet duty
Was but to sing,
In voices of surpassing beauty,
The wit and wisdom of their king.

V.

But evil things, in robes of sorrow,
Assailed the monarch's high estate;
(Ah, let us mourn, for never morrow
Shall dawn upon him, desolate!)
And, round about his home, the glory
That blushed and bloomed
Is but a dim-remembered story
Of the old time entombed.

VI.

And travellers now within that valley,
Through the red-litten windows, see
Vast forms that move fantastically
To a discordant melody;
While, like a rapid ghastly river,
Through the pale door,
A hideous throng rush out forever,
And laugh—but smile no more.

I well remember that suggestions arising from this ballad, led us into a train of thought wherein there became manifest an opinion of Usher's which I mention not so much on account of its novelty (for other men* have thought thus), as on account of the pertinacity with which he maintained it. This opinion, in its general form, was that of the sentience of all vegetable things. But, in his disordered fancy, the idea had assumed a more daring character, and trespassed, under certain conditions, upon the kingdom of inorganization. I lack words to express the full extent, or the earnest *abandon* of his persuasion. The belief, however, was connected (as I have previously hinted) with the gray stones of the home of his forefathers. The conditions of the sentience had been here, he imagined, fulfilled, in the method of collocation of these stones—in the order of their arrangement, as well as in that of the many fungi which overspread them,

* Watson, Dr. Percival, Spallanzani, and especially the Bishop of Landaff—See "Chemical Essays," vol. v. [Poe's note]

and of the decayed trees which stood around—above all, in the long undisturbed endurance of this arrangement, and in its reduplication in the still waters of the tarn. Its evidence—the evidence of the sentience—was to be seen, he said (and I here started as he spoke), in the gradual yet certain condensation of an atmosphere of their own about the waters and the walls. The result was discoverable, he added, in that silent, yet importunate and terrible influence which for centuries had moulded the destinies of his family, and which made *him* what I now saw him—what he was. Such opinions need no comment, and I will make none.

Our books—the books which, for years, had formed no small portion of the mental existence of the invalid—were, as might be supposed, in strict keeping with this character of phantasm. We pored together over such works as the Ververt et Chartreuse of Gresset; the Belphegor of Machiavelli; the Heaven and Hell of Swedenborg; the Subterranean Voyage of Nicholas Klimm by Holberg; the Chiromancy of Robert Flud, of Jean D'Indaginé, and of De la Chambre; the Journey into the Blue Distance of Tieck; and the City of the Sun of Campanella. One favorite volume was a small octavo edition of the *Directorium Inquisitorium,* by the Dominican Eymeric de Gironne; and there were passages in Pomponius Mela, about the old African Satyrs and Œgipans, over which Usher would sit dreaming for hours. His chief delight, however, was found in the perusal of an exceedingly rare and curious book in quarto Gothic—the manual of a forgotten church—the *Vigiliae Mortuorum secundum Chorum Ecclesiae Maguntinae.*

I could not help thinking of the wild ritual of this work, and of its probable influence upon the hypochondriac, when, one evening, having informed me abruptly that the lady Madeline was no more, he stated his intention of preserving her corpse for a fortnight (previously to its final interment), in one of the numerous vaults within the main walls of the building. The worldly reason, however, assigned for this singular proceeding, was one which I did not feel at liberty to dispute. The brother had been led to his resolution (so he told me) by consideration of the unusual character of the malady of the deceased, of certain obtrusive and eager inquiries on the part of her medical men, and of the remote and exposed situation of the burial-ground of the family. I will not deny that when I called to mind the sinister countenance of the person whom I met upon the staircase, on the day of my arrival at the house, I had no desire to oppose what I regarded as at best but a harmless, and by no means an unnatural, precaution.

At the request of Usher, I personally aided him in the arrangements for the temporary entombment. The body having been encoffined, we two

Vigiliae Mortuorum secundum...: Vigils for the dead according to the musical rites of the Maguntian Church.

alone bore it to its rest. The vault in which we placed it (and which had been so long unopened that our torches, half smothered in its oppressive atmosphere, gave us little opportunity for investigation) was small, damp, and entirely without means of admission for light; lying, at great depth, immediately beneath that portion of the building in which was my own sleeping apartment. It had been used, apparently, in remote feudal times, for the worst purposes of a donjon-keep, and, in later days, as a place of deposit for powder, or some other highly combustible substance, as a portion of its floor, and the whole interior of a long archway through which we reached it, were carefully sheathed with copper. The door, of massive iron, had been, also, similarly protected. Its immense weight caused an unusually sharp grating sound, as it moved upon its hinges.

Having deposited our mournful burden upon tressels within this region of horror, we partially turned aside the yet unscrewed lid of the coffin, and looked upon the face of the tenant. A striking similitude between the brother and sister now first arrested my attention; and Usher, divining, perhaps, my thoughts, murmured out some few words from which I learned that the deceased and himself had been twins, and that sympathies of a scarcely intelligible nature had always existed between them. Our glances, however, rested not long upon the dead—for we could not regard her un-awed. The disease which had thus entombed the lady in the maturity of youth, had left, as usual in all maladies of a strictly cataleptical character, the mockery of a faint blush upon the bosom and the face, and that suspiciously lingering smile upon the lip which is so terrible in death. We replaced and screwed down the lid, and, having secured the door of iron, made our way, with toil, into the scarcely less gloomy apartments of the upper portion of the house.

And now, some days of bitter grief having elapsed, an observable change came over the features of the mental disorder of my friend. His ordinary manner had vanished. His ordinary occupations were neglected or forgotten. He roamed from chamber to chamber with hurried, unequal, and objectless step. The pallor of his countenance had assumed, if possible, a more ghastly hue—but the luminousness of his eye had utterly gone out. The once occasional huskiness of his tone was heard no more; and a tremulous quaver, as if of extreme terror, habitually characterized his utterance. There were times, indeed, when I thought his unceasingly agitated mind was laboring with some oppressive secret, to divulge which he struggled for the necessary courage. At times, again, I was obliged to resolve all into the mere inexplicable vagaries of madness, for I beheld him gazing upon vacancy for long hours, in an attitude of the profoundest attention, as if listening to some imaginary sound. It was no wonder that his condition terrified—that it infected me. I felt creeping upon me, by slow yet certain degrees, the wild influences of his own fantastic yet impressive superstitions.

It was, especially, upon retiring to bed late in the night of the seventh or eighth day after the placing of the lady Madeline within the donjon, that I experienced the full power of such feelings. Sleep came not near my couch—while the hours waned and waned away. I struggled to reason off the nervousness which had dominion over me. I endeavored to believe that much, if not all of what I felt, was due to the bewildering influence of the gloomy furniture of the room—of the dark and tattered draperies, which, tortured into motion by the breath of a rising tempest, swayed fitfully to and fro upon the walls, and rustled uneasily about the decorations of the bed. But my efforts were fruitless. An irrepressible tremor gradually pervaded my frame; and, at length, there sat upon my very heart an incubus of utterly causeless alarm. Shaking this off with a gasp and a struggle, I uplifted myself upon the pillows, and, peering earnestly within the intense darkness of the chamber, harkened—I know not why, except that an instinctive spirit prompted me—to certain low and indefinite sounds which came, through the pauses of the storm, at long intervals, I knew not whence. Overpowered by an intense sentiment of horror, unaccountable yet unendurable, I threw on my clothes with haste (for I felt that I should sleep no more during the night), and endeavored to arouse myself from the pitiable condition into which I had fallen, by pacing rapidly to and fro through the apartment.

I had taken but few turns in this manner, when a light step on an adjoining staircase arrested my attention. I presently recognised it as that of Usher. In an instant afterward he rapped, with a gentle touch, at my door, and entered, bearing a lamp. His countenance was, as usual, cadaverously wan—but, moreover, there was a species of mad hilarity in his eyes—an evidently restrained hysteria in his whole demeanor. His air appalled me—but anything was preferable to the solitude which I had so long endured, and I even welcomed his presence as a relief.

"And you have not seen it?" he said abruptly, after having stared about him for some moments in silence—"you have not then seen it?—but, stay! you shall." Thus speaking, and having carefully shaded his lamp, he hurried to one of the casements, and threw it freely open to the storm.

The impetuous fury of the entering gust nearly lifted us from our feet. It was, indeed, a tempestuous yet sternly beautiful night, and one wildly singular in its terror and its beauty. A whirlwind had apparently collected its force in our vicinity; for there were frequent and violent alterations in the direction of the wind; and the exceeding density of the clouds (which hung so low as to press upon the turrets of the house) did not prevent our perceiving the life-like velocity with which they flew careering from all points against each other, without passing away into the distance. I say that even their exceeding density did not prevent our perceiving this—yet we had no glimpse of the moon or stars—nor was there any flashing forth of the lightning. But the under surfaces of the huge masses of agitated vapor, as well as all terrestrial objects immediately around us, were glowing in the unnatural light of a faintly luminous and distinctly visible gaseous exhalation which hung about and enshrouded the mansion.

"You must not—you shall not behold this!" said I, shudderingly, to Usher, as I led him, with a gentle violence, from the window to a seat. "These appearances, which bewilder you, are merely electrical phenomena not uncommon—or it may be that they have their ghastly origin in the rank miasma of the tarn. Let us close this casement;—the air is chilling and dangerous to your frame. Here is one of your favorite romances. I will read, and you shall listen;—and so we will pass away this terrible night together."

The antique volume which I had taken up was the "Mad Trist" of Sir Launcelot Canning; but I had called it a favorite of Usher's more in sad jest than in earnest; for, in truth, there is little in its uncouth and unimaginative prolixity which could have had interest for the lofty and spiritual ideality of my friend. It was, however, the only book immediately at hand; and I indulged a vague hope that the excitement which now agitated the hypochondriac, might find relief (for the history of mental disorder is full of similar anomalies) even in the extremeness of the folly which I should read. Could I have judged, indeed, by the wild overstrained air of vivacity with which he harkened, or apparently harkened, to the words of the tale, I might well have congratulated myself upon the success of my design.

I had arrived at that well-known portion of the story where Ethelred, the hero of the Trist, having sought in vain for peaceable admission into the dwelling of the hermit, proceeds to make good an entrance by force. Here, it will be remembered, the words of the narrative run thus:

"And Ethelred, who was by nature of a doughty heart, and who was now mighty withal, on account of the powerfulness of the wine which he had drunken, waited no longer to hold parley with the hermit, who, in sooth, was of an obstinate and maliceful turn, but, feeling the rain upon his shoulders, and fearing the rising of the tempest, uplifted his mace outright, and, with blows, made quickly room in the plankings of the door for his gauntleted hand; and now pulling therewith sturdily, he so cracked, and ripped, and tore all asunder, that the noise of the dry and hollow-sounding wood alarummed and reverberated throughout the forest."

At the termination of this sentence I started, and for a moment, paused; for it appeared to me (although I at once concluded that my excited fancy had deceived me)—it appeared to me that, from some very remote portion of the mansion, there came, indistinctly, to my ears, what might have been, in its exact similarity of character, the echo (but a stifled and dull one certainly) of the very cracking and ripping sound which Sir Launcelot had so particularly described. It was, beyond doubt, the coincidence alone which had arrested my attention for, amid the rattling of the sashes of the casements, and the ordinary commingled noises of the still increasing storm, the sound, in itself, had nothing surely, which should have interested or disturbed me. I continued the story:

"But the good champion Ethelred, now entering within the door, was sore enraged and amazed to perceive no signal of the maliceful hermit; but, in the stead thereof, a dragon of a scaly and prodigious demeanor, and of a fiery tongue, which sate in guard before a palace of gold, with a floor of silver; and upon the wall there hung a shield of shining brass with this legend enwritten—

Who entereth herein, a conqueror hath bin;
Who slayeth the dragon, the shield he shall win;

And Ethelred uplifted his mace, and struck upon the head of the dragon, which fell before him, and gave up his pesty breath, with a shriek so horrid and harsh, and withal so piercing, that Ethelred had fain to close his ears with his hands against the dreadful noise of it, the like whereof was never before heard."

Here again I paused abruptly, and now with a feeling of wild amazement—for there could be no doubt whatever that, in this instance, I did actually hear (although from what direction it proceeded I found it impossible to say) a low and apparently distant, but harsh, protracted, and most unusual screaming or grating sound—the exact counterpart of what my fancy had already conjured up for the dragon's unnatural shriek as described by the romancer.

Oppressed, as I certainly was, upon the occurrence of this second and most extraordinary coincidence, by a thousand conflicting sensations, in which wonder and extreme terror were predominant, I still retained sufficient presence of mind to avoid exciting by any observation, the sensitive nervousness of my companion. I was by no means certain that he had noticed the sounds in question; although, assuredly, a strange alteration had, during the last few minutes, taken place in his demeanor. From a position fronting my own, he had gradually brought round his chair, so as to sit with his face to the door of the chamber; and thus I could but partially perceive his features, although I saw that his lips trembled as if he were murmuring inaudibly. His head had dropped upon his breast—yet I knew that he was not asleep, from the wide and rigid opening of the eye as I caught a glance of it in profile. The motion of his body, too, was at variance with this idea—for he rocked from side to side with a gentle yet constant and uniform sway. Having rapidly taken notice of all this, I resumed the narrative of Sir Launcelot, which thus proceeded:

"And now, the champion, having escaped from the terrible fury of the dragon, bethinking himself of the brazen shield, and of the breaking up of the enchantment which was upon it, removed the carcass from out of the way before him, and approached valorously over the silver pavement of the castle to where the shield was upon the wall; which in sooth tarried not for his full coming, but fell down at his feet upon the silver floor, with a mighty great and terrible ringing sound."

No sooner had these syllables passed my lips, than—as if a shield of brass had indeed, at the moment, fallen heavily upon a floor of silver—I became aware of a distinct, hollow, a metallic, and clangorous, yet apparently muffled reverberation. Completely unnerved, I leaped to my feet; but the measured rocking movement of Usher was undisturbed. I rushed to the chair in which he sat. His eyes were bent fixedly before him, and throughout his whole countenance there reigned a stony rigidity. But, as I placed my hand upon his shoulder, there came a strong shudder over his whole person; a sickly smile quivered about his lips; and I saw that he spoke in a low, hurried, and gibbering murmur, as if unconscious of my presence. Bending closely over him, I at length drank in the hideous import of his words.

"Not hear it?—yes, I hear it, and *have* heard it. Long—long—long— many minutes, many hours, many days, have I heard it—yet I dared not —oh, pity me, miserable wretch that I am!—I dared not—I *dared* not speak! *We have put her living in the tomb!* Said I not that my senses were acute? I *now* tell you that I heard her first feeble movements in the hollow coffin. I heard them—many, many days ago—yet I dared not—*I dared not speak!* And now—to-night—Ethelred—ha! ha!—the breaking of the hermit's door, and the death-cry of the dragon, and the clangor of the shield!—say, rather, the rending of her coffin, and the grating of the iron hinges of her prison, and her struggles within the coppered archway of the vault! Oh whither shall I fly? Will she not be here anon? Is she not hurrying to upbraid me for my haste? Have I not heard her footsteps on the stair? Do I not distinguish that heavy and horrible beating of her heart? Madman!"—here he sprang furiously to his feet, and shrieked out his syllables, as if in the effort he were giving up his soul—*"Madman! I tell you that she now stands without the door!"*

As if in the superhuman energy of his utterance there had been found the potency of a spell—the huge antique panels to which the speaker pointed, threw slowly back, upon the instant, their ponderous and ebony jaws. It was the work of the rushing gust—but then without those doors there *did* stand the lofty and enshrouded figure of the lady Madeline of Usher. There was blood upon her white robes, and the evidence of some bitter struggle upon every portion of her emaciated frame. For a moment she remained trembling and reeling to and fro upon the threshold—then, with a low moaning cry, fell heavily inward upon the person of her brother, and in her violent and now final death-agonies, bore him to the floor a corpse, and a victim to the terrors he had anticipated.

From that chamber, and from that mansion, I fled aghast. The storm was still abroad in all its wrath as I found myself crossing the old causeway. Suddenly there shot along the path a wild light, and I turned to see whence a gleam so unusual could have issued; for the vast house and its shadows were alone behind me. The radiance was that of the full, setting, and blood-red moon, which now shone vividly through that once barely-discernible fissure, of which I have before spoken as extending from the roof of the building, in a zigzag direction, to the base. While I gazed, this fissure rapidly widened—there came a fierce breath of the whirlwind—the entire orb of the satellite burst at once upon my sight—my brain reeled as I saw the mighty walls rushing asunder—there was a long tumultuous shouting sound like the voice of a thousand waters—and the deep and dank tarn at my feet closed sullenly and silently over the fragments of the *"House of Usher."*

A STORY
Dylan Thomas

If you can call it a story. There's no real beginning or end and there's very little in the middle. It is all about a day's outing, by charabanc, to Porthcawl, which, of course, the charabanc never reached, and it happened when I was so high and much nicer.

I was staying at the time with my uncle and his wife. Although she was my aunt, I never thought of her as anything but the wife of my uncle, partly because he was so big and trumpeting and red-hairy and used to fill every inch of the hot little house like an old buffalo squeezed into an airing cupboard, and partly because she was so small and silk and quick and made no noise at all as she whisked about on padded paws, dusting the china dogs, feeding the buffalo, setting the mousetraps that never caught her; and once she sleaked out of the room, to squeak in a nook or nibble in the hayloft, you forgot she had ever been there.

But there he was, always, a steaming hulk of an uncle, his braces straining like hawsers, crammed behind the counter of the tiny shop at the front of the house, and breathing like a brass band; or guzzling and blustery in the kitchen over his gutsy supper, too big for everything except the great black boats of his boots. As he ate, the house grew smaller; he billowed out over the furniture, the loud check meadow of his waistcoat littered, as though after a picnic, with cigarette ends, peelings, cabbage stalks, birds' bones, gravy; and the forest fire of his hair crackled among the hooked hams from the ceiling. She was so small she could hit him only if she stood on a chair; and every Saturday night at half-past ten he would lift her up, under his arm, onto a chair in the kitchen so that she could hit him on the head with whatever was handy, which was always a china dog. On Sundays, and when pickled, he sang high tenor, and had won many cups.

The first I heard of the annual outing was when I was sitting one evening on a bag of rice behind the counter, under one of my uncle's stomachs, reading an advertisement for sheep-dip, which was all there was to read. The shop was full of my uncle, and when Mr. Benjamin Franklyn, Mr.

Porthcawl: a popular seaside resort in Southern Wales.

Weazley, Noah Bowen, and Will Sentry came in, I thought it would burst. It was like all being together in a drawer that smelled of cheese and turps, and twist tobacco and sweet biscuits and snuff and waistcoat. Mr. Benjamin Franklyn said that he had collected enough money for the charabanc and twenty cases of pale ale and a pound apiece over that he would distribute among the members of the outing when they first stopped for refreshment, and he was about sick and tired, he said, of being followed by Will Sentry.

"All day long, wherever I go," he said, "he's after me like a collie with one eye. I got a shadow of my own *and* a dog. I don't need no Tom, Dick or Harry pursuing me with his dirty muffler on."

Will Sentry blushed, and said, "It's only oily. I got a bicycle."

"A man has no privacy at all," Mr. Franklyn went on. "I tell you he sticks so close I'm afraid to go out the back in case I sit in his lap. It's a wonder to me," he said, "he don't follow me into bed at night."

"Wife won't let," Will Sentry said.

And that started Mr. Franklyn off again, and they tried to soothe him down by saying, "Don't you mind Will Sentry." "No harm in old Will." "He's only keeping an eye on the money, Benjie."

"Aren't I honest?" asked Mr. Franklyn in surprise. There was no answer for some time; then Noah Bowen said, "You know what the committee is. Ever since Bob the Fiddle they don't feel safe with a new treasurer."

"Do you think *I'm* going to drink the outing funds, like Bob the Fiddle did?" said Mr. Franklyn.

"You *might*," said my uncle, slowly.

"I resign," said Mr. Franklyn.

"Not with our money you won't," Will Sentry said.

"Who put the dynamite in the salmon pool?" said Mr. Weazley, but nobody took any notice of him. And, after a time, they all began to play cards in the thickening dusk of the hot, cheesy shop, and my uncle blew and bugled whenever he won, and Mr. Weazley grumbled like a dredger, and I fell to sleep on the gravy-scented mountain meadow of uncle's waistcoat.

On Sunday evening, after Bethesda, Mr. Franklyn walked into the kitchen where my uncle and I were eating sardines from the tin with spoons because it was Sunday and his wife would not let us play draughts. She was somewhere in the kitchen, too. Perhaps she was inside the grandmother clock, hanging from the weights and breathing. Then, a second later, the door opened again and Will Sentry edged into the room, twiddling his hard, round hat. He and Mr. Franklyn sat down on the settee, stiff and moth-balled and black in their chapel and funeral suits.

to go out the back: to use the outhouse.

"I brought the list," said Mr. Franklyn. "Every member fully paid. You ask Will Sentry."

My uncle put on his spectacles, wiped his whiskery mouth with a handkerchief big as a Union Jack, laid down his spoon of sardines, took Mr. Franklyn's list of names, removed the spectacles so that he could read, and then ticked the names off one by one.

"Enoch Davies. Aye. He's good with his fists. You never know. Little Gerwain. Very melodious bass. Mr. Cadwalladwr. That's right. He can tell opening time better than my watch. Mr. Weazley. Of course. He's been to Paris. Pity he suffers so much in the charabanc. Stopped us nine times last year between the Beehive and the Red Dragon. Noah Bowen. Ah, very peaceable. He's got a tongue like a turtledove. Never a argument with Noah Bowen. Jenkins Loughor. Keep him off economics. It cost us a plate-glass window. And ten pints for the Sergeant. Mr. Jervis. Very tidy."

"He tried to put a pig in the charra," Will Sentry said.

"Live and let live," said my uncle.

Will Sentry blushed.

"Sinbad the Sailor's Arms. Got to keep in with him. Old O. Jones."

"Why old O. Jones?" said Will Sentry.

"Old O. Jones always goes," said my uncle.

I looked down at the kitchen table. The tin of sardines was gone. By Gee, I said to myself, Uncle's wife is quick as a flash.

"Cuthbert Johnny Fortnight. Now there's a card," said my uncle.

"He whistles after women," Will Sentry said.

"So do you," said Mr. Benjamin Franklyn, "in your mind."

My uncle at last approved the whole list, pausing only to say, when he came across one name, "If we weren't a Christian community, we'd chuck that Bob the Fiddle in the sea."

"We can do that in Porthcawl," said Mr. Franklyn, and soon after that he went, Will Sentry no more than an inch behind him, their Sunday-bright boots squeaking on the kitchen cobbles.

And then, suddenly, there was my uncle's wife standing in front of the dresser, with a china dog in one hand. By Gee, I said to myself again, did you ever see such a woman, if that's what she is. The lamps were not lit yet in the kitchen and she stood in a wood of shadows, with the plates on the dresser behind her shining—like pink-and-white eyes.

"If you go on that outing on Saturday, Mr. Thomas," she said to my uncle in her small, silk voice, "I'm going home to my mother's."

Holy Mo, I thought, she's got a mother. Now that's one old bald mouse· of a hundred and five I won't be wanting to meet in a dark lane.

"It's me or the outing, Mr. Thomas."

I would have made my choice at once, but it was almost half a minute

boots: shoes.

before my uncle said, "Well, then, Sarah, it's the outing, my love." He lifted her up, under his arm, onto a chair in the kitchen, and she hit him on the head with the china dog. Then he lifted her down again, and then I said good night.

For the rest of the week my uncle's wife whisked quiet and quick round the house with her darting duster, my uncle blew and bugled and swole, and I kept myself busy all the time being up to no good. And then at breakfast time on Saturday morning, the morning of the outing, I found a note on the kitchen table. It said, "There's some eggs in the pantry. Take your boots off before you go to bed." My uncle's wife had gone, as quick as a flash.

When my uncle saw the note, he tugged out the flag of his handkerchief and blew such a hubbub of trumpets that the plates on the dresser shook. "It's the same every year," he said. And then he looked at me. "But this year it's different. *You'll* have to come on the outing, too, and what the members will say I dare not think."

The charabanc drew up outside, and when the members of the outing saw my uncle and me squeeze out of the shop together, both of us cat-licked and brushed in our Sunday best, they snarled like a zoo.

"Are you bringing a *boy*?" asked Mr. Benjamin Franklyn as we climbed into the charabanc. He looked at me with horror.

"Boys is nasty," said Mr. Weazley.

"He hasn't paid his contributions," Will Sentry said.

"No room for boys. Boys get sick in charabancs."

"So do you, Enoch Davies," said my uncle.

"Might as well bring *women*."

The way they said it, women were worse than boys.

"Better than bringing grandfathers."

"Grandfathers is nasty too," said Mr. Weazley.

"What can we do with him when we stop for refreshments?"

"I'm a grandfather," said Mr. Weazley.

"Twenty-six minutes to opening time," shouted an old man in a panama hat, not looking at a watch. They forgot me at once.

"Good old Mr. Cadwalladwr," they cried, and the charabanc started off down the village street.

A few cold women stood at their doorways, grimly watching us go. A very small boy waved goodbye, and his mother boxed his ears. It was a beautiful August morning.

We were out of the village, and over the bridge, and up the hill toward Steeplehat Wood when Mr. Franklyn, with his list of names in his hand, called out loud, "Where's old O. Jones?"

"Where's old O.?"

"We've left old O. behind."

"Can't go without old O."

And though Mr. Weazley hissed all the way, we turned and drove back to the village, where, outside the Prince of Wales, old O. Jones was waiting patiently and alone with a canvas bag.

"I didn't want to come at all," old O. Jones said as they hoisted him into the charabanc and clapped him on the back and pushed him on a seat and stuck a bottle in his hand, "but I always go." And over the bridge and up the hill and under the deep green wood and along the dusty road we wove, slow cows and ducks flying by, until "Stop the bus!" Mr. Weazley cried, "I left my teeth on the mantelpiece."

"Never you mind," they said, "you're not going to bite nobody," and they gave him a bottle with a straw.

"I might want to smile," he said.

"Not you," they said.

"What's the time, Mr. Cadwalladwr?"

"Twelve minutes to go," shouted back the old man in the panama, and they all began to curse him.

The charabanc pulled up outside the Mountain Sheep, a small, unhappy public house with a thatched roof like a wig with ringworm. From a flag-pole by the Gents fluttered the flag of Siam. I knew it was the flag of Siam because of cigarette cards. The landlord stood at the door to welcome us, simpering like a wolf. He was a long, lean, black-fanged man with a greased love-curl and pouncing eyes. "What a beautiful August day!" he said, and touched his love-curl with a claw. That was the way he must have welcomed the Mountain Sheep before he ate it, I said to myself. The members rushed out, bleating, and into the bar.

"You keep an eye on the charra," my uncle said, "see nobody steals it now."

"There's nobody to steal it," I said, "except some cows," but my uncle was gustily blowing his bugle in the bar. I looked at the cows opposite, and they looked at me. There was nothing else for us to do. Forty-five minutes passed, like a very slow cloud. The sun shone down on the lonely road, the lost, unwanted boy, and the lake-eyed cows. In the dark bar they were so happy they were breaking glasses. A Shoni-Onion Breton man, with a beret and a necklace of onions, bicycled down the road and stopped at the door.

"*Quelle un grand matin, monsieur,*" I said.

"There's French, boy bach!" he said.

I followed him down the passage, and peered into the bar. I could hardly recognize the members of the outing. They had all changed color. Beetroot, rhubarb and puce, they hollered and rollicked in that dark,

---

Quelle un grand...: schoolboy French for "What a lovely morning, sir."

damp hole like enormous ancient bad boys, and my uncle surged in the middle, all red whiskers and bellies. On the floor was broken glass and Mr. Weazley.

"Drinks all round," cried Bob the Fiddle, a small, absconding man with bright blue eyes and a plump smile.

"Who's been robbing the orphans?"

"Who sold his little babby to the gyppoes?"

"Trust old Bob, he'll let you down."

"You will have your little joke," said Bob the Fiddle, smiling like a razor, "but I forgive you, boys."

Out of the fug and babel I heard: "Where's old O. Jones?" "Where are you old O.?" "He's in the kitchen cooking his dinner." "He never forgets his dinner time." "Good old O. Jones." "Come out and fight." "No, not now, later." "No, now when I'm in a temper." "Look at Will Sentry, he's proper snobbled." "Look at his willful feet." "Look at Mr. Weazley lording it on the floor."

Mr. Weazley got up, hissing like a gander. "That boy pushed me down deliberate," he said, pointing to me at the door, and I slunk away down the passage and out to the mild, good cows.

Time clouded over, the cows wondered, I threw a stone at them and they wandered, wondering, away. Then out blew my Uncle, ballooning, and one by one the members lumbered after him in a grizzle. They had drunk the Mountain Sheep dry. Mr. Weazley had won a string of onions that the Shoni-Onion man had raffled in the bar.

"What's the good of onions if you left your teeth on the mantelpiece?" he said. And when I looked through the back window of the thundering charabanc, I saw the pub grow smaller in the distance. And the flag of Siam, from the flagpole by the Gents, fluttered now at half mast.

The Blue Bull, the Dragon, the Star of Wales, the Twll in the Wall, the Sour Grapes, the Shepherd's Arms, the Bells of Aberdovey: I had nothing to do in the whole wild August world but remember the names where the outing stopped and keep an eye on the charabanc. And whenever it passed a public house, Mr. Weazley would cough like a billy goat and cry, "Stop the bus, I'm dying of breath." And back we would all have to go.

Closing time meant nothing to the members of that outing. Behind locked doors, they hymned and rumpused all the beautiful afternoon. And, when a policeman entered the Druid's Tap by the back door, and found them all choral with beer, "Sssh!" said Noah Bowen, "the pub is shut."

"Where do you come from?" he said in his buttoned, blue voice.

They told him.

gyppoes: gypsies.
proper snobbled: pleasantly drunk.

"I got a auntie there," the policeman said. And very soon he was singing "Asleep in the Deep."

Off we drove again at last, the charabanc bouncing with tenors and flagons, and came to a river that rushed along among willows.

"Water!" they shouted.

"Porthcawl!" sang my uncle.

"Where's the donkeys?" said Mr. Weazley.

And out they lurched, to paddle and whoop in the cool, white, winding water. Mr. Franklyn, trying to polka on the slippery stones, fell in twice. "Nothing is simple," he said with dignity as he oozed up the bank.

"It's cold!" they cried.

"It's lovely!"

"It's smooth as a moth's nose!"

"It's *better* than Porthcawl!"

And dusk came down warm and gentle on thirty wild, wet, pickled, splashing men without a care in the world at the end of the world in the west of Wales. And, "Who goes there?" called Will Sentry to a wild duck flying.

They stopped at the Hermit's Nest for a rum to keep out the cold. "I played for Aberavon in 1898," said a stranger to Enoch Davies.

"Liar," said Enoch Davies.

"I can show you photos," said the stranger.

"Forged," said Enoch Davies.

"And I'll show you my cap at home."

"Stolen."

"I got friends to prove it," the stranger said in a fury.

"Bribed," said Enoch Davies.

On the way home, through the simmering moon-splashed dark, old O. Jones began to cook his supper on a primus stove in the middle of the charabanc. Mr. Weazley coughed himself blue in the smoke. "Stop the bus!" he cried, "I'm dying of breath." We all climbed down into the moonlight. There was not a public house in sight. So they carried out the remaining cases, and the primus stove, and old O. Jones himself, and took them into a field, and sat down in a circle in the field and drank and sang while old O. Jones cooked sausage and mash and the moon flew above us. And there I drifted to sleep against my uncle's mountainous waistcoat, and, as I slept, "Who goes there?" called out Will Sentry to the flying moon.

MY KINSMAN,
MAJOR MOLINEUX
Nathaniel Hawthorne

After the kings of Great Britain had assumed the right of appointing the colonial governors, the measures of the latter seldom met with the ready and general approbation which had been paid to those of their predecessors, under the original charters. The people looked with most jealous scrutiny to the exercise of power which did not emanate from themselves, and they usually rewarded their rulers with slender gratitude for the compliances by which, in softening their instructions from beyond the sea, they had incurred the reprehension of those who gave them. The annals of Massachusetts Bay will inform us, that of six governors in the space of about forty years from the surrender of the old charter, under James II, two were imprisoned by a popular insurrection; a third, as Hutchinson inclines to believe, was driven from the province by the whizzing of a musket-ball; a fourth, in the opinion of the same historian, was hastened to his grave by continual bickerings with the House of Representatives; and the remaining two, as well as their successors, till the Revolution, were favored with few and brief intervals of peaceful sway. The inferior members of the court party, in times of high political excitement, led scarcely a more desirable life. These remarks may serve as a preface to the following adventures, which chanced upon a summer night, not far from a hundred years ago. The reader, in order to avoid a long and dry detail of colonial affairs, is requested to dispense with an account of the train of circumstances that had caused much temporary inflammation of the popular mind.

It was near nine o'clock of a moonlight evening, when a boat crossed the ferry with a single passenger, who had obtained his conveyance at that unusual hour by the promise of an extra fare. While he stood on the landing-place, searching in either pocket for the means of fulfilling his agreement, the ferryman lifted a lantern, by the aid of which, and the newly risen moon, he took a very accurate survey of the stranger's figure. He was a youth of barely eighteen years, evidently country-bred, and now, as it should seem, upon his first visit to town. He was clad in a coarse gray coat, well worn, but in excellent repair; his under garments were durably constructed of leather, and fitted tight to a pair of serviceable and well-shaped limbs; his stockings of blue yarn were the incontrovertible work of a mother or a sister; and on his head was a three-cornered hat, which in its better days had perhaps sheltered the graver brow of the lad's father. Under his left arm was a heavy cudgel formed of an oak sapling, and retaining a part of the hardened root; and his equipment was completed by a wallet, not so abundantly stocked as to incommode the vigorous shoulders on which it hung. Brown, curly hair, well-shaped features, and bright, cheerful eyes were nature's gifts, and worth all that art could have done for his adornment.

The youth, one of whose names was Robin, finally drew from his pocket the half of a little province bill of five shillings, which, in the depreciation in that sort of currency, did but satisfy the ferryman's demand, with the surplus of a sexangular piece of parchment, valued at three-pence. He then walked forward into the town, with as light a step as if his day's journey had not already exceeded thirty miles, and with as eager an eye as if he were entering London city, instead of the little metropolis of a New England colony. Before Robin had proceeded far, however, it occurred to him that he knew not whither to direct his steps; so he paused, and looked up and down the narrow street, scrutinizing the small and mean wooden buildings that were scattered on either side.

"This low hovel cannot be my kinsman's dwelling," thought he, "nor yonder old house, where the moonlight enters at the broken casement; and truly I see none hereabouts that might be worthy of him. It would have been wise to inquire my way of the ferryman, and doubtless he would have gone with me, and earned a shilling from the Major for his pains. But the next man I meet will do as well."

He resumed his walk, and was glad to perceive that the street now became wider, and the houses more respectable in their appearance. He soon discerned a figure moving on moderately in advance, and hastened his steps to overtake it. As Robin drew nigh, he saw that the passenger was a man in years, with a full periwig of gray hair, a wide-skirted coat of dark cloth, and silk stockings rolled above his knees. He carried a long and polished cane, which he struck down perpendicularly before him at every step; and at regular intervals he uttered two successive hems, of a peculiarly solemn and sepulchral intonation. Having made these observations, Robin laid hold of the skirt of the old man's coat, just when the light from the open door and windows of a barber's shop fell upon both their figures.

"Good-evening to you, honored sir," said he, making a low bow, and still retaining his hold of the skirt. "I pray you tell me whereabouts is the dwelling of my kinsman, Major Molineux."

The youth's question was uttered very loudly; and one of the barbers, whose razor was descending on a well-soaped chin, and another who was dressing a Ramillies wig, left their occupations, and came to the door. The citizen, in the mean time, turned a long-favored countenance upon Robin, and answered him in a tone of excessive anger and annoyance. His two sepulchral hems, however, broke into the very centre of his rebuke, with most singular effect, like a thought of the cold grave obtruding among wrathful passions.

"Let go my garments, fellow! I tell you, I know not the man you speak of. What! I have authority, I have—hem, hem—authority; and if this be the respect you show for your betters, your feet shall be brought acquainted with the stocks by daylight, to-morrow morning!"

Robin released the old man's skirt, and hastened away, pursued by an ill-mannered roar of laughter from the barber's shop. He was at first considerably surprised by the result of his question, but, being a shrewd youth, soon thought himself able to account for the mystery.

"This is some country representative," was his conclusion, "who has never seen the inside of my kinsman's door, and lacks the breeding to answer a stranger civilly. The man is old, or verily—I might be tempted to turn back and smite him on the nose. Ah, Robin, Robin! even the barber's boys laugh at you for choosing such a guide! You will be wiser in time, friend Robin."

He now became entangled in a succession of crooked and narrow streets, which crossed each other, and meandered at no great distance from the water-side. The smell of tar was obvious to his nostrils, the masts of vessels pierced the moonlight above the tops of the buildings, and the numerous signs, which Robin paused to read, informed him that he was near the centre of business. But the streets were empty, the shops were closed, and lights were visible only in the second stories of a few dwelling-houses. At length, on the corner of a narrow lane, through which he was passing, he beheld the broad countenance of a British hero swinging before the door of an inn, whence proceeded the voices of many guests. The casement of one of the lower windows was thrown back, and a very thin curtain permitted Robin to distinguish a party at supper, round a well-furnished table. The fragrance of the good cheer steamed forth into the outer air, and the youth could not fail to recollect that the last remnant of his travelling stock of provisions had yielded to his morning appetite, and that noon had found and left him dinnerless.

"O, that a parchment three-penny might give me a right to sit down at yonder table!" said Robin with a sigh. "But the Major will make me welcome to the best of his victuals; so I will even step boldly in, and inquire my way to his dwelling."

He entered the tavern, and was guided by the murmur of voices and the fumes of tobacco to the public-room. It was a long and low apartment, with oaken walls, grown dark in the continual smoke, and a floor which was thickly sanded, but of no immaculate purity. A number of persons—the larger part of whom appeared to be mariners, or in some way connected with the sea—occupied the wooden benches, or leather-bottomed chairs, conversing on various matters, and occasionally lending their attention to some topic of general interest. Three or four little groups were draining as many bowls of punch, which the West India trade had long since made a familiar drink in the colony. Others, who had the appearance of men who lived by regular and laborious handicraft, preferred the insulated bliss of an unshared potation, and became more taciturn under its influence. Nearly all, in short, evinced a predilection for the Good Creature in some of its various shapes, for this is a vice to which, as Fast Day sermons of a hundred years ago will testify, we have a long hereditary claim. The only guests to whom Robin's sympathies inclined him were two or three sheepish countrymen, who were using the inn somewhat after the fashion of a Turkish caravansary; they had gotten themselves into the darkest corner of the room, and, heedless of the Nicotian atmosphere, were supping on the bread of their own ovens, and the bacon cured in their own chimney smoke. But though Robin felt a sort of brotherhood with these strangers, his eyes were attracted from them to a person who stood near the door, holding whispered conversation with a group of ill-dressed associates. His features were separately striking almost to grotesqueness, and the whole face left a deep impression on the memory. The forehead bulged out into a double prominence, with a vale between; the nose came boldly forth in an irregular curve, and its bridge was of more than a finger's breadth; the eyebrows were deep and shaggy, and the eyes glowed beneath them like fire in a cave.

While Robin deliberated of whom to inquire respecting his kinsman's dwelling, he was accosted by the innkeeper, a little man in a stained white apron, who had come to pay his professional welcome to the stranger. Being in the second generation from a French Protestant, he seemed to have inherited the courtesy of his parent nation; but no variety of circumstances was ever known to change his voice from the one shrill note in which he now addressed Robin.

"From the country, I presume, sir?" said he, with a profound bow. "Beg leave to congratulate you on your arrival, and trust you intend a long stay with us. Fine town here, sir, beautiful buildings, and much that may interest a stranger. May I hope for the honor of your commands in respect to supper?"

"The man sees a family likeness! the rogue has guessed that I am related to the Major!" thought Robin, who had hitherto experienced little superfluous civility.

All eyes were now turned on the country lad, standing at the door, in his worn three-cornered hat, gray coat, leather breeches, and blue yarn stockings, leaning on an oaken cudgel, and bearing a wallet on his back.

Robin replied to the courteous innkeeper, with such an assumption of confidence as befitted the Major's relative. "My honest friend," he said, "I shall make it a point to patronize your house on some occasion, when" —here he could not help lowering his voice—"when I may have more than a parchment three-pence in my pocket. My present business," continued he, speaking with lofty confidence, "is merely to inquire my way to the dwelling of my kinsman, Major Molineux."

There was a sudden and general movement in the room, which Robin interpreted as expressing the eagerness of each individual to become his guide. But the innkeeper turned his eyes to a written paper on the wall, which he read, or seemed to read, with occasional recurrences to the young man's figure.

"What have we here?" said he, breaking his speech into little dry fragments. " 'Left the house of the subscriber, bounden servant, Hezekiah Mudge,—had on, when he went away, gray coat, leather breeches, master's third-best hat. One pound currency reward to whosoever shall lodge him in any jail of the province.' Better trudge, boy; better trudge!"

Robin had begun to draw his hand towards the lighter end of the oak cudgel, but a strange hostility in every countenance induced him to relinquish his purpose of breaking the courteous innkeeper's head. As he turned to leave the room, he encountered a sneering glance from the bold-featured personage whom he had before noticed; and no sooner was he beyond the door, than he heard a general laugh, in which the innkeeper's voice might be distinguished, like the dropping of small stones into a kettle.

"Now, is it not strange," thought Robin, with his usual shrewdness,— "is it not strange that the confession of an empty pocket should outweigh the name of my kinsman, Major Molineux? O, if I had one of those grinning rascals in the woods, where I and my oak sapling grew up together, I would teach him that my arm is heavy, though my purse be light!"

On turning the corner of the narrow lane, Robin found himself in a spacious street, with an unbroken line of lofty houses on each side, and a steepled building at the upper end, whence the ringing of a bell announced the hour of nine. The light of the moon, and the lamps from the numerous shop-windows, discovered people promenading on the pavement, and amongst them Robin hoped to recognize his hitherto inscrutable relative. The result of his former inquiries made him unwilling to hazard another, in a scene of such publicity, and he determined to walk slowly and silently up the street, thrusting his face close to that of every elderly gentleman, in search of the Major's lineaments. In his progress, Robin encountered many gay and gallant figures. Embroidered garments of showy colors, enormous periwigs, gold-laced hats, and silver-hilted swords glided past him and dazzled his optics. Travelled youths, imitators of the European fine gentlemen of the period, trod jauntily along, half dancing to the fashionable tunes which they hummed, and making poor Robin ashamed of his quiet and natural gait. At length, after many pauses to examine the gorgeous display of goods in the shop-windows, and after suffering some rebukes for the impertinence of his scrutiny into people's faces, the Major's kinsman found himself near the steepled building, still unsuccessful in his search. As yet, however, he had seen only one side of the thronged street; so Robin crossed, and continued the same sort of inquisition down the opposite pavement, with stronger hopes than the philosopher seeking an honest man, but with no better fortune. He had arrived about midway towards the lower end, from which his course began, when he overheard the approach of some one who struck down a cane on the flagstones at every step, uttering, at regular intervals, two sepulchral hems.

"Mercy on us!" quoth Robin, recognizing the sound.

Turning a corner, which chanced to be close at his right hand, he hastened to pursue his researches in some other part of the town. His patience now was wearing low, and he seemed to feel more fatigue from his rambles since he crossed the ferry, than from his journey of several days on the other side. Hunger also pleaded loudly within him, and Robin began to balance the propriety of demanding, violently, and with lifted cudgel, the necessary guidance from the first solitary passenger whom he should meet. While a resolution to this effect was gaining strength, he entered a street of mean appearance, on either side of which a row of ill-built houses was straggling towards the harbor. The moonlight fell upon no passenger along the whole extent, but in the third domicile which Robin passed there was a half-opened door, and his keen glance detected a woman's garment within.

"My luck may be better here," said he to himself.

Accordingly, he approached the door, and beheld it shut closer as he did so; yet an open space remained, sufficing for the fair occupant to observe the stranger, without a corresponding display on her part. All that Robin could discern was a strip of scarlet petticoat, and the occasional sparkle of an eye, as if the moonbeams were trembling on some bright thing.

"Pretty mistress," for I may call her so with a good conscience, thought the shrewd youth, since I know nothing to the contrary,—"my sweet pretty mistress, will you be kind enough to tell me whereabouts I must seek the dwelling of my kinsman, Major Molineux?"

Robin's voice was plaintive and winning, and the female, seeing nothing to be shunned in the handsome country youth, thrust open the door, and came forth into the moonlight. She was a dainty little figure, with a white neck, round arms, and a slender waist, at the extremity of which her scarlet petticoat jutted out over a hoop, as if she were standing in a balloon. Moreover, her face was oval and pretty, her hair dark beneath the little cap, and her bright eyes possessed a sly freedom, which triumphed over those of Robin.

"Major Molineux dwells here," said this fair woman.

Now, her voice was the sweetest Robin had heard that night, the airy counterpart of a stream of melted silver; yet he could not help doubting whether that sweet voice spoke Gospel truth. He looked up and down the mean street, and then surveyed the house before which they stood. It was a small, dark edifice of two stories, the second of which projected over the lower floor, and the front apartment had the aspect of a shop for petty commodities.

"Now, truly, I am in luck," replied Robin cunningly, "and so indeed is my kinsman, the Major, in having so pretty a housekeeper. But I prithee trouble him to step to the door; I will deliver him a message from his friends in the country, and then go back to my lodgings at the inn."

"Nay, the Major has been abed this hour or more," said the lady of the scarlet petticoat; "and it would be to little purpose to disturb him to-night, seeing his evening draught was of the strongest. But he is a kind-hearted man, and it would be as much as my life's worth to let a kinsman of his turn away from the door. You are the good old gentleman's very picture, and I could swear that was his rainy-weather hat. Also he has garments very much resembling those leather small-clothes. But come in, I pray, for I bid you hearty welcome in his name."

So saying, the fair and hospitable dame took our hero by the hand; and the touch was light, and the force was gentleness, and though Robin read in her eyes what he did not hear in her words, yet the slender-waisted woman in the scarlet petticoat proved stronger than the athletic country youth. She had drawn his half-willing footsteps nearly to the threshold, when the opening of a door in the neighborhood startled the Major's housekeeper, and, leaving the Major's kinsman, she vanished speedily into her own domicile. A heavy yawn preceded the appearance of a man, who, like the Moonshine of Pyramus and Thisbe, carried a lantern needlessly aiding his sister luminary in the heavens. As he walked sleepily up the street, he turned his broad, dull face on Robin, and displayed a long staff, spiked at the end.

"Home, vagabond, home!" said the watchman, in accents that seemed to fall asleep as soon as they were uttered. "Home, or we'll set you in the stocks by peep of day!"

"This is the second hint of the kind," thought Robin. "I wish they would end my difficulties, by setting me there to-night."

Nevertheless, the youth felt an instinctive antipathy towards the guardian of midnight order, which at first prevented him from asking his usual question. But just when the man was about to vanish behind the corner, Robin resolved not to lose the opportunity, and shouted lustily after him,—

"I say, friend! will you guide me to the house of my kinsman, Major Molineux?"

The watchman made no reply, but turned the corner and was gone; yet Robin seemed to hear the sound of drowsy laughter stealing along the solitary street. At that moment, also, a pleasant titter saluted him from the open window above his head; he looked up, and caught the sparkle of a saucy eye; a round arm beckoned to him, and next he heard light footsteps descending the staircase within. But Robin, being of the household of a New England clergyman, was a good youth, as well as a shrewd one; so he resisted temptation, and fled away.

He now roamed desperately, and at random, through the town, almost ready to believe that a spell was on him, like that by which a wizard of his country had once kept three pursuers wandering, a whole winter night, within twenty paces of the cottage which they sought. The streets lay before him, strange and desolate, and the lights were extinguished in almost every house. Twice, however, little parties of men, among whom Robin distinguished individuals in outlandish attire, came hurrying along; but, though on both occasions they paused to address him, such intercourse did not at all enlighten his perplexity. They did but utter a few words in some language of which Robin knew nothing, and perceiving his inability to answer, bestowed a curse upon him in plain English and hastened away. Finally, the lad determined to knock at the door of every mansion that might appear worthy to be occupied by his kinsman, trusting that perseverance would overcome the fatality that had hitherto thwarted him. Firm in this resolve, he was passing beneath the walls of a church, which formed the corner of two streets, when, as he turned into the shade of its steeple, he encountered a bulky stranger, muffled in a cloak. The man was proceeding with the speed of earnest business, but Robin planted himself full before him, holding the oak cudgel with both hands across his body as a bar to further passage.

"Halt, honest man, and answer me a question," said he very resolutely. "Tell me, this instant, whereabouts is the dwelling of my kinsman, Major Molineux!"

"Keep your tongue between your teeth, fool, and let me pass!" said a deep, gruff voice, which Robin partly remembered. "Let me pass, I say, or I'll strike you to the earth!"

"No, no, neighbor!" cried Robin, flourishing his cudgel, and then thrusting its larger end close to the man's muffled face. "No, no, I'm not the fool you take me for, nor do you pass till I have an answer to my question. Whereabouts is the dwelling of my kinsman, Major Molineux?"

The stranger, instead of attempting to force his passage, stepped back into the moonlight, unmuffled his face, and stared full into that of Robin.

"Watch here an hour, and Major Molineux will pass by," said he.

Robin gazed with dismay and astonishment on the unprecedented physiognomy of the speaker. The forehead with its double prominence, the broad hooked nose, the shaggy eyebrows, and fiery eyes were those which he had noticed at the inn, but the man's complexion had undergone a singular, or, more properly, a twofold change. One side of the face blazed an intense red, while the other was black as midnight, the division line being in the broad bridge of the nose; and a mouth which seemed to extend from ear to ear was black or red, in contrast to the color of the cheek. The effect was as if two individual devils, a fiend of fire and a fiend of darkness, had united themselves to form this infernal visage. The stranger grinned in Robin's face, muffled his party-colored features, and was out of sight in a moment.

"Strange things we travellers see!" ejaculated Robin.

He seated himself, however, upon the steps of the church door, resolving to wait the appointed time for his kinsman. A few moments were consumed in philosophical speculations upon the species of man who had just left him; but having settled this point shrewdly, rationally, and satisfactorily, he was compelled to look elsewhere for his amusement. And first he threw his eyes along the street. It was of more respectable appearance than most of those into which he had wandered; and the moon, creating, like the imaginative power, a beautiful strangeness in familiar objects, gave something of romance to a scene that might not have possessed it in the light of day. The irregular and often quaint architecture of the houses, some of whose roofs were broken into numerous little peaks, while others ascended, steep and narrow, into a single point, and others again were square; the pure snow-white of some of their complexions, the aged darkness of others, and the thousand sparklings, reflected from bright substances in the walls of many; these matters engaged Robin's attention for a while, and then began to grow wearisome. Next he endeavored to define the forms of distant objects, starting away, with almost ghostly indistinctness, just as his eye appeared to grasp them; and finally he took a minute survey of an edifice which stood on the opposite side of the street, directly in front of the church door, where he was stationed. It was a large, square mansion, distinguished from its neighbors by a balcony, which rested on tall pillars, and by an elaborate Gothic window, communicating therewith.

"Perhaps this is the very house I have been seeking," thought Robin.

Then he strove to speed away the time, by listening to a murmur which swept continually along the street, yet was scarcely audible, except to an unaccustomed ear like his; it was a low, dull, dreamy sound, compounded of many noises, each of which was at too great a distance to be separately heard. Robin marvelled at this snore of a sleeping town, and marvelled more whenever its continuity was broken by now and then a distant shout, apparently loud where it originated. But altogether it was a sleep-inspiring sound, and, to shake off its drowsy influence, Robin arose, and climbed a window frame, that he might view the interior of the church. There the moonbeams came trembling in, and fell down upon the deserted pews, and extended along the quiet aisles. A fainter yet more awful radiance was hovering around the pulpit, and one solitary ray had dared to rest upon the open page of the great Bible. Had nature, in that deep hour, become a worshipper in the house which man had builded? Or was that heavenly light the visible sanctity of the place,—visible because no earthly and impure feet were within the walls? The scene made Robin's heart shiver with a sensation of loneliness stronger than he had ever felt in the remotest depths of his native woods; so he turned away and sat down again before the door. There were graves around the church, and now an uneasy thought obtruded into Robin's breast. What if the object of his search, which had been so often and so strangely thwarted, were all the time mouldering in his shroud? What if his kinsman should glide through yonder gate, and nod and smile to him in dimly passing by?

"O that any breathing thing were here with me!" said Robin.

Recalling his thoughts from this uncomfortable track, he sent them over forest, hill, and stream, and attempted to imagine how that evening of ambiguity and weariness had been spent by his father's household. He pictured them assembled at the door, beneath the tree, the great old tree, which had been spared for its huge twisted trunk and venerable shade, when a thousand leafy brethren fell. There, at the going down of the summer sun, it was his father's custom to perform domestic worship, that the neighbors might come and join with him like brothers of the family, and that the wayfaring man might pause to drink at that fountain, and keep his heart pure by freshening the memory of home. Robin distinguished the seat of every individual of the little audience; he saw the good man in the midst, holding the Scriptures in the golden light that fell from the western clouds; he beheld him close the book and all rise up to pray. He heard the old thanksgivings for daily mercies, the old supplications for their continuance, to which he had so often listened in weariness, but which were now among his dear remembrances. He perceived the slight inequality of his father's voice when he came to speak of the absent one; he noted how his mother turned her face to the broad and knotted trunk; how his elder brother scorned, because the beard was rough upon his upper lip, to permit his features to be moved; how the younger sister drew down a low hanging branch before her eyes; and how the little one of all, whose sports had hitherto broken the decorum of the scene, understood the prayer for her playmate, and burst into clamorous grief. Then he saw them go in at the door; and when Robin would have entered also, the latch tinkled into its place, and he was excluded from his home.

"Am I here, or there?" cried Robin, starting; for all at once, when his thoughts had become visible and audible in a dream, the long, wide, solitary street shone out before him.

He aroused himself, and endeavored to fix his attention steadily upon the large edifice which he had surveyed before. But still his mind kept vibrating between fancy and reality; by turns, the pillars of the balcony lengthened into the tall, bare stems of pines, dwindled down to human figures, settled again into their true shape and size, and then commenced a new succession of changes. For a single moment, when he deemed himself awake, he could have sworn that a visage—one which he seemed to remember, yet could not absolutely name as his kinsman's—was looking towards him from the Gothic window. A deeper sleep wrestled with and nearly overcame him, but fled at the sound of footsteps along the opposite pavement. Robin rubbed his eyes, discerned a man passing at the foot of the balcony, and addressed him in a loud, peevish, and lamentable cry.

"Hallo, friend! must I wait here all night for my kinsman, Major Molineux?"

The sleeping echoes awoke, and answered the voice; and the passenger, barely able to discern a figure sitting in the oblique shade of the steeple, traversed the street to obtain a nearer view. He was himself a gentleman in his prime, of open, intelligent, cheerful, and altogether prepossessing countenance. Perceiving a country youth, apparently homeless and without friends, he accosted him in a tone of real kindness, which had become strange to Robin's ears.

"Well, my good lad, why are you sitting here?" inquired he. "Can I be of service to you in any way?"

"I am afraid not, sir," replied Robin despondingly; "yet I shall take it kindly, if you'll answer me a single question. I've been searching, half the night, for one Major Molineux; now, sir, is there really such a person in these parts, or am I dreaming?"

"Major Molineux! The name is not altogether strange to me," said the gentleman, smiling. "Have you any objection to telling me the nature of your business with him?"

Then Robin briefly related that his father was a clergyman, settled on a small salary, at a long distance back in the country, and that he and Major Molineux were brothers' children. The Major, having inherited riches, and acquired civil and military rank, had visited his cousin, in great pomp, a year or two before; had manifested much interest in Robin and an elder brother, and, being childless himself, had thrown out hints respecting the future establishment of one of them in life. The elder brother was destined to succeed to the farm which his father cultivated in the interval of sacred duties; it was therefore determined that Robin should profit by his kinsman's generous intentions, especially as he seemed to be rather the favorite, and was thought to possess other necessary endowments.

"For I have the name of being a shrewd youth," observed Robin, in this part of his story.

"I doubt not you deserve it," replied his new friend good-naturedly; "but pray proceed."

"Well, sir, being nearly eighteen years old, and well grown, as you see," continued Robin, drawing himself up to his full height, "I thought it high time to begin the world. So my mother and sister put me in handsome trim, and my father gave me half the remnant of his last year's salary, and five days ago I started for this place, to pay the Major a visit. But, would you believe it, sir! I crossed the ferry a little after dark, and have yet found nobody that would show me the way to his dwelling; only, an hour or two since, I was told to wait here, and Major Molineux would pass by."

"Can you describe the man who told you this?" inquired the gentleman.

"O, he was a very ill-favored fellow, sir," replied Robin, "with two great bumps on his forehead, a hook nose, fiery eyes; and, what struck me as the strangest, his face was of two different colors. Do you happen to know such a man, sir?"

"Not intimately," answered the stranger, "but I chanced to meet him a little time previous to your stopping me. I believe you may trust his word, and that the Major will very shortly pass through this street. In the mean time, as I have a singular curiosity to witness your meeting, I will sit down here upon the steps and bear you company."

He seated himself accordingly, and soon engaged his companion in animated discourse. It was but of brief continuance, however, for a noise of shouting, which had long been remotely audible, drew so much nearer that Robin inquired its cause.

"What may be the meaning of this uproar?" asked he. "Truly, if your town be always as noisy, I shall find little sleep while I am an inhabitant."

"Why, indeed, friend Robin, there do appear to be three or four riotous fellows abroad to-night," replied the gentleman. "You must not expect all the stillness of your native woods here in our streets. But the watch will shortly be at the heels of these lads and"—

"Ay, and set them in the stocks by peep of day," interrupted Robin, recollecting his own encounter with the drowsy lantern-bearer. "But, dear sir, if I may trust my ears, an army of watchmen would never make head against such a multitude of rioters. There were at least a thousand voices went up to make that one shout."

"May not a man have several voices, Robin, as well as two complexions?" said his friend.

"Perhaps a man may; but Heaven forbid that a woman should!" responded the shrewd youth, thinking of the seductive tones of the Major's housekeeper.

The sounds of a trumpet in some neighboring street now became so evident and continual, that Robin's curiosity was strongly excited. In addition to the shouts, he heard frequent bursts from many instruments of discord, and a wild and confused laughter filled up the intervals. Robin rose from the steps, and looked wistfully towards a point whither people seemed to be hastening.

"Surely some prodigious merry-making is going on," exclaimed he. "I have laughed very little since I left home, sir, and should be sorry to lose an opportunity. Shall we step round the corner by that darkish house, and take our share of the fun?"

"Sit down again, sit down, good Robin," replied the gentleman, laying his hand on the skirt of the gray coat. "You forget that we must wait here for your kinsman; and there is reason to believe that he will pass by, in the course of a very few moments."

The near approach of the uproar had now disturbed the neighborhood; windows flew open on all sides; and many heads, in the attire of the pillow, and confused by sleep suddenly broken, were protruded to the gaze of whoever had leisure to observe them. Eager voices hailed each other from house to house, all demanding the explanation, which not a soul could give. Half-dressed men hurried towards the unknown commotion, stumbling as they went over the stone steps that thrust themselves into the narrow footwalk. The shouts, the laughter, and the tuneless bray, the antipodes of music, came onwards with increasing din, till scattered individuals, and then denser bodies, began to appear round a corner at the distance of a hundred yards.

"Will you recognize your kinsman, if he passes in this crowd?" inquired the gentleman.

"Indeed, I can't warrant it, sir; but I'll take my stand here, and keep a bright lookout," answered Robin, descending to the outer edge of the pavement.

A mighty stream of people now emptied into the street, and came rolling slowly towards the church. A single horseman wheeled the corner in the midst of them, and close behind him came a band of fearful wind-instruments, sending forth a fresher discord now that no intervening buildings kept it from the ear. Then a redder light disturbed the moonbeams, and a dense multitude of torches shone along the street, concealing, by their glare, whatever object they illuminated. The single horseman, clad in a military dress, and bearing a drawn sword, rode onward as the leader, and, by his fierce and variegated countenance, appeared like war personified; the red of one cheek was an emblem of fire and sword; the blackness of the other betokened the mourning that attends them. In his train were wild figures in the Indian dress, and many fantastic shapes without a model, giving the whole march a visionary air, as if a dream had broken forth from some feverish brain, and were sweeping visibly through the midnight streets. A mass of people, inactive, except as applauding spectators, hemmed the procession in; and several women ran along the sidewalk, piercing the confusion of heavier sounds with their shrill voices of mirth or terror.

"The double-faced fellow has his eye upon me," muttered Robin, with an indefinite but an uncomfortable idea that he was himself to bear a part in the pageantry.

The leader turned himself in the saddle, and fixed his glance full upon the country youth, as the steed went slowly by. When Robin had freed his eyes from those fiery ones, the musicians were passing before him, and the torches were close at hand; but the unsteady brightness of the latter formed a veil which he could not penetrate. The rattling of wheels over the stones sometimes found its way to his ear, and confused traces of a human form appeared at intervals, and then melted into the vivid light. A moment more, and the leader thundered a command to halt: the trumpets vomited a horrid breath, and then held their peace; the shouts and laughter of the people died away, and there remained only a universal hum, allied to silence. Right before Robin's eyes was an uncovered cart. There the torches blazed the brightest, there the moon shone out like day, and there, in tar-and-feathery dignity, sat his kinsman, Major Molineux!

He was an elderly man, of large and majestic person, and strong, square features, betokening a steady soul; but steady as it was, his enemies had found means to shake it. His face was pale as death, and far more ghastly; the broad forehead was contracted in his agony, so that his eyebrows formed one grizzled line; his eyes were red and wild, and the foam hung white upon his quivering lip. His whole frame was agitated by a quick and continual tremor, which his pride strove to quell, even in those circumstances of overwhelming humiliation. But perhaps the bitterest pang of all was when his eyes met those of Robin; for he evidently knew him on the instant, as the youth stood witnessing the foul disgrace of a head grown gray in honor. They stared at each other in silence, and Robin's knees shook, and his hair bristled, with a mixture of pity and terror. Soon, however, a bewildering excitement began to seize upon his mind; the preceding adventures of the night, the unexpected appearance of the crowd, the torches, the confused din and the hush that followed, the spectre of his kinsman reviled by that great multitude,—all this, and, more than all, a perception of tremendous ridicule in the whole scene, affected him with a sort of mental inebriety. At that moment a voice of sluggish merriment saluted Robin's ears; he turned instinctively, and just behind the corner of the church stood the lantern-bearer, rubbing his eyes, and drowsily enjoying the lad's amazement. Then he heard a peal of laughter like the ringing of silvery bells; a woman twitched his arm, a saucy eye met his, and he saw the lady of the scarlet petticoat. A sharp, dry cachinnation appealed to his memory, and, standing on tiptoe in the crowd, with his white apron over his head, he beheld the courteous little innkeeper. And lastly, there sailed over the heads of the multitude a great, broad laugh, broken in the midst by two sepulchral hems; thus, "Haw, haw, haw,—hem, hem,—haw, haw haw, haw!"

The sound proceeded from the balcony of the opposite edifice, and thither Robin turned his eyes. In front of the Gothic window stood the old citizen, wrapped in a wide gown, his gray periwig exchanged for a nightcap, which was thrust back from his forehead, and his silk stockings hanging about his legs. He supported himself on his polished cane in a fit of convulsive merriment, which manifested itself on his solemn old features like a funny inscription on a tombstone. Then Robin seemed to hear the voices of the barbers, of the guests of the inn, and of all who had made sport of him that night. The contagion was spreading among the multitude, when all at once it seized upon Robin, and he sent forth a shout of laughter that echoed through the street,—every man shook his sides, every man emptied his lungs, but Robin's shout was the loudest there. The cloud-spirits peeped from their silvery islands, as the congregated mirth went roaring up the sky! The Man in the Moon heard the far bellow. "Oho," quoth he, "the old earth is frolicsome to-night!"

When there was a momentary calm in that tempestuous sea of sound, the leader gave the sign, the procession resumed its march. On they went, like fiends that throng in mockery around some dead potentate, mighty no more, but majestic still in his agony. On they went, in counterfeited pomp, in senseless uproar, in frenzied merriment, trampling all on an old man's heart. On swept the tumult, and left a silent street behind.

.   .   .   .

"Well, Robin, are you dreaming?" inquired the gentleman, laying his hand on the youth's shoulder.

Robin started, and withdrew his arm from the stone post to which he had instinctively clung, as the living stream rolled by him. His cheek was somewhat pale, and his eye not quite as lively as in the earlier part of the evening.

"Will you be kind enough to show me the way to the ferry?" said he, after a moment's pause.

"You have, then, adopted a new subject of inquiry?" observed his companion with a smile.

"Why, yes, sir," replied Robin rather dryly. "Thanks to you, and to my other friends, I have at last met my kinsman, and he will scarce desire to see my face again. I begin to grow weary of a town life, sir. Will you show me the way to the ferry?"

"No, my good friend Robin,—not to-night, at least," said the gentleman. "Some few days hence, if you wish it, I will speed you on your journey. Or, if you prefer to remain with us, perhaps, as you are a shrewd youth, you may rise in the world without the help of your kinsman, Major Molineux."

THERE WILL COME SOFT RAINS
Ray Bradbury

In the living room the voice-clock sang, *Tick-tock, seven o'clock, time to get up, time to get up, seven o'clock!* as if it were afraid that nobody would. The morning house lay empty. The clock ticked on, repeating and repeating its sounds into the emptiness. *Seven-nine, breakfast time, seven-nine!*

In the kitchen the breakfast stove gave a hissing sigh and ejected from its warm interior eight pieces of perfectly browned toast, eight eggs sunnyside up, sixteen slices of bacon, two coffees, and two cool glasses of milk.

"Today is August 4, 2026," said a second voice from the kitchen ceiling, "in the city of Allendale, California." It repeated the date three times for memory's sake. "Today is Mr. Featherstone's birthday. Today is the anniversary of Tilita's marriage. Insurance is payable, as are the water, gas, and light bills."

Somewhere in the walls, relays clicked, memory tapes glided under electric eyes.

Eight-one, tick-tock, eight-one o'clock, off to school, off to work, run, run, eight-one! But no doors slammed, no carpets took the soft tread of rubber heels. It was raining outside. The weather box on the front door sang quietly: "Rain, rain, go away; rubbers, raincoats for today..." And the rain tapped on the empty house, echoing.

Outside, the garage chimed and lifted its door to reveal the waiting car. After a long wait the door swung down again.

At eight-thirty the eggs were shriveled and the toast was like stone. An aluminum wedge scraped them into the sink, where hot water whirled them down a metal throat which digested and flushed them away to the distant sea. The dirty dishes were dropped into a hot washer and emerged twinkling dry.

Nine-fifteen, sang the clock, *time to clean.*

Out of warrens in the wall, tiny robot mice darted. The rooms were acrawl with the small cleaning animals, all rubber and metal. They thudded

175

against chairs, whirling their mustached runners, kneading the rug nap, sucking gently at hidden dust. Then, like mysterious invaders, they popped into their burrows. Their pink electric eyes faded. The house was clean.

Ten o'clock. The sun came out from behind the rain. The house stood alone in a city of rubble and ashes. This was the one house left standing. At night the ruined city gave off a radioactive glow which could be seen for miles.

Ten-fifteen. The garden sprinklers whirled up in golden founts, filling the soft morning air with scatterings of brightness. The water pelted windowpanes, running down the charred west side where the house had been burned evenly free of its white paint. The entire west face of the house was black, save for five places. Here the silhouette in paint of a man mowing a lawn. Here, as in a photograph, a woman bent to pick flowers. Still farther over, their images burned on wood in one titanic instant, a small boy, hands flung into the air; higher up, the image of a thrown ball, and opposite him a girl, hands raised to catch a ball which never came down.

The five spots of paint—the man, the woman, the children, the ball—remained. The rest was a thin charcoaled layer.

The gentle sprinkler rain filled the garden with falling light.

Until this day, how well the house had kept its peace. How carefully it had inquired, "Who goes there? What's the password?" and, getting no answer from lonely foxes and whining cats, it had shut up its windows and drawn shades in an old-maidenly preoccupation with self-protection which bordered on a mechanical paranoia.

It quivered at each sound, the house did. If a sparrow brushed a window, the shade snapped up. The bird, startled, flew off! No, not even a bird must touch the house!

The house was an altar with ten thousand attendants, big, small, servicing, attending, in choirs. But the gods had gone away, and the ritual of the religion continued senselessly, uselessly.

Twelve noon.

A dog whined, shivering, on the front porch.

The front door recognized the dog voice and opened. The dog, once huge and fleshy, but now gone to bone and covered with sores, moved in and through the house, tracking mud. Behind it whirred angry mice, angry at having to pick up mud, angry at inconvenience.

For not a leaf fragment blew under the door but what the wall panels flipped open and the copper scrap rats flashed swiftly out. The offending dust, hair, or paper, seized in miniature steel jaws, was raced back to the burrows. There, down tubes which fed into the cellar, it was dropped into the sighing vent of an incinerator which sat like evil Baal in a dark corner.

The dog ran upstairs, hysterically yelping to each door, at last realizing, as the house realized, that only silence was here.

It sniffed the air and scratched the kitchen door. Behind the door, the stove was making pancakes which filled the house with a rich baked odor and the scent of maple syrup.

The dog frothed at the mouth, lying at the door, sniffing, its eyes turned to fire. It ran wildly in circles, biting at its tail, spun in a frenzy, and died. It lay in the parlor for an hour.

Two o'clock, sang a voice.

Delicately sensing decay at last, the regiments of mice hummed out as softly as blown gray leaves in an electrical wind.

Two-fifteen.

The dog was gone.

In the cellar, the incinerator glowed suddenly and a whirl of sparks leaped up the chimney.

Two thirty-five.

Bridge tables sprouted from patio walls. Playing cards fluttered onto pads in a shower of pips. Martinis manifested on an oaken bench with egg-salad sandwiches. Music played.

But the tables were silent and the cards untouched.

At four o'clock the tables folded like great butterflies back through the paneled walls.

Four-thirty.

The nursery walls glowed.

Animals took shape: yellow giraffes, blue lions, pink antelopes, lilac panthers cavorting in crystal substance. The walls were glass. They looked out upon color and fantasy. Hidden films clocked through well-oiled sprockets, and the walls lived. The nursery floor was woven to resemble a crisp, cereal meadow. Over this ran aluminum roaches and iron crickets, and in the hot still air butterflies of delicate red tissue wavered among the sharp aroma of animal spoors! There was the sound like a great matted yellow hive of bees within a dark bellows, the lazy bumble of a purring lion. And there was the patter of okapi feet and the murmur of a fresh jungle rain, like other hoofs, falling upon the summer-starched grass. Now the walls dissolved into distances of parched weed, mile on mile, and warm endless sky. The animals drew away into thorn brakes and water holes.

It was the children's hour.

Five o'clock. The bath filled with clear hot water.

Six, seven, eight o'clock. The dinner dishes manipulated like magic tricks, and in the study a *click.* In the metal stand opposite the hearth where a fire now blazed up warmly, a cigar popped out, half an inch of soft gray ash on it, smoking, waiting.

Nine o'clock. The beds warmed their hidden circuits, for nights were cool here.

Nine-five. A voice spoke from the study ceiling:

"Mrs. McClellan, which poem would you like this evening?"

The house was silent.

The voice said at last, "Since you express no preference, I shall select a poem at random." Quiet music rose to back the voice. "Sara Teasdale. As I recall, your favorite. . . .

"There will come soft rains and the smell of the ground,
And swallows circling with their shimmering sound;

And frogs in the pools singing at night,
And wild plum trees in tremulous white;

Robins will wear their feathery fire,
Whistling their whims on a low fence-wire;

And not one will know of the war, not one
Will care at last when it is done.

Not one would mind, neither bird nor tree,
If mankind perished utterly;

And Spring herself, when she woke at dawn
Would scarcely know that we were gone."

The fire burned on the stone hearth and the cigar fell away into a mound of quiet ash on its tray. The empty chairs faced each other between the silent walls, and the music played.

At ten o'clock the house began to die.

The wind blew. A falling tree bough crashed through the kitchen window. Cleaning solvent, bottled, shattered over the stove. The room was ablaze in an instant!

"Fire!" screamed a voice. The house lights flashed, water pumps shot water from the ceilings. But the solvent spread on the linoleum, licking, eating, under the kitchen door, while the voices took it up in chorus: "Fire, fire, fire!"

The house tried to save itself. Doors sprang tightly shut, but the windows were broken by the heat and the wind blew and sucked upon the fire.

The house gave ground as the fire in ten billion angry sparks moved with flaming ease from room to room and then up the stairs. While scurrying water rats squeaked from the walls, pistoled their water, and ran for more. And the wall sprays let down showers of mechanical rain.

But too late. Somewhere, sighing, a pump shrugged to a stop. The quenching rain ceased. The reserve water supply which had filled baths and washed dishes for many quiet days was gone.

The fire crackled up the stairs. It fed upon Picassos and Matisses in the upper halls, like delicacies, baking off the oily flesh, tenderly crisping the canvases into black shavings.

Now the fire lay in beds, stood in windows, changed the colors of drapes! And then, reinforcements.

From attic trapdoors, blind robot faces peered down with faucet mouths gushing green chemical.

The fire backed off, as even an elephant must at the sight of a dead snake. Now there were twenty snakes whipping over the floor, killing the fire with a clear cold venom of green froth.

But the fire was clever. It had sent flame outside the house, up through the attic to the pumps there. An explosion! The attic brain which directed the pumps was shattered into bronze shrapnel on the beams.

The fire rushed back into every closet and felt of the clothes hung there.

The house shuddered, oak bone on bone, its bared skeleton cringing from the heat, its wire, its nerves revealed as if a surgeon had torn the skin off to let the red veins and capillaries quiver in the scalded air. Help, help! Fire! Run, run! Heat snapped mirrors like the first brittle winter ice. And the voices wailed Fire, fire, run, run, like a tragic nursery rhyme, a dozen voices, high, low, like children dying in a forest alone, alone. And the voices fading as the wires popped their sheathings like hot chestnuts. One two, three, four, five voices died.

In the nursery the jungle burned. Blue lions roared, purple giraffes bounded off. The panthers ran in circles, changing color, and ten million animals, running before the fire, vanished off toward a distant steaming river. . . .

Ten more voices died. In the last instant under the fire avalanche, other choruses, oblivious, could be heard announcing the time, playing music, cutting the lawn by remote-control mower, or setting an umbrella frantically out and in the slamming and opening front door, a thousand things happening, like a clock shop when each clock strikes the hour insanely before or after the other, a scene of maniac confusion, yet unity; singing, screaming, a few last cleaning mice darting bravely out to carry the horrid ashes away! And one voice, with sublime disregard for the situation, read poetry aloud in the fiery study, until all the film spools burned, until all the wires withered and the circuits cracked.

The fire burst the house and let it slam flat down, puffing out skirts of spark and smoke.

In the kitchen, an instant before the rain of fire and timber, the stove could be seen making breakfasts at a psychopathic rate, ten dozen eggs, six loaves of toast, twenty dozen bacon strips, which, eaten by fire, started the stove working again, hysterically hissing!

The crash. The attic smashing into kitchen and parlor. The parlor into cellar, cellar into sub-cellar. Deep freeze, armchair, film tapes, circuits, beds, and all like skeletons thrown in a cluttered mound deep under.

Smoke and silence. A great quantity of smoke.

Dawn showed faintly in the east. Among the ruins, one wall stood alone. Within the wall, a last voice said, over and over again and again, even as the sun rose to shine upon the heaped rubble and steam:

"Today is August 5, 2026, today is August 5, 2026, today is. . ."

WASH
William Faulkner

Sutpen stood above the pallet bed on which the mother and child lay. Between the shrunken planking of the wall the early sunlight fell in long pencil strokes, breaking upon his straddled legs and upon the riding whip in his hand, and lay across the still shape of the mother, who lay looking up at him from still, inscrutable, sullen eyes, the child at her side wrapped in a piece of dingy though clean cloth. Behind them an old Negro woman squatted beside the rough hearth where a meager fire smoldered.

"Well, Milly," Sutpen said, "too bad you're not a mare. Then I could give you a decent stall in the stable."

Still the girl on the pallet did not move. She merely continued to look up at him without expression, with a young, sullen, inscrutable face still pale from recent travail. Sutpen moved, bringing into the splintered pencils of sunlight the face of a man of sixty. He said quietly to the squatting Negress, "Griselda foaled this morning."

"Horse or mare?" the Negress said.

"A horse. A damned fine colt. . . . What's this?" He indicated the pallet with the hand which held the whip.

"That un's a mare, I reckon."

"Hah," Sutpen said. "A damned fine colt. Going to be the spit and image of old Rob Roy when I rode him North in '61. Do you remember?"

"Yes, Marster."

"Hah." He glanced back towards the pallet. None could have said if the girl still watched him or not. Again his whip hand indicated the pallet. "Do whatever they need with whatever we've got to do it with." He went out, passing out the crazy doorway and stepping down into the rank weeds (there yet leaned rusting against the corner of the porch the scythe which Wash had borrowed from him three months ago to cut them with) where his horse waited, where Wash stood holding the reins.

When Colonel Sutpen rode away to fight the Yankees, Wash did not go. "I'm looking after the Kernel's place and niggers," he would tell all who asked him and some who had not asked—a gaunt, malaria-ridden man with pale, questioning eyes, who looked about thirty-five, though it was known that he had not only a daughter but an eight-year-old granddaughter as well. This was a lie, as most of them—the few remaining men between eighteen and fifty—to whom he told it, knew, though there were some who believed that he himself really believed it, though even these believed that he had better sense than to put it to the test with Mrs. Sutpen or the Sutpen slaves. Knew better or was just too lazy and shiftless to try it, they said, knowing that his sole connection with the Sutpen plantation lay in the fact that for years now Colonel Sutpen had allowed him to squat in a crazy shack on a slough in the river bottom on the Sutpen place, which Sutpen had built for a fishing lodge in his bachelor days and which had since fallen in dilapidation from disuse, so that now it looked like an aged or sick wild beast crawled terrifically there to drink in the act of dying.

The Sutpen slaves themselves heard of his statement. They laughed. It was not the first time they had laughed at him, calling him white trash behind his back. They began to ask him themselves, in groups, meeting him in the faint road which led up from the slough and the old fish camp, "Why ain't you at de war, white man?"

Pausing, he would look about the ring of black faces and white eyes and teeth behind which derision lurked. "Because I got a daughter and family to keep," he said. "Git out of my road, niggers."

"Niggers?" they repeated; "niggers?" laughing now. "Who him, calling us niggers?"

"Yes," he said. "I ain't got no niggers to look after my folks if I was gone."

"Nor nothing else but dat shack down yon dat Cunnel wouldn't *let* none of us live in."

Now he cursed them; sometimes he rushed at them, snatching up a stick from the ground while they scattered before him, yet seeming to surround him still with that black laughing, derisive, evasive, inescapable, leaving him panting and impotent and raging. Once it happened in the very back yard of the big house itself. This was after bitter news had come down from the Tennessee mountains and from Vicksburg, and Sherman had passed through the plantation, and most of the Negroes had followed him. Almost everything else had gone with the Federal troops, and Mrs. Sutpen had sent word to Wash that he could have the scuppernongs ripening in the arbor in the back yard. This time it was a house servant, one of the few Negroes who remained; this time the Negress had to retreat up the kitchen steps, where she turned. "Stop right dar, white man. Stop right whar you is. You ain't never crossed dese steps whilst Cunnel here, and you ain't ghy' do hit now."

This was true. But there was this of a kind of pride: he had never tried to enter the big house, even though he believed that if he had, Sutpen would have received him, permitted him. "But I ain't going to give no black nigger the chance to tell me I can't go nowhere," he said to himself. "I ain't even going to give Kernel the chance to have to cuss a nigger on my account." This, though he and Sutpen had spent more than one afternoon together on those rare Sundays when there would be no company in the house. Perhaps his mind knew that it was because Sutpen had nothing else to do, being a man who could not bear his own company. Yet the fact remained that the two of them would spend whole afternoons in the scuppernong arbor, Sutpen in the hammock and Wash squatting against a post, a pail of cistern water between them, taking drink for drink from the same demijohn. Meanwhile on weekdays he would see the fine figure of the man—they were the same age almost to a day, though neither of them (perhaps because Wash had a grandchild while Sutpen's son was a youth in school) ever thought of himself as being so—on the fine figure of the black stallion, galloping about the plantation. For that moment his heart would be quiet and proud. It would seem to him that the world in which Negroes, whom the Bible told him had been created and cursed by God to be brute and vassal to all men of white skin, were better found and housed and even clothed than he and his; that world in which he sensed always about him mocking echoes of black laughter was but a dream and an illusion, and that the actual world was this one across which his own lonely apotheosis seemed to gallop on the black thoroughbred, thinking how the Book said also that all men were created in the image of God and hence all men made the same image in God's eyes at least; so that he could say, as though speaking of himself, "A fine proud man. If God Himself was to come down and ride the natural earth, that's what He would aim to look like."

Sutpen returned in 1865, on the black stallion. He seemed to have aged ten years. His son had been killed in action the same winter in which his wife had died. He returned with his citation for gallantry from the hand of General Lee to a ruined plantation, where for a year now his daughter had subsisted partially on the meager bounty of the man to whom fifteen years ago he had granted permission to live in that tumbledown fishing camp whose very existence he had at the time forgotten. Wash was there to meet him, unchanged: still gaunt, still ageless, with his pale, questioning gaze, his air diffident, a little servile, a little familiar. "Well, Kernel," Wash said, "they kilt us but they ain't whupped us yit, air they?"

That was the tenor of their conversation for the next five years. It was inferior whisky which they drank now together from a stoneware jug, and it was not in the scuppernong arbor. It was in the rear of the little store which Sutpen managed to set up on the highroad: a frame shelved room where, with Wash for clerk and porter, he dispensed kerosene and staple foodstuffs and stale gaudy candy and cheap beads and ribbons to Negroes or poor whites of Wash's own kind, who came afoot or on gaunt mules to haggle tediously for dimes and quarters with a man who at one time could gallop (the black stallion was still alive; the stable in which his jealous get lived was in better repair than the house where the master himself lived) for ten miles across his own fertile land and who had led troops gallantly in battle; until Sutpen in fury would empty the store, close and lock the doors from the inside. Then he and Wash would repair to the rear and the jug. But the talk would not be quiet now, as when Sutpen lay in the hammock, delivering an arrogant monologue while Wash squatted guffawing against his post. They both sat now, though Sutpen had the single chair while Wash used whatever box or keg was handy, and even this for just a little while, because soon Sutpen would reach that stage of impotent and furious undefeat in which he would rise, swaying and plunging, and declare again that he would take his pistol and the black stallion and ride single-handed into Washington and kill Lincoln, dead now, and Sherman, now a private citizen. "Kill them!" he would shout. "Shoot them down like the dogs they are—"

"Sho, Kernel; sho, Kernel," Wash would say, catching Sutpen as he fell. Then he would commandeer the first passing wagon or, lacking that, he would walk the mile to the nearest neighbor and borrow one and return and carry Sutpen home. He entered the house now. He had been doing so for a long time, taking Sutpen home in whatever borrowed wagon might be, talking him into locomotion with cajoling murmurs as though he were a horse, a stallion himself. The daughter would meet them and hold open the door without a word. He would carry his burden through the once white formal entrance, surmounted by a fanlight imported piece by piece from Europe and with a board now nailed over a missing pane, across a velvet carpet from which all nap was now gone, and up a formal stairs, now but a fading ghost of bare boards between two strips of fading paint, and into the bedroom. It would be dusk by now, and he would let his burden sprawl onto the bed and undress it and then he would sit quietly in a chair beside. After a time the daughter would come to the door. "We're all right now," he would tell her. "Don't you worry none, Miss Judith."

Then it would become dark, and after a while he would lie down on the floor beside the bed, though not to sleep, because after a time—sometimes before midnight—the man on the bed would stir and groan and then speak. "Wash?"

"Hyer I am, Kernel. You go back to sleep. We ain't whupped yit, air we? Me and you kin do hit."

Even then he had already seen the ribbon about his granddaughter's waist. She was now fifteen, already mature, after the early way of her kind. He knew where the ribbon came from; he had been seeing it and its kind daily for three years, even if she had lied about where she got it, which she did not, at once bold, sullen, and fearful. "Sho now," he said. "Ef Kernel wants to give hit to you, I hope you minded to thank him."

His heart was quiet, even when he saw the dress, watching her secret, defiant, frightened face when she told him that Miss Judith, the daughter, had helped her to make it. But he was quite grave when he approached Sutpen after they closed the store that afternoon, following the other to the rear.

"Get the jug," Sutpen directed.

"Wait," Wash said. "Not yit for a minute."

Neither did Sutpen deny the dress. "What about it?" he said.

But Wash met his arrogant stare; he spoke quietly. "I've knowed you for going on twenty years. I ain't never yit denied to do what you told me to do. And I'm a man nigh sixty. And she ain't nothing but a fifteen-year-old gal."

"Meaning that I'd harm a girl? I, a man as old as you are?"

"If you was ara other man, I'd say you was as old as me. And old or no old, I wouldn't let her keep that dress nor nothing else that come from your hand. But you are different."

"How different?" But Wash merely looked at him with his pale, questioning, sober eyes. "So that's why you are afraid of me?"

Now Wash's gaze no longer questioned. It was tranquil, serene. "I ain't afraid. Because you air brave. It ain't that you were a brave man at one minute or day of your life and got a paper to show hit from General Lee. But you air brave, the same as you air alive and breathing. That's where hit's different. Hit don't need no ticket from nobody to tell me that. And I know that whatever you handle or tech, whether hit's a regiment of men or a ignorant gal or just a hound dog, that you will make hit right."

Now it was Sutpen who looked away, turning suddenly, brusquely. "Get the jug," he said sharply.

"Sho, Kernel," Wash said.

So on that Sunday dawn two years later, having watched the Negro midwife, which he had walked three miles to fetch, enter the crazy door beyond which his granddaughter lay wailing, his heart was still quiet though concerned. He knew what they had been saying—the Negroes in cabins about the land, the white men who loafed all day long about the store, watching quietly the three of them: Sutpen, himself, his granddaughter with her air of brazen and shrinking defiance as her condition became daily more and more obvious, like three actors that came and went upon a stage. "I know what they say to one another," he thought. "I can almost hyear them: *Wash Jones has fixed old Sutpen at last. Hit taken him twenty years, but he has done hit at last.*"

It would be dawn after a while, though not yet. From the house, where the lamp shone dim beyond the warped door-frame, his granddaughter's voice came steadily as though run by a clock, while thinking went slowly and terrifically, fumbling, involved somehow with a sound of galloping hooves, until there broke suddenly free in mid-gallop the fine proud figure of the man on the fine proud stallion, galloping; and then that at which thinking fumbled, broke free too and quite clear, not in justification nor even explanation, but as the apotheosis, lonely, explicable, beyond all fouling by human touch: "He is bigger than all them Yankees that kilt his son and his wife and taken his niggers and ruined his land, bigger than this hyer durn country that he fit for and that has denied him into keeping a little country store; bigger than the denial which hit helt to his lips like the bitter cup in the Book. And how could I have lived this nigh to him for twenty years without being teched and changed by him? Maybe I ain't as big as him and maybe I ain't done none of the galloping. But at least I done been drug along. Me and him kin do hit, if so be he will show me what he aims for me to do."

Then it was dawn. Suddenly he could see the house, and the old Negress in the door looking at him. Then he realized that his granddaughter's voice had ceased. "It's a girl," the Negress said. "You can go tell him if you want to." She re-entered the house.

"A girl," he repeated; "a girl"; in astonishment, hearing the galloping hooves, seeing the proud galloping figure emerge again. He seemed to watch it pass, galloping through avatars which marked the accumulation of years, time, to the climax where it galloped beneath a brandished saber and a shot-torn flag rushing down a sky in color like thunderous sulphur, thinking for the first time in his life that perhaps Sutpen was an old man like himself. "Gittin a gal," he thought in that astonishment; then he thought with the pleased surprise of a child: "Yes, sir. Be dawg if I ain't lived to be a great-grandpaw after all."

He entered the house. He moved clumsily, on tiptoe, as if he no longer lived there, as if the infant which had just drawn breath and cried in light had dispossessed him, be it of his own blood too though it might. But even above the pallet he could see little save the blur of his granddaughter's exhausted face. Then the Negress squatting at the hearth spoke, "You better gawn tell him if you going to. Hit's daylight now."

But this was not necessary. He had no more than turned the corner of the porch where the scythe leaned which he had borrowed three months ago to clear away the weeds through which he walked, when Sutpen himself rode up on the old stallion. He did not wonder how Sutpen had got the word. He took it for granted that this was what had brought the other out at this hour on Sunday morning, and he stood while the other dismounted, and he took the reins from Sutpen's hand, an expression on his gaunt face almost imbecile with a kind of weary triumph, saying, "Hit's a gal, Kernel. I be dawg if you ain't as old as I am—" until Sutpen passed him and entered the house. He stood there with the reins in his hand and heard Sutpen cross the floor to the pallet. He heard what Sutpen said, and something seemed to stop dead in him before going on.

The sun was now up, the swift sun of Mississippi latitudes, and it seemed to him that he stood beneath a strange sky, in a strange scene, familiar only as things are familiar in dreams, like the dreams of falling to one who has never climbed. "I kain't have heard what I thought I heard," he thought quietly. "I know I kain't." Yet the voice, the familiar voice which had said the words was still speaking, talking now to the old Negress about a colt foaled that morning. "That's why he was up so early," he thought. "That was hit. Hit ain't me and mine. Hit ain't even hisn that got him outen bed."

Sutpen emerged. He descended into the weeds, moving with that heavy deliberation which would have been haste when he was younger. He had not yet looked full at Wash. He said, "Dicey will stay and tend to her. You better—" Then he seemed to see Wash facing him and paused. "What?" he said.

"You said—" To his own ears Wash's voices sounded flat and ducklike, like a deaf man's. "You said if she was a mare, you could give her a good stall in the stable."

"Well?" Sutpen said. His eyes widened and narrowed, almost like a man's fists flexing and shutting, as Wash began to advance towards him, stooping a little. Very astonishment kept Sutpen still for the moment, watching that man whom in twenty years he had no more known to make any motion save at command than he had the horse which he rode. Again his eyes narrowed and widened; without moving he seemed to rear suddenly upright. "Stand back," he said suddenly and sharply. "Don't you touch me."

"I'm going to tech you, Kernel," Wash said in that flat, quiet, almost soft voice, advancing.

Sutpen raised the hand which held the riding whip; the old Negress peered around the crazy door with her black gargoyle face of a worn gnome. "Stand back, Wash," Sutpen said. Then he struck. The old Negress leaped down into the weeds with the agility of a goat and fled. Sutpen slashed Wash again across the face with the whip, striking him to his knees. When Wash rose and advanced once more he held in his hands the scythe which he had borrowed from Sutpen three months ago and which Sutpen would never need again.

When he re-entered the house his granddaughter stirred on the pallet bed and called his name fretfully. "What was that?" she said.

"What was what, honey?"

"That ere racket out there."

" 'Twarn't nothing," he said gently. He knelt and touched her hot forehead clumsily. "Do you want ara thing?"

"I want a sup of water," she said querulously. "I been laying here wanting a sup of water a long time, but don't nobody care enough to pay me no mind."

"Sho now," he said soothingly. He rose stiffly and fetched the dipper of water and raised her head to drink and laid her back and watched her turn to the child with an absolutely stonelike face. But a moment later he saw that she was crying quietly. "Now, now," he said, "I wouldn't do that. Old Dicey says hit's a right fine gal. Hit's all right now. Hit's all over now. Hit ain't no need to cry now."

But she continued to cry quietly, almost sullenly, and he rose again and stood uncomfortably above the pallet for a time, thinking as he had thought when his own wife lay so and then his daughter in turn: "Women. Hit's a mystry to me. They seem to want em, and yit when they git em they cry about hit. Hit's a mystry to me. To ara man." Then he moved away and drew a chair up to the window and sat down.

Through all that long, bright sunny forenoon he sat at the window, waiting. Now and then he rose and tiptoed to the pallet. But his granddaughter slept now, her face sullen and calm and weary, the child in the crook of her arm. Then he returned to the chair and sat again, waiting, wondering why it took them so long, until he remembered that it was Sunday. He was sitting there at mid-afternoon when a half-grown white boy came around the corner of the house upon the body and gave a choked cry and looked up and glared for a mesmerized instant at Wash in the window before he turned and fled. Then Wash rose and tiptoed again to the pallet.

The granddaughter was awake now, wakened perhaps by the boy's cry without hearing it. "Milly," he said, "air you hungry?" She didn't answer, turning her face away. He built up the fire on the hearth and cooked the food which he had brought home the day before: fatback it was, and cold corn pone; he poured water into the stale coffee pot and heated it. But she would not eat when he carried the plate to her, so he ate himself, quietly, alone, and left the dishes as they were and returned to the window.

Now he seemed to sense, feel, the men who would be gathering with horses and guns and dogs—the curious, and the vengeful: men of Sutpen's own kind, who had made the company about Sutpen's table in the time when Wash himself had yet to approach nearer to the house than the scuppernong arbor—men who had also shown the lesser ones how to fight in battle, who maybe also had signed papers from the generals saying that they were among the first of the brave; who had also galloped in the old days arrogant and proud on the fine horses across the fine plantations—symbols also of admiration and hope; instruments too of despair and grief.

That was whom they would expect him to run from. It seemed to him that he had no more to run from than he had to run to. If he ran, he would merely be fleeing one set of bragging and evil shadows for another just like them, since they were all of a kind throughout all the earth which he knew, and he was old, too old to flee far even if he were to flee. He could never escape them, no matter how much or how far he ran: a man going on sixty could not run that far. Not far enough to escape beyond the boundaries of earth where such men lived, set the order and the rule of living. It seemed to him that he now saw for the first time, after five years, how it was that Yankees or any other living armies had managed to whip them: the gallant, the proud, the brave; the acknowledged and chosen best among them all to carry courage and honor and pride. Maybe if he had gone to the war with them he would have discovered them sooner. But if he had discovered them sooner, what would he have done with his life since? How could he have borne to remember for five years what his life had been before?

Now it was getting toward sunset. The child had been crying; when he went to the pallet he saw his granddaughter nursing it, her face still bemused, sullen, inscrutable. "Air you hungry yit?" he said.

"I don't want nothing."

"You ought to eat."

This time she did not answer at all, looking down at the child. He returned to his chair and found that the sun had set. "Hit kain't be much longer," he thought. He could feel them quite near now, the curious and the vengeful. He could even seem to hear what they were saying about him, the undercurrent of believing beyond the immediate fury: *Old Wash Jones he come a tumble at last. He thought he had Sutpen, but Sutpen fooled him. He thought he had Kernel where he would have to marry the gal or pay up. And Kernel refused.* "But I never expected that, Kernel!" he cried aloud, catching himself at the sound of his own voice, glancing quickly back to find his granddaughter watching him.

"Who you talking to now?" she said.

"Hit ain't nothing. I was just thinking and talked out before I knowed hit."

Her face was becoming indistinct again, again a sullen blur in the twilight. "I reckon so. I reckon you'll have to holler louder than that before he'll hear you, up yonder at that house. And I reckon you'll need to do more than holler before you get him down here too."

"Sho now," he said. "Don't you worry none." But already thinking was going smoothly on: "You know I never. You know how I ain't never expected or asked nothing from ara living man but what I expected from you. And I never asked that. I didn't think hit would need. I said, *I don't need to. What need has a fellow like Wash Jones to question or doubt the man that General Lee himself says in a handwrote ticket that he was brave?* Brave," he thought. "Better if nara one of them had never rid back home in '65"; thinking *Better if his kind and mine too had never drawn the breath of life on this earth. Better that all who remain of us be blasted from the face of earth than that another Wash Jones should see his whole life shredded from him and shrivel away like a dried shuck thrown onto the fire.*

He ceased, became still. He heard the horses, suddenly and plainly; presently he saw the lantern and the movement of men, the glint of gun barrels, in its moving light. Yet he did not stir. It was quite dark now, and he listened to the voices and the sounds of underbrush as they surrounded the house. The lantern itself came on; its light fell upon the quiet body in the weeds and stopped, the horses tall and shadowy. A man descended and stooped in the lantern light, above the body. He held a pistol; he rose and faced the house. "Jones," he said.

"I'm here," Wash said quietly from the window. "That you, Major?"

"Come out."

"Sho," he said quietly. "I just want to see to my granddaughter."

"We'll see to her. Come on out."

"Sho, Major. Just a minute."

"Show a light. Light your lamp."

"Sho. In just a minute." They could hear his voice retreat into the house, though they could not see him as he went swiftly to the crack in the chimney where he kept the butcher knife: the one thing in his slovenly life and house in which he took pride, since it was razor sharp. He approached the pallet, his granddaughter's voice:

"Who is it? Light the lamp, grandpaw."

"Hit won't need no light, honey. Hit won't take but a minute," he said, kneeling, fumbling toward her voice, whispering now. "Where air you?"

"Right here," she said fretfully. "Where would I be? What is..." His hand touched her face. "What is...Grandpaw! Grand...."

"Jones!" the sheriff said. "Come out of there!"

"In just a minute, Major," he said. Now he rose and moved swiftly. He knew where in the dark the can of kerosene was, just as he knew that it was full, since it was not two days ago that he had filled it at the store and held it there until he got a ride home with it, since the five gallons were heavy. There were still coals on the hearth; besides, the crazy building itself was like tinder: the coals, the hearth, the walls exploding in a single blue glare. Against it the waiting men saw him in a wild instant springing toward them with the lifted scythe before the horses reared and whirled. They checked the horses and turned them back toward the glare, yet still in wild relief against it the gaunt figure ran toward them with the lifted scythe.

"Jones!" the sheriff shouted; "stop! Stop, or I'll shoot. Jones! *Jones!*" Yet still the gaunt, furious figure came on against the glare and roar of the flames. With the scythe lifted, it bore down upon them, upon the wild glaring eyes of the horses and the swinging glints of gun barrels, without any cry, any sound.

FOUR
The Language
of Fiction

Words are a writer's medium so he must choose them as carefully as a composer selecting his note-patterns or a sculptor picking out a block of marble. Given the brevity of most stories, it is no wonder that William Faulkner once remarked that "in a short story...almost every word has got to be exactly right." Language will reveal a character's personality and values by how something is said as well as by what is said. This is most obvious in two first-person narratives which follow: "Son in the Afternoon" and "Why I Live at the P.O.," where the story is told as if the person were simply speaking aloud to us. It is equally true, however, for most other stories. In "Wash," Faulkner has Wash Jones first recall his days with Sutpen, then reflect accurately upon his wasted life which he knows will soon end violently. Jones contrasts the superficial way others will view him: *"Old Wash Jones he come a tumble at last,"* with his own considered judgment: *"Better if his kind and mine too had never drawn the breath of life on this earth. Better that all who remain of us be blasted from the face of earth than that another Wash Jones should see his whole life shredded from him and shrivel away like a dried shuck thrown onto the fire."* There is a striking contrast between the cliché response he imagines his friends saying and his own fierce eloquence as his thoughts acquire dignity and force through the sophisticated use of alliteration (*should...shredded...shr*ivel...*dried sh*uck). The parallel construction (*Better* if...*Better* that) links past and present to an impossible future. Our final view of his character and action must be tempered by this terrible clarity with which he summarizes his life and records his negative judgment of it.

In choosing his words, a writer draws upon the vast resources of language. If he wants his reader to see, touch, taste, smell or hear something in his imagination, then he will use images. An image is a sense impression: the *red* wagon, the *stink* of garbage, the *rough* sandpaper, the *noisy* drill, the *sweet* candy bar are all images. Each appeals to one of the senses through imagination. The Sara Teasdale poem in Ray Bradbury's story, "There Will Come Soft Rains," employs imagery that appeals to four of our five senses: "There will come soft rains [sight and touch] and the smell of the ground [smell] / And swallows circling [sight] with their shimmering sound [hearing]." In "The Sculptor's Funeral," Willa Cather brings the activity at the railway station vividly before us through her carefully chosen sense impressions:

Just then a distant whistle sounded [hearing], and there was a shuffling of feet on the platform [hearing and sight]. A number of lanky boys of all ages appeared [sight] as suddenly and slimily as eels wakened [sight and touch] by the crack of thunder [hearing].

Cather adds to the picture of the "lanky boys" the tactile sensations associated with "slimily." The reader's reaction against the eels then transfers to the boys: they are as unpredictable and unpleasant as the eels would be. In contrast to this use of image and comparison, Dylan Thomas in "A Story" evokes a smile from the reader as he compares the large uncle to a buffalo or says Mr. Weazley hisses "like a gander" or "coughs like a goat." Such comparisons are an integral part of Thomas' warm, gently comic style and have none of the negative connotations of the eels.

There is another important type of comparison: "As slimily...as eels," "hisses like a gander" and "coughs like a goat" are all similes, whereas "feeding the buffalo" and "the loud check meadow" of the uncle's waistcoat in "A Story" are metaphors. A simile states a comparison, as in "hisses *like* a gander," while a metaphor only implies one, as in the aunt "feeding the buffalo." Similes do the work for the reader, while metaphors demand his involvement. Thomas does not say in the metaphor that his uncle is *like* a buffalo, but that his aunt feeds "the buffalo." Neither does he say that the waistcoat stretched across his uncle's huge stomach is *like* a meadow, but describes "the loud check meadow of his waistcoat." Instead of observing a ready-made comparison, the reader helps create one. There is an instant in every metaphor in which the identities of the objects being compared fuse. As readers, we must then separate the objects (buffalo/uncle; meadow/waistcoat) and make the comparison ourselves. This process of fusion followed by comparison in which the reader actively participates gives metaphor its unique imaginative power.

Another potential source of imaginative power for the writer lies in symbolism and allusion. In "My Kinsman, Major Molineux," the narrator emphasizes the distance between Robin and the townsfolk by identifying the young man with the country, which symbolizes innocence and goodness, and then exposing him to the city, which symbolizes evil and corruption. The linking of the city with danger, death and decayed morality goes back at least as far as the story of Cain, the first murderer, who also founded the first city. Light in "My Kinsman, Major Molineux" also functions symbolically to intensify the opposition between city and country: instead of the clarity of country sunlight, Robin finds only ambiguous moonlight. When torchlight flares in the city, it brings not comfort but more confusion as the tortured features of Robin's kinsman are thrown into harsh relief.

Closely allied with the symbolism are the allusions Hawthorne suggests to other familiar tales. In Greek mythology, dead souls pay the ferryman, Charon, to take them across the river Styx from the known land of the living to the underworld. When Robin pays the ferryman to take him alone across the river, his actions parallel those in the ancient myth; for although he travels physically but from the country to the town, he moves symbolically from the known to the unknown, from innocence to experience. At the end of the tale he exchanges his naïveté about the world and his forthright way of confronting people for knowledge of himself and his society. Never again will he be quite so eager to proclaim himself a "shrewd youth," nor will he be quite so eager to search for kinsmen to help him make his way in the world. Turning to his kind acquaintance of the night, Robin speaks ironically from experience: "Thanks to you, and to my other friends, I have at last met my kinsman, and he will scarce desire to see my face again. I begin to grow weary of a town life, sir. Will you show me the way to the ferry?" His language reveals that he accepts the complexities of life and now knows that "a man [may] have several voices as well as two complexions." In Hawthorne's story, symbolism, allusion and language coalesce to clarify and deepen the dilemma faced by a young man taking his first halting step into maturity. (Compare Hawthorne's use of symbolism and allusion to that of Joyce in "Araby" or Lawrence in "The Man Who Loved Islands.")

Through his choice of words a writer arrives at a distinctive way of speaking which we call his style. A story by Faulkner, Dylan Thomas or Edgar Allan Poe sounds like no one else's because of their readily identifiable voice. The style of the following story, for instance, is so individual that readers of modern fiction will recognize it immediately as Franz Kafka's.

A COMMON CONFUSION

A common experience, resulting in a common confusion. A has to transact important business with B in H. He goes to H for a preliminary interview, accomplishes the journey there in ten minutes, and the journey back in the same time, and on returning boasts to his family of his expedition. Next day he goes again to H, this time to settle his business finally. As that by all appearances will require several hours, A leaves very early in the morning. But although all the accessory circumstances, at least in A's estimation, are exactly the same as the day before, it takes him ten hours this time to reach H. When he arrives there quite exhausted in the evening he is informed that B, annoyed at his absence, had left half an hour before to go to A's village, and that they must have passed each other on the road. A is advised to wait. But in his anxiety about his business he sets off at once and hurries home.

This time he achieves the journey, without paying any particular attention to the fact, exactly in a second. At home he learns that B had arrived quite early, immediately after A's departure, indeed that he had met A on the threshold and reminded him of his business; but A had replied that he had no time to spare, he must go at once.

In spite of this incomprehensible behavior of A, however, B had stayed on to wait for A's return. It is true, he had asked several times whether A was not back yet, but he was still sitting up in A's room. Overjoyed at the opportunity of seeing B at once and explaining everything to him, A rushes upstairs. He is almost at the top, when he stumbles, twists a sinew, and almost fainting with the pain, incapable even of uttering a cry, only able to moan faintly in the darkness, he hears B—impossible to tell whether at a great distance or quite near him—stamping down the stairs in a violent rage and vanishing for good.

Kafka's story provokes thought and teases the imagination because of its unexpected juxtaposition of subject and language. By distilling into one brief sequence the many incidents, mistakes and false assumptions which typically contribute to human failure, the story becomes, as one critic says, "not the report of a confusing event, but the model of confusion itself." Although the style is that of a test which measures mathematical aptitude or problem-solving ability, the story's events, such as "A" passing "B" on the road or failing to recognize him on the doorstep, are taken from slapstick comic routines. "Sorry I can't stay," says the comic, "but I have to meet you in ten minutes." We laugh at the joke, in part, because the speaker thoroughly confuses means with ends. "A" becomes so absorbed in his journey that he forgets why he set out in the first place! As a result he fails to recognize "B," the object of his travels, when he passes him on the road. Besides not separating his means from ends, "A" mistakenly assumes that coming within sight of his goal is equivalent to reaching it. His premature joy dissolves into excruciating pain as "B" stamps "down the stairs in a violent rage . . . vanishing for good." The objective-sounding language of the story contrasts with the absurd sequence of events and the pathetic ending, and this precise description of impossible events is a characteristic of Kafka's stories and style. (Compare to his "The Great Wall of China," in Chapter Five.) Slightly different, yet in a similar vein, is the last story in this section, "Tlön, Uqbar, Orbis Tertius" where Jorge Luis Borges, the Argentine writer, combines—somewhat improbably—science fiction fantasy with an all-too-precise, pedantic scholarship. The results are by turns puzzling, outrageous, boring and amusing.

By using the resources of language including imagery, metaphor, simile, symbolism and allusion, but above all by developing their distinctive styles, writers such as Hawthorne, Thomas, Cather, Bradbury, Kafka and those in this section create stories which give us pleasure long after we have finished reading them. To read well, as Thoreau observes, may be one of the most difficult and rewarding tasks a person can accomplish, but how much more difficult it is to write well.

ARABY
James Joyce

North Richmond Street, being blind, was a quiet street except at the hour when the Christian Brothers' School set the boys free. An uninhabited house of two storeys stood at the blind end, detached from its neighbours in a square ground. The other houses of the street, conscious of decent lives within them, gazed at one another with brown imperturbable faces.

The former tenant of our house, a priest, had died in the back drawing-room. Air, musty from having been long enclosed, hung in all the rooms, and the waste room behind the kitchen was littered with old useless papers. Among these I found a few paper-covered books, the pages of which were curled and damp: *The Abbot,* by Walter Scott, *The Devout Communicant* and *The Memoirs of Vidocq*. I liked the last best because its leaves were yellow. The wild garden behind the house contained a central apple-tree and a few straggling bushes under one of which I found the late tenant's rusty bicycle-pump. He had been a very charitable priest; in his will he had left all his money to institutions and the furniture of his house to his sister.

When the short days of winter came dusk fell before we had well eaten our dinners. When we met in the street the houses had grown sombre. The space of sky above us was the colour of ever-changing violet and towards it the lamps of the street lifted their feeble lanterns. The cold air stung us and we played till our bodies glowed. Our shouts echoed in the silent street. The career of our play brought us through the dark muddy lanes behind the houses where we ran the gantlet of the rough tribes from the cottages, to the back doors of the dark dripping gardens where odours arose from the ashpits, to the dark odorous stables where a coachman smoothed and combed the horse or shook music from the buckled harness. When we returned to the street light from the kitchen windows had filled the areas. If my uncle was seen turning the corner we hid in the shadow until we had seen him safely housed. Or if Mangan's sister came out on the doorstep to call her brother in to his tea we watched her from our shadow peer up and down the street. We waited to see whether she would remain or go in and, if she remained, we left our shadow and walked up to Mangan's steps resignedly. She was waiting for us, her figure defined by the light from the half-opened door. Her brother always teased her before he obeyed and I stood by the railings looking at her. Her dress swung as she moved her body and the soft rope of her hair tossed from side to side.

Every morning I lay on the floor in the front parlour watching her door. The blind was pulled down to within an inch of the sash so that I could not be seen. When she came out on the doorstep my heart leaped. I ran to the hall, seized my books and followed her. I kept her brown figure always in my eye and, when we came near the point at which our ways diverged, I quickened my pace and passed her. This happened morning after morning. I had never spoken to her, except for a few casual words, and yet her name was like a summons to all my foolish blood.

Her image accompanied me even in places the most hostile to romance. On Saturday evenings when my aunt went marketing I had to go to carry some of the parcels. We walked through the flaring streets, jostled by drunken men and bargaining women, amid the curses of labourers, the shrill litanies of shop-boys who stood on guard by the barrels of pigs' cheeks, the nasal chanting of street-singers, who sang a *come-all-you* about O'Donovan Rossa, or a ballad about the troubles in our native land. These noises converged in a single sensation of life for me: I imagined that I bore my chalice safely through a throng of foes. Her name sprang to my lips at moments in strange prayers and praises which I myself did not understand. My eyes were often full of tears (I could not tell why) and at times a flood from my heart seemed to pour itself out into my bosom. I thought little of the future. I did not know whether I would ever speak to her or not or, if I spoke to her, how I could tell her of my confused adoration. But my body was like a harp and her words and gestures were like fingers running upon the wires.

One evening I went into the back drawing-room in which the priest had died. It was a dark rainy evening and there was no sound in the house. Through one of the broken panes I heard the rain impinge upon the earth, the fine incessant needles of water playing in the sodden beds. Some distant lamp or lighted window gleamed below me. I was thankful that I could see so little. All my senses seemed to desire to veil themselves and, feeling that I was about to slip from them, I pressed the palms of my hands together until they trembled, murmuring: *O love! O love!* many times.

At last she spoke to me. When she addressed the first words to me I was so confused that I did not know what to answer. She asked me was I going to *Araby*. I forget whether I answered yes or no. It would be a splendid bazaar, she said; she would love to go.

—And why can't you? I asked.

While she spoke she turned a silver bracelet round and round her wrist. She could not go, she said, because there would be a retreat that week in her convent. Her brother and two other boys were fighting for their caps and I was alone at the railings. She held one of the spikes, bowing her head towards me. The light from the lamp opposite our door caught the white curve of her neck, lit up her hair that rested there and, falling, lit up the hand upon the railing. It fell over one side of her dress and caught the white border of a petticoat, just visible as she stood at ease.

—It's well for you, she said.

—If I go, I said, I will bring you something.

What innumerable follies laid waste my waking and sleeping thoughts after that evening! I wished to annihilate the tedious intervening days. I chafed against the work of school. At night in my bedroom and by day in the classroom her image came between me and the page I strove to read. The syllables of the word *Araby* were called to me through the silence in which my soul luxuriated and cast an Eastern enchantment over me. I asked for leave to go to the bazaar on Saturday night. My aunt was surprised and hoped it was not some Freemason affair. I answered few questions in class. I watched my master's face pass from amiability to sternness; he hoped I was not beginning to idle. I could not call my wandering thoughts together. I had hardly any patience with the serious work of life which, now that it stood between me and my desire, seemed to me child's play, ugly monotonous child's play.

On Saturday morning I reminded my uncle that I wished to go to the bazaar in the evening. He was fussing at the hallstand, looking for the hat-brush, and answered me curtly:

—Yes, boy, I know.

As he was in the hall I could not go into the front parlour and lie at the window. I left the house in bad humour and walked slowly towards the school. The air was pitilessly raw and already my heart misgave me.

When I came home to dinner my uncle had not yet been home. Still it was early. I sat staring at the clock for some time and, when its ticking began to irritate me, I left the room. I mounted the staircase and gained the upper part of the house. The high cold empty gloomy rooms liberated me and I went from room to room singing. From the front window I saw my companions playing below in the street. Their cries reached me weakened and indistinct and, leaning my forehead against the cool glass, I looked over at the dark house where she lived. I may have stood there for an hour, seeing nothing but the brown-clad figure cast by my imagination, touched discreetly by the lamplight at the curved neck, at the hand upon the railings and at the border below the dress.

When I came downstairs again I found Mrs. Mercer sitting at the fire. She was an old garrulous woman, a pawnbroker's widow, who collected used stamps for some pious purpose. I had to endure the gossip of the tea-table. The meal was prolonged beyond an hour and still my uncle did not come. Mrs. Mercer stood up to go: she was sorry she couldn't wait any longer, but it was after eight o'clock and she did not like to be out late, as the night air was bad for her. When she had gone I began to walk up and down the room, clenching my fists. My aunt said:

—I'm afraid you may put off your bazaar for this night of Our Lord.

At nine o'clock I heard my uncle's latchkey in the halldoor. I heard him talking to himself and heard the hallstand rocking when it had received the weight of his overcoat. I could interpret these signs. When he was midway through his dinner I asked him to give me the money to go to the bazaar. He had forgotten.

—The people are in bed and after their first sleep now, he said.

I did not smile. My aunt said to him energetically:

—Can't you give him the money and let him go? You've kept him late enough as it is.

My uncle said he was very sorry he had forgotten. He said he believed in the old saying: *All work and no play makes Jack a dull boy.* He asked me where I was going and, when I had told him a second time he asked me did I know *The Arab's Farewell to his Steed.* When I left the kitchen he was about to recite the opening lines of the piece to my aunt.

I held a florin tightly in my hand as I strode down Buckingham Street towards the station. The sight of the streets thronged with buyers and glaring with gas recalled to me the purpose of my journey. I took my seat in a third-class carriage of a deserted train. After an intolerable delay the train moved out of the station slowly. It crept onward among ruinous houses and over the twinkling river. At Westland Row Station a crowd of people pressed to the carriage doors; but the porters moved them back, saying that it was a special train for the bazaar. I remained alone in the bare carriage. In a few minutes the train drew up beside an improvised wooden platform. I passed out on the road and saw by the lighted dial of a clock that it was ten minutes to ten. In front of me was a large building which displayed the magical name.

I could not find any sixpenny entrance and, fearing that the bazaar would be closed, I passed in quickly through a turnstile, handing a shilling to a weary-looking man. I found myself in a big hall girdled at half its height by a gallery. Nearly all the stalls were closed and the greater part of the hall was in darkness. I recognised a silence like that which pervades a church after a service. I walked into the centre of the bazaar timidly. A few people were gathered about the stalls which were still open. Before a curtain, over which the words *Café Chantant* were written in coloured lamps, two men were counting money on a salver. I listened to the fall of the coins.

Remembering with difficulty why I had come I went over to one of the stalls and examined porcelain vases and flowered tea-sets. At the door of the stall a young lady was talking and laughing with two young gentlemen. I remarked their English accents and listened vaguely to their conversation.

—O, I never said such a thing!

—O, but you did!

—O, but I didn't!

—Didn't she say that?

—Yes. I heard her.

—O, there's a...fib!

Observing me the young lady came over and asked me did I wish to buy anything. The tone of her voice was not encouraging; she seemed to have spoken to me out of a sense of duty. I looked humbly at the great jars that stood like eastern guards at either side of the dark entrance to the stall and murmured:

—No, thank you.

The young lady changed the position of one of the vases and went back to the two young men. They began to talk of the same subject. Once or twice the young lady glanced at me over her shoulder.

I lingered before her stall, though I knew my stay was useless, to make my interest in her wares seem the more real. Then I turned away slowly and walked down the middle of the bazaar. I allowed the two pennies to fall against the sixpence in my pocket. I heard a voice call from one end of the gallery that the light was out. The upper part of the hall was now completely dark.

Gazing up into the darkness I saw myself as a creature driven and derided by vanity; and my eyes burned with anguish and anger.

SON IN THE AFTERNOON
John A. Williams

It was hot and I'm a bitch when it's hot. I goosed the Ford over Sepulveda Boulevard toward Santa Monica until I got stuck in the traffic that pours from Elay into the surrounding towns. I'd had a lousy day at the studio.

I was—and still am—a writer and this studio had hired me to check scripts and films with Negroes in them to make sure the Negro movie-goer wouldn't be offended. I'm a Negro writer, you see. Anyway, the day had been tough because of a couple of verbs—slink and walk. One of those Yale guys had done a script calling for a Negro waiter to slink away from this table where a dinner party was glaring at him. I had said the waiter shouldn't slink, but walk. This Yale guy said it was essential to the plot that the waiter slink, because later on he becomes a hero. I said you don't slink one minute and be a hero the next; there has to be some consistency. The actor who played the waiter agreed with me, and so did the director. I knew this Yale guy's stuff. It was all the same, that one subtle scene packed with prejudice that usually registered subliminally. I wondered how come the guy didn't hate himself, but then, I heard he did.

Anyway...hear me out now. I was on my way to Santa Monica to pick up my mother, Nora. Sometimes I call her mother; sometimes I call her Nora. It was a long haul for such a hot day. I had planned a quiet evening; a nice shower, fresh clothes, and then I would have dinner at the Watkins and talk with some of the musicians making it on the scene for a quick one before they cut out to their sets to blow. After, I was going by the Pigalle down on Figueroa and catch Earl Grant. The boy really plays; he'll make it big one day. And still later, if nothing exciting happened, I'd pick up Scottie and make it to the Lighthouse on the Beach or to the Strollers and listen to some sounds. I looked forward to hearing Sleepy Stein's show on the way out.

So you see, this picking up Nora was a little inconvenient because we had to drive all the way into West Los Angeles. My mother was a maid for the Couchman's. Ronald Couchman was an architect, a good one I understood from Nora who has a fine sense for this sort of thing; you don't work in some hundred-odd houses during your life and not get some idea of the way a house or even a building should be laid out, if you're Nora. Couchman's wife, Kay, was a playgirl who drove a white Jaguar from one elbow-bending function to another. My mother didn't like her much; she didn't seem to care much for her son, Ronald, junior. The Couchman's lived in a real fine residential section, of course. In the neighborhood there also lived a number of actors my mother knew quite well, like the guy who used to play Dagwood.

Somehow it is very funny. I mean that the maids and butlers know everything about these people and these people, like the Yale guy, know nothing about butlers or maids. Through Nora we knew who was laying whose wife; who had money and who *really* had money; we knew about the wild parties hours before the police, and we knew who smoked marijuana, when they smoked it and where they got it. We knew all about them.

To get to the Couchman's driveway I had to go three blocks up one side of a palm-planted center strip and back down the other. The drive bent gently, swept out of sight of the main road. The house, sheltered by slim palms, looked like a transplanted Colonial only with ugly brown shingles. I parked and walked to the kitchen door, skirting the growling Great Dane tied to a tree. I don't like kitchen doors. Entering people's houses by them, I mean. I'd done this sort of thing most of my life when I called at the places where Nora worked to pick up the patched sheets or the half-used meats and tarnished silver—the fringe benefits of a housemaid. As a teenager I'd told Nora I was through with that crap; that I was not going through anybody's kitchen door. She only laughed and said I'd learn. One day I called for her—I was still a kid—and without knocking walked through the front door of this house, right through the living room. I was almost out of the room when I saw feet behind a couch. I leaned over and there was Mr. Jorgensen and his wife making out like crazy. I guess it hit them sort of sudden and they went at it like the Hell-bomb was due to drop any minute. I've been like that too, mostly in the Spring. Of course, when Mr. Jorgensen looked over his shoulder and saw me, you know what happened. I was thrown out and Nora was right behind me. In the middle of winter, the old man sick and the coal bill three months overdue. Nora was right; I learned.

My mother saw me before I could ring the bell. She opened the door. "Hello," she said. She was breathing hard like she was out of breath. "Come in and sit down. I don't know *where* that Kay is. Little Ronald is sick and she's prob'ly out gettin' drunk again." She left me and half-walked, half-ran back through the house, I guess to be with Ronnie. I disliked the combination of her white nylon uniform, her dark brown face and the streaks of gray in her hair. Nora had married this guy from Texas a few years after the old man died. He was all right, I guess, and he made out okay. Nora didn't have to work, but she couldn't be still; she always had to be doing something. I suggested she quit work, but like her husband, I had little luck. It would have been good for her to take an extended trip around the country visiting my brothers and sisters, and once she got to Philly, she'd probably go right out to the cemetery and sit awhile with the old man.

I walked through the house. I liked Couchman's library. I thought if I knew him I'd like him. The room made me feel like that. I left it and went into the big living room. You could tell Couchman had let his wife do it. Everything in it was fast, moving, dart-like with no sense of ease. But on the walls were several of Couchman's conceptions of buildings and homes. His lines were neat, well-paced and functional.

My mother walked rapidly through the room and without looking at me said, "Just be patient, Wendell. She should be here real soon."

"Yeah," I said, "with a snootful." I had turned back to the drawings when Ronnie scampered into the room, his face twisted with rage.

"Nora!" he tried to roar, perhaps as he'd seen the parents of some of his friends roar at their maids; I'm quite sure Kay didn't shout at Nora, and I don't think Couchman would. But then, no one shouts at Nora. That is implicit in her posture, her speech and manner. "Nora you come right back here this minute!" and the little bastard stamped and pointed to a spot on the floor where my mother was supposed to come to roost.

I have a nasty temper. Sometimes it lies dormant for ages and at other times, like when the weather is hot and nothing seems to be going right, it stands poised on a springboard. It dived off. "Don't talk to *my* mother like that you little—!" I said sharply, breaking off just before I cursed. I took a step forward, wishing he'd been big enough for me to strike. "How'd you like for me to talk to *your* mother like that?"

The nine-year-old looked up at me in surprise and confusion. He hadn't expected me to say anything; I was just another piece of furniture or something. Tears rose in his eyes and spilled out onto his pale cheeks. He put his hands behind him, twisted them. He moved backwards, away from me. He looked at my mother with a "Nora, come help me," look. And sure, there was Nora, speeding back across the room, gathering the kid in her arms, tucking his robe together.

I was almost too angry to feel hatred for myself.

Ronnie was the Couchman's only kid. Nora loved him; I suppose that was the trouble, she loved him. Couchman was gone ten, twelve hours a day; the mother didn't stay around the house any longer than necessary, so Ronnie had only my mother. You know, I think kids should have someone to love, and Nora wasn't a bad sort. But somehow, when the six of us were growing up we never had her. She was gone, out scuffling to get those crumbs to put into our mouths and shoes for our feet and praying for something to happen so that all the space in between would be taken care of. Nora's affection for us took the form of rushing out into the morning's five o'clock blackness to wake some silly bitch and get her coffee; took form in her trudging five miles home every night instead of taking the streetcar because we always needed tablets for school, we said. But the truth was all of us liked to draw and we went through a tablet in a couple of hours every day. Can you imagine? There's not a goddamn artist among us. We never had the physical affection, the pat on the head, the quick, smiling kiss, the "gimmee a hug" routine. All of this Ronnie was getting.

He buried his little blond head in Nora's breast and sobbed. "There, there now," Nora said. "Don't you cry, Ronnie. Ol' Wendell is just jealous, and he hasn't got much sense either. He didn't mean nuthin'."

I left the room. Nora had hit it of course; hit it and passed on. I looked back. It didn't look so incongruous, the white and black together, I mean. Ronnie was still sobbing, his head now on Nora's shoulder. The only time I ever got that close to her was when she trapped me with a bearhug so she could whale the daylights out of me after I put an iceball through Mrs. Grant's window.

I walked outside and lighted a cigarette. When Ronnie was in the hospital the month before Nora got me to run her way the hell over in Hollywood every night to see him. I didn't like it worth a damn. All right, I'll admit it; it did upset me. All that affection I didn't get nor my brothers and sisters going to that little white boy who without a doubt, when away from her called her "our nigger maid." I spat at the Great Dane. He snarled and then I bounced a rock off his fanny. "Lay down you bastard," I muttered. He strained at his leash. It was a good thing he was tied up.

I heard the low cough of the Jaguar slapping against the road. The car was throttled down and with a muted roar swung into the driveway. The woman aimed it for me. I didn't move. At the last moment, grinning, she swung the wheel over and braked to a jolting stop. She bounded out of the car like a tennis player vaulting over a net. "Hi," she said. She tugged at her shorts.

"Hello."

"You're Nora's boy?"

"I'm Nora's son." I can't stand that word "boy."

We stood looking at each other while the dog whined. Kay had a nice tan, a nice body. She was high. Looking at her, I could feel myself going into my sexy-looking bastard role; sometimes I can swing it great, and I guess this was one of the time. Maybe it all had to do with the business inside. Kay took off her sunglasses and took a good look at me.

"May I have a cigarette?"

I gave her one and lighted it.

"Nice tan," I said. Most white people I know think it's a big, big deal if a Negro compliments them on their tans. It's a large laugh, honest. You have all this volleyball about color and come summer you can't hold the white folks back from the beaches and the country, anyplace where they can get sun. And of course, the blacker they get, the more pleased they are. Crazy.

"You like it?" she asked. She was pleased. She placed her arm next to mine. "Almost the same color," she said.

"Ronnie isn't feeling well," I said.

"Oh, the poor kid. I'm so glad we have Nora. She's such a charm. I'll run right in and look at him. Have a drink in the bar. Fix me one too."

Kay skipped inside and I went to the bar and poured out two drinks. I made hers three times stronger than mine. She was back soon. "Nora was trying to put him to sleep and she made me stay out." She giggled. I leaned over the bar and peered down her breasts as she gulped her drink. "Fix me another, would you?" For one second I was angry; I wasn't her damned servingman. I held my temper.

While I was fixing her drink she was saying how amazing it was for Nora to have a son who was a writer. What she was really saying was that it was amazing for a servant to have a son who was not also a servant. "Anything can happen in a democracy," I said. "Servant's sons drink with the madam and so on."

"Oh, Nora isn't a servant," Kay said. "She's part of the family."

Yeah, I thought. Where and how many times had I heard *that* jazz before? We were silent again and she said after it, "You like my tan, huh?"

This time I went close to her, held her arm and we compared the colors. I placed one arm around her. She pretended not to see or feel it, but she wasn't trying to get away either. In fact, while trying to appear not to, she pressed just a bit closer and the register in my brain which tells me I've got it made clicked and inwardly I grinned. I looked at her. She was very high. I put both arms around her and she wrapped her arms around me, running her hands up and down the back of my neck. Then I kissed her; she responded quickly, completely.

"Mom!"

"Ronnie, come to bed," I heard Nora shout from the other room. We could hear Ronnie out there too, running over the rug. Kay tried to get away from me, push me to one side because Ronnie was coming right for the bar. "Oh, *please*," she said, "don't let him see us." I wouldn't let her push me away. "Stop!" she hissed. "He'll *see* us!" We stopped struggling, just for an instant, and we listened to the echo of the word *see*. She gritted her teeth and renewed her efforts to get away.

Me? I had the scene laid right out before me. The kid breaks in and sees his mother in this real wriggly clinch with this nigger who's just hollered at him and no matter how his mother explains it away, the kid has the image for the rest of his life.

That's the way it happened. The kid's mother hissed under her breath, *"You're crazy!"* and she looked at me as though she were seeing me or something about me for the very first time. I'd released her as soon as Ronnie, romping into the bar, saw us and came to a full, open-mouthed halt. Kay went to him. He looked first at me, then at his mother. Kay turned to me, but she couldn't speak.

Outside in the main room my mother called with her clear, loud voice, "Wendell, where are you? We can go now."

I started to move past Kay and Ronnie. I wasn't angry any longer; I felt as though I might throw up. I was beginning to feel sorry for it all, but I made myself think, *"There, you little bastard, there."*

My mother thrust her face inside the door and said, "Goodbye, Mrs. Couchman, see you tomorrow. 'Bye, Ronnie."

"Yes, Nora," Kay said, sort of stunned. "Tomorrow." She was reaching for Ronnie's hand as we left. I turned and saw that the kid was slapping her hand away. I hurried quickly after Nora.

THE MAN WHO LOVED ISLANDS
D. H. Lawrence

I

There was a man who loved islands. He was born on one, but it didn't suit him, as there were too many other people on it, besides himself. He wanted an island all of his own: not necessarily to be alone on it, but to make it a world of his own.

An island, if it is big enough, is no better than a continent. It has to be really quite small, before it *feels* like an island; and this story will show how tiny it has to be, before you can presume to fill it with your own personality.

Now circumstances so worked out that this lover of islands, by the time he was thirty-five, actually acquired an island of his own. He didn't own it as freehold property, but he had a ninety-nine years' lease of it, which, as far as a man and an island are concerned, is as good as everlasting. Since, if you are like Abraham, and want your offspring to be numberless as the sands of the sea-shore, you don't choose an island to start breeding on. Too soon there would be over-population, overcrowding, and slum conditions. Which is a horrid thought, for one who loves an island for its insulation. No, an island is a nest which holds one egg, and one only. This egg is the islander himself.

The island acquired by our potential islander was not in the remote oceans. It was quite near at home, no palm trees nor boom of surf on the reef, nor any of that kind of thing; but a good solid dwelling-house, rather gloomy, above the landing-place, and beyond, a small farmhouse with sheds, and a few outlying fields. Down on the little landing-bay were three cottages in a row, like coastguards' cottages, all neat and whitewashed.

What could be more cosy and home-like? It was four miles if you walked all round your island, through the gorse and the blackthorn bushes, above the steep rocks of the sea and down in the little glades where the primroses grew. If you walked straight over the two humps of hills, the length of it, through the rocky fields where the cows lay chewing, and through the rather sparse oats, on into the gorse again, and so to the low cliffs' edge, it took you only twenty minutes. And when you came to the edge, you could see another, bigger island lying beyond. But the sea was between you and it. And as you returned over the turf where the short, downland cowslips nodded, you saw to the east still another island, a tiny one this time, like the calf of the cow. This tiny island also belonged to the islander.

Thus it seems that even islands like to keep each other company.

Our islander loved his island very much. In early spring, the little ways and glades were a snow of blackthorn, a vivid white among the Celtic stillness of close green and grey rock, blackbirds calling out in the whiteness their first long, triumphant calls. After the blackthorn and the nestling primroses came the blue apparition of hyacinths, like elfin lakes and slipping sheets of blue, among the bushes and under the glade of trees. And many birds with nests you could peep into, on the island all your own. Wonderful what a great world it was!

Followed summer, and the cowslips gone, the wild roses faintly fragrant through the haze. There was a field of hay, the foxgloves stood looking down. In a little cove, the sun was on the pale granite where you bathed, and the shadow was in the rocks. Before the mist came stealing, you went home through the ripening oats, the glare of the sea fading from the high air as the fog-horn started to moo on the other island. And then the sea-fog went, it was autumn, the oat-sheaves lying prone, the great moon, another island, rose golden out of the sea, and rising higher, the world of the sea was white.

So autumn ended with rain, and winter came, dark skies and dampness and rain, but rarely frost. The island, your island, cowered dark, holding away from you. You could feel, down in the wet, sombre hollows, the resentful spirit coiled upon itself, like a wet dog coiled in gloom, or a snake that is neither asleep nor awake. Then in the night, when the wind left off blowing in great gusts and volleys, as at sea, you felt that your island was a universe, infinite and old as the darkness; not an island at all, but an infinite dark world where all the souls from all the other bygone nights lived on, and the infinite distance was near.

Strangely, from your little island in space, you were gone forth into the dark, great realms of time, where all the souls that never die veer and swoop on their vast, strange errands. The little earthly island has dwindled, like a jumping-off place, into nothingness, for you have jumped off, you know not how, into the dark wide mystery of time, where the past is vastly alive, and the future is not separated off.

This is the danger of becoming an islander. When, in the city, you wear your white spats and dodge the traffic with the fear of death down your spine, then you are quite safe from the terrors of infinite time. The moment is your little islet in time, it is the spatial universe that careers round you.

But once isolate yourself on a little island in the sea of space, and the moment begins to heave and expand in great circles, the solid earth is gone, and your slippery, naked dark soul finds herself out in the timeless world, where the chariots of the so-called dead dash down the old streets of centuries, and souls crowd on the footways that we, in the moment, call bygone years. The souls of all the dead are alive again, and pulsating actively around you. You are out in the other infinity.

Something of this happened to our islander. Mysterious 'feelings' came upon him that he wasn't used to; strange awarenesses of old, far-gone men, and other influences; men of Gaul, with big moustaches, who had been on his island, and had vanished from the face of it, but not out of the air of night. They were there still, hurtling their big, violent, unseen bodies through the night. And there were priests, with golden knives and mistletoe; then other priests with a crucifix; then pirates with murder on the sea.

Our islander was uneasy. He didn't believe, in the day-time, in any of this nonsense. But at night it just was so. He had reduced himself to a single point in space, and, a point being that which has neither length nor breadth, he had to step off it into somewhere else. Just as you must step into the sea, if the waters wash your foothold away, so he had, at night, to step off into the other worlds of undying time.

He was uncannily aware, as he lay in the dark, that the blackthorn grove that seemed a bit uncanny even in the realm of space and day, at night was crying with old men of an invisible race, around the altar stone. What was a ruin under the hornbeam trees by day, was a moaning of blood-stained priests with crucifixes, on the ineffable night. What was a cave and a hidden beach between coarse rocks, became in the invisible dark the purple-lipped imprecation of pirates.

To escape any more of this sort of awareness, our islander daily concentrated upon his material island. Why should it not be the Happy Isle at last? Why not the last small isle of the Hesperides, the perfect place, all filled with his own gracious, blossom-like spirit? A minute world of pure perfection, made by man himself.

He began, as we begin all our attempts to regain Paradise, by spending money. The old, semi-feudal dwelling-house he restored, let in more light, put clear lovely carpets on the floor, clear, flower-petal curtains at the sullen windows, and wines in the cellars of rock. He brought over a buxom housekeeper from the world, and a soft-spoken, much-experienced butler. These two were to be islanders.

In the farmhouse he put a bailiff, with two farm-hands. There were Jersey cows, tinkling a slow bell, among the gorse. There was a call to meals at midday, and the peaceful smoking of chimneys at evening, when rest descended.

A jaunty sailing-boat with a motor accessory rode in the shelter in the bay, just below the row of three white cottages. There was also a little yawl, and two row-boats drawn up on the sand. A fishing-net was drying on its supports, a boatload of new white planks stood criss-cross, a woman was going to the well with a bucket.

In the end cottage lived the skipper of the yacht, and his wife and son. He was a man from the other, large island, at home on this sea. Every fine day he went out fishing, with his son, every fair day there was fresh fish in the island.

In the middle cottage lived an old man and wife, a very faithful couple. The old man was a carpenter, and man of many jobs. He was always working, always the sound of his plane or his saw; lost in his work, he was another kind of islander.

In the third cottage was a mason, a widower with a son and two daughters. With the help of his boy, this man dug ditches and built fences, raised buttresses and erected a new outbuilding, and hewed stone from the little quarry. One daughter worked at the big house.

It was a quiet, busy little world. When the islander brought you over as his guest, you met first the dark-bearded, thin, smiling skipper, Arnold, then his boy Charles. At the house, the smooth-lipped butler who had lived all over the world valeted you, and created that curious creamy-smooth, disarming sense of luxury around you which only a perfect and rather untrustworthy servant can create. He disarmed you and had you at his mercy. The buxom housekeeper smiled and treated you with the subtly respectful familiarity that is only dealt out to the true gentry. And the rosy maid threw a glance at you, as if you were very wonderful, coming from the great outer world. Then you met the smiling but watchful bailiff, who came from Cornwall, and the shy farm-hand from Berkshire, with his clean wife and two little children: then the rather sulky farm-hand from Suffolk. The mason, a Kent man, would talk to you by the yard if you let him. Only the old carpenter was gruff and elsewhere absorbed.

Well then, it was a little world to itself, and everybody feeling very safe, and being very nice to you, as if you were really something special. But it was the islander's world, not yours. He was the Master. The special smile, the special attention was to the Master. They all knew how well off they were. So the islander was no longer Mr. So-and-so. To everyone on the island, even to you yourself, he was 'the Master'.

Well, it was ideal. The Master was no tyrant. Ah, no! He was a delicate, sensitive, handsome Master, who wanted everything perfect and everybody happy. Himself, of course, to be the fount of this happiness and perfection.

But in his way, he was a poet. He treated his guests royally, his servants liberally. Yet he was shrewd, and very wise. He never came the boss over his people. Yet he kept his eye on everything, like a shrewd, blue-eyed young Hermes. And it was amazing what a lot of knowledge he had at hand. Amazing what he knew about Jersey cows, and cheese-making, ditching and fencing, flowers and gardening, ships and the sailing of ships. He

was a fount of knowledge about everything, and this knowledge he imparted to his people in an odd, half-ironical, half-portentous fashion, as if
he really belonged to the quaint, half-real world of the gods.

They listened to him with their hats in their hands. He loved white
clothes; or creamy white; and cloaks, and broad hats. So, in fine weather,
the bailiff would see the elegant tall figure in creamy-white serge coming
like some bird over the fallow, to look at the weeding of the turnips. Then
there would be a doffing of hats, and a few minutes of whimsical, shrewd,
wise talk, to which the bailiff answered admiringly, and the farm-hands
listened in silent wonder, leaning on their hoes. The bailiff was almost
tender, to the Master.

Or, on a windy morning, he would stand with his cloak blowing in the
sticky sea-wind, on the edge of the ditch that was being dug to drain a
little swamp, talking in the teeth of the wind to the man below, who looked
up at him with steady and inscrutable eyes.

Or at evening in the rain he would be seen hurrying across the yard,
the broad hat turned against the rain. And the farm-wife would hurriedly
exclaim: "The Master! Get up, John, and clear him a place on the sofa."
And then the door opened, and it was a cry of: "Why, of all things, if it
isn't the Master! Why, have ye turned out then, of a night like this, to
come across to the like of we?" And the bailiff took his cloak, and the
farm-wife his hat, the two farm-hands drew their chairs to the back, he
sat on the sofa and took a child up near him. He was wonderful with
children, talked to them simply wonderful, made you think of Our Saviour
Himself, said the woman.

He was always greeted with smiles, and the same peculiar deference, as
if he were a higher, but also frailer being. They handled him almost tenderly, and almost with adulation. But when he left, or when they spoke of
him, they had often a subtle, mocking smile on their faces. There was no
need to be afriad of 'the Master'. Just let him have his own way. Only the
old carpenter was sometimes sincerely rude to him; so he didn't care for
the old man.

It is doubtful whether any of them really liked him, man to man, or
even woman to man. But then it is doubtful if he really liked any of
them, as man to man, or man to woman. He wanted them to be happy, and
the little world to be perfect. But anyone who wants the world to be perfect must be careful not to have real likes or dislikes. A general goodwill is
all you can afford.

The sad fact is, alas, that general goodwill is always felt as something
of an insult, by the mere object of it; and so it breeds a quite special
brand of malice. Surely general goodwill is a form of egoism, that it should
have such a result!

Our islander, however, had his own resources. He spent long hours in his library, for he was compiling a book of references to all the flowers mentioned in the Greek and Latin authors. He was not a great classical scholar; the usual public-school equipment. But there are such excellent translations nowadays. And it was so lovely, tracing flower after flower as it blossomed in the ancient world.

So the first year on the island passed by. A great deal had been done. Now the bills flooded in, and the Master, conscientious in all things, began to study them. The study left him pale and breathless. He was not a rich man. He knew he had been making a hole in his capital to get the island into running order. When he came to look, however, there was hardly anything left but hole. Thousands and thousands of pounds had the island swallowed into nothingness.

But surely the bulk of the spending was over! Surely the island would now begin to be self-supporting, even if it made no profit! Surely he was safe. He paid a good many of the bills, and took a little heart. But he had had a shock, and the next year, the coming year, there must be economy, frugality. He told his people so in simple and touching language. And they said: "Why, surely! Surely!"

So, while the wind blew and the rain lashed outside, he would sit in his library with the bailiff over a pipe and pot of beer, discussing farm projects. He lifted his narrow, handsome face, and his blue eyes became dreamy. "*What* a wind!" It blew like cannon-shots. He thought of his island, lashed with foam, and inaccessible, and he exulted. . . . No, he must not lose it. He turned back to the farm projects with the zest of genius, and his hands flicked white emphasis, while the bailiff intoned: "Yes, sir! Yes, sir! You're right, Master!"

But the man was hardly listening. He was looking at the Master's blue lawn shirt and curious pink tie with the fiery red stone, at the enamel sleeve-links, and at the ring with the peculiar scarab. The brown searching eyes of the man of the soil glanced repeatedly over the fine, immaculate figure of the Master, with a sort of slow, calculating wonder. But if he happened to catch the Master's bright, exalted glance, his own eye lit up with a careful cordiality and deference, as he bowed his head slightly.

Thus between them they decided what crops should be sown, what fertilizers should be used in different places, which breed of pigs should be imported, and which line of turkeys. That is to say, the bailiff, by continually cautiously agreeing with the Master, kept out of it, and let the young man have his own way.

The Master knew what he was talking about. He was brilliant at grasping the gist of a book, and knowing how to apply his knowledge. On the whole, his ideas were sound. The bailiff even knew it. But in the man of the soil there was no answering enthusiasm. The brown eyes smiled their cordial deference, but the thin lips never changed. The Master pursed his own flexible mouth in a boyish versatility, as he cleverly sketched in his ideas to the other man, and the bailiff made eyes of admiration, but in his heart he was not attending, he was only watching the Master as he would have watched a queer, caged animal, quite without sympathy, not implicated.

So, it was settled, and the Master rang for Elvery, the butler, to bring a sandwich. He, the Master, was pleased. The butler saw it, and came back with anchovy and ham sandwiches, and a newly opened bottle of vermouth. There was always a newly opened bottle of something.

It was the same with the mason. The Master and he discussed the drainage of a bit of land, and more pipes were ordered, more special bricks, more this, more that.

Fine weather came at last; there was a little lull in the hard work on the island. The Master went for a short cruise in his yacht. It was not really a yacht, just a little bit of a thing. They sailed along the coast of the mainland, and put in at the ports. At every port some friend turned up, the butler made elegant little meals in the cabin. Then the Master was invited to villas and hotels, his people disembarked him as if he were a prince.

And oh, how expensive it turned out! He had to telegraph to the bank for money. And he went home again to economise.

The marsh-marigolds were blazing in the little swamp where the ditches were being dug for drainage. He almost regretted, now, the work in hand. The yellow beauties would not blaze again.

Harvest came, and a bumper crop. There must be a harvest-home supper. The long barn was now completely restored and added to. The carpenter had made long tables. Lanterns hung from the beams of the highpitched roof. All the people of the island were assembled. The bailiff presided. It was a gay scene.

Towards the end of the supper the Master, in a velvet jacket, appeared with his guests. Then the bailiff rose and proposed "The Master! Long life and health to the Master!" All the people drank the health with great enthusiasm and cheering. The Master replied with a little speech: They were on an island in a little world of their own. It depended on them all to make this world a world of true happiness and content. Each must do his part. He hoped he himself did what he could, for his heart was in his island, and with the people of his island.

The butler responded: As long as the island had such a Master, it could not help but be a little heaven for all the people on it. This was seconded with virile warmth by the bailiff and the mason, the skipper was beside himself. Then there was dancing, the old carpenter was fiddler.

But under all this, things were not well. The very next morning came the farm-boy to say that a cow had fallen over the cliff. The Master went to look. He peered over the not very high declivity, and saw her lying dead on a green ledge under a bit of late-flowering broom. A beautiful, expensive creature, already looking swollen. But what a fool, to fall so unnecessarily!

It was a question of getting several men to haul her up the bank, and then of skinning and burying her. No one would eat the meat. How repulsive it all was!

This was symbolic of the island. As sure as the spirits rose in the human breast, with a movement of joy, an invisible hand struck malevolently out of the silence. There must not be any joy, nor even any quiet peace. A man broke a leg, another was crippled with rheumatic fever. The pigs had some strange disease. A storm drove the yacht on a rock. The mason hated the butler, and refused to let his daughter serve at the house.

Out of the very air came a stony, heavy malevolence. The island itself seemed malicious. It would go on being hurtful and evil for weeks at a time. Then suddenly again one morning it would be fair, lovely as a morning in Paradise, everything beautiful and flowing. And everybody would begin to feel a great relief, and a hope for happiness.

Then as soon as the Master was opened out in spirit like an open flower, some ugly blow would fall. Somebody would send him an anonymous note, accusing some other person on the island. Somebody else would come hinting things against one of his servants.

"Some folks think they've got an easy job out here, with all the pickings they make!" the mason's daughter screamed at the suave butler, in the Master's hearing. He pretended not to hear.

"My man says this island is surely one of the lean kine of Egypt, it would swallow a sight of money, and you'd never get anything back out of it," confided the farm-hand's wife to one of the Master's visitors.

The people were not contented. They were not islanders. "We feel we're not doing right by the children," said those who had children. "We feel we're not doing right by ourselves," said those who had no children. And the various families fairly came to hate one another.

Yet the island was so lovely. When there was a scent of honeysuckle and the moon brightly flickering down on the sea, then even the grumblers felt a strange nostalgia for it. It set you yearning, with a wild yearning; perhaps for the past, to be far back in the mysterious past of the island, when the blood had a different throb. Strange floods of passion came over you, strange violent lusts and imaginations of cruelty. The blood and the passion and the lust which the island had known. Uncanny dreams, half-dreams, half-evocated yearnings.

The Master himself began to be a little afraid of his island. He felt here strange, violent feelings he had never felt before, and lustful desires that he had been quite free from. He knew quite well now that his people didn't love him at all. He knew that their spirits were secretly against him, malicious, jeering, envious, and lurking to down him. He became just as wary and secretive with regard to them.

But it was too much. At the end of the second year, several departures took place. The housekeeper went. The Master always blamed self-important women most. The mason said he wasn't going to be monkeyed about any more, so he took his departure, with his family. The rheumatic farmhand left.

And then the year's bills came in, the Master made up his accounts. In spite of good crops, the assets were ridiculous, against the spending. The island had again lost, not hundreds but thousands of pounds. It was incredible. But you simply couldn't believe it! Where had it all gone?

The Master spent gloomy nights and days going through accounts in the library. He was thorough. It became evident, now the housekeeper had gone, that she had swindled him. Probably everybody was swindling him. But he hated to think it, so he put the thought away.

He emerged, however, pale and hollow-eyed from his balancing of unbalanceable accounts, looking as if something had kicked him in the stomach. It was pitiable. But the money had gone, and there was an end of it. Another great hole in his capital. How could people be so heartless?

It couldn't go on, that was evident. He would soon be bankrupt. He had to give regretful notice to his butler. He was afraid to find out how much his butler had swindled him. Because the man was such a wonderful butler, after all. And the farm bailiff had to go. The Master had no regrets in that quarter. The losses on the farm had almost embittered him.

The third year was spent in rigid cutting down of expenses. The island was still mysterious and fascinating. But it was also treacherous and cruel, secretly, fathomlessly malevolent. In spite of all its fair show of white blossom and bluebells, and the lovely dignity of foxgloves bending their rose-red bells, it was your implacable enemy.

With reduced staff, reduced wages, reduced splendour, the third year went by. But it was fighting against hope. The farm still lost a good deal. And once more there was a hole in that remnant of capital. Another hole in that which was already a mere remnant round the old holes. The island was mysterious in this also: it seemed to pick the very money out of your pocket, as if it were an octopus with invisible arms stealing from you in every direction.

Yet the Master still loved it. But with a touch of rancour now.

He spent, however, the second half of the fourth year intensely working on the mainland, to be rid of it. And it was amazing how difficult he found it, to dispose of an island. He had thought that everybody was pining for such an island as his; but not at all. Nobody would pay any price for it. And he wanted now to get rid of it, as a man who wants a divorce at any cost.

It was not till the middle of the fifth year that he transferred it, at a considerable loss to himself, to an hotel company who were willing to speculate in it. They were to turn it into a handy honeymoon-and-golf island.

There, take that, island which didn't know when it was well off. Now be a honeymoon-and-golf island!

II

The Second Island

The islander had to move. But he was not going to the mainland. Oh, no! He moved to the smaller island, which still belonged to him. And he took with him the faithful old carpenter and wife, the couple he never really cared for; also a widow and daughter, who had kept house for him the last year; also an orphan lad, to help the old man.

The small island was very small; but being a hump of rock in the sea, it was bigger than it looked. There was a little track among the rocks and bushes, winding and scrambling up and down around the islet, so that it took you twenty minutes to do the circuit. It was more than you would have expected.

Still, it was an island. The islander moved himself, with all his books, into the commonplace six-roomed house up to which you had to scramble from the rocky landing-place. There were also two joined-together cottages. The old carpenter lived in one, with his wife and the lad, the widow and daughter lived in the other.

At last all was in order. The Master's books filled two rooms. It was already autumn, Orion lifting out of the sea. And in the dark nights, the Master could see the lights on his late island, where the hotel company were entertaining guests who would advertise the new resort for honey-moon-golfers.

On his lump of rock, however, the Master was still master. He explored the crannies, the odd hand-breadths of grassy level, the steep little cliffs where the last harebells hung and the seeds of summer were brown above the sea, lonely and untouched. He peered down the old well. He examined the stone pen where the pig had been kept. Himself, he had a goat.

Yes, it was an island. Always, always underneath among the rocks the Celtic sea sucked and washed and smote its feathery greyness. How many different noises of the sea! Deep explosions, rumblings, strange long sighs and whistling noises; then voices, real voices of people clamouring as if tehy were in a market, under the waters: and again, the far-off ringing of a bell, surely an actual bell! Then a tremendous trilling noise, very long and alarming, and an undertone of hoarse gasping.

On this island there were no human ghosts, no ghosts of any ancient race. The sea, and the spume and the weather, had washed them all out, washed them out so there was only the sound of the sea itself, its own ghost, myriad-voiced, communing and plotting and shouting all winter long. And only the smell of the sea, with a few bristly bushes of gorse and coarse tufts of heather, among the grey, pellucid rocks, in the grey, more-pellucid air. The coldness, the greyness, even the soft, creeping fog of the sea, and the islet of rock humped up in it all, like the last point in space.

Green star Sirius stood over the sea's rim. The island was a shadow. Out at sea a ship showed small lights. Below, in the rocky cove, the row-boat and the motor-boat were safe. A light shone in the carpenter's kitchen. That was all.

Save, of course, that the lamp was lit in the house, where the widow was preparing supper, her daughter helping. The islander went in to his meal. Here he was no longer the Master, he was an islander again and he had peace. The old carpenter, the widow and daughter were all faithfulness itself. The old man worked while ever there was light to see, because he had a passion for work. The widow and her quiet, rather delicate daughter of thirty-three worked for the Master, because they loved looking after him, and they were infinitely grateful for the haven he provided them. But they didn't call him 'the Master'. They gave him his name: 'Mr. Cathcart, sir!' softly and reverently. And he spoke back to them also softly, gently, like people far from the world, afraid to make a noise.

The island was no longer a 'world'. It was a sort of refuge. The islander no longer struggled for anything. He had no need. It was as if he and his few dependents were a small flock of sea-birds alighted on this rock, as they travelled through space, and keeping together without a word. The silent mystery of travelling birds.

He spent most of his day in his study. His book was coming along. The widow's daughter could type out his manuscript for him, she was not un-educated. It was the one strange sound on the island, the typewriter. But soon even its spattering fitted in with the sea's noises, and the wind's.

The months went by. The islander worked away in his study, the people of the island went quietly about their concerns. The goat had a little black kid with yellow eyes. There were mackerel in the sea. The old man went fishing in the row-boat with the lad, when the weather was calm enough; they went off in the motor-boat to the biggest island for the post. And they brought supplies, never a penny wasted. And the days went by, and the nights, without desire, without ennui.

The strange stillness from all desire was a kind of wonder to the islander. He didn't want anything. His soul at last was still in him, his spirit was like a dim-lit cave under water, where strange sea-foliage expands upon the watery atmosphere, and scarcely sways, and a mute fish shadowily slips in and slips away again. All still and soft and uncrying, yet alive as rooted seaweed is alive.

The islander said to himself: "Is this happiness?" He said to himself: "I am turned into a dream. I feel nothing, or I don't know what I feel. Yet it seems to me I am happy."

Only he had to have something upon which his mental activity could work. So he spent long, silent hours in his study, working not very fast, nor very importantly, letting the writing spin softly from him as if it were drowsy gossamer. He no longer fretted whether it were good or not, what he produced. He slowly, softly spun it like gossamer, and if it were to melt away as gossamer in autumn melts, he would not mind. It was only the soft evanescence of gossamy things which now seemed to him permanent. The very mist of eternity was in them. Whereas stone buildings, cathedrals for example, seemed to him to howl with temporary resistance, knowing they must fall at last; the tension of their long endurance seemed to howl forth from them all the time.

Sometimes he went to the mainland and to the city. Then he went elegantly, dressed in the latest style, to his club. He sat in a stall at the theatre, he shopped in Bond Street. He discussed terms for publishing his book. But over his face was that gossamy look of having dropped out of the race of progress, which made the vulgar city people feel they had won it over him, and made him glad to go back to his island.

He didn't mind if he never published his book. The years were blending into a soft mist, from which nothing obtruded. Spring came. There was never a primrose on his island, but he found a winter-aconite. There were two little sprayed bushes of blackthorn, and some wind-flowers. He began to make a list of the flowers of his islet, and that was absorbing. He noted a wild currant bush and watched for the elder flowers on a stunted little tree, then for the first yellow rags of the broom, and wild roses. Bladder campion, orchids stitchwort, celandine, he was prouder of them than if they had been people on his island. When he came across the golden saxifrage, so inconspicuous in a damp corner, he crouched over it in a trance, he knew not for how long, looking at it. Yet it was nothing to look at. As the widow's daughter found, when he showed it her.

He had said to her in real triumph:

"I found the golden saxifrage this morning."

The name sounded splendid. She looked at him with fascinated brown eyes, in which was a hollow ache that frightened him a little.

"Did you, sir? Is it a nice flower?"

He pursed his lips and tilted his brows.

"Well—not showy exactly. I'll show it you if you like."

"I should like to see it."

She was so quiet, so wistful. But he sensed in her a persistency which made him uneasy. She said she was so happy: really happy. She followed him quietly, like a shadow, on the rocky track where there was never room for two people to walk side by side. He went first, and could feel her there, immediately behind him, following so submissively, gloating on him from behind.

It was a kind of pity for her which made him become her lover: though he never realised the extent of the power she had gained over him, and how *she* willed it. But the moment he had fallen, a jangling feeling came upon him, that it was all wrong. He felt a nervous dislike of her. He had not wanted it. And it seemed to him, as far as her physical self went, she had not wanted it either. It was just her will. He went away, and climbed at the risk of his neck down to a ledge near the sea. There he sat for hours, gazing all jangled at the sea, and saying miserably to himself: "We didn't want it. We didn't really want it."

It was the automatism of sex that had caught him again. Not that he hated sex. He deemed it, as the Chinese do, one of the great life-mysteries. But it had become mechanical, automatic, and he wanted to escape that. Automatic sex shattered him, and filled him with a sort of death. He thought he had come through, to a new stillness of desirelessness. Perhaps beyond that there was a new fresh delicacy of desire, an unentered frail communion of two people meeting on untrodden ground.

Be that as it might, this was not it. This was nothing new or fresh. It was automatic, and driven from the will. Even she, in her true self, hadn't wanted it. It was automatic in her.

When he came home, very late, and saw her face white with fear and apprehension of his feeling against her, he pitied her, and spoke to her delicately, reassuringly. But he kept himself remote from her.

She gave no sign. She served him with the same silence, the same hidden hunger to serve him, to be near where he was. He felt her love following him with strange, awful persistency. She claimed nothing. Yet now, when he met her bright, brown, curiously vacant eyes, he saw in them the mute question. The question came direct at him, with a force and a power of will he never realised.

So he succumbed, and asked her again.

"Not," she said, "if it will make you hate me."

"Why should it?" he replied, nettled. "Of course not."

"You know I would do anything on earth for you."

It was only afterwards, in his exasperation, he remembered what she said, and was more exasperated. Why should she pretend to do this for *him*? Why not herself? But in his exasperation, he drove himself deeper in. In order to achieve some sort of satisfaction, which he never did achieve, he abandoned himself to her. Everybody on the island knew. But he did not care.

Then even what desire he had left him, and he felt only shattered. He felt that only with her will had she wanted him. Now he was shattered and full of self-contempt. His island was smirched and spoiled. He had lost his place in the rare, desireless levels of Time to which he had at last arrived, and he had fallen right back. If only it had been true, delicate desire between them, and a delicate meeting on the third rare place where a man might meet a woman, when they were both true to the frail, sensitive, crocus-flame of desire in them. But it had been no such thing: automatic, an act of will, not of true desire, it left him feeling humiliated.

He went away from the islet, in spite of her mute reproach. And he wandered about the continent, vainly seeking a place where he could stay. He was out of key; he did not fit in the world any more.

There came a letter from Flora—her name was Flora—to say she was afraid she was going to have a child. He sat down as if he were shot, and he remained sitting. But he replied to her: "Why be afraid? If it is so, it is so, and we should rather be pleased than afraid."

At this very moment, it happened there was an auction of islands. He got the maps, and studied them. And at the auction he bought, for very little money, another island. It was just a few acres of rock away in the north, on the outer fringe of the isles. It was low, it rose low out of the great ocean. There was not a building, not even a tree on it. Only northern sea-turf, a pool of rain-water, a bit of sedge, rock, and sea-birds. Nothing else. Under the weeping wet western sky.

He made a trip to visit his new possession. For several days, owing to the seas, he could not approach it. Then, in a light sea-mist, he landed, and saw it hazy, low, stretching apparently a long way. But it was illusion. He walked over the wet, springy turf, and dark-grey sheep tossed away from him, spectral, bleating hoarsely. And he came to the dark pool, with the sedge. Then on in the dampness, to the grey sea sucking angrily among the rocks.

This was indeed an island.

So he went home to Flora. She looked at him with guilty fear, but also with a triumphant brightness in her uncanny eyes. And again he was gentle, he reassured her, even he wanted her again, with that curious desire that was almost like toothache. So he took her to the mainland, and they were married, since she was going to have his child.

They returned to the island. She still brought in his meals, her own along with then. She sat and ate with him. He would have it so. The widowed mother preferred to stay in the kitchen. And Flora slept in the guest-room of his house, mistress of his house.

His desire, whatever it was, died in him with nauseous finality. The child would still be months coming. His island was hateful to him, vulgar, a suburb. He himself had lost all his finer distinction. The weeks passed in a sort of prison, in humiliation. Yet he stuck it out, till the child was born. But he was meditating escape. Flora did not even know.

A nurse appeared, and ate at table with them. The doctor came sometimes, and, if the sea were rough, he too had to stay. He was cheery over his whisky.

They might have been a young couple in Golders Green.

The daughter was born at last. The father looked at the baby, and felt depressed, almost more than he could bear. The millstone was tied round his neck. But he tried not to show what he felt. And Flora did not know. She still smiled with a kind of half-witted triumph in her joy, as she got well again. Then she began again to look at him with those aching, suggestive, somehow impudent eyes. She adored him so.

This he could not stand. He told her that he had to go away for a time. She wept, but she thought she had got him. He told her he had settled the best part of his property on her, and wrote down for her what income it would produce. She hardly listened, only looked at him with those heavy, adoring, impudent eyes. He gave her a cheque-book, with the amount of her credit duly entered. This did arouse her interest. And he told her, if she got tired of the island, she could choose her home wherever she wished.

She followed him with those aching, persistent brown eyes, when he left, and he never even saw her weep.

He went straight north, to prepare his third island.

III

The Third Island

The third island was soon made habitable. With cement and the big pebbles from the shingle beach, two men built him a hut, and roofed it with corrugated iron. A boat brought over a bed and table, and three chairs, with a good cupboard, and a few books. He laid in a supply of coal and paraffin and food—he wanted so little.

The house stood near the flat shingle bay where he landed, and where he pulled up his light boat. On a sunny day in August the men sailed away and left him. The sea was still and pale blue. On the horizon he saw the small mail-steamer slowly passing northwards, as if she were walking. She served the outer isles twice a week. He could row out to her if need be, in calm weather, and he could signal her from a flagstaff behind his cottage.

Half a dozen sheep still remained on the island, as company; and he had a cat to rub against his legs. While the sweet, sunny days of the northern autumn lasted, he would walk among the rocks, and over the springy turf of his small domain, always coming to the ceaseless, restless sea. He looked at every leaf, that might be different from another, and he watched the endless expansion and contraction of the water-tossed seaweed. He had never a tree, not even a bit of heather to guard. Only the turf, and tiny turf-plants, and the sedge by the pool, the seaweed in the ocean. He was glad. He didn't want trees or bushes. They stood up like people, too assertive. His bare, low-pitched island in the pale blue sea was all he wanted.

He no longer worked at his book. The interest had gone. He liked to sit on the low elevation of his island, and see the sea; nothing but the pale, quiet sea. And to feel his mind turn soft and hazy, like the hazy ocean. Sometimes, like a mirage, he would see the shadow of land rise hovering to northwards. It was a big island beyond. But quite without substance.

He was soon almost startled when he perceived the steamer on the near horizon, and his heart contracted with fear, lest it were going to pause and molest him. Anxiously he watched it go, and not till it was out of sight did he feel truly relieved, himself again. The tension of waiting for human approach was cruel. He did not want to be approached. He did not want to hear voices. He was shocked by the sound of his own voice, if he inadvertently spoke to his cat. He rebuked himself for having broken the great silence. And he was irritated when his cat would look up at him and mew faintly, plaintively. He frowned at her. And she knew. She was becoming wild, lurking in the rocks, perhaps fishing.

But what he disliked most was when one of the lumps of sheep opened its mouth and baa-ed its hoarse, raucous baa. He watched it, and it looked to him hideous and gross. He came to dislike the sheep very much.

He wanted only to hear the whispering sound of the sea, and the sharp cries of the gulls, cries that came out of another world to him. And best of all, the great silence.

He decided to get rid of the sheep when the boat came. They were accustomed to him now, and stood and stared at him with yellow or colourless eyes, in an insolence that was almost cold ridicule. There was a suggestion of cold indecency about them. He disliked them very much. And when they jumped with staccato jumps off the rocks, and their hoofs made the dry, sharp hit, and the fleece flopped on their square backs, he found them repulsive, degrading.

The fine weather passed, and it rained all day. He lay a great deal on his bed, listening to the water trickling from his roof into the zinc waterbutt, looking through the open door at the rain, the dark rocks, the hidden sea. Many gulls were on the island now: many sea-birds of all sorts. It was another world of life. Many of the birds he had never seen before. His old impulse came over him, to send for a book, to know their names. In a flicker of the old passion, to know the name of everything he saw, he even decided to row out to the steamer. The names of these birds! He must know their names, otherwise he had not got them, they were not quite alive to him.

But the desire left him, and he merely watched the birds as they wheeled or walked around him, watched them vaguely, without discrimination. All interest had left him. Only there was one gull, a big, handsome fellow, who would walk back and forth, back and forth in front of the open door of the cabin, as if he had some mission there. He was big, and pearl-grey, and his roundnesses were as smooth and lovely as a pearl. Only the folded wings had shut black pinions, and on the closed black feathers were three very distinct white dots, making a pattern. The islander wondered very much, why this bit of trimming on the bird out of the far, cold seas. And as the gull walked back and forth, back and forth in front of the cabin, strutting on pale-dusky gold feet, holding up his pale yellow beak, that was curved at the tip, with curious alien importance, the man wondered over him. He was portentous, he had a meaning.

Then the bird came no more. The island, which had been full of sea-birds, the flash of wings, the sound and cut of wings and sharp eerie cries in the air, began to be deserted again. No longer they sat like living eggs on the rocks and turf, moving their heads, but scarcely rising into flight round his feet. No longer they ran across the turf among the sheep, and lifted themselves upon low wings. The host had gone. But some remained, always.

The days shortened, and the world grew eerie. One day the boat came: as if suddenly, swooping down. The islander found it a violation. It was torture to talk to those two men, in their homely clumsy clothes. The air of familiarity around them was very repugnant to him. Himself, he was neatly dressed, his cabin was neat and tidy. He resented any intrusion, the clumsy homeliness, the heavy-footedness of the two fishermen was really repulsive to him.

The letters they had brought he left lying unopened in a little box. In one of them was his money. But he could not bear to open even that one. Any kind of contact was repulsive to him. Even to read his name on an envelope. He hid the letters away.

And the hustle and horror of getting the sheep caught and tied and put in the ship made him loathe with profound repulsion the whole of the animal creation. What repulsive god invented animals and evil-smelling men? To his nostrils, the fishermen and the sheep alike smelled foul; an uncleanness on the fresh earth.

He was still nerve-racked and tortured when the ship at last lifted sail and was drawing away, over the still sea. And sometimes, days after, he would start with repulsion, thinking he heard the munching of sheep.

The dark days of winter drew on. Sometimes there was no real day at all. He felt ill, as if he were dissolving, as if dissolution had already set in inside him. Everything was twilight, outside, and in his mind and soul. Once, when he went to the door, he saw black heads of men swimming in his bay. For some moments he swooned unconscious. It was the shock, the horror of unexpected human approach. The horror in the twilight! And not till the shock had undermined him and left him disembodied, did he realise that the black heads were the heads of seals swimming in. A sick relief came over him. But he was barely conscious, after the shock. Later on, he sat and wept with gratitude, because they were not men. But he never realised that he wept. He was too dim. Like some strange, ethereal animal, he no longer realised what he was doing.

Only he still derived his single satisfaction from being alone, absolutely alone, with the space soaking into him. The grey sea alone, and the footing of his sea-washed island. No other contact. Nothing human to bring its horror into contact with him. Only space, damp, twilit, sea-washed space! This was the bread of his soul.

For this reason, he was most glad when there was a storm, or when the sea was high. Then nothing could get at him. Nothing could come through to him from the outer world. True, the terrific violence of the wind made him suffer badly. At the same time, it swept the world utterly out of existence for him. He always liked the sea to be heavily rolling and tearing. Then no boat could get at him. It was like eternal ramparts round his island.

He kept no track of time, and no longer thought of opening a book. The print, the printed letters, so like the depravity of speech, looked obscene. He tore the brass label from his paraffin stove. He obliterated any bit of lettering in his cabin.

His cat had disappeared. He was rather glad. He shivered at her thin, obtrusive call. She had lived in the coal-shed. And each morning he had put her a dish of porridge, the same as he ate. He washed her saucer with repulsion. He did not like her writhing about. But he fed her scrupulously. Then one day she did not come for her porridge; she always mewed for it. She did not come again.

He prowled about his island in the rain, in a big oilskin coat, not knowing what he was looking at, nor what he went out to see. Time had ceased to pass. He stood for long spaces, gazing from a white, sharp face, with those keen, far-off blue eyes of his, gazing fiercely and almost cruelly at the dark sea under the dark sky. And if he saw the labouring sail of a fishing-boat away on the cold waters, a strange malevolent anger passed over his features.

Sometimes he was ill. He knew he was ill, because he staggered as he walked, and easily fell down. Then he paused to think what it was. And he went to his stores and took out dried milk and malt, and ate that. Then he forgot again. He ceased to register his own feelings.

The days were beginning to lengthen. All winter the weather had been comparatively mild, but with much rain, much rain. He had forgotten the sun. Suddenly, however, the air was very cold, and he began to shiver. A fear came over him. The sky was level and grey, and never a star appeared at night. It was very cold. More birds began to arrive. The island was freezing. With trembling hands he made a fire in his grate. The cold frightened him.

And now it continued, day after day, a dull, deathly cold. Occasional crumblings of snow were in the air. The days were greyly longer, but no change in the cold. Frozen grey daylight. The birds passed away, flying away. Some he saw lying frozen. It was as if all life were drawing away, contracting away from the north, contracting southwards. "Soon," he said to himself, "it will all be gone, and in all these regions nothing will be alive." He felt a cruel satisfaction in the thought.

Then one night there seemed to be a relief; he slept better, did not tremble half-awake, and writhe so much, half-conscious. He had become so used to the quaking and writhing of his body, he hardly noticed it. But when for once it slept deep, he noticed that.

He woke in the morning to a curious whiteness. His window was muffled. It had snowed. He got up and opened his door, and shuddered. Ugh! How cold! All white, with a dark leaden sea, and black rocks curiously speckled with white. The foam was no longer pure. It seemed dirty. And the sea ate at the whiteness of the corpse-like land. Crumbles of snow were silting down the dead air.

On the ground the snow was a foot deep, white and smooth and soft, windless. He took a shovel to clear round his house and shed. The pallor of morning darkened. There was a strange rumbling of far-off thunder in the frozen air, and through the newly-falling snow, a dim flash of lightning. Snow now fell steadily down in the motionless obscurity.

He went out for a few minutes. But it was difficult. He stumbled and fell in the snow, which burned his face. Weak, faint, he toiled home. And when he recovered, took the trouble to make hot milk.

It snowed all the time. In the afternoon again there was a muffled rumbling of thunder, and flashes of lightning blinking reddish through the falling snow. Uneasy, he went to bed and lay staring fixedly at nothingness.

Morning seemed never to come. An eternity long he lay and waited for one alleviating pallor on the night. And at last it seemed the air was paler. His house was a cell faintly illuminated with white light. He realised the snow was walled outside his window. He got up, in the dead cold. When he opened his door, the motionless snow stopped him in a wall as high as his breast. Looking over the top of it, he felt the dead wind slowly driving, saw the snow-powder lift and travel like a funeral train. The blackish sea churned and champed, seeming to bite at the snow, impotent. The sky was grey, but luminous.

He began to work in a frenzy, to get at his boat. If he was to be shut in, it must be by his own choice, not by the mechanical power of the elements. He must get to the sea. He must be able to get at his boat.

But he was weak, and at times the snow overcame him. It fell on him, and he lay buried and lifeless. Yet every time he struggled alive before it was too late, and fell upon the snow with the energy of fever. Exhausted, he would not give in. He crept indoors and made coffee and bacon. Long since he had cooked so much. Then he went at the snow once more. He must conquer the snow, this new, white brute force which had accumulated against him.

He worked in the awful, dead wind, pushing the snow aside, pressing it with his shovel. It was cold, freezing hard in the wind, even when the sun came out for a while, and showed him his white, lifeless surroundings, the black sea rolling sullen, flecked with dull spume, away to the horizons. Yet the sun had power on his face. It was March.

He reached the boat. He pushed the snow away, then sat down under the lee of the boat, looking at the sea, which swirled nearly to his feet, in the high tide. Curiously natural the pebbles looked, in a world gone all uncanny. The sun shone no more. Snow was falling in hard crumbs, that vanished as if by a miracle as they touched the hard blackness of the sea. Hoarse waves rang in the shingle, rushing up at the snow. The wet rocks were brutally black. And all the time the myriad swooping crumbs of snow, demonish, touched the dark sea and disappeared.

During the night there was a great storm. It seemed to him he could hear the vast mass of snow striking all the world with a ceaseless thud; and over it all, the wind roared in strange hollow volleys, in between which came a jump of blindfold lightning, then the low roll of thunder heavier than the wind. When at last the dawn faintly discoloured the dark, the storm had more or less subsided, but a steady wind drove on. The snow was up to the top of his door.

Sullenly, he worked to dig himself out. And he managed through sheer persistency to get out. He was in the tail of a great drift, many feet high. When he got through, the frozen snow was not more than two feet deep. But his island was gone. Its shape was all changed, great heaping white hills rose where no hills had been, inaccessible, and they fumed like volcanoes, but with snow powder. He was sickened and overcome.

His boat was in another, smaller drift. But he had not the strength to clear it. He looked at it helplessly. The shovel slipped from his hands, and he sank in the snow, to forget. In the snow itself, the sea resounded.

Something brought him to. He crept to his house. He was almost without feeling. Yet he managed to warm himself, just that part of him which leaned in snow-sleep over the coal fire. Then again he made hot milk. After which, carefully, he built up the fire.

The wind dropped. Was it night again? In the silence, it seemed he could hear the panther-like dropping of infinite snow. Thunder rumbled nearer, crackled quick after the bleared reddened lightning. He lay in bed in a kind of stupor. The elements! The elements! His mind repeated the word dumbly. You can't win against the elements.

How long it went on, he never knew. Once, like a wraith, he got out and climbed to the top of a white hill on his unrecognisable island. The sun was hot. "It is summer," he said to himself, "and the time of leaves." He looked stupidly over the whiteness of his foreign island, over the waste of the lifeless sea. He pretended to imagine he saw the wink of a sail. Because he knew too well there would never again be a sail on that stark sea.

As he looked, the sky mysteriously darkened and chilled. From far off came the mutter of the unsatisfied thunder, and he knew it was the signal of the snow rolling over the sea. He turned, and felt its breath on him.

A CLEAN, WELL-LIGHTED PLACE
Ernest Hemingway

It was late and every one had left the café except an old man who sat in the shadow the leaves of the tree made against the electric light. In the day time the street was dusty, but at night the dew settled the dust and the old man liked to sit late because he was deaf and now at night it was quiet and he felt the difference. The two waiters inside the café knew that the old man was a little drunk, and while he was a good client they knew that if he became too drunk he would leave without paying, so they kept watch on him.

"Last week he tried to commit suicide," one waiter said.

"Why?"

"He was in despair."

"What about?"

"Nothing."

"How do you know it was nothing?"

"He has plenty of money."

They sat together at a table that was close against the wall near the door of the café and looked at the terrace where the tables were all empty except where the old man sat in the shadow of the leaves of the tree that moved slightly in the wind. A girl and a soldier went by in the street. The street light shone on the brass number on his collar. The girl wore no head covering and hurried beside him.

"The guard will pick him up," one waiter said.

"What does it matter if he gets what he's after?"

"He had better get off the street now. The guard will get him. They went by five minutes ago."

The old man sitting in the shadow rapped on his saucer with his glass. The younger waiter went over to him.

"What do you want?"

The old man looked at him. "Another brandy," he said.

"You'll be drunk," the waiter said. The old man looked at him. The waiter went away.

"He'll stay all night," he said to his colleague. "I'm sleepy now. I never get into bed before three o'clock. He should have killed himself last week."

The waiter took the brandy bottle and another saucer from the counter inside the café and marched out to the old man's table. He put down the saucer and poured the glass full of brandy.

"You should have killed yourself last week," he said to the deaf man. The old man motioned with his finger. "A little more," he said. The waiter poured on into the glass so that the brandy slopped over and ran down the stem into the top saucer of the pile. "Thank you," the old man said. The waiter took the bottle back inside the café. He sat down at the table with his colleague again.

"He's drunk now," he said.

"He's drunk every night."

"What did he want to kill himself for?"

"How should I know."

"How did he do it?"

"He hung himself with a rope."

"Who cut him down?"

"His niece."

"Why did they do it?"

"Fear for his soul."

"How much money has he got?"

"He's got plenty."

"He must be eighty years old."

"Anyway I should say he was eighty."

"I wish he would go home. I never get to bed before three o'clock. What kind of hour is that to go to bed?"

"He stays up because he likes it."

"He's lonely. I'm not lonely. I have a wife waiting in bed for me."

"He had a wife once too."

"A wife would be no good to him now."

"You can't tell. He might be better with a wife."

"His niece looks after him. You said she cut him down."

"I know."

"I wouldn't want to be that old. An old man is a nasty thing."

"Not always. This old man is clean. He drinks without spilling. Even now, drunk. Look at him."

"I don't want to look at him. I wish he would go home. He has no regard for those who must work."

The old man looked from his glass across the square, then over at the waiters.

"Another brandy," he said, pointing to his glass. The waiter who was in a hurry came over.

"Finished," he said, speaking with that omission of syntax stupid people employ when talking to drunken people or foreigners. "No more tonight. Close now."

"Another," said the old man.

"No. Finished." The waiter wiped the edge of the table with a towel and shook his head.

The old man stood up, slowly counted the saucers, took a leather coin purse from his pocket and paid for the drinks, leaving half a peseta tip.

The waiter watched him go down the street, a very old man walking unsteadily but with dignity.

"Why didn't you let him stay and drink?" the unhurried waiter asked. They were putting up the shutters. "It is not half-past two."

"I want to go home to bed."

"What is an hour?"

"More to me than to him."

"An hour is the same."

"You talk like an old man yourself. He can buy a bottle and drink at home."

"It's not the same."

"No, it is not," agreed the waiter with a wife. He did not wish to be unjust. He was only in a hurry.

"And you? You have no fear of going home before your usual hour?"

"Are you trying to insult me?"

"No, hombre, only to make a joke."

"No," the waiter who was in a hurry said, rising from pulling down the metal shutters. "I have confidence. I am all confidence."

"You have youth, confidence, and a job," the older waiter said. "You have everything."

"And what do you lack?"

"Everything but work."

"You have everything I have."

"No. I have never had confidence and I am not young."

"Come on. Stop talking nonsense and lock up."

"I am of those who like to stay late at the café," the older waiter said. "With all those who do not want to go to bed. With all those who need a light for the night."

"I want to go home and into bed."

"We are of two different kinds," the older waiter said. He was now dressed to go home. "It is not only a question of youth and confidence although those things are very beautiful. Each night I am reluctant to close up because there may be some one who needs the café."

"Hombre, there are bodegas open all night long."

"You do not understand. This is a clean and pleasant café. It is well lighted. The light is very good and also, now, there are shadows of the leaves."

"Good night," said the younger waiter.

"Good night," the other said. Turning off the electric light he continued the conversation with himself. It is the light of course but it is necessary that the place be clean and pleasant. You do not want music. Certainly you do not want music. Nor can you stand before a bar with dignity although that is all that is provided for these hours. What did he fear? It was not fear or dread. It was a nothing that he knew too well. It was all a nothing and a man was nothing too. It was only that and light was all it needed and a certain cleanness and order. Some lived in it and never felt it but he knew it all was nada y pues nada y nada y pues nada. Our nada who art in nada, nada be thy name thy kingdom nada thy will be nada in nada as it is in nada. Give us this nada our daily nada and nada us our nada as we nada our nadas and nada us not into nada but deliver us from nada; pues nada. Hail nothing full of nothing, nothing is with thee. He smiled and stood before a bar with a shining steam pressure coffee machine.

"What's yours?" asked the barman.

"Nada."

"Otro loco mas," said the barman and turned away.

"A little cup," said the waiter.

The barman poured it for him.

"The light is very bright and pleasant but the bar is unpolished," the waiter said.

The barman looked at him but did not answer. It was too late at night for conversation.

"You want another copita?" the barman asked.

"No, thank you," said the waiter and went out. He disliked bars and bodegas. A clean, well-lighted café was a very different thing. Now, without thinking further, he would go home to his room. He would lie in the bed and finally, with daylight, he would go to sleep. After all, he said to himself, it is probably only insomnia. Many must have it.

nada: nothing.
nada y pues nada: nothing and, well, nothing.
Otro loco mas: another crazy man.
bodegas: small Spanish bars.

WHY I LIVE AT THE P.O.
Eudora Welty

I was getting along fine with Mama, Papa-Daddy and Uncle Rondo until my sister Stella-Rondo just separated from her husband and came back home again. Mr. Whitaker! Of course I went with Mr. Whitaker first, when he first appeared here in China Grove, taking "Pose Yourself" photos, and Stella-Rondo broke us up. Told him I was one-sided. Bigger on one side than the other, which is a deliberate, calculated falsehood: I'm the same. Stella-Rondo is exactly twelve months to the day younger than I am and for that reason she's spoiled.

She's always had anything in the world she wanted and then she'd throw it away. Papa-Daddy gave her this gorgeous Add-a-Pearl necklace when she was eight years old and she threw it away playing baseball when she was nine, with only two pearls.

So as soon as she got married and moved away from home the first she did was separate! From Mr. Whitaker! This photographer with the pop-eyes she said she trusted. Came home from one of those towns up in Illinois and to our complete surprise brought this child of two.

Mama said she like to made her drop dead for a second. "Here you had this marvelous blonde child and never so much as wrote your mother a word about it," says Mama. "I'm thoroughly ashamed of you." But of course she wasn't.

Stella-Rondo just calmly takes off this *hat*, I wish you could see it. She says, "Why, Mama, Shirley-T.'s adopted, I can prove it."

"How?" says Mama, but all I says was, "H'm!" There I was over the hot stove, trying to stretch two chickens over five people and a completely unexpected child into the bargain, without one moment's notice.

"What do you mean—'H'm!'?" says Stella-Rondo, and Mama says, "I heard that, Sister."

I said that oh, I didn't mean a thing, only that whoever Shirley-T. was, she was the spit-image of Papa-Daddy if he'd cut off his beard, which of course he'd never do in the world. Papa-Daddy's Mama's papa and sulks.

Stella-Rondo got furious! She said, "Sister, I don't need to tell you you got a lot of nerve and always did have and I'll thank you to make no future reference to my adopted child whatsoever."

"Very well," I said. "Very well, very well. Of course I noticed at once she looks like Mr. Whitaker's side too. That frown. She looks like a cross between Mr. Whitaker and Papa-Daddy."

"Well, all I can say is she isn't."

"She looks exactly like Shirley Temple to me," says Mama, but Shirley-T. just ran away from her.

So the first thing Stella-Rondo did at the table was turn Papa-Daddy against me.

"Papa-Daddy," she says. He was trying to cut up his meat. "Papa-Daddy!" I was taken completely by surprise. Papa-Daddy is about a million years old and's got this long-long beard. "Papa-Daddy, Sister says she fails to understand why you don't cut off your beard."

So Papa-Daddy l-a-y-s down his knife and fork! He's real rich. Mama says he is, he says he isn't. So he says, "Have I heard correctly? You don't understand why I don't cut off my beard?"

"Why," I says, "Papa-Daddy, of course I understand, I did not say any such of a thing, the idea!"

He says, "Hussy!"

I says, "Papa-Daddy, you know I wouldn't any more want you to cut off your beard than the man in the moon. It was the farthest thing from my mind! Stella-Rondo sat there and made that up while she was eating breast of chicken."

But he says, "So the postmistress fails to understand why I don't cut off my beard. Which job I got you through my influence with the government. 'Bird's nest'—is that what you call it?"

Not that it isn't the next to smallest P.O. in the entire state of Mississippi.

I says, "Oh, Papa-Daddy," I says, "I didn't say any such of a thing, I never dreamed it was a bird's nest, I have always been grateful though this is the next to smallest P.O. in the state of Mississippi, and I do not enjoy being referred to as a hussy by my own grandfather."

But Stella-Rondo says, "Yes, you did say it too. Anybody in the world could of heard you, that had ears."

"Stop right there," says Mama, looking at *me*.

So I pulled my napkin straight back through the napkin ring and left the table.

As soon as I was out of the room Mama says, "Call her back, or she'll starve to death," but Papa-Daddy says, "This is the beard I started growing on the Coast when I was fifteen years old." He would of gone on till nightfall if Shirley-T. hadn't lost the Milky Way she ate in Cairo.

So Papa-Daddy says, "I am going out and lie in the hammock, and you can all sit here and remember my words: I'll never cut off my beard as long as I live, even one inch, and I don't appreciate it in you at all." Passed right by me in the hall and went straight out and got in the hammock.

It would be a holiday. It wasn't five minutes before Uncle Rondo suddenly appeared in the hall in one of Stella-Rondo's flesh-colored kimonos, all cut on the bias, like something Mr. Whitaker probably thought was gorgeous.

"Uncle Rondo!" I says. "I didn't know who that was! Where are you going?"

"Sister," he says, "get out of my way, I'm poisoned."

"If you're poisoned stay away from Papa-Daddy," I says. "Keep out of the hammock. Papa-Daddy will certainly beat you on the head if you come within forty miles of him. He thinks I deliberately said he ought to cut off his beard after he got me the P.O., and I've told him and told him and told him, and he acts like he just don't hear me. Papa-Daddy must of gone stone deaf."

"He picked a fine day to do it then," says Uncle Rondo, and before you could say "Jack Robinson" flew out in the yard.

What he'd really done, he'd drunk another bottle of that prescription. He does it every single Fourth of July as sure as shooting, and it's horribly expensive. Then he falls over in the hammock and snores. So he insisted on zigzagging right on out to the hammock, looking like a half-wit.

Papa-Daddy woke up with this horrible yell and right there without moving an inch he tried to turn Uncle Rondo against me. I heard every word he said. Oh, he told Uncle Rondo I didn't learn to read till I was eight years old and he didn't see how in the world I ever got the mail put up at the P.O., much less read it all, and he said if Uncle Rondo could only fathom the lengths he had gone to to get me that job! And he said on the other hand he thought Stella-Rondo had a brilliant mind and deserved credit for getting out of town. All the time he was just lying there swinging as pretty as you please and looping out his beard, and poor Uncle Rondo was *pleading* with him to slow down the hammock, it was making him as dizzy as a witch to watch it. But that's what Papa-Daddy likes about a hammock. So Uncle Rondo was too dizzy to get turned against me for the time being. He's Mama's only brother and is a good case of a one-track mind. Ask anybody. A certified pharmacist.

Just then I heard Stella-Rondo raising the upstairs window. While she was married she got this peculiar idea that it's cooler with the windows shut and locked. So she has to raise the window before she can make a soul hear her outdoors.

So she raises the window and says, *"Oh!"* You would have thought she was mortally wounded.

Uncle Rondo and Papa-Daddy didn't even look up, but kept right on with what they were doing. I had to laugh.

I flew up the stairs and threw the door open! I says, "What in the wide world's the matter, Stella-Rondo? You mortally wounded?"

"No," she says, "I am not mortally wounded but I wish you would do me the favor of looking out that window there and telling me what you see."

So I shade my eyes and look out the window.

"I see the front yard," I says.

"Don't you see any human beings?" she says.

"I see Uncle Rondo trying to run Papa-Daddy out of the hammock," I says. "Nothing more. Naturally, it's so suffocating-hot in the house, with all the windows shut and locked, everybody who cares to stay in their right mind will have to go out and get in the hammock before the Fourth of July is over."

"Don't you notice anything different about Uncle Rondo?" asks Stella-Rondo.

"Why, no, except he's got on some terrible-looking flesh-colored contraption I wouldn't be found dead in, is all I can see," I says.

"Never mind, you won't be found dead in it, because it happens to be part of my trousseau, and Mr. Whitaker took several dozen photographs of me in it," says Stella-Rondo. "What on earth could Uncle Rondo *mean* by wearing part of my trousseau out in the broad open daylight without saying so much as 'Kiss my foot,' *knowing* I only got home this morning after my separation and hung my negligee up on the bathroom door, just as nervous as I could be?"

"I'm sure I don't know, and what do you expect me to do about it?" I says. "Jump out the window?"

"No, I expect nothing of the kind. I simply declare that Uncle Rondo looks like a fool in it, that's all," she says. "It makes me sick to my stomach."

"Well, he looks as good as he can," I says. "As good as anybody in reason could." I stood up for Uncle Rondo, please remember. And I said to Stella-Rondo, "I think I would do well not to criticize so freely if I were you and came home with a two-year-old child I had never said a word about, and no explanation whatever about my separation."

"I asked you the instant I entered this house not to refer one more time to my adopted child, and you gave me your word of honor you would not," was all Stella-Rondo would say, and started pulling out every one of her eyebrows with some cheap Kress tweezers.

So I merely slammed the door behind me and went down and made some green-tomato pickle. Somebody had to do it. Of course Mama had turned both the niggers loose; she always said no earthly power could hold one anyway on the Fourth of July, so she wouldn't even try. It turned out that Jaypan fell in the lake and came within a very narrow limit of drowning.

So Mama trots in. Lifts up the lid and says, "H'm! Not very good for your Uncle Rondo in his precarious condition, I must say. Or poor little adopted Shirley-T. Shame on you!"

That made me tired. I says, "Well, Stella-Rondo had better thank her lucky stars it was her instead of me came trotting in with that very peculiar-looking child. Now if it had been me that trotted in from Illinois and brought a peculiar-looking child of two, I shudder to think of the reception I'd of got, much less controlled the diet of an entire family."

"But you must remember, Sister, that you were never married to Mr. Whitaker in the first place and didn't go up to Illinois to live," says Mama, shaking a spoon in my face. "If you had I would of been just as overjoyed to see you and your little adopted girl as I was to see Stella-Rondo, when you wound up with your separation and came on back home."

"You would not," I says.

"Don't contradict me, I would," says Mama.

But I said she couldn't convince me though she talked till she was blue in the face. Then I said, "Besides, you know as well as I do that that child is not adopted."

"She most certainly is adopted," says Mama, stiff as a poker.

I says, "Why, Mama, Stella-Rondo had her just as sure as anything in this world, and just too stuck up to admit it."

"Why, Sister," said Mama. "Here I thought we were going to have a pleasant Fourth of July, and you start right out not believing a word your own baby sister tells you!"

"Just like Cousin Annie Flo. Went to her grave denying the facts of life," I remind Mama.

"I told you if you ever mentioned Annie Flo's name I'd slap your face," says Mama, and slaps my face.

"All right, you wait and see," I says.

"I," says Mama, "I prefer to take my children's word for anything when it's humanly possible." You ought to see Mama, she weighs two hundred pounds and has real tiny feet.

Just then something perfectly horrible occurred to me.

"Mama," I says, "can that child talk?" I simply had to whisper! "Mama, I wonder if that child can be—you know—in any way? Do you realize," I says, "that she hasn't spoken one single, solitary word to a human being up to this minute? This is the way she looks," I says, and I looked like this.

Well, Mama and I just stood there and stared at each other. It was horrible!

"I remember well that Joe Whitaker frequently drank like a fish," says Mama. "I believed to my soul he drank *chemicals*." And without another word she marches to the foot of the stairs and calls Stella-Rondo.

"Stella-Rondo? O-o-o-o-o! Stella-Rondo!"

"What?" says Stella-Rondo from upstairs. Not even the grace to get up off the bed.

"Can that child of yours talk?" asks Mama.

Stella-Rondo says, "Can she what?"

"Talk! Talk!" says Mama. "Burdyburdyburdyburdy!"

So Stella-Rondo yells back, "Who says she can't talk?"

"Sister says so," says Mama.

"You didn't have to tell me, I know whose word of honor don't mean a thing in this house," says Stella-Rondo.

And in a minute the loudest Yankee voice I ever heard in my life yells out, "OE'm Pop-OE the Sailor-r-r-r Ma-a-an!" and then somebody jumps up and down in the upstairs hall. In another second the house would of fallen down.

"Not only talks, she can tap-dance!" calls Stella-Rondo. "Which is more than some people I won't name can do."

"Why, the little precious darling thing!" Mama says, so surprised. "Just as smart as she can be!" Starts talking baby talk right there. Then she turns on me. "Sister, you ought to be thoroughly ashamed! Run upstairs this instant and apologize to Stella-Rondo and Shirley-T."

"Apologize for what?" I says. "I merely wondered if the child was normal, that's all. Now that she's proved she is, why, I have nothing further to say."

But Mama just turned on her heel and flew out, furious. She ran right upstairs and hugged the baby. She believed it was adopted. Stella-Rondo hadn't done a thing but turn her against me from upstairs while I stood there helpless over the hot stove. So that made Mama, Papa-Daddy and the baby all on Stella-Rondo's side.

Next, Uncle Rondo.

I must say that Uncle Rondo has been marvelous to me at various times in the past and I was completely unprepared to be made to jump out of my skin, the way it turned out. Once Stella-Rondo did something perfectly horrible to him—broke a chain letter from Flanders Field—and he took the radio back he had given her and gave it to me. Stella-Rondo was furious! For six months we all had to call her Stella instead of Stella-Rondo, or she wouldn't answer. I always thought Uncle Rondo had all the brains of the entire family. Another time he sent me to Mammoth Cave, with all expenses paid.

But this would be the day he was drinking that prescription, the Fourth of July.

So at supper Stella-Rondo speaks up and says she thinks Uncle Rondo ought to try to eat a little something. So finally Uncle Rondo said he would try a little cold biscuits and ketchup, but that was all. So *she* brought it to him.

"Do you think it wise to disport with ketchup in Stella-Rondo's flesh-colored kimono?" I says. Trying to be considerate! If Stella-Rondo couldn't watch out for her trousseau, somebody had to.

"Any objections?" asks Uncle Rondo, just about to pour out all the ketchup.

"Don't mind what she says, Uncle Rondo," says Stella-Rondo. "Sister has been devoting this solid afternoon to sneering out my bedroom window at the way you look."

"What's that?" says Uncle Rondo. Uncle Rondo has got the most terrible temper in the world. Anything is liable to make him tear the house down if it comes at the wrong time.

So Stella-Rondo says, "Sister says, 'Uncle Rondo certainly does look like a fool in that pink kimono!' "

Do you remember who it was really said that?

Uncle Rondo spills out all the ketchup and jumps out of his chair and tears off the kimono and throws it down on the dirty floor and puts his foot on it. It had to be sent all the way to Jackson to the cleaners and re-pleated.

"So that's your opinion of your Uncle Rondo, it is?" he says. "I look like a fool, do I? Well, that's the last straw. A whole day in this house with nothing to do, and then to hear you come out with a remark like that behind my back!"

"I didn't say any such of a thing, Uncle Rondo," I says, "and I'm not saying who did, either. Why, I think you look all right. Just try to take care of yourself and not talk and eat at the same time," I says. "I think you better go lie down."

"Lie down my foot," says Uncle Rondo. I ought to of known by that he was fixing to do something perfectly horrible.

So he didn't do anything that night in the precarious state he was in— just played Casino with Mama and Stella-Rondo and Shirley-T. and gave Shirley-T. a nickel with a head on both sides. It tickled her nearly to death, and she called him "Papa." But at 6:30 A.M. the next morning, he threw a whole five-cent package of some unsold one-inch firecrackers from the store as hard as he could into my bedroom and they every one went off. Not one bad one in the string. Anybody else, there'd be one that wouldn't go off.

Well, I'm just terribly susceptible to noise of any kind, the doctor has always told me I was the most sensitive person he had ever seen in his whole life, and I was simply prostrated. I couldn't eat! People tell me they heard it as far as the cemetery, and old Aunt Jep Patterson, that had been holding her own so good, thought it was Judgment Day and she was going to meet her whole family. It's usually so quiet here.

And I'll tell you it didn't take me any longer than a minute to make up my mind what to do. There I was with the whole entire house on Stella-Rondo's side and turned against me. If I have anything at all I have pride.

So I just decided I'd go straight down to the P.O. There's plenty of room there in the back, I says to myself.

Well! I made no bones about letting the family catch on to what I was up to. I didn't try to conceal it.

The first thing they knew, I marched in where they were all playing Old Maid and pulled the electric oscillating fan out by the plug, and everything got real hot. Next I snatched the pillow I'd done the needle-point on right off the davenport from behind Papa-Daddy. He went "Ugh!" I beat Stella-Rondo up the stairs and finally found my charm bracelet in her bureau drawer under a picture of Nelson Eddy.

"So that's the way the land lies," says Uncle Rondo. There he was, piecing on the ham. "Well, Sister, I'll be glad to donate my army cot if you got any place to set it up, providing you'll leave right this minute and let me get some peace." Uncle Rondo was in France.

"Thank you kindly for the cot and 'peace' is hardly the word I would select if I had to resort to firecrackers at 6:30 A.M. in a young girl's bedroom," I says back to him. "And as to where I intend to go, you seem to forget my position as postmistress of China Grove, Mississippi," I says. "I've always got the P.O."

Well, that made them all sit up and take notice.

I went out front and started digging up some four-o'clocks to plant around the P.O.

"Ah-ah-ah!" says Mama, raising the window. "Those happen to be my four-o'clocks. Everything planted in that star is mine. I've never known you to make anything grow in your life."

"Very well," I says. "But I take the fern. Even you, Mama, can't stand there and deny that I'm the one watered that fern. And I happen to know where I can send in a box top and get a packet of one thousand mixed seeds, no two the same kind, free."

"Oh, where?" Mama wants to know.

But I says, "Too late. You 'tend to your house, and I'll 'tend to mine. You hear things like that all the time if you know how to listen to the radio. Perfectly marvelous offers. Get anything you want free."

So I hope to tell you I marched in and got that radio, and they could of all bit a nail in two, especially Stella-Rondo, that it used to belong to, and she well knew she couldn't get it back, I'd sue for it like a shot. And I very politely took the sewing-machine motor I helped pay the most on to give Mama for Christmas back in 1929, and a good big calendar, with the first-aid remedies on it. The thermometer and the Hawaiian ukulele certainly were rightfully mine, and I stood on the step-ladder and got all my watermelon-rind preserves and every fruit and vegetable I'd put up, every jar. Then I began to pull the tacks out of the bluebird wall vases on the archway to the dining room.

"Who told you you could have those, Miss Priss?" says Mama, fanning as hard as she could.

"I bought 'em and I'll keep track of 'em," I says. "I'll tack 'em up one on each side the postoffice window, and you can see 'em when you come to ask me for your mail, if you're so dead to see 'em."

"Not I! I'll never darken the door to that post office again if I live to be a hundred," Mama says. "Ungrateful child! After all the money we spent on you at the Normal."

"Me either," says Stella-Rondo. "You can just let my mail lie there and *rot*, for all I care. I'll never come and relieve you of a single, solitary piece."

"I should worry," I says. "And who you think's going to sit down and write you all those big fat letters and postcards, by the way? Mr. Whitaker? Just because he was the only man ever dropped down in China Grove and you got him—unfairly—is he going to sit down and write you a lengthy correspondence after you come home giving no rhyme nor reason whatsoever for your separation and no explanation for the presence of that child? I may not have your brilliant mind, but I fail to see it."

So Mama says, "Sister, I've told you a thousand times that Stella-Rondo simply got homesick, and this child is far too big to be hers," and she says, "Now, why don't you all just sit down and play Casino?"

Then Shirley-T. sticks out her tongue at me in this perfectly horrible way. She has no more manners than the man in the moon. I told her she was going to cross her eyes like that some day and they'd stick.

"It's too late to stop me now," I says. "You should have tried that yesterday. I'm going to the P.O. and the only way you can possibly see me is to visit me there."

So Papa-Daddy says, "You'll never catch me setting foot in that post office, even if I should take a notion into my head to write a letter some place." He says, "I won't have you reachin' out of that little old window with a pair of shears and cuttin' off any beard of mine. I'm too smart for you!"

"We all are," says Stella-Rondo.

But I said, "If you're so smart, where's Mr. Whitaker?"

So then Uncle Rondo says, "I'll thank you from now on to stop reading all the orders I get on postcards and telling everybody in China Grove what you think is the matter with them," but I says, "I draw my own conclusions and will continue in the future to draw them." I says, "If people want to write their inmost secrets on penny postcards, there's nothing in the wide world you can do about it, Uncle Rondo."

"And if you think we'll ever *write* another postcard you're sadly mistaken," says Mama.

"Cutting off your nose to spite your face then," I says. "But if you're all determined to have no more to do with the U. S. mail, think of this: What will Stella-Rondo do now, if she wants to tell Mr. Whitaker to come after her?"

"Wah!" says Stella-Rondo. I knew she'd cry. She had a conniption fit right there in the kitchen.

"It will be interesting to see how long she holds out," I says. "And now— I am leaving."

"Good-bye," says Uncle Rondo.

"Oh, I declare," says Mama, "to think that a family of mine should quarrel on the Fourth of July, or the day after, over Stella-Rondo leaving old Mr. Whitaker and having the sweetest little adopted child! It looks like we'd all be glad!"

"Wah!" says Stella-Rondo, and has a fresh conniption fit.

"*He* left *her*—you mark my words," I says. "That's Mr. Whitaker. I know Mr. Whitaker. After all, I knew him first. I said from the beginning he'd up and leave her. I foretold every single thing that's happened."

"Where did he go?" asks Mama.

"Probably to the North Pole, if he knows what's good for him," I says.

But Stella-Rondo just bawled and wouldn't say another word. She flew to her room and slammed the door.

"Now look what you've gone and done, Sister," says Mama. "You go apologize."

"I haven't got time, I'm leaving," I says.

"Well, what are you waiting around for?" asks Uncle Rondo.

So I just picked up the kitchen clock and marched off, without saying "Kiss my foot" or anything, and never did tell Stella-Rondo good-bye.

There was a nigger girl going along on a little wagon right in front.

"Nigger girl," I says, "come help me haul these things down the hill, I'm going to live in the post office."

Took her nine trips in her express wagon. Uncle Rondo came out on the porch and threw her a nickel.

And that's the last I've laid eyes on any of my family or my family laid eyes on me for five solid days and nights. Stella-Rondo may be telling the most horrible tales in the world about Mr. Whitaker, but I haven't heard them. As I tell everybody, I draw my own conclusions.

But oh, I like it here. It's ideal, as I've been saying. You see, I've got everything cater-cornered, the way I like it. Hear the radio? All the war news. Radio, sewing machine, book ends, ironing board and that great big piano lamp—peace, that's what I like. Butter-bean vines planted all along the front where the strings are.

Of course, there's not much mail. My family are naturally the main people in China Grove, and if they prefer to vanish from the face of the earth, for all the mail they get or the mail they write, why, I'm not going to open my mouth. Some of the folks here in town are taking up for me and some turned against me. I know which is which. There are always people who will quit buying stamps just to get on the right side of Papa-Daddy.

But here I am, and here I'll stay. I want the world to know I'm happy.

And if Stella-Rondo should come to me this minute, on bended knees, and *attempt* to explain the incidents of her life with Mr. Whitaker, I'd simply put my fingers in both my ears and refuse to listen.

UPON THE SWEEPING FLOOD
Joyce Carol Oates

One day in Eden County, in the remote marsh and swamplands to the south, a man named Walter Stuart was stopped in the rain by a sheriff's deputy along a country road. Stuart was in a hurry to get home to his family—his wife and two daughters—after having endured a week at his father's old farm, arranging for his father's funeral, surrounded by aging relatives who had sucked at him for the strength of his youth. He was a stern, quiet man of thirty-nine, beginning now to lose some of the muscular hardness that had always baffled others, masking as it did Stuart's remoteness, his refinement, his faith in discipline and order that seem to have belonged, even in his youth, to a person already grown safely old. He was a district vice-president for one of the gypsum mining plants, a man to whom financial success and success in love had come naturally, without fuss. When only a child he had shifted his faith with little difficulty from the unreliable God of his family's tradition to the things and emotions of this world, which he admired in his thoughtful, rather conservative way, and this faith had given him access, as if by magic, to a communion with persons vastly different from himself—with someone like the sheriff's deputy, for example, who approached him that day in the hard, cold rain. "Is something wrong?" Stuart said. He rolled down the window and had nearly opened the door when the deputy, an old man with gray eyebrows and a slack, sunburned face, began shouting against the wind. "Just the weather, mister. You plan on going far? How far are you going?"

"Two hundred miles," Stuart said. "What about the weather? Is it a hurricane?"

"A hurricane—yes—a hurricane," the man said, bending to shout at Stuart's face. "You better go back to town and stay put. They're evacuating up there. We're not letting anyone through."

A long line of cars and pickup trucks, tarnished and gloomy in the rain, passed them on the other side of the road. "How bad is it?" said Stuart. "Do you need help?"

"Back at town, maybe, they need help," the man said. "They're putting up folks at the schoolhouse and the churches, and different families— The eye was spost to come by here, but last word we got it's veered further south. Just the same, though—"

"Yes, it's good to evacuate them," Stuart said. At the back window of an automobile passing them two children's faces peered out at the rain, white and blurred. "The last hurricane here—"

"Ah, God, leave off of that!" the old man said, so harshly that Stuart felt, inexplicably, hurt. "You better turn around now and get on back to town. You got money they can put you up somewheres good—not with these folks coming along here."

This was said without contempt, but Stuart flinched at its assumptions and, years afterward, he was to remember the old man's remark as the beginning of his adventure. The man's twisted face and unsteady, jumping eyes, his wind-snatched voice, would reappear to Stuart when he puzzled for reasons—but along with the deputy's face there would be the sad line of cars, the children's faces turned toward him, and, beyond them in his memory, the face of his dead father with skin wrinkled and precise as a withered apple.

"I'm going in to see if anybody needs help," Stuart said. He had the car going again before the deputy could even protest. "I know what I'm doing! I know what I'm doing!" Stuart said.

The car lunged forward into the rain, drowning out the deputy's out-raged shouts. The slashing of rain against Stuart's face excited him. Faces staring out of oncoming cars were pale and startled, and Stuart felt rising in him a strange compulsion to grin, to laugh madly at their alarm. . . . He passed cars for some time. Houses looked deserted, yards bare. Things had the look of haste about them, even trees—in haste to rid themselves of their leaves, to be stripped bare. Grass was twisted and wild. A ditch by the road was overflowing and at spots the churning, muddy water stretched across the red clay road. Stuart drove, splashing, through it. After a while his enthusiasm slowed, his foot eased up on the gas pedal. He had not passed any cars or trucks for some time.

The sky had darkened and the storm had increased. Stuart thought of turning back when he saw, a short distance ahead, someone standing in the road. A car approached from the opposite direction. Stuart slowed, bearing to the right. He came upon a farm—a small, run-down one with just a few barns and a small pasture in which a horse stood drooping in the rain. Behind the roofs of the buildings a shifting edge of foliage from the trees beyond curled in the wind, now dark, now silver. In a neat harsh line against the bottom of the buildings the wind had driven up dust and red clay. Rain streamed off roofs, plunged into fat, tilted rain barrels, and exploded back out of them. As Stuart watched, another figure appeared, running out of the house. Both persons—they looked like children—jumped about in the road, waving their arms. A spray of leaves was driven against them and against the muddy windshield of the car that approached and passed them. They turned: a girl and a boy, waving their fists in rage, their faces white and distorted. As the car sped past Stuart, water and mud splashed up in a vicious wave.

When Stuart stopped and opened the door the girl was already there, shouting, "Going the wrong way! Wrong way!" Her face was coarse, pimply about her forehead and chin. The boy pounded up behind her, straining for air. "Where the hell are you going, mister?" the girl cried. "The storm's coming from this way. Did you see that bastard, going right by us? Did you see him? If I see him when I get to town—" A wall of rain struck. The girl lunged forward and tried to push her way into the car; Stuart had to hold her back. "Where are your folks?" he shouted. "Let me in," cried the girl savagely. "We're getting out of here!" "Your folks," said Stuart. He had to cup his mouth to make her hear. "Your folks in there!" "There ain't anybody there— *Goddamn* you," she said, twisting about to slap her brother, who had been pushing at her from behind. She whirled upon Stuart again. "You letting us in, mister? You letting us in?" she screamed, raising her hands as if to claw him. But Stuart's size must have calmed her, for she shouted hoarsely and mechanically: "There ain't nobody in there. Our pa's been gone the last two days. *Last two days.* Gone into town *by himself.* Gone drunk somewhere. He ain't here. He left us here. LEFT US HERE!" Again she rushed at Stuart, and he leaned forward against the steering wheel to let her get in back. The boy was about to follow when something caught his eye back at the farm. "Get in," said Stuart. "Get in. Please. Get in." "My horse there," the boy muttered. "You little bastard! You get in here!" his sister screamed.

But once the boy got in, once the door was closed, Stuart knew that it was too late. Rain struck the car in solid walls and the road, when he could see it, had turned to mud. "Let's go! Let's go!" cried the girl, pounding on the back of the seat. "Turn it around! Go up on our drive and turn it around!" The engine and the wind roared together. "Turn it! Get it going!" cried the girl. There was a scuffle and someone fell against Stuart. "It ain't no good," the boy said. "Let me out." He lunged for the door and Stuart grabbed him. "I'm going back to the house," the boy cried, appealing to Stuart with his frightened eyes, and his sister, giving up suddenly, pushed him violently forward. "It's no use," Stuart said. "Goddamn fool," the girl screamed, "goddamn fool!"

The water was ankle deep as they ran to the house. The girl splashed ahead of Stuart, running with her head up and her eyes wide open in spite of the flying scud. When Stuart shouted to the boy, his voice was slammed back to him as if he were being mocked. "Where are you going? Go to the house! Go to the house!" The boy had turned and was running toward the pasture. His sister took no notice but ran to the house. "Come back, kid!" Stuart cried. Wind tore at him, pushing him back. "What are you—"

The horse was undersized, skinny and brown. It ran to the boy as if it wanted to run him down but the boy, stooping through the fence, avoided the frightened hoofs and grabbed the rope that dangled from the horse's halter. "That's it! That's it!" Stuart shouted as if the boy could hear. At the gate the boy stopped and looked around wildly, up to the sky—he might have been looking for someone who had just called him; then he shook the gate madly. Stuart reached the gate and opened it, pushing it back against the boy, who now turned to gape at him. "What? What are you doing here?" he said.

The thought crossed Stuart's mind that the child was insane. "Bring the horse through!" he said. "We don't have much time."

"What are you doing here?" the boy shouted. The horse's eyes rolled, its mane lifted and haloed about its head. Suddenly it lunged through the gate and jerked the boy off the ground. The boy ran in the air, his legs kicking. "Hang on and bring him around!" Stuart shouted. "Let me take hold!" He grabbed the boy instead of the rope. They stumbled together against the horse. It had stopped now and was looking intently at something just to the right of Stuart's head. The boy pulled himself along the rope, hand over hand, and Stuart held onto him by the strap of his overalls. "He's scairt of you!" the boy said. "He's scairt of you!" Stuart reached over and took hold of the rope above the boy's fingers and tugged gently at it. His face was about a foot away from the horse's. "Watch out for him," said the boy. The horse reared and broke free, throwing Stuart back against the boy. "Hey, hey," screamed the boy, as if mad. The horse turned in mid-air as if whirled about by the wind, and Stuart looked up through his fingers to see its hoofs and a vicious flicking of its tail, and the face of the boy being yanked past him and away with incredible speed. The boy fell heavily on his side in the mud, arms outstretched above him, hands still gripping the rope with wooden fists. But he scrambled to his feet at once and ran alongside the horse. He flung one arm up around its neck as Stuart shouted, "Let him go! Forget about him!" Horse and boy pivoted together back toward the fence, slashing wildly at the earth, feet and hoofs together. The ground erupted beneath them. But the boy landed upright, still holding the rope, still with his arm about the horse's neck. "Let me help," Stuart said. "No," said the boy, "he's my horse, he knows me—" "Have you got him good?" Stuart shouted. "We got—we got each other here," the boy cried, his eyes shut tight.

Stuart went to the barn to open the door. While he struggled with it, the boy led the horse forward. When the door was open far enough, Stuart threw himself against it and slammed it around to the side of the barn. A cloud of hay and scud filled the air. Stuart stretched out his arms, as if pleading with the boy to hurry, and he murmured, "Come on. Please. Come on." The boy did not hear him or even glance at him: his own lips were moving as he caressed the horse's neck and head. The horse's muddy hoof had just begun to grope about the step before the door when something like an explosion came against the back of Stuart's head, slammed his back, and sent him sprawling out at the horse.

"Damn you! Damn you!" the boy screamed. Stuart saw nothing except rain. Then something struck him, his shoulder and hand, and his fingers were driven down into the mud. Something slammed beside him in the mud and he seized it—the horse's foreleg—and tried to pull himself up, insanely, lurching to his knees. The horse threw him backwards. It seemed to emerge out of the air before and above him, coming into sight as though out of a cloud. The boy he did not see at all—only the hoofs—and then the boy appeared, inexplicably, under the horse, peering intently at Stuart, his face struck completely blank. "Damn you!" Stuart heard, "he's my horse! My horse! I hope he kills you!" Stuart crawled back in the water, crab fashion, watching the horse form and dissolve, hearing its vicious tattoo against the barn. The door, swinging madly back and forth, parodied the horse's rage, seemed to challenge its frenzy; then the door was all Stuart heard, and he got to his feet, gasping, to see that the horse was out of sight.

The boy ran bent against the wind, out toward nowhere, and Stuart ran after him. "Come in the house, kid! Come on! Forget about it, kid!" He grabbed the boy's arm. The boy struck at him with his elbow. "He was my horse!" he cried.

In the kitchen of the house they pushed furniture against the door. Stuart had to stand between the boy and the girl to keep them from fighting. "Goddamn sniffling fool," said the girl. "So your goddamn horse run off for the night!" The boy crouched down on the floor, crying steadily. He was about thirteen: small for his age, with bony wrists and face. "We're all going to be blownt to hell, let alone your horse," the girl said. She sat with one big thigh and leg outstretched on the table, watching Stuart. He thought her perhaps eighteen. "Glad you come down to get us?" she said. "Where are you from, mister?" Stuart's revulsion surprised him; he had not supposed there was room in his stunned mind for emotion of this sort. If the girl noticed it she gave no sign, but only grinned at him. "I was—I was on my way home," he said. "My wife and daughters—" It occurred to him that he had forgotten about them entirely. He had not thought of them until now and, even now, no image came to his mind: no woman's face, no little girls' faces. Could he have imagined their lives, their love for him? For an instant he doubted everything. "Wife and daughters," said the girl, as if wondering whether to believe him. "Are they in this storm too?" "No—no," Stuart said. To get away from her he went to the window. He could no longer see the road. Something struck the house and he flinched away. "Them trees!" chortled the girl. "I knew it! Pa always said how he ought to cut them down, so close to the house like they are!

I knew it! I knew it! And the old bastard off safe now where they can't get him!"

"Trees?" said Stuart slowly.

"Them trees! Old oak trees!" said the girl.

The boy, struck with fear, stopped crying suddenly. He crawled on the floor to a woodbox beside the big old iron stove and got in, patting the disorderly pile of wood as if he were blind. The girl ran to him and pushed him. "What are you doing?" Stuart cried in anguish. The girl took no notice of him. "What am I doing?" he said aloud. "What the hell am I doing here?" It seemed to him that the end would come in a minute or two, that the howling outside could get no louder, that the howling inside his mind could get no more intense, no more accusing. A goddamn fool! A goddamn fool! he thought. The deputy's face came to mind, and Stuart pictured himself groveling before the man, clutching at his knees, asking forgiveness and for time to be turned back. . . . Then he saw himself back at the old farm, the farm of his childhood, listening to tales of his father's agonizing sickness, the old peoples' heads craning around, seeing how he took it, their eyes charged with horror and delight. . . . "My wife and daughters," Stuart muttered.

The wind made a hollow, drumlike sound. It seemed to be tolling. The boy, crouching back in the woodbox, shouted: "I ain't scairt! I ain't scairt!" The girl gave a shriek. "Our chicken coop, I'll be gahdammed!" she cried. Try as he could, Stuart could see nothing out the window. "Come away from the window," Stuart said, pulling the girl's arm. She whirled upon him. "Watch yourself, mister," she said, "you want to go out to your gahdamn bastardly worthless car?" Her body was strong and big in her men's clothing; her shoulders looked muscular beneath the filthy shirt. Cords in her young neck stood out. Her hair had been cut short and was now wet, plastered about her blemished face. She grinned at Stuart as if she were about to poke him in the stomach, for fun. "I ain't scairt of what God can do!" the boy cried behind them.

When the water began to bubble up through the floor boards they decided to climb to the attic. "There's an ax!" Stuart exclaimed, but the boy got on his hands and knees and crawled to the corner where the ax was propped before Stuart could reach it. The boy cradled it in his arms. "What do you want with that?" Stuart said, and for an instant his heart was pierced with fear. "Let me take it. I'll take it." He grabbed it out of the boy's dazed fingers.

The attic was about half as large as the kitchen and the roof jutted down sharply on either side. Tree limbs rubbed and slammed against the roof on all sides. The three of them crouched on the middle beam, Stuart with the ax tight in his embrace, the boy pushing against him as if for warmth, and the girl kneeling, with her thighs straining her overalls. She watched the little paneless window at one end of the attic without much emotion or interest, like a large, wet turkey. The house trembled beneath them. "I'm going to the window," Stuart said, and was oddly relieved when the girl did not sneer at him. He crawled forward along the dirty beam, dragging the ax with him, and lay full length on the floor about a yard from the window. There was not much to see. At times the rain relaxed, and objects beneath in the water took shape: tree stumps, parts of buildings, junk whirling about in the water. The thumping on the roof was so loud at that end that he had to crawl backwards to the middle again. "I ain't scairt, nothing God can do!" the boy cried. "Listen to the sniveling baby," said the girl. "He thinks God pays him any mind! Hah!" Stuart crouched beside them, waiting for the boy to press against him again. "As if God gives a good damn about him," the girl said. Stuart looked at her. In the near dark her face did not seem so coarse; the set of her eyes was almost attractive. "You don't think God cares about you?" Stuart said slowly. "No, not specially," the girl said, shrugging her shoulders. "The hell with it. You seen the last one of these?" She tugged at Stuart's arm. "Mister? It was something to see. Me an' Jackie was little then—him just a baby. We drove a far ways north to get out of it. When we come back the roads was so thick with sightseers from the cities! They took all the dead ones floating in the water and put them in one place, part of a swamp they cleared out. The families and things—they were mostly fruit pickers—had to come by on rafts and rowboats to look and see could they find the ones they knew. That was there for a day. The bodies would turn round and round in the wash from the boats. Then the faces all got alike and they wouldn't let anyone come any more and put oil on them and set them afire. We stood on top of the car and watched all that day. I wasn't but nine then."

When the house began to shake, some time later, Stuart cried aloud: "This is it!" He stumbled to his feet, waving the ax. He turned around and around as if he were in a daze. "You goin' to chop somethin' with that?" the boy said, pulling at him. "Hey, no, that ain't yours to—it ain't yours to chop—" They struggled for the ax. The boy sobbed, "It ain't yours! It ain't yours!" and Stuart's rage at his own helplessness, at the folly of his being here, for an instant almost made him strike the boy with the ax. But the girl slapped him furiously. "Get away from him! I swear I'll kill you!" she screamed.

Something exploded beneath them. "That's the windows," the girl muttered, clinging to Stuart, " and how am I to clean it again! The old bastard will want it clean, and mud over everything!" Stuart pushed her away so that he could swing the ax. Pieces of soft, rotted wood exploded back onto his face. The boy screamed insanely as the boards gave way to a deluge of wind and water, and even Stuart wondered if he had made a mistake. The three of them fell beneath the onslaught and Stuart lost the ax, felt the handle slam against his leg. "You! You" Stuart cried, pulling at the girl—

for an instant, blinded by pain, he could not think who he was, what he was doing, whether he had any life beyond this moment. The big-faced, husky girl made no effort to hide her fear and cried, "wait, wait!" But he dragged her to the hole and tried to force her out. "My brother—" she gasped. She seized his wrists and tried to get away. "Get out there! There isn't any time!" Stuart muttered. The house seemed about to collapse at any moment. He was pushing her through the hole, against the shattered wood, when she suddenly flinched back against him and he saw that her cheek was cut and she was choking. He snatched her hands away from her mouth as if he wanted to see something secret: blood welled out between her lips. She coughed and spat blood onto him. "You're all right," he said, oddly pleased. "Now get out there and I'll get the kid. I'll take care of him." This time she managed to crawl through the hole, with Stuart pushing her from behind; when he turned to seize the boy, the boy clung to his neck, sobbing something about God. "God loves you!" Stuart yelled. "Loves the least of you! The least of you!" The girl pulled her brother up in her great arms and Stuart was free to climb through himself.

It was actually quite a while—perhaps an hour—before the battering of the trees and the wind pushed the house in. The roof fell slowly, and the section to which they clung was washed free. "We're going somewheres!" shouted the girl. "Look at the house! That gahdamn old shanty seen the last storm!"

The boy lay with his legs pushed in under Stuart's and had not spoken for some time. When the girl cried, "Look at that!" he tried to burrow in farther. Stuart wiped his eyes to see the wall of darkness dissolve. The rain took on another look—a smooth, piercing, metallic glint, like nails driving against their faces and bodies. There was no horizon. They could see nothing except the rushing water and a thickening mist that must have been rain, miles and miles of rain, slammed by the wind into one great wall that moved remorselessly upon them. "Hang on," Stuart said, gripping the girl. "Hang on to me."

Waves washed over the roof, pushing objects at them with soft, muted thuds—pieces of fence, boards, branches heavy with foliage. Stuart tried to ward them off with his feet. Water swirled around them, sucking at them, sucking the roof, until they were pushed against one of the farm buildings. Something crashed against the roof—another section of the house—and splintered, flying up against the girl. She was thrown backwards, away from Stuart, who lunged after her. They fell into the water while the boy screamed. The girl's arms threshed wildly against Stuart. The water was cold, and its aliveness, its sinister energy, surprised him more than the thought that he would drown—that he would never endure the night. Struggling with the girl, he forced her back to the roof, pushed her up. Bare, twisted nails raked his hands. "Gahdamn you, Jackie, you give a hand!" the girl said as Stuart crawled back up. He lay, exhausted, flat on his stomach and let the water and debris slosh over him.

His mind was calm beneath the surface buzzing. He liked to think that his mind was a clear, sane circle of quiet carefully preserved inside the chaos of the storm—that the three of them were safe within the sanctity of this circle; this was how man always conquered nature, how he subdued things greater than himself. But whenever he did speak to her it was in short grunts, in her own idiom: "This ain't so bad!" or "It'll let up pretty soon!" Now the girl held him in her arms as if he were a child, and he did not have the strength to pull away. Of his own free will he had given himself to this storm, or to the strange desire to save someone in it—but now he felt grateful for the girl, even for her brother, for they had saved him as much as he had saved them. Stuart thought of his wife at home, walking through the rooms, waiting for him; he thought of his daughters in their twin beds, two glasses of water on their bureau. . . . But these people knew nothing of him: in his experience now he did not belong to them. Perhaps he had misunderstood his role, his life? Perhaps he had blundered out of his way, drawn into the wrong life, surrendered to the wrong role. What had blinded him to the possibility of many lives, many masks, many arms that might so embrace him? A word not heard one day, a gesture misinterpreted, a leveling of someone's eyes in a certain unmistakable manner, which he had mistaken just the same! The consequences of such errors might trail insanely into the future, across miles of land, across worlds. He only now sensed the incompleteness of his former life. . . . "Look! Look!" the girl cried, jostling him out of his stupor. "Take a look at that, mister!"

He raised himself on one elbow. A streak of light broke out of the dark. Lanterns, he thought, a rescue party already. . . . But the rain dissolved the light; then it reappeared with a beauty that startled him. "What is it?" the boy screamed. "How come it's here?" They watched it filter through the rain, rays knifing through and showing, now, how buildings and trees crouched close about them. "It's the sun, the sun going down," the girl said. "The sun!" said Stuart, who had thought it was night. "The sun!" They stared at it until it disappeared.

The waves calmed sometime before dawn. By then the roof had lost its peak and water ran unchecked over it, in generous waves and then in thin waves, alternately, as the roof bobbed up and down. The three huddled together with their backs to the wind. Water came now in slow drifts. "It's just got to spread itself out far enough so's it will be even," said the girl, "then it'll go down." She spoke without sounding tired, only a little disgusted—as if things weren't working fast enough to suit her. "Soon as it goes down we'll start toward town and see if there ain't somebody coming out to get us in a boat," she said, chattily and comfortably, into

Stuart's ear. Her manner astonished Stuart, who had been thinking all night of the humiliation and pain he had suffered. "Bet the old bastard will be glad to see us," she said, "even if he did go off like that. Well, he never knew a storm was coming. Me and him get along pretty well—he ain't so bad." She wiped her face; it was filthy with dirt and blood. "He'll buy you a drink, mister, for saving us how you did. That was something to have happen—a man just driving up to get us!" And she poked Stuart in the ribs.

The wind warmed as the sun rose. Rain turned to mist and back to rain again, still falling heavily, and now objects were clear about them. The roof had been shoved against the corner of the barn and a mound of dirt, and eddied there without much trouble. Right about them, in a kind of halo, a thick blanket of vegetation and filth bobbed. The fence had disappeared and the house had collapsed and been driven against a ridge of land. The barn itself had fallen in, but the stone support looked untouched, and it was against this they had been shoved. Stuart thought he could see his car—or something over there where the road used to be.

"I bet it ain't deep. Hell," said the girl, sticking her foot into the water. The boy leaned over the edge and scooped up some of the filth in his hands. "Lookit all the spiders," he said. He wiped his face slowly. "Leave them gahdamn spiders alone," said the girl. "You want me to shove them down your throat?" She slid to the edge and lowered her legs. "Yah, I touched bottom. It ain't bad." But then she began coughing and drew herself back. Her coughing made Stuart cough: his chest and throat were ravaged, shaken. He lay exhausted when the fit left him and realized, suddenly, that they were all sick—that something had happened to them. They had to get off the roof. Now, with the sun up, things did not look so bad: there was a ridge of trees a short distance away on a long, red clay hill. "We'll go over there," Stuart said. "Do you think you can make it?"

The boy played in the filth, without looking up, but the girl gnawed at her lip to show she was thinking. "I spose so," she said. "But him—I don't know about him."

"Your brother? What's wrong?"

"Turn around. Hey, stupid. Turn around." She prodded the boy, who jerked around, terrified, to stare at Stuart. His thin bony face gave way to a drooping mouth. "Gone loony, it looks like," the girl said with a touch of regret. "Oh, he had times like this before. It might go away."

Stuart was transfixed by the boy's stare. The realization of what had happened struck him like a blow, sickening his stomach. "We'll get him over there," he said, making his words sound good. "We can wait there for someone to come. Someone in a boat. He'll be better there."

"I spose so," said the girl vaguely.

Stuart carried the boy while the girl splashed eagerly ahead. The water was sometimes up to his thighs. "Hold on another minute," he pleaded.

The boy stared out at the water as if he thought he were taken somewhere to be drowned. "Put your arms around my neck. Hold on," Stuart said. He shut his eyes and every time he looked up the girl was still a few yards ahead and the hill looked no closer. The boy breathed hollowly, coughing into Stuart's face. His own face and neck were covered with small red bites. Ahead, the girl walked with her shoulders lunged forward as if to hurry her there, her great thighs straining against the water, more than a match for it. As Stuart watched her, something was on the side of his face—in his ear—and with a scream he slapped at it, nearly dropping the boy. The girl whirled around. Stuart slapped at his face and must have knocked it off—probably a spider. The boy, upset by Stuart's outcry, began sucking in air faster and faster as if he were dying. "I'm all right, I'm all right," Stuart whispered, "just hold on another minute. . . ."

When he finally got to the hill the girl helped pull him up. He set the boy down with a grunt, trying to put the boy's legs under him so he could stand. But the boy sank to the ground and turned over and vomited into the water; his body shook as if he were having convulsions. Again the thought that the night had poisoned them, their own breaths had sucked germs into their bodies, struck Stuart with an irresistible force. "Let him lay down and rest," the girl said, pulling tentatively at the back of her brother's belt, as if she were thinking of dragging him farther up the slope. "We sure do thank you, mister," she said.

Stuart climbed to the crest of the hill. His heart pounded madly, blood pounded in his ears. What was going to happen? Was anything going to happen? How disappointing it looked—ridges of land showing through the water and the healthy sunlight pushing back the mist. Who would believe him when he told of the night, of the times when death seemed certain. . . ? Anger welled up in him already as he imagined the tolerant faces of his friends, his children's faces ready to turn to other amusements, other oddities. His wife would believe him; she would shudder, holding him, burying her small face in his neck. But what could she understand of his experience, having had no part in it? . . . Stuart cried out; he had nearly stepped on a tangle of snakes. Were they alive? He backed away in terror. The snakes gleamed wetly in the morning light, heads together as if conspiring. Four . . . five of them—they too had swum for this land, they too had survived the night, they had as much reason to be proud of themselves as Stuart.

He gagged and turned away. Down by the water line the boy lay flat on his stomach and the girl squatted nearby, wringing out her denim jacket. The water behind them caught the sunlight and gleamed mightily, putting them into silhouette. The girl's arms moved slowly, hard with muscle. The boy lay coughing gently. Watching them, Stuart was beset by a strange desire: he wanted to run at them, demand their gratitude, their love. Why should they not love him, when he had saved their lives? When he had lost what he was just the day before, turned now into a different person, a stranger even to himself? Stuart stooped and picked up a rock. A broad hot hand seemed to press against his chest. He threw the rock out into the water and said, "Hey!"

The girl glanced around but the boy did not move. Stuart sat down on the soggy ground and waited. After a while the girl looked away; she spread the jacket out to dry. Great banked clouds rose into the sky, reflected in the water—jagged and bent in the waves. Stuart waited as the sun took over the sky. Mist at the horizon glowed, thinned, gave way to solid shapes. Light did not strike cleanly across the land, but was marred by ridges of trees and parts of buildings, and around a corner at any time Stuart expected to see a rescuing party—in a rowboat or something.

"Hey, mister." He woke; he must have been dozing. The girl had called him. "Hey. Whyn't you come down here? There's all them snakes up there."

Stuart scrambled to his feet. When he stumbled downhill, embarrassed and frightened, the girl said chattily, "The sons of bitches are crawling all over here. He chast some away." The boy was on his feet and looking around with an important air. His coming alive startled Stuart—indeed, the coming alive of the day, of the world, evoked alarm in him. All things came back to what they were. The girl's alert eyes, the firm set of her mouth, had not changed—the sunlight had not changed, or the land, really; only Stuart had been changed. He wondered at it...and the girl must have seen something in his face that he himself did not yet know about, for her eyes narrowed, her throat gulped a big swallow, her arms moved slowly up to show her raw elbows. "We'll get rid of them," Stuart said, breaking the silence. "Him and me. We'll do it."

The boy was delighted. "I got a stick," he said, waving a thin whiplike branch. "There's some over here."

"We'll get them," Stuart said. But when he started to walk, a rock slipped loose and he fell back into the mud. He laughed aloud. The girl, squatting a few feet away, watched him silently. Stuart got to his feet, still laughing. "You know much about it, kid?" he said, cupping his hand on the boy's head.

"About what?" said the boy.

"Killing snakes," said Stuart.

"I spose—I spose you just kill them."

The boy hurried alongside Stuart. "I need a stick," Stuart said; they got him one from the water, about the size of an ax. "Go by that bush," Stuart said, "there might be some there."

The boy attacked the bush in a frenzy. He nearly fell into it. His enthusiasm somehow pleased Stuart, but there were no snakes in the bush. "Go down that way," Stuart ordered. He glanced back at the girl: she watched them. Stuart and the boy went on with their sticks held in mid-air. "God put them here to keep us awake," the boy said brightly. "See we don't forget about Him." Mud sucked at their feet. "Last year we couldn't fire the woods on account of it so dry. This year can't either on account of the water. We got to get the snakes like this."

Stuart hurried as if he had somewhere to go. The boy, matching his steps, went faster and faster, panting, waving his stick angrily in the air. The boy complained about snakes and, listening to him, fascinated by him, in that instant Stuart saw everything. He saw the conventional dawn that had mocked the night, had mocked his desire to help people in trouble; he saw, beyond that, his father's home emptied now even of ghosts. He realized that the God of these people had indeed arranged things, had breathed the order of chaos into forms, had animated them, had animated even Stuart himself forty years ago. The knowledge of this fact struck him about the same way as the nest of snakes had struck him —an image leaping right to the eye, pouncing upon the mind, joining itself with the perceiver. "Hey, hey!" cried the boy, who had found a snake: the snake crawled noisily and not very quickly up the slope, a brown-speckled snake. The boy ran clumsily after it. Stuart was astonished at the boy's stupidity, at his inability to see, now, that the snake had vanished. Still he ran along the slope, waving his stick, shouting, "I'll get you! I'll get you!" This must have been the sign Stuart was waiting for. When the boy turned, Stuart was right behind him. "It got away up there," the boy said. "We got to get it." When Stuart lifted his stick the boy fell back a step but went on in mechanical excitement, "It's up there, gotten hid in the weeds. It ain't me," he said, "it ain't me that—" Stuart's blow struck the boy on the side of the head, and the rotted limb shattered into soft wet pieces. The boy stumbled down toward the water. He was coughing when Stuart took hold of him and began shaking him madly, and he did nothing but cough, violently and with all his concentration, even when Stuart bent to grab a rock and brought it down on his head. Stuart let him fall into the water. He could hear him breathing and he could see, about the boy's lips, tiny flecks or bubbles of blood appearing and disappearing with his breath.

When the boy's eyes opened, Stuart fell upon him. They struggled savagely in the water. Again the boy went limp; Stuart stood, panting, and waited. Nothing happened for a minute or so. But then he saw something—the boy's fingers moving up through the water, soaring to the surface! "Will you quit it!" Stuart screamed. He was about to throw himself upon the boy again when the thought of the boy's life, bubbling out between his lips, moving his fingers, filled him with such outraged disgust that he backed away. He threw the rock out into the water and ran back, stumbling, to where the girl stood.

She had nothing to say: her jaw was hard, her mouth a narrow line, her thick nose oddly white against her dirty face. Only her eyes moved, and these were black, lustrous, at once demanding and terrified. She held a board in one hand. Stuart did not have time to think, but, as he lunged toward her, he could already see himself grappling with her in the mud, forcing her down, tearing her ugly clothing from her body—"Lookit!" she cried, the way a person might speak to a horse, cautious and coaxing, and pointed behind him. Stuart turned to see a white boat moving toward them, a half mile or so away. Immediately his hands dropped, his mouth opened in awe. The girl still pointed, breathing carefully, and Stuart, his mind shattered by the broken sunshine upon the water, turned to the boat, raised his hands, cried out, "Save me! Save me!" He had waded out a short distance by the time the men arrived.

TLÖN, UQBAR, ORBIS TERTIUS
Jorge Luis Borges

translated by james e. irby

I

I owe the discovery of Uqbar to the conjunction of a mirror and an encyclopedia. The mirror troubled the depths of a corridor in a country
house on Gaona Street in Ramos Mejía; the encyclopedia is fallaciously
called *The Anglo-American Cyclopaedia* (New York, 1917) and is a literal but delinquent reprint of the *Encyclopaedia Britannica* of 1902. The
event took place some five years ago. Bioy Casares had had dinner with
me that evening and we became lengthily engaged in a vast polemic concerning the composition of a novel in the first person, whose narrator
would omit or disfigure the facts and indulge in various contradictions
which would permit a few readers—very few readers—to perceive an atro-
cious or banal reality. From the remote depths of the corridor, the mirror
spied upon us. We discovered (such a discovery is inevitable in the late
hours of the night) that mirrors have something monstrous about them.
Then Bioy Casares recalled that one of the heresiarchs of Uqbar had
declared that mirrors and copulation are abominable, because they increase
the number of men. I asked him the origin of this memorable observation
and he answered that it was reproduced in *The Anglo-American Cyclopaedia,* in its article on Uqbar. The house (which we had rented furnished)
had a set of this work. On the last pages of Volume XLVI we found an
article on Upsala; on the first pages of Volume XLVII, one on Ural-Altaic
Languages, but not a word about Uqbar. Bioy, a bit taken aback, consulted the volumes of the index. In vain he exhausted all of the imaginable
spellings: Ukbar, Ucbar, Ooqbar, Ookbar, Oukbahr...Before leaving, he
told me that it was a region of Iraq or of Asia Minor. I must confess that
I agreed with some discomfort. I conjectured that this undocumented
country and its anonymous heresiarch were a fiction devised by Bioy's
modesty in order to justify a statement. The fruitless examination of one
of Justus Perthes' atlases fortified my doubt.

The following day, Bioy called me from Buenos Aires. He told me he had before him the article on Uqbar, in Volume XLVI of the encyclopedia. The heresiarch's name was not forthcoming, but there was a note on his doctrine, formulated in words almost identical to those he had repeated, though perhaps literarily inferior. He had recalled: *Copulation and mirrors are abominable*. The text of the encyclopedia said: *For one of those gnostics, the visible universe was an illusion or (more precisely) a sophism. Mirrors and fatherhood are abominable because they multiply and disseminate that universe*. I told him, in all truthfulness, that I should like to see that article. A few days later he brought it. This surprised me, since the scrupulous cartographical indices of Ritter's *Erdkunde* were plentifully ignorant of the name Uqbar.

The tome Bioy brought was, in fact, Volume XLVI of the *Anglo-American Cyclopaedia*. On the half-title page and the spine, the alphabetical marking (Tor-Ups) was that of our copy, but, instead of 917, it contained 921 pages. These four additional pages made up the article on Uqbar, which (as the reader will have noticed) was not indicated by the alphabetical marking. We later determined that there was no other difference between the volumes. Both of them (as I believe I have indicated) are reprints of the tenth *Encyclopaedia Britannica*. Bioy had acquired his copy at some sale or other.

We read the article with some care. The passage recalled by Bioy was perhaps the only surprising one. The rest of it seemed very plausible, quite in keeping with the general tone of the work and (as is natural) a bit boring. Reading it over again, we discovered beneath its rigorous prose a fundamental vagueness. Of the fourteen names which figured in the geographical part, we only recognized three—Khorasan, Armenia, Erzerum—interpolated in the text in an ambiguous way. Of the historical names, only one: the impostor magician Smerdis, invoked more as a metaphor. The note seemed to fix the boundaries of Uqbar, but its nebulous reference points were rivers and craters and mountain ranges of that same region. We read, for example, that the lowlands of Tsai Khaldun and the Axa Delta marked the southern frontier and that on the islands of the delta wild horses procreate. All this, on the first part of page 918. In the historical section (page 920) we learned that as a result of the religious persecutions of the thirteenth century, the orthodox believers sought refuge on these islands, where to this day their obelisks remain and where it is not uncommon to unearth their stone mirrors. The section on Language and Literature was brief. Only one trait is worthy of recollection: it noted that the literature of Uqbar was one of fantasy and that its epics and legends never referred to reality, but to the two imaginary regions of Mlejnas and Tlön... The bibliography enumerated four volumes which we have not yet found, though the third—Silas Haslam: *History of the Land Called Uqbar*, 1874—figures in the catalogues of Bernard Quaritch's book shop.[1] The first, *Lesbare und lesenswerthe Bemerkungen über das Land Ukkbar in Klein-Asien,* dates from 1641 and is the work of Johannes Valentinus Andreä. This fact is significant; a few years later, I came upon that name in the unsuspected pages of De Quincey (*Writings,* Volume XIII) and learned that it belonged to a German theologian who, in the early seventeenth century, described the imaginary community of Rosae Crucis—a community that others founded later, in imitation of what he had prefigured.

That night we visited the National Library. In vain we exhausted atlases, catalogues, annuals of geographical societies, travelers' and historians' memoirs: no one had ever been in Uqbar. Neither did the general index of Bioy's encyclopedia register that name. The following day, Carlos Mastronardi (to whom I had related the matter) noticed the black and gold covers of the *Anglo-American Cyclopaedia* in a bookshop on Corrientes and Talcahuano...He entered and examined Volume XLVI. Of course, he did not find the slightest indication of Uqbar.

II

Some limited and waning memory of Herbert Ashe, an engineer of the southern railways, persists in the hotel at Adrogué, amongst the effusive honeysuckles and in the illusory depths of the mirrors. In his lifetime, he suffered from unreality, as do so many Englishmen; once dead, he is not even the ghost he was then. He was tall and listless and his tired rectangular beard had once been red. I understand he was a widower, without children. Every few years he would go to England, to visit (I judge from some photographs he showed us) a sundial and a few oaks. He and my father had entered into one of those close (the adjective is excessive) English friendships that begin by excluding confidences and very soon dispense with dialogue. They used to carry out an exchange of books and newspapers and engage in taciturn chess games...I remember him in the hotel corridor, with a mathematics book in his hand, sometimes looking at the irrecoverable colors of the sky. One afternoon, we spoke of the duodecimal system of numbering (in which twelve is written as 10). Ashe said that he was converting some kind of tables from the duodecimal to the sexagesimal system (in which sixty is written as 10). He added that the task had been entrusted to him by a Norwegian, in Rio Grande do Sul. We had known him for eight years and he had never mentioned his sojourn in that region...We talked of country life, of the *capangas,* of the Brazilian etymology of the word *gaucho* (which some old Uruguayans still pronounce *gaúcho*) and nothing more was said—may God forgive me—of duodecimal functions. In September of 1937 (we were not at the

---

[1] Haslam has also published *A General History of Labyrinths.* [Author's note.]

hotel), Herbert Ashe died of a ruptured aneurysm. A few days before, he had received a sealed and certified package from Brazil. It was a book in large octavo. Ashe left it at the bar, where—months later—I found it. I began to leaf through it and experienced an astonished and airy feeling of vertigo which I shall not describe, for this is not the story of my emotions but of Uqbar and Tlön and Orbis Tertius. On one of the nights of Islam called the Night of Nights, the secret doors of heaven open wide and the water in the jars becomes sweeter; if those doors opened, I would not feel what I felt that afternoon. The book was written in English and contained 1001 pages. On the yellow leather back I read these curious words which were repeated on the title page: *A First Encyclopaedia of Tlön. Vol. XI. Hlaer to Jangr.* There was no indication of date or place. On the first page and on a leaf of silk paper that covered one of the color plates there was stamped a blue oval with this inscription: *Orbis Tertius.* Two years before I had discovered, in a volume of a certain pirated encyclopedia, a superficial description of a nonexistent country; now chance afforded me something more precious and arduous. Now I held in my hands a vast methodical fragment of an unknown planet's entire history, with its architecture and its playing cards, with the dread of its mythologies and the murmur of its languages, with its emperors and its seas, with its minerals and its birds and its fish, with its algebra and its fire, with its theological and metaphysical controversy. And all of it articulated, coherent, with no visible doctrinal intent or tone of parody.

In the "Eleventh Volume" which I have mentioned, there are allusions to preceding and succeeding volumes. In an article in the *N. R. F.* which is now classic, Néstor Ibarra has denied the existence of those companion volumes; Ezequiel Martínez Estrada and Drieu La Rochelle have refuted that doubt, perhaps victoriously. The fact is that up to now the most diligent inquiries have been fruitless. In vain we have upended the libraries of the two Americas and of Europe. Alfonso Reyes, tired of these subordinate sleuthing procedures, proposes that we should all undertake the task of reconstructing the many and weighty tomes that are lacking: *ex ungue leonem.* He calculates, half in earnest and half jokingly, that a generation of *tlönistas* should be sufficient. This venturesome computation brings us back to the fundamental problem: Who are the inventors of Tlön? The plural is inevitable, because the hypothesis of a lone inventor—an infinite Leibniz laboring away darkly and modestly—has been unanimously discounted. It is conjectured that this brave new world is the work of a secret society of astronomers, biologists, engineers, metaphysicians, poets, chemists, algebraists, moralists, painters, geometers... directed by an obscure man of genius. Individuals mastering these diverse disciplines are abundant, but not so those capable of inventiveness and

ex ungue leonem: out of the lion's jaws.

less so those capable of subordinating that inventiveness to a rigorous and systematic plan. This plan is so vast that each writer's contribution is infinitesimal. At first it was believed that Tlön was a mere chaos, an irresponsible license of the imagination; now it is known that it is a cosmos and that the intimate laws which govern it have been formulated, at least provisionally. Let it suffice for me to recall that the apparent contradictions of the Eleventh Volume are the fundamental basis for the proof that the other volumes exist, so lucid and exact is the order observed in it. The popular magazines, with pardonable excess, have spread news of the zoology and topography of Tlön; I think its transparent tigers and towers of blood perhaps do not merit the continued attention of *all* men. I shall venture to request a few minutes to expound its concept of the universe.

Hume noted for all time that Berkeley's arguments did not admit the slightest refutation nor did they cause the slightest conviction. This dictum is entirely correct in its application to the earth, but entirely false in Tlön. The nations of this planet are congenitally idealist. Their language and the derivations of their language—religion, letters, metaphysics—all presuppose idealism. The world for them is not a concourse of objects in space; it is a heterogeneous series of independent acts. It is successive and temporal, not spatial. There are no nouns in Tlön's conjectural *Ursprache,* from which the "present" languages and the dialects are derived: there are impersonal verbs, modified by monosyllabic suffixes (or prefixes) with an adverbial value. For example: there is no word corresponding to the word "moon," but there is a verb which in English would be "to moon" or "to moonate." "The moon rose above the river" is *hlör u fang axaxaxas mlö,* or literally: "upward behind the onstreaming it mooned."

The preceding applies to the languages of the southern hemisphere. In those of the northern hemisphere (on whose *Ursprache* there is very little data in the Eleventh Volume) the prime unit is not the verb, but the monosyllabic adjective. The noun is formed by an accumulation of adjectives. They do not say "moon," but rather "round airy-light on dark" or "pale-orange-of-the-sky" or any other such combination. In the example selected the mass of adjectives refers to a real object, but this is purely fortuitous. The literature of this hemisphere (like Meinong's subsistent world) abounds in ideal objects, which are convoked and dissolved in a moment, according to poetic needs. At times they are determined by mere simultaneity. There are objects composed of two terms, one of visual and another of auditory character: the color of the rising sun and the faraway cry of a bird. There are objects of many terms: the sun and the water on a swimmer's chest, the vague tremulous rose color we see with our eyes closed, the sensation of being carried along by a river and also by sleep.

Ursprache: primeval language.

These second-degree objects can be combined with others; through the use of certain abbreviations, the process is practically infinite. There are famous poems made up of one enormous word. This word forms a *poetic object* created by the author. The fact that no one believes in the reality of nouns paradoxically causes their number to be unending. The languages of Tlön's northern hemisphere contain all the nouns of the Indo-European languages—and many others as well.

It is no exaggeration to state that the classic culture of Tlön comprises only one discipline: psychology. All others are subordinated to it. I have said that the men of this planet conceive the universe as a series of mental processes which do not develop in space but successively in time. Spinoza ascribes to his inexhaustible divinity the attributes of extension and thought; no one in Tlön would understand the juxtaposition of the first (which is typical only of certain states) and the second—which is a perfect synonym of the cosmos. In other words, they do not conceive that the spatial persists in time. The perception of a cloud of smoke on the horizon and then of the burning field and then of the half-extinguished cigarette that produced the blaze is considered an example of association of ideas.

This monism or complete idealism invalidates all science. If we explain (or judge) a fact, we connect it with another; such linking, in Tlön, is a later state of the subject which cannot affect or illuminate the previous state. Every mental state is irreducible: the mere fact of naming it—i.e., of classifying it—implies a falsification. From which it can be deduced that there are no sciences on Tlön, not even reasoning. The paradoxical truth is that they do exist, and in almost uncountable number. The same thing happens with philosophies as happens with nouns in the northern hemisphere. The fact that every philosophy is by definition a dialectical game, a *Philosophie des Als Ob,* has caused them to multiply. There is an abundance of incredible systems of pleasing design or sensational type. The metaphysicians of Tlön do not seek for the truth or even for verisimilitude, but rather for the astounding. They judge that metaphysics is a branch of fantastic literature. They know that a system is nothing more than the subordination of all aspects of the universe to any one such aspect. Even the phrase "all aspects" is rejectable, for it supposes the impossible addition of the present and of all past moments. Neither is it licit to use the plural "past moments," since it supposes another impossible operation...One of the schools of Tlön goes so far as to negate time: it reasons that the present is indefinite, that the future has no reality other than as a present hope, that the past has no reality other than as a present memory.[2] Another school declares that *all time* has already transpired and

2 Russell (*The Analysis of Mind,* 1921, page 159) supposes that the planet has been created a few minutes ago, furnished with a humanity that "remembers" an illusory past. [Author's note.]

that our life is only the crepuscular and no doubt falsified and mutilated memory or reflection of an irrecoverable process. Another, that the history of the universe—and in it our lives and the most tenuous detail of our lives—is the scripture produced by a subordinate god in order to communicate with a demon. Another, that the universe is comparable to those cryptographs in which not all the symbols are valid and that only what happens every three hundred nights is true. Another, that while we sleep here, we are awake elsewhere and that in this way every man is two men.

Amongst the doctrines of Tlön, none has merited the scandalous reception accorded to materialism. Some thinkers have formulated it with less clarity than fervor, as one might put forth a paradox. In order to facilitate the comprehension of this inconceivable thesis, a heresiarch of the eleventh century[3] devised the sophism of the nine copper coins, whose scandalous renown is in Tlön equivalent to that of the Eleatic paradoxes. There are many versions of this "specious reasoning," which vary the number of coins and the number of discoveries; the following is the most common:

On Tuesday, X crosses a deserted road and loses nine copper coins. On Thursday, Y finds in the road four coins, somewhat rusted by Wednesday's rain. On Friday, Z discovers three coins in the road. On Friday morning, X finds two coins in the corridor of his house. The heresiarch would deduce from this story the reality—i.e., the continuity—of the nine coins which were recovered. *It is absurd* (he affirmed) *to imagine that four of the coins have not existed between Tuesday and Thursday, three between Tuesday and Friday afternoon, two between Tuesday and Friday morning. It is logical to think that they have existed—at least in some secret way, hidden from the comprehension of men—at every moment of those three periods.*

The language of Tlön resists the formulation of this paradox; most people did not even understand it. The defenders of common sense at first did no more than negate the veracity of the anecdote. They repeated that it was a verbal fallacy, based on the rash application of two neologisms not authorized by usage and alien to all rigorous thought: the verbs "find" and "lose," which beg the question, because they presuppose the identity of the first and of the last nine coins. They recalled that all nouns (man, coin, Thursday, Wednesday, rain) have only a metaphorical value. They denounced the treacherous circumstance "somewhat rusted by Wednesday's rain," which presupposes what is trying to be demonstrated: the persistence of the four coins from Tuesday to Thursday. They explained that *equality* is one thing and *identity* another, and formulated a kind of *reductio ad absurdum:* the hypothetical case of nine men who on nine successive nights suffer a severe pain. Would it not be ridiculous—they

[3] A century, according to the duodecimal system, signifies a period of a hundred and forty-four years. [Author's note.]

questioned—to pretend that this pain is one and the same?[4] They said that the heresiarch was prompted only by the blasphemous intention of attributing the divine category of *being* to some simple coins and that at times he negated plurality and at other times did not. They argued: if equality implies identity, one would also have to admit that the nine coins are one.

Unbelievably, these refutations were not definitive. A hundred years after the problem was stated, a thinker no less brilliant than the heresiarch but of orthodox tradition formulated a very daring hypothesis. This happy conjecture affirmed that there is only one subject, that this indivisible subject is every being in the universe and that these beings are the organs and masks of the divinity. X is Y and is Z. Z discovers three coins because he remembers that X lost them; X finds two in the corridor because he remembers that the others have been found...The Eleventh Volume suggests that three prime reasons determind the complete victory of this idealist pantheism. The first, its repudiation of solipsism; the second, the possibility of preserving the psychological basis of the sciences; the third, the possibility of preserving the cult of the gods. Schopenhauer (the passionate and lucid Schopenhauer) formulates a very similar doctrine in the first volume of *Parerga und Paralipomena.*

The geometry of Tlön comprises two somewhat different disciplines: the visual and the tactile. The latter corresponds to our own geometry and is subordinated to the first. The basis of visual geometry is the surface, not the point. This geometry disregards parallel lines and declares that man in his movement modifies the forms which surround him. The basis of its arithmetic is the notion of indefinite numbers. They emphasize the importance of the concepts of greater and lesser, which our mathematicians symbolize as $>$ and $<$. They maintain that the operation of counting modifies quantities and converts them from indefinite into definite sums. The fact that several individuals who count the same quantity should obtain the same result is, for the psychologists, an example of association of ideas or of a good exercise of memory. We already know that in Tlön the subject of knowledge is one and eternal.

In literary practices the idea of a single subject is also all-powerful. It is uncommon for books to be signed. The concept of plagiarism does not exist: it has been established that all works are the creation of one author, who is atemporal and anonymous. The critics often invent authors: they select two dissimilar works—the *Tao Te Ching* and the *1001 Nights,* say—attribute them to the same writer and then determine most scrupulously the psychology of this interesting *homme de lettres...*

Their books are also different. Works of fiction contain a single plot,

---

[4] Today, one of the churches of Tlön Platonically maintains that a certain pain, a certain greenish tint of yellow, a certain temperature, a certain sound, are the only reality. All men, in the vertiginous moment of coitus, are the same man. All men who repeat a line from Shakespeare *are* William Shakespeare. [Author's note.]

with all its imaginable permutations. Those of a philosophical nature invariably include both the thesis and the antithesis, the rigorous pro and con of a doctrine. A book which does not contain its counterbook is considered incomplete.

Centuries and centuries of idealism have not failed to influence reality. In the most ancient regions of Tlön, the duplication of lost objects is not infrequent. Two persons look for a pencil; the first finds it and says nothing; the second finds a second pencil, no less real, but closer to his expectations. These secondary objects are called *hrönir* and are, though awkward in form, somewhat longer. Until recently, the *hrönir* were the accidental products of distraction and forgetfulness. It seems unbelievable that their methodical production dates back scarcely a hundred years, but this is what the Eleventh Volume tells us. The first efforts were unsuccessful. However, the *modus operandi* merits description. The director of one of the state prisons told his inmates that there were certain tombs in an ancient river bed and promised freedom to whoever might make an important discovery. During the months preceding the excavation the inmates were shown photographs of what they were to find. This first effort proved that expectation and anxiety can be inhibitory; a week's work with pick and shovel did not manage to unearth anything in the way of a *hrön* except a rusty wheel of a period posterior to the experiment. But this was kept in secret and the process was repeated later in four schools. In three of them the failure was almost complete; in the fourth (whose director died accidentally during the first excavations) the students unearthed—or produced—a gold mask, an archaic sword, two or three clay urns and the moldy and mutilated torso of a king whose chest bore an inscription which it has not yet been possible to decipher. Thus was discovered the unreliability of witnesses who knew of the experimental nature of the search... Mass investigations produce contradictory objects; now individual and almost improvised jobs are preferred. The methodical fabrication of *hrönir* (says the Eleventh Volume) has performed prodigious services for archaeologists. It has made possible the interrogation and even the modification of the past, which is now no less plastic and docile than the future. Curiously, the *hrönir* of second and third degree—the *hrönir* derived from another *hrön*, those derived from the *hrön* of a *hrön*—exaggerate the aberrations of the initial one; those of fifth degree are almost uniform; those of ninth degree become confused with those of the second; in those of the eleventh there is a purity of line not found in the original. The process is cyclical: the *hrön* of twelfth degree begins to fall off in quality. Stranger and more pure than any *hrön* is, at times, the *ur:* the object produced through suggestion, educed by hope. The great golden mask I have mentioned is an illustrious example.

Things become duplicated in Tlön; they also tend to become effaced and lose their details when they are forgotten. A classic example is the doorway which survived so long as it was visited by a beggar and disappeared at his death. At times some birds, a horse, have saved the ruins of an amphitheater.

Postscript (1947). I reproduce the preceding article just as it appeared in the *Anthology of Fantastic Literature* (1940), with no omission other than that of a few metaphors and a kind of sarcastic summary which now seems frivolous. So many things have happened since then...I shall do no more than recall them here.

In March of 1941 a letter written by Gunnar Erfjord was discovered in a book by Hinton which had belonged to Herbert Ashe. The envelope bore a cancellation from Ouro Preto; the letter completely elucidated the mystery of Tlön. Its text corroborated the hypotheses of Martínez Estrada. One night in Lucerne or in London, in the early seventeenth century, the splendid history has its beginning. A secret and benevolent society (amongst whose members were Dalgarno and later George Berkeley) arose to invent a country. Its vague initial program included "hermetic studies," philanthropy and the cabala. From this first period dates the curious book by Andreä. After a few years of secret conclaves and premature syntheses it was understood that one generation was not sufficient to give articulate form to a country. They resolved that each of the masters should elect a disciple who would continue his work. This hereditary arrangement prevailed; after an interval of two centuries the persecuted fraternity sprang up again in America. In 1824, in Memphis (Tennessee), one of its affiliates conferred with the ascetic millionaire Ezra Buckley. The latter, somewhat disdainfully, let him speak—and laughed at the plan's modest scope. He told the agent that in America it was absurd to invent a country and proposed the invention of a planet. To this gigantic idea he added another, a product of his nihilism:[5] that of keeping the enormous enterprise secret. At that time the twenty volumes of the *Encyclopaedia Britannica* were circulating in the United States; Buckley suggested that a methodical encyclopedia of the imaginary planet be written. He was to leave them his mountains of gold, his navigable rivers, his pasture lands roamed by cattle and buffalo, his Negroes, his brothels and his dollars, on one condition: "The work will make no pact with the impostor Jesus Christ." Buckley did not believe in God, but he wanted to demonstrate to this nonexistent God that mortal man was capable of conceiving a world. Buckley was poisoned in Baton Rouge in 1828; in 1914 the society delivered to its collaborators, some three hundred in number, the last volume of the First Encyclopedia of Tlön. The edition was a secret one; its forty volumes (the vastest undertaking ever carried out by man) would be the basis for another more detailed edition, written not in English but in one of the languages of Tlön. This revision of an illusory world, was called, provisionally, *Orbis Tertius* and one of its modest demiurgi was Herbert Ashe,

[5] Buckley was a freethinker, a fatalist and a defender of slavery. [Author's note.]

whether as an agent of Gunnar Erfjord or as an affiliate, I do not know. His having received a copy of the Eleventh Volume would seem to favor the latter assumption. But what about the others?

In 1942 events became more intense. I recall one of the first of these with particular clarity and it seems that I perceived then something of its premonitory character. It happened in an apartment on Laprida Street, facing a high and light balcony which looked out toward the sunset. Princess Faucigny Lucinge had received her silverware from Poitiers. From the vast depths of a box embellished with foreign stamps, delicate immobile objects emerged: silver from Utrecht and Paris covered with hard heraldic fauna, and a samovar. Amongest them—with the perceptible and tenuous tremor of a sleeping bird—a compass vibrated mysteriously. The Princess did not recognize it. Its blue needle longed for magnetic north; its metal case was concave in shape; the letters around its edge corresponded to one of the alphabets of Tlön. Such was the first intrusion of this fantastic world into the world of reality.

I am still troubled by a stroke of chance which made me the witness of the second intrusion as well. It happened some months later, at a country store owned by a Brazilian in Cuchilla Negra. Amorim and I were returning from Sant' Anna. The River Tacuarembó had flooded and we were obliged to sample (and endure) the proprietor's rudimentary hospitality. He provided us with some creaking cots in a large room cluttered with barrels and hides. We went to bed, but were kept from sleeping until dawn by the drunken ravings of an unseen neighbor, who intermingled inextricable insults with snatches of *milongas*—or rather with snatches of the same *milonga*. As might be supposed, we attributed this insistent uproar to the store owner's fiery cane liquor. By daybreak, the man was dead in the hallway. The roughness of his voice had deceived us: he was only a youth. In his delirium a few coins had fallen from his belt, along with a cone of bright metal, the size of a die. In vain a boy tried to pick up this cone. A man was scarcely able to raise it from the ground. I held it in my hand for a few minutes; I remember that its weight was intolerable and that after it was removed, the feeling of oppressiveness remained. I also remember the exact circle it pressed into my palm. This sensation of a very small and at the same time extremely heavy object produced a disagreeable impression of repugnance and fear. One of the local men suggested we throw it into the swollen river; Amorim acquired it for a few pesos. No one knew anything about the dead man, except that "he came from the border." These small, very heavy cones (made from a metal which is not of this world) are images of the divinity in certain regions of Tlön.

Here I bring the personal part of my narrative to a close. The rest is in the memory (if not in the hopes or fears) of all my readers. Let it suffice for me to recall or mention the following facts, with a mere brevity of

milonga: a kind of song.

words which the reflective recollection of all will enrich or amplify. Around 1944, a person doing research for the newspaper *The American* (of Nashville, Tennessee) brought to light in a Memphis library the forty volumes of the First Encyclopedia of Tlön. Even today there is a controversy over whether this discovery was accidental or whether it was permitted by the directors of the still nebulous *Orbis Tertius*. The latter is most likely. Some of the incredible aspects of the Eleventh Volume (for example, the multiplication of the *hrönir*) have been eliminated or attenuated in the Memphis copies; it is reasonable to imagine that these omissions follow the plan of exhibiting a world which is not too incompatible with the real world. The dissemination of objects from Tlön over different countries would complement this plan...[6] The fact is that the international press infinitely proclaimed the "find." Manuals, anthologies, summaries, literal versions, authorized re-editions and pirated editions of the Greatest Work of Man flooded and still flood the earth. Almost immediately, reality yielded on more than one account. The truth is that it longed to yield. Ten years ago any symmetry with a semblance of order—dialectical materialism, anti-Semitism, Nazism—was sufficient to entrance the minds of men. How could one do other than submit to Tlön, to the minute and vast evidence of an orderly planet? It is useless to answer that reality is also orderly. Perhaps it is, but in accordance with divine laws—I translate: inhuman laws—which we never quite grasp. Tlön is surely a labyrinth, but it is a labyrinth devised by men, a labyrinth destined to be deciphered by men.

The contact and the habit of Tlön have disintegrated this world. Enchanted by its rigor, humanity forgets over and again that it is a rigor of chess masters, not of angels. Already the schools have been invaded by the (conjectural) "primitive language" of Tlön; already the teaching of its harmonious history (filled with moving episodes) has wiped out the one which governed in my childhood; already a fictitious past occupies in our memories the place of another, a past of which we know nothing with certainty—not even that it is false. Numismatology, pharmacology and archaeology have been reformed. I understand that biology and mathematics also await their avatars...A scattered dynasty of solitary men has changed the face of the world. Their task continues. If our forecasts are not in error, a hundred years from now someone will discover the hundred volumes of the Second Encyclopedia of Tlön.

Then English and French and mere Spanish will disappear from the globe. The world will be Tlön. I pay no attention to all this and go on revising, in the still days at the Adrogué hotel, an uncertain Quevedian translation (which I do not intend to publish) of Browne's *Urn Burial*.

6 There remains, of course, the problem of the *material* of some objects. [Author's note.]

FIVE
Artist, Theme
and Story

When the Irish writer Tom Mac Intyre defines an artist as "someone who has been savaged to a terrible degree and managed to recover and sing about it," he implies that an artist must be able to take his chaotic—often personally painful—experience and transform it into something accessible, entertaining and worthwhile for his audience, such as a song. While there are many contrasting views on what constitutes an artist, almost all views have in common this belief that the artist speaks to his audience by first winnowing his experience: selecting, rejecting, adding to and subtracting from, until he has chosen what he wants to communicate. He then submits this raw material to his artistic medium which, if he is a writer, is words on a page. Unlike life, where events appear to occur at random, stories have an order imposed upon them. By carefully choosing the setting, characters, events, narrator and language, the writer creates a world that is at the same time familiar and strange: familiar because it is constructed out of reflections and refractions of human experience, and strange because of the shape and form imposed upon it.

In the three stories read thus far about a youth's initiation into the world of experience, "A Trifling Occurrence," "My Kinsman, Major Molineux" and "Araby," none contains the kind of vaguely significant childhood incident which most adults recollect at least occasionally. Instead, the incidents and characters are so clearly focused that the reader shares the writer's perception. Each story has at its core an unpleasant incident of great importance to the youngster involved, but one which the adult world may not happen to notice or may choose to ignore. In Chekhov's tale, the children learn that an adult's selfishness, duplicity and pride can cause them great pain, but for the older person remain "a trifling occurrence" hardly worth mentioning. In Joyce's story, the young boy's idealized romantic love contrasts with a saleswoman's casual flirtation with two Englishmen at the bazaar. In this story's commercial setting with its music of coins falling on a silver salver, the boy feels "driven and derided"; tears start to his eyes over his failure to accomplish his knightly errand. Leaving some of his childhood innocence behind, he begins to understand that he has been betrayed by circumstances beyond his control, as well as by his own unwarranted idealism. In "My Kinsman, Major Molineux," Robin has a clear intimation of the price experience costs, for he sees the scorn, ridicule and physical torment his kinsman undergoes at the hands of the mob. Whether the young man realizes now or will realize in the future how much he adds to the pain with his laughter remains unclear. In Mac Intyre's story, "Stallions," a boy discovers the forces of procreation latent in himself and rampant in the world: "It was like watching the start of the world," he exclaims. No wonder he feels flushed and confused finding at night that "the stallion roiled my dreams." For him the occasion is momentous, for the watching men it is amusing, while for his disapproving mother it is distasteful and immoral.

Because stories have order and form they leave us with a sense of completion—a sense which nearly always eludes us in life—and whatever we perceive of human life through experiencing the complete story is its theme. As Frank O'Connor liked to say, a story's theme is "something which is worth something to everybody." Even if physically young, we may, through reading "A Clean Well-Lighted Place," begin to appreciate the difficulty that many people, especially the elderly, have in maintaining their dignity and sense of personal worth in the face of hostility or indifference. The reality of living and dying alone, or of achieving a personal identity, or of fostering deep love relationships knows no national, social, cultural or physical boundaries, as illustrated by stories such as Tillie Olsen's "Tell Me a Riddle," Isaac Bashevis Singer's "The Spinoza of Market Street" and Ralph Ellison's "King of the Bingo Game." The theme of each story is "worth something to everybody."

A theme does not summarize a story's action but attempts to capture in a few words the perception of human life discoverable in the whole story. In "Upon the Sweeping Flood," the careful use of character, event, motivation, setting, language and narrator moves us powerfully into the eye of the storm until we vicariously experience the flood in nature and in man. The hurricane's wind and rain anticipates, then mirrors, the characters' violence. The girl openly expresses her hostility for her absent father and her recalcitrant brother; the boy alternates between willfully asserting himself and submissively withdrawing; Stuart's civilized veneer cracks as he allies himself through murder with "the God [who] . . . had breathed the order of chaos into forms, had animated them, had animated even Stuart himself." Convention, codes of behavior, rational action are all left behind when Stuart surrenders to the chaos that wells up within him. After surviving the ordeal of the stormy night spent on a partially submerged roof, his mind no longer controls nor recognizes the nature of his urge to kill and rape. Like Cain, he murders in a fit of rage and frustration, and "the order of chaos" leaves "his mind shattered by the broken sunshine upon the water." The girl tries to calm him by speaking "the way a person might speak to a horse, cautious and coaxing," for she knows he is a dangerous, maddened animal. His forlorn cry at the end, "Save me! Save me!" further clarifies the theme; for in the context of the whole story Stuart asks to be saved from the unheroic world of work and family, from further physical terror and killing, but above all from what he has become this night.

The theme of "Upon the Sweeping Flood" lies in acknowledging the high price people pay in confronting relentless forces of nature within and without themselves. When pushed beyond endurance they go mad. The narrator of Oates's story economically states this theme when he speaks of "the order of chaos" which asserts itself in the natural world through the devastating storm, and in the human world through the external violence and internal madness of all the characters, but especially through Stuart.

Many stories, such as the ones which open and close *The Choices of Fiction*, remain memorable through repeated readings and tellings, not because they say something new, original or especially profound, but because they describe familiar human desires and situations in an entertaining way. The story Petronius tells of the overly virtuous widow existed long before he retold it, but because of his deft handling of incident, his sharp eye for human weakness and, above all, his artistry which enabled him to invent the surprising, anticlimactic ending, the story is now securely associated with his name.

The concluding selection, "Tale of the Laughing Fish," has amused and instructed audiences for hundreds of years. Handed down orally from generation to generation by storytellers living near the biblical Mount Ararat, and now worn as smooth as pebbles which the ocean polishes for centuries, it exemplifies the concision and surprise which many such ancient stories have. There are no rough edges, no extraneous elements, but everything joins together to delight, entertain and instruct. Before we stop marvelling at a fish that can laugh, our attention is diverted to the boy's prescience, then to his stories of loyal, self-sacrificing pets. Like Scheherazade, the storyteller in *The Thousand and One Nights*, the wise child uses his tales to prolong, then to save, his life. When suspense can no longer be sustained, he concludes swiftly, dramatically and happily. Most of us, hopefully, will never find ourselves in a predicament where a story might save our life, nor are many of us likely to become king for three hours; yet through the magic of stories such as this one, we can enlarge our experience and enrich our lives.

Before men wrote, they told stories, and as long as human beings gather together to entertain or instruct one another there will be the sharing of stories. Reading "Tale of the Laughing Fish" or any other well-told tale is like biting into one of the fabled apples of immortality: while we are absorbed in the imaginative world of the story, our mundane world fades in importance and time waits suspended. The proverb with which "Tale of the Laughing Fish" concludes applies equally well to all good stories: "Three apples fell from heaven; one for the teller of this tale, one for the listener, and one for him who heeds the teller's words."

FINAL REQUEST
Machado de Assis

translated by helen caldwell

"...Item, it is my last wish that the coffin in which my body is buried be made in the shop of Joaquim Soares on the Rua da Alfândega. I wish him to be informed of this disposition, which shall also be made public. Joaquim Soares does not know me; but he is worthy of the honor, as one of our finest craftsmen and one of the most highly respected men in the land..."

This provision of the will was carried out to the letter. Joaquim Soares made the coffin in which poor Nicolau B. de C.'s body was placed. He made it *con amore,* and, finally, in an access of cordiality he begged to be allowed to do it without pay. He was already paid, he said: the mark of favor shown him by the deceased was in itself a notable prize. All he wanted was an exact copy of the paragraph in the will. They gave it to him. He had it framed, and hung it up on a nail in his shop. The other coffinmakers, once their astonishment had passed, protested that the will was a piece of nonsense. Happily—and this is one of the advantages of an organized society—happily, all the other trades and professions thought that this hand, reaching forth from the pit to bless the work of a modest craftsman, performed an act of rare magnanimity. It was in 1855: people were closer then, nobody talked of anything else. The name of Nicolau reverberated for many days in the press of the imperial capital; from there it passed to the provinces. But the life of all of us is full of change, events crowd one upon the other so fast, and, finally, the memory of men is so flimsy, that a day arrived when Nicolau's act was completely sunk in oblivion.

I am not here to restore it. To forget is a necessity. Life is a slate, which destiny, in order to write down a new event, must wipe clean of the one written there. A matter of pencil and sponge. No, no, I am not here to restore it. There are thousands of actions just as handsome, or even more handsome than Nicolau's, that have been eaten away by forgetfulness. I

con amore: with love.

273

have come to tell you that the provision in the will was not an effect without a cause. I have come to describe one of the most morbid curiosities of this century.

Yes, dear reader, we are going to enter full blast into pathology. That little boy you see there toward the end of the last century (when Nicolau died in 1855 he was sixty-eight years old), that little boy was not a sound fruit, he was not a perfect organism. On the contrary, from his tenderest years, he showed by acts repeated time and again that there was deep within him a hidden deformity, an organic flaw. One cannot explain in any other way the persistence with which he would run to destroy the play-things of other little boys. I do not mean toys as good as his or worse than his, but ones that were better or more expensive than his. Still less can one understand why, when the toy was unique or perhaps only rare he consoled the victim with two or three kicks, never less than one. All this is obscure. It could not have been his father's fault. His father was an honest shopkeeper or commission man (most of the persons in this city that are given the title of *merchants*, the Marquis de Lavradio used to say, are nothing more than simple commission men) who lived with a certain pomp in the last quarter of the century, a gruff, austere man, who admonished his son, and, when necessary, punished him. But neither admonishings nor punishments had any effect. Nicolau's inner urge produced more effect than any paternal cane, and once or twice a week the little boy slipped back into his criminal ways. The family was deeply disturbed. There was one instance which, in view of its grave consequences, deserves to be told.

The viceroy, at that time the Count de Rezende, was plagued by the necessity of constructing a dock at Dom Manuel beach. This, which today would be a simple municipal episode, was, in those days in a city of sparse population, an important undertaking. The viceroy had no funds; the public coffers could scarcely meet the ordinary demands upon them. A statesman, and probably a philosopher, the count devised an expedient no less pleasant than profitable: namely, the distribution, in exchange for pecuniary donations, of the posts of captain, lieutenant, and second lieutenant.

When the decree was made public, Nicolau's father saw at once that this was an opportunity to figure, without personal danger, in the military gallery of the age and at the same time to disprove one of the teachings of the Brahmins. For it is written in the laws of Manu that from the arms of Brahma were born the warriors, and from his belly the farmers and merchants. When Nicolau's father received his captain's commission he corrected this point of class anatomy.

Another merchant, who competed with him in everything, though they were close friends, heard of the appointment and went to take his stone to

Manu: One of Classical India's greatest law-givers and philosophers.

the dock also. Unluckily, pique at being a few days behind, prompted him to make a request that was not only in bad taste but, as it turned out, most unfortunate. *He* asked the viceroy to grant a second dock officer's commission (this was the title given to those decorated by this system) to his seven-year-old son. The viceroy hesitated; but the applicant, in addition to the double donation, had influence, and the child came away with the rank of second lieutenant.

It was all done in the greatest secrecy. Nicolau's father did not get wind of the matter till the next Sunday at the Carmo church, where he saw the two of them, father and son, and the boy decked out in a small-size but dashing uniform. Nicolau, who was also there, became livid. In a flash, he threw himself on the young lieutenant and tore his uniform before the parents could come to the rescue. A scandal. The clamor of the mob, the indignation of the devout, and the groans of the victim interrupted the divine service for several minutes. The fathers exchanged several sharp words outside the church door, and remained enemies for life.

"That boy of ours will be the death of us!" shouted Nicolau's father when they got home.

Nicolau got a thrashing, suffered great pain, wept, sobbed; but in the way of improvement? Nothing. Other little boys' playthings were in no less danger. It was the same with their clothes. The more wealthy children of the neighborhood never went outside except in the most inexpensive play clothes, the only way of escaping Nicolau's nails. With the passing of time he extended his aversion to the faces themselves when they were handsome, or considered as such. The street on which he lived boasted an untold number of bruised, scratched, spat-upon faces. Things reached such a pass that his father decided to keep him shut up in the house for three or four months. It was a palliative, and as such excellent. As long as the incarceration lasted, Nicolau was nothing less than angelic. Aside from that morbid habit of his, he was gentle, docile, obedient, fond of his family, regular in his prayers. At the end of four months his father let him loose. It was time to put him in grammar school.

"Leave him with me," said the teacher, "and with that." He pointed to the ferule…"With that it is unlikely he will have an urge to mistreat his companions."

Frivolous, thrice-frivolous teacher! Yes, there is no doubt he succeeded in protecting the handsome little boys and the fancy clothes by punishing poor Nicolau's first onslaughts, but in what respect did this cure him of the malady? On the contrary, obliged to hold himself in, to swallow his impulse, he suffered double, he would become more livid than before—with an overtone of verdigris. Sometimes he was forced to turn away his eyes, or close them, so as not to burst, he said. And, if he left off persecuting the best-looking or best-dressed, he did not spare those who were ahead in their studies: he pommeled them, snatched their books and threw them away on the beach or into the swamp. Brawls, bloodshed, hatreds—these were life's fruits for him, and besides he suffered cruel pain—pain that his family refused to understand. If we add that he could not study anything continuously but only piecemeal and poorly, as tramps eat, nothing regular, nothing methodical, we will have seen some of the distressing consequences of this hidden, morbid condition. His father had cherished the idea of sending his son to the university. When he found himself forced to strangle this dream also, he was ready to curse Nicolau; it was his mother who saved him.

One century departed, another came into being, but the lesion in Nicolau's organism remained. His father died in 1807, his mother in 1809. Three months later his sister married a Dutch physician. Nicolau now lived by himself. He was twenty-three years old, a dandy and man about town—but of a peculiar sort. He could not meet another of his set who either had more noble features or was wearing a specially fine waistcoat, without experiencing a violent pain, so violent that he sometimes had to bite his lip till it bled. Other times his legs grew wobbly and he reeled, or from the corner of his mouth there trickled an almost imperceptible thread of foam. The rest was no less cruel. He would be disgruntled; at home everything seemed bad, uncomfortable, loathsome. He hit the slaves on the head with plates, which were also broken, and kicked the dogs; he was not quiet ten minutes; he did not eat, or only a little. Finally he would go to bed. Sleep repaired everything. He woke up affable and kind, soul of a patriarch blessing all, kissing the dogs between the ears, letting them lick his face, giving them the best he had, calling the slaves the most intimate and endearing things. And all, dogs and slaves, forgot the blows of the night before, and ran at his call, obedient, adoring, as if this were the true master, and not that other man.

One day when he was at his sister's she asked him why he did not take up some career or other, something to occupy his...

"You are right," he said, "I'll look into it."

His brother-in-law chimed in and suggested the diplomatic service. The brother-in-law had begun to suspect he was suffering from some illness and thought a change of climate would restore him to health. Nicolau secured a letter of introduction and went to see the Minister of Foreign Affairs. He found him surrounded by several subsecretaries, on the point of leaving for the palace to bring the news of the second fall of Napoleon, news that had arrived a few minutes before. The presence of the minister, the solemnity of the moment, the bowing and scraping of the secretaries, all this so struck at Nicolau's heart that he could not look the minister in the face. He tried, six or eight times, to lift his eyes, and the one time he succeeded they were so crossed that he saw no one, or only a shadow, a shape, that hurt his pupils; at the same time, his face turned green. He stepped back, extended a trembling hand to the draperies in the doorway, and fled.

"I don't want to be anything," he said to his sister when he got home. "I have you and my friends."

The "friends" were the most obnoxious young men in the city, commonplace and coarse. Nicolau had chosen them carefully. To live without the company of the important men of the community was a great sacrifice for him, but, since he would have suffered much more living with them, he put up with it. This proves that he had a certain empirical understanding of his malady and of the way to relieve it. With those companions of his, all Nicolau's physiological disorders vanished. He could gaze at them without becoming livid, without squinting, without his legs giving way, without anything. Besides, they not only spared his natural irritability, they exerted themselves to render his life, if not pleasant, at least calm. And to this end they kept paying him the finest compliments in the world, in fawning attitudes, or with a certain obsequious familiarity. Nicolau loved inferior natures in general, as the sick love the drug that restores them to health: he petted them in a fatherly manner, heaped them with affectionate praise, lent them money, presented them with delicate and thoughtful gifts, opened up his heart to them...

Then came the Shout of Independence at Ypiringa. Nicolau entered politics. The year 1823 found him in the Constituent Assembly. Words cannot describe the way he fulfilled the duties of his post. An upright, disinterested patriot! But it was not without cost that he practiced these public virtues; it was only at the price of great spiritual turbulence. Speaking metaphorically, one may say that the meetings of the assembly cost him precious blood. It was not only because the debates seemed intolerable, but also because it was hard for him to look at certain men, especially on certain days. Montezuma, for example, seemed flabby to him, Vergueiro crude, the Andradas detestable. Each speech, not only of the leading orators, but even of the second-rate ones, was a genuine torture for him. Still, he remained steadfast, punctual. The balloting never found him absent, his name never sounded through the august chamber without an echo. Whatever might be his own desperation, he was able to contain himself and place the idea of country above his own comfort. It may be that in his heart he applauded the decree for dissolution. I do not affirm it, but there is good reason to believe that Nicolau, in spite of outward appearances, enjoyed seeing the assembly dispersed. And, if that conjecture is true, this one will be no less so—that the deportation of some of the Constituent leaders, who were declared enemies of the people, damped that pleasure. Nicolau, who had suffered from their speeches, suffered no less from their exile, inasmuch as it gave them a certain importance. If only he, too, had been exiled!

"You could get married, brother," his sister said to him.

"I don't have a bride."

"I'll get you one. Shall I?"

It was a scheme of her husband's. In his opinion the nature of Nicolau's malady was plain: it was a worm in his spleen that fed on the pain of the patient, that is to say, on a special secretion produced by the sight of certain acts, situations, or persons. It was only a question of killing the worm; but, since he did not know of any chemical substance capable of destroying it, his only recourse was to prevent the secretion—which would produce the same effect. He therefore urged Nicolau to marry some pretty and accomplished girl, to leave the city, and get a place in the country, to which he would take his finest table ware, finest furniture, most disreputable friends, et cetera.

"Every morning," the brother-in-law confided to his wife, "Nicolau will receive a newspaper that I shall have specially printed for the sole purpose of telling him the most agreeable things in the world, and naming them one by one, recalling his modest but helpful labors in the Constituent Assembly, and imputing to him many amorous adventures, flashes of keen-wittedness, and acts of courage. I have already spoken to the Dutch admiral about having some of our officers wait on Nicolau, from time to time, to tell him they cannot return to The Hague without having the honor of meeting such an eminent and charming citizen, in whom are united rare qualities ordinarily scattered over many individuals. Now you, if you can get some modiste, Gudin for example, to name a hat or a little ruffled cape after Nicolau, it would be of great help in the cure of your dear brother. Anonymous love letters sent through the mail are an effective remedy...But let us begin with the beginning, that is, to marry him."

Never was a plan more conscientiously carried out. The bride chosen for him was the most elegant, or one of the most elegant, in the capital. The bishop himself married them. When they withdrew to the country, only some of Nicolau's most worthless friends went along. The newspaper was fabricated, the love letters sent, the official visits duly paid. For three months everything worked like a charm. But nature, sworn to cheat and cozen man, once more showed that she possesses surprising hidden powers.

One of the ways of giving pleasure to Nicolau was to praise the beauty, elegance, and virtues of his wife; but the disease had progressed, and what should have been an excellent medicine was a simple aggravation of the complaint. After a certain length of time Nicolau began to find all these eulogies of his wife otiose and excessive. And this was enough to exasperate him, and exasperation produced the deadly secretion. It seems he even reached a point where he could not look at her for very long, and scarcely ever did look at her. Then there occurred several rows, which would have been the beginning of a separation if she had not shortly died. Nicolau's grief was profound and genuine, but the cure was interrupted because he went back to Rio de Janeiro, where we find him some time later among the revolutionaries of 1831.

Although it may seem rash to suggest the reasons that led Nicolau to the Campo da Acclamação on the night of the sixth of April, I believe one will not be far from the truth if he supposes (it is the reasoning of a famous though anonymous Athenian) that those who spoke well and those who spoke ill of the Emperor Pedro I were equally satisfactory to Nicolau. That man, who inspired enthusiasms and hatreds, whose name was repeated wherever Nicolau went, on the street, in the theater, in other people's houses, became a real, morbid persecution. Hence the fervor with which he joined the sedition of 1831. The abdication brought him relief. The truth is, however, that the Regency soon found him among its opponents. And there are those who claim he joined the Caramurú or restoration party, even though there is no proof of it. What is certain is that Nicolau's public life ceased with the majority of Pedro II.

The disease had now definitely taken control of the organism. Little by little Nicolau went into seclusion. He could not pay certain calls, visit certain houses. The theater failed to distract him. The state of his auditory organs was so delicate that the sound of applause caused him excruciating pains. The enthusiasm of the Rio population for the famous Candiani, and also for Meréa, but mainly for Candiani, whose carriage was drawn by human arms—a civility all the more remarkable in that they would not have done it for Plato himself—this enthusiasm was one of Nicolau's greatest torments. Finally, he almost stopped going to the theater, found Candiani intolerable, and preferred the *Norma* of the hurdy-gurdies to that of the prima donna. It was not from an exaggerated patriotism that he enjoyed seeing João Caetano in the early days. But finally he abandoned him too, and along with him well nigh all the theater.

"He is lost!" thought his brother-in-law. "If we could only give him a new spleen..."

How could he imagine such a foolish thing? Nicolau was lost, naturally —destroyed by nature herself. Domestic pleasures no longer contented him. His literary attempts—family verses, prize impromptu poems, political stanzas—had not lasted long, and it may even be that they hastened the progress of the malady. In any case, it struck him one day that this occupation was the most ridiculous thing in the world and the adulation of Gonçalves Dias, for example, showed him a nation of vulgarity and bad taste. This literary sentiment, result of an organic lesion, reacted on this lesion in such a way as to produce serious crises that confined him to his bed for a time. His brother-in-law seized the moment to clear the house of all books of a certain caliber.

More difficult to explain is the sloppy way he began to dress a few months thereafter. Brought up in habits of stylish elegance, he was an old customer of one of the leading court tailors, Plum, and he never let a day pass without having his hair dressed at the establishment of Demarais & Gérard, *coiffeurs de la cour,* on the Rua do Ouvidor. It seems he found this designation of "hairdressers to the court" conceited, and rebuked them by going to a low-class barber to have his hair dressed. As for the motive that led him to change his way of dress, I repeat, it is entirely obscure, and, unless it can be attributed to age, inexplicable.

The dismissal of his cook is another enigma. At the urging of his brother-in-law, who wanted to keep him diverted, Nicolau gave two dinners a week, and the guests were unanimous in the opinion that his cook surpassed all the others of the capital. Actually his dishes were good, a few excellent, but the praise was a bit emphatic, a bit excessive, for the very purpose of giving pleasure to Nicolau, and it did for a certain length of time. How can you explain then the fact that one Sunday, as soon as dinner was over, a magnificent dinner, he fired this worthy and remarkable man who had been the indirect cause of some of his most delightful moments on earth? An impenetrable mystery.

"He was a thief!" was the reply Nicolau gave his brother-in-law.

Neither the efforts of the latter, nor those of his sister and of his friends, nor his wealth, or anything, improved our poor Nicolau. The secretion in the spleen became incessant, and the worm multiplied by the millions...I do not know whether this theory is the true one, but after all it was his brother-in-law's. His last years were excruciating. He turned green, was constantly irritated, squint-eyed, suffering more himself than he made others suffer. The least or greatest thing pulverized his nerves: a good speech, a clever artist, a carriage, a cravat, a sonnet, a witty remark, an interesting dream, everything, brought on an attack.

Had he determined to let himself die? One would imagine so to see the impassivity which he refused the remedies of the leading physicians of the capital. Finally it was necessary to resort to deception and give them as if they had been prescribed by some quack. But it was too late. Death carried him off in a couple of weeks.

"Joaquim Soares?" shouted the brother-in-law in astonishment when he learned of the provision in the dead man's will specifying that his coffin be made by this workman. "But that fellow's coffins aren't worth a damn, and..."

"Hush!" interrupted his wife. "Our dear brother's wish must be respected."

NO FLIES ON FRANK
John Lennon

There were no flies on Frank that morning—after all why not? He was a responsible citizen with a wife and child, wasn't he? It was a typical Frank morning and with an agility that defies description he leapt into the barthroom onto the scales. To his great harold he discovered he was twelve inches more tall heavy! He couldn't believe it and his blood raised to his head causing a mighty red colouring.

'I carn't not believe this incredible fact of truth about my very body which has not gained fat since mother begat me at childburn. Yea, though I wart through the valet of thy shadowy hut I will feed no norman. What grate qualmsy hath taken me thus into such a fatty hardbuckle."

Again Frank looked down at the awful vision which clouded his eyes with fearful weight. 'Twelve inches more heavy, Lo!, but am I not more fatty than my brother Geoffery whose father Alec came from Kenneth —through Leslies, who begat Arthur, son of Eric, by the house of Ronald and April—keepers of James of Newcastle who ran Madeline at 2–1 by Silver Flower, (10–2) past Wot-ro-Wot at 4/3d a pound?'

He journeyed downstairs crestfallen and defective—a great wait on his boulders—not even his wife's battered face could raise a smile on poor Frank's head—who as you know had no flies on him. His wife, a former beauty queer, regarded him with a strange but burly look.

'What ails thee, Frank?', she asked stretching her prune. 'You look dejected if not informal,' she addled.

'Tis nothing but wart I have gained but twelve inches more tall heavy than at the very clock of yesterday at this time—am I not the most miserable of men? Suffer ye not to spake to me or I might thrust you a mortal injury; I must traddle this trial alone.'

'Lo! Frank—thou hast smote me harshly with such grave talk—am I to blame for this vast burton?'

Frank looked sadly at his wife—forgetting for a moment the cause of his misery. Walking slowly but slowly toward her, he took his head in his hands and with a few swift blows had clubbed her mercifully to the ground dead.

'She shouldn't see me like this,' he mubbled, 'not all fat and on her thirtysecond birthday.'

Frank had to get his own breakfast that morning and also on the following mornings.

Two, (or was it three?) weeks later Frank awake again to find that there were *still* no flies on him.

'No flies on this Frank boy,' he thought; but to his amazement there seemed to be a lot of flies on his wife—who was still lying about the kitchen floor.

'I carn't not partake of bread and that with her lying about the place,' he thought allowed, writing as he spoke. 'I must deliver her to her home where she will be made welcome.'

He gathered her in a small sack (for she was only four foot three) and headed for her rightful home. Frank knocked on the door of his wife's mothers house. She opened the door.

'I've brought Marian home, Mrs. Sutherskill' (he could never call her Mum). He opened the sack and placed Marian on the doorstep.

'I'm not having all those flies in my home,' shouted Mrs. Sutherskill (who was very houseproud), shutting the door. 'She could have at least offered me a cup of tea,' thought Frank lifting the problem back on his boulders.

STALLIONS
Tom Mac Intyre

One afternoon the housekeeper pounced—

"You're going to the creamery"—the can pushed at me—"two shillings worth of cream and hurry back."

She slapped shut the door.

I went down the avenue and on to the road where tar oozed and gleamed after hours of sun. It was four o'clock. It was May.

The town lay a good shout off, the creamery half a mile beyond. I set out, past Jack Traynor's who had been a schoolmaster, was now old, and came abroad only to walk in the downpour; past Miss Farnan's who snatched kindling from behind hedges and had seen The Blessed Virgin; past Tom Millar's who housed a motor-bike and greyhounds but was Protestant. I stopped at Carroll's archway, that day a funnel of shadows. My eyes pricked. Among the shadows, sloping round the curve which hid the gap of the other end, was Albert McElwaine.

There was something up in Carroll's yard.

McElwaine was about my age, his curiosity mine. The cut of him lured me, the lie of his back, the drag of his hand as he took the bend—blurring himself to the wall. I followed, hastening through, round the blind curve and into the yard, a square, which held the light like a bowl.

Ten or twenty men were standing about, talking in groups, smoking, testing the ground with ashplants or nubbly blackthorns. A line of carts to one side, cherry and blue, shafts down, backsides up, harness slack in their bellies, had gone to sleep. There was a green whiff of droppings, and the stomping and tossing of horses fidgety in the dark stables. Nothing was happening. McElwaine, by himself in a far corner, hadn't seen me yet.

The creamery?—should I go on?—full of ramshackle noises, flood-waters, pipes which sang and sneezed, churns with portholes and hatches, ladders, platforms, ramps, and a gloom of ice and snow where they stored the butter...Maybe I should go on?

From behind the row of carts, someone brought out a black mare, shivery patches of sweat slick on her rump. In the middle of the yard they

ashplants or blackthorns: walking sticks.

stopped, waiting, the middle their own. The space had grown while they moved into it. The mare jibbed and wheeled.

I stole to the edge of the ashplant and blackthorn ring.

As if a thousand locks had snapped, a door to the left flew open. A stallion ricochetted into the sun, pawed for the sky, and let out a whinny that flared over the town.

Dread turned inside me. Between those great open haunches guilt swayed.

Chestnut against the whitewash walls he rose again, fetlock to crest shining like fire and, twenty feet up, two polished hooves flailing my body with velvet blows.

Excited and glancing, the mare waited. For the first time, I saw the ostler, puny, and the reins. Flanks in a quiver, the stallion broke forward, closed, reared and plunged. Guiding in the reek and sweat flashed the red hand of the ostler. The stallion, straddled, pumped like his taut hamstrings must split. Then the ostler again, parting them, the spill passed on. The mare was led away. Snorting and champing, the chestnut was stalled.

Against the butt of a hobnailed boot, a farmer near me rapped his pipe—

"Well, boy, what d'ye make of it?"

He grinned down over a porter belly.

Flushed and floundering, I left. I was smeared—at the same time dazed by the pounding of velvet hooves.

Every Monday I escaped to the yard. McElwaine was always there. And a few others I knew in school. Here we never spoke. Singly, privately, we awaited each loud unbolting and the rush that followed. It was like watching the start of the world.

Curried and ribboned and bobbed, the stallion roiled my dreams.

At home no one noticed.

I saw the future: fifty-two Mondays bright and luscious in the year.

On my fourth visit, Lil Carroll, ladling sugar into two-pound bags, looked out a spidery window, saw me criminal among the men. And told.

When Mother called I was eating in the kitchen.

"Come up here you."

Fearful, I rose and followed her up to the parlour.

First she stood with her back to me, staring out on the flower-garden, said nothing. Then she turned, making a slow sign of the cross, and met me with a dead face.

"Where were you this afternoon?"

"Playing football."

"Football!" she mocked. "In Carroll's yard?"

a porter belly: Porter is a dark beer, hence a "beer belly."

I eyed the garden behind her.

"May," she said, "Our Lady's Month."

I shrank to a culprit.

"If I ever hear of you being there again, you'll get a dose you won't forget."

I said nothing.

"Promise," she commanded, "Come on."

"I promise"—

Too fast.

There was a pause while she studied me, a long one, and with it I could feel driving between us the fury of the yard, the glare and the ripeness, the sling of that door's opening, the stallion loosed again.

"Go back to your tea."

I left the room.

"Stallions," I heard her say on my way down the hall.

THE SPINOZA
OF MARKET STREET
Isaac Bashevis Singer

translated by martha glicklich and cecil hemley

I

Dr. Nahum Fischelson paced back and forth in his garret room in Market Street, Warsaw. Dr. Fischelson was a short, hunched man with a grayish beard, and was quite bald except for a few wisps of hair remaining at the nape of the neck. His nose was as crooked as a beak and his eyes were large, dark, and fluttering like those of some huge bird. It was a hot summer evening, but Dr. Fischelson wore a black coat which reached to his knees, and he had on a stiff collar and a bow tie. From the door he paced slowly to the dormer window set high in the slanting room and back again. One had to mount several steps to look out. A candle in a brass holder was burning on the table and a variety of insects buzzed around the flame. Now and again one of the creatures would fly too close to the fire and sear its wings, or one would ignite and glow on the wick for an instant. At such moments Dr. Fischelson grimaced. His wrinkled face would twitch and beneath his disheveled moustache he would bite his lips. Finally he took a handkerchief from his pocket and waved it at the insects.

"Away from there, fools and imbeciles," he scolded. "You won't get warm here; you'll only burn yourself."

The insects scattered but a second later returned and once more circled the trembling flame. Dr. Fischelson wiped the sweat from his wrinkled forehead and sighed, "Like men they desire nothing but the pleasure of the moment." On the table lay an open book written in Latin, and on its broad-margined pages were notes and comments printed in small letters by Dr. Fischelson. The book was Spinoza's *Ethics* and Dr. Fischelson had been studying it for the last thirty years. He knew every proposition, every proof, every corollary, every note by heart. When he wanted to find a particular passage, he generally opened to the place immediately without having to search for it. But, nevertheless, he continued to study the *Ethics* for hours every day with a magnifying glass in his bony hand, murmuring and nodding his head in agreement. The truth was that the more Dr. Fischelson studied, the more puzzling sentences, unclear passages, and cryptic remarks he found. Each sentence contained hints unfathomed by any of the students of Spinoza. Actually the philosopher had anticipated all of the criticisms of pure reason made by Kant and his followers. Dr. Fischelson was writing a commentary on the *Ethics*. He had drawers full of notes and drafts, but it didn't seem that he would ever be able to complete his work. The stomach ailment which had plagued him for years was growing worse from day to day. Now he would get pains in his stomach after only a few mouthfuls of oatmeal. "God in Heaven, it's difficult, very difficult," he would say to himself using the same intonation as had his father, the late Rabbi of Tishevitz. "It's very, very hard."

Dr. Fischelson was not afraid of dying. To begin with, he was no longer a young man. Secondly, it is stated in the fourth part of the *Ethics* that "a free man thinks of nothing less than of death and his wisdom is a meditation not of death, but of life." Thirdly, it is also said that "the human mind cannot be absolutely destroyed with the human body but there is some part of it that remains eternal." And yet Dr. Fischelson's ulcer (or perhaps it was a cancer) continued to bother him. His tongue was always coated. He belched frequently and emitted a different foul-smelling gas each time. He suffered from heartburn and cramps. At times he felt like vomiting and at other times he was hungry for garlic, onions, and fried foods. He had long ago discarded the medicines prescribed for him by the doctors and had sought his own remedies. He found it beneficial to take grated radish after meals and lie on his bed, belly down, with his head hanging over the side. But these home remedies offered only temporary relief. Some of the doctors he consulted insisted there was nothing the matter with him. "It's just nerves," they told him. "You could live to be a hundred."

But on this particular hot summer night, Dr. Fischelson felt his strength ebbing. His knees were shaky, his pulse weak. He sat down to read and his vision blurred. The letters on the page turned from green to gold. The lines became waved and jumped over each other, leaving white gaps as if the text had disappeared in some mysterious way. The heat was unbearable, flowing down directly from the tin roof; Dr. Fischelson felt he was inside of an oven. Several times he climbed the four steps to the window and thrust his head out into the cool of the evening breeze. He would remain in that position for so long his knees would become wobbly. "Oh it's a fine breeze," he would murmur, "really delightful," and he would recall that according to Spinoza, morality and happiness were identical, and that the most moral deed a man could perform was to indulge in some pleasure which was not contrary to reason.

II

Dr. Fischelson, standing on the top step at the window and looking out, could see into two worlds. Above him were the heavens, thickly strewn with stars. Dr. Fischelson had never seriously studied astronomy but he could differentiate between the planets, those bodies which like the earth, revolve around the sun, and the fixed stars, themselves distant suns, whose light reaches us a hundred or even a thousand years later. He recognized the constellations which mark the path of the earth in space and that nebulous sash, the Milky Way. Dr. Fischelson owned a small telescope he had bought in Switzerland where he had studied and he particularly enjoyed looking at the moon through it. He could clearly make out on the moon's surface the volcanoes bathed in sunlight and the dark, shadowy craters. He never wearied of gazing at these cracks and crevasses. To him they seemed both near and distant, both substantial and insubstantial. Now and then he would see a shooting star trace a wide arc across the sky and disappear, leaving a fiery trail behind it. Dr. Fischelson would know then that a meteorite had reached our atmosphere, and perhaps some unburned fragment of it had fallen into the ocean or had landed in the desert or perhaps even in some inhabited region. Slowly the stars which had appeared from behind Dr. Fischelson's roof rose until they were shining above the house across the street. Yes, when Dr. Fischelson looked up into the heavens, he became aware of that infinite extension which is, according to Spinoza, one of God's attributes. It comforted Dr. Fischelson to think that although he was only a weak, puny man, a changing mode of the absolutely infinite Substance, he was nevertheless a part of the cosmos, made of the same matter as the celestial bodies; to the extent that he was a part of the Godhead, he knew he could not be destroyed. In such moments, Dr. Fischelson experienced the *Amor Dei Intellectualis* which is, according to the philosopher of Amsterdam, the highest perfection of the mind. Dr. Fischelson breathed deeply, lifted his head as high as his stiff collar permitted and actually felt he was whirling in company with the earth, the sun, the stars of the Milky Way, and the infinite host of galaxies known only to infinite thought. His legs became light and weightless and he grasped the window frame with both hands as if afraid he would lose his footing and fly out into eternity.

When Dr. Fischelson tired of observing the sky, his glance dropped to Market Street below. He could see a long strip extending from Yanash's market to Iron Street with the gas lamps lining it merged into a string of fiery dots. Smoke was issuing from the chimneys on the black, tin roofs; the bakers were heating their ovens, and here and there sparks mingled with the black smoke. The street never looked so noisy and crowded as on

Amor Dei Intellectualis: the intellectual's love of God.

a summer evening. Thieves, prostitutes, gamblers, and fences loafed in the square which looked from above like a pretzel covered with poppy seeds. The young men laughed coarsely and the girls shrieked. A peddler with a keg of lemonade on his back pierced the general din with his intermittent cries. A watermelon vendor shouted in a savage voice, and the long knife which he used for cutting the fruit dripped with the blood-like juice. Now and again the street became even more agitated. Fire engines, their heavy wheels clanging, sped by; they were drawn by sturdy black horses which had to be tightly curbed to prevent them from running wild. Next came an ambulance, its siren screaming. Then some thugs had a fight among themselves and the police had to be called. A passerby was robbed and ran about shouting for help. Some wagons loaded with firewood sought to get through into the courtyards where the bakeries were located but the horses could not lift the wheels over the steep curbs and the drivers berated the animals and lashed them with their whips. Sparks rose from the clanging hoofs. It was now long after seven, which was the prescribed closing time for stores, but actually business had only begun. Customers were led in stealthily through back doors. The Russian policemen on the street, having been paid off, noticing nothing of this. Merchants continued to hawk their wares, each seeking to outshout the others.

"Gold, gold, gold," a woman who dealt in rotten oranges shrieked.

"Sugar, sugar, sugar," croaked a dealer of overripe plums.

"Heads, heads, heads," a boy who sold fishheads roared.

Through the window of a *Chassidic* study house across the way, Dr. Fischelson could see boys with long sidelocks swaying over holy volumes, grimacing and studying aloud in sing-song voices. Butchers, porters, and fruit dealers were drinking beer in the tavern below. Vapor drifted from the tavern's open door like steam from a bathhouse, and there was the sound of loud music. Outside of the tavern, streetwalkers snatched at drunken soldiers and at workers on their way home from the factories. Some of the men carried bundles of wood on their shoulders, reminding Dr. Fischelson of the wicked who are condemned to kindle their own fires in Hell. Husky record players poured out their raspings through open windows. The liturgy of the high holidays alternated with vulgar vaudeville songs.

Dr. Fischelson peered into the half-lit bedlam and cocked his ears. He knew that the behavior of this rabble was the very antithesis of reason. These people were immersed in the vainest of passions, were drunk with emotions, and, according to Spinoza, emotion was never good. Instead of the pleasure they ran after, all they succeeded in obtaining was disease and prison, shame and the suffering that resulted from ignorance. Even the cats which loitered on the roofs here seemed more savage and pas-

Chassidic: belonging to a pietistic, joy-filled, enthusiastic Jewish sect.

sionate than those in other parts of the town. They caterwauled with the voices of women in labor, and like demons scampered up walls and leaped onto eaves and balconies. One of the toms paused at Dr. Fischelson's window and let out a howl which made Dr. Fischelson shudder. The doctor stepped from the window and, picking up a broom, brandished it in front of the black beast's glowing, green eyes. "Scat, begone, you ignorant savage!"—and he rapped the broom handle against the roof until the tom ran off.

III

When Dr. Fischelson had returned to Warsaw from Zurich where he had studied philosophy, a great future had been predicted for him. His friends had known that he was writing an important book on Spinoza. A Jewish Polish journal had invited him to be a contributor; he had been a frequent guest at several wealthy households and he had been made head librarian at the Warsaw synagogue. Although even then he had been considered an old bachelor, the matchmakers had proposed several rich girls for him. But Dr. Fischelson had not taken advantage of these opportunities. He had wanted to be as independent as Spinoza himself. And he had been. But because of his heretical ideas he had come into conflict with the rabbi and had had to resign his post as librarian. For years after that, he had supported himself by giving private lessons in Hebrew and German. Then, when he had become sick, the Berlin Jewish community had voted him a subsidy of five hundred marks a year. This had been made possible through the intervention of the famous Dr. Hildesheimer with whom he corresponded about philosophy. In order to get by on so small a pension, Dr. Fischelson had moved into the attic room and had begun cooking his own meals on a kerosene stove. He had a cupboard which had many drawers, and each drawer was labelled with the food it contained—buckwheat, rice, barley, onions, carrots, potatoes, mushrooms. Once a week Dr. Fischelson put on his widebrimmed black hat, took a basket in one hand and Spinoza's *Ethics* in the other, and went off to the market for his provisions. While he was waiting to be served, he would open the *Ethics*. The merchants knew him and would motion him to their stalls.

"A fine piece of cheese, Doctor—just melts in your mouth."

"Fresh mushrooms, Doctor, straight from the woods."

"Make way for the Doctor, ladies," the butcher would shout. "Please don't block the entrance."

During the early years of his sickness, Dr. Fischelson had still gone in the evening to a café which was frequented by Hebrew teachers and other intellectuals. It had been his habit to sit there and play chess while drinking a half a glass of black coffee. Sometimes he would stop at the bookstores on Holy Cross Street where all sorts of old books and magazines could be purchased cheap. On one occasion a former pupil of his had arranged to meet him at a restaurant one evening. When Dr. Fischelson arrived, he had been surprised to find a group of friends and admirers who forced him to sit at the head of the table while they made speeches about him. But these were things that had happened long ago. Now people were no longer interested in him. He had isolated himself completely and had become a forgotten man. The events of 1905 when the boys of Market Street had begun to organize strikes, throw bombs at police stations, and shoot strike breakers so that the stores were closed even on weekdays had greatly increased his isolation. He began to despise everything associated with the modern Jew—Zionism, socialism, anarchism. The young men in question seemed to him nothing but an ignorant rabble intent on destroying society, society without which no reasonable existence was possible. He still read a Hebrew magazine occasionally, but he felt contempt for modern Hebrew which had no roots in the Bible or the Mishnah. The spelling of Polish words had changed also. Dr. Fischelson concluded that even the so-called spiritual men had abandoned reason and were doing their utmost to pander to the mob. Now and again he still visited a library and browsed through some of the modern histories of philosophy, but he found that the professors did not understand Spinoza, quoted him incorrectly, attributed their own muddled ideas to the philosopher. Although Dr. Fischelson was well aware that anger was an emotion unworthy of those who walk the path of reason, he would become furious, and would quickly close the book and push it from him. "Idiots," he would mutter, "asses, upstarts." And he would vow never again to look at modern philosophy.

IV

Every three months a special mailman who only delivered money orders brought Dr. Fischelson eighty rubles. He expected his quarterly allotment at the beginning of July but as day after day passed and the tall man with the blond moustache and the shiny buttons did not appear, the Doctor grew anxious. He had scarcely a groshen left. Who knows—possibly the Berlin Community had rescinded his subsidy; perhaps Dr. Hildesheimer had died, God forbid; the post office might have made a mistake. Every event has its cause, Dr. Fischelson knew. All was determined, all necessary, and a man of reason had no right to worry. Nevertheless, worry invaded his brain, and buzzed about like the flies. If the worst came to the worst, it occurred to him, he could commit suicide, but then he remembered that Spinoza did not approve of suicide and compared those who took their own lives to the insane.

One day when Dr. Fischelson went out to a store to purchase a composition book, he heard people talking about war. In Serbia somewhere, an Austrian Prince had been shot and the Austrians had delivered an ultimatum to the Serbs. The owner of the store, a young man with a yellow beard and shifty yellow eyes, announced, "We are about to have a small war," and he advised Dr. Fischelson to store up food because in the near future there was likely to be a shortage.

Everything happened so quickly. Dr. Fischelson had not even decided whether it was worthwhile to spend four groshen on a newspaper, and already posters had been hung up announcing mobilization. Men were to be seen walking on the street with round, metal tags on their lapels, a sign that they were being drafted. They were followed by their crying wives. One Monday when Dr. Fischelson descended to the street to buy some food with his last kopecks, he found the stores closed. The owners and their wives stood outside and explained that merchandise was unobtainable. But certain special customers were pulled to one side and let in through back doors. On the street all was confusion. Policemen with swords unsheathed could be seen riding on horseback. A large crowd had gathered around the tavern where, at the command of the Tsar, the tavern's stock of whiskey was being poured into the gutter.

Dr. Fischelson went to his old café. Perhaps he would find some acquaintances there who would advise him. But he did not come across a single person he knew. He decided, then, to visit the rabbi of the synagogue where he had once been librarian, but the sexton with the six-sided skull cap informed him that the rabbi and his family had gone off to the spas. Dr. Fischelson had other old friends in town but he found no one at home. His feet ached from so much walking; black and green spots appeared before his eyes and he felt faint. He stopped and waited for the giddiness to pass. The passers-by jostled him. A dark-eyed high school girl tried to give him a coin. Although the war had just started, soldiers eight abreast were marching in full battle dress—the men were covered with dust and were sunburnt. Canteens were strapped to their sides and they wore rows of bullets across their chests. The bayonets on their rifles gleamed with a cold, green light. They sang with mournful voices. Along with the men came cannons, each pulled by eight horses; their blind muzzles breathed gloomy terror. Dr. Fischelson felt nauseous. His stomach ached; his intestines seemed about to turn themselves inside out. Cold sweat appeared on his face.

"I'm dying," he thought. "This is the end." Nevertheless, he did manage to drag himself home where he lay down on the iron cot and remained, panting and gasping. He must have dozed off because he imagined that he was in his home town, Tishvitz. He had a sore throat and his mother was busy wrapping a stocking stuffed with hot salt around his neck. He could hear talk going on in the house; something about a candle and about how a frog had bitten him. He wanted to go out into the street but they wouldn't let him because a Catholic procession was passing by. Men in long robes, holding double edged axes in their hands, were intoning in

Latin as they sprinkled holy water. Crosses gleamed; sacred pictures waved in the air. There was an odor of incense and corpses. Suddenly the sky turned a burning red and the whole world started to burn. Bells were ringing; people rushed madly about. Flocks of birds flew overhead, screeching. Dr. Fischelson awoke with a start. His body was covered with sweat and his throat was now actually sore. He tried to meditate about his extraordinary dream, to find its rational connection with what was happening to him and to comprehend it *sub specie eternitatis,* but none of it made sense. "Alas, the brain is a receptacle for nonsense," Dr. Fischelson thought. "This earth belongs to the mad."

And he once more closed his eyes; once more he dozed; once more he dreamed.

V

The eternal laws, apparently, had not yet ordained Dr. Fischelson's end.

There was a door to the left of Dr. Fischelson's attic room which opened off a dark corridor, cluttered with boxes and baskets, in which the odor of fried onions and laundry soap was always present. Behind this door lived a spinster whom the neighbors called Black Dobbe. Dobbe was tall and lean, and as black as a baker's shovel. She had a broken nose and there was a mustache on her upper lip. She spoke with the hoarse voice of a man and she wore men's shoes. For years Black Dobbe had sold breads, rolls, and bagels which she had bought from the baker at the gate of the house. But one day she and the baker had quarreled and she had moved her business to the market place and now she dealt in what were called "wrinklers" which was a synonym for cracked eggs. Black Dobbe had no luck with men. Twice she had been engaged to baker's apprentices but in both instances they had returned the engagement contract to her. Some time afterwards she had received an engagement contract from an old man, a glazier who claimed that he was divorced, but it had later come to light that he still had a wife. Black Dobbe had a cousin in America, a shoemaker, and repeatedly she boasted that this cousin was sending her passage, but she remained in Warsaw. She was constantly being teased by the women who would say, "There's no hope for you, Dobbe. You're fated to die an old maid." Dobbe always answered, "I don't intend to be a slave for any man. Let them all rot."

That afternoon Dobbe received a letter from America. Generally she would go to Leizer the Tailor and have him read it to her. However, that day Leizer was out and so Dobbe thought of Dr. Fischelson whom the other tenants considered a convert since he never went to prayer. She knocked on the door of the doctor's room but there was no answer. "The

sub specie eternitatis: under the aspect of eternity or in its essential form.

heretic is probably out," Dobbe thought but, nevertheless, she knocked once more, and this time the door moved slightly. She pushed her way in and stood there frightened. Dr. Fischelson lay fully clothed on his bed; his face was as yellow as wax; his Adam's apple stuck out prominently; his beard pointed upward. Dobbe screamed; she was certain that he was dead, but—no—his body moved. Dobbe picked up a glass which stood on the table, ran into the corridor, filled the glass with water from the faucet, hurried back, and threw the water into the face of the unconscious man. Dr. Fischelson shook his head and opened his eyes.

"What's wrong with you?" Dobbe asked. "Are you sick?"

"Thank you very much. No."

"Have you a family? I'll call them."

"No family," Dr. Fischelson said.

Dobbe wanted to fetch the barber from across the street but Dr. Fischelson signified that he didn't wish the barber's assistance. Since Dobbe was not going to the market that day, no "wrinklers" being available, she decided to do a good deed. She assisted the sick man to get off the bed and smoothed down the blanket. Then she undressed Dr. Fischelson and prepared some soup for him on the kerosene stove. The sun never entered Dobbe's room, but here squares of sunlight shimmered on the faded walls. The floor was painted red. Over the bed hung a picture of a man who was wearing a broad frill around his neck and had long hair. "Such an old fellow and yet he keeps his place so nice and clean," Dobbe thought approvingly. Dr. Fischelson asked for the *Ethics,* and she gave it to him disapprovingly. She was certain it was a gentile prayer book. Then she began bustling about, brought in a pail of water, swept the floor. Dr. Fischelson ate; after he had finished, he was much stronger and Dobbe asked him to read her the letter.

He read it slowly, the paper trembling in his hands. It came from New York, from Dobbe's cousin. Once more he wrote that he was about to send her a "really important letter" and a ticket to America. By now, Dobbe knew the story by heart and she helped the old man decipher her cousin's scrawl. "He's lying," Dobbe said. "He forgot about me a long time ago." In the evening, Dobbe came again. A candle in a brass holder was burning on the chair next to the bed. Reddish shadows trembled on the walls and ceiling. Dr. Fischelson sat propped up in bed, reading a book. The candle threw a golden light on his forehead which seemed as if cleft in two. A bird had flown in through the window and was perched on the table. For a moment Dobbe was frightened. This man made her think of witches, of black mirrors and corpses wandering around at night and terrifying women. Nevertheless, she took a few steps toward him and inquired, "How are you? Any better?"

"A little, thank you."

"Are you really a convert?" she asked although she wasn't quite sure what the word meant.

"Me, a convert? No, I'm a Jew like any other Jew," Dr. Fischelson answered.

The doctor's assurances made Dobbe feel more at home. She found the bottle of kerosene and lit the stove, and after that she fetched a glass of milk from her room and began cooking kasha. Dr. Fischelson continued to study the *Ethics,* but that evening he could make no sense of the theorems and proofs with their many references to axioms and definitions and other theorems. With trembling hand he raised the book to his eyes and read, "The idea of each modification of the human body does not involve adequate knowledge of the human body itself. . . . The idea of the idea of each modification of the human mind does not involve adequate knowledge of the human mind."

VI

Dr. Fischelson was certain he would die any day now. He made out his will, leaving all of his books and manuscripts to the synagogue library. His clothing and furniture would go to Dobbe since she had taken care of him. But death did not come. Rather his health improved. Dobbe returned to her business in the market, but she visited the old man several times a day, prepared soup for him, left him a glass of tea, and told him news of the war. The Germans had occupied Kalish, Bendin, and Cestechow, and they were marching on Warsaw. People said that on a quiet morning one could hear the rumblings of the cannon. Dobbe reported that the casualties were heavy. "They're falling like flies," she said. "What a terrible misfortune for the women."

She couldn't explain why, but the old man's attic room attracted her. She liked to remove the gold-rimmed books from the bookcase, dust them, and then air them on the window sill. She would climb the few steps to the window and look out through the telescope. She also enjoyed talking to Dr. Fischelson. He told her about Switzerland where he had studied, of the great cities he had passed through, of the high mountains that were covered with snow even in the summer. His father had been a rabbi, he said, and before he, Dr. Fischelson, had become a student, he had attended a yeshiva. She asked him how many languages he knew and it turned out that he could speak and write Hebrew, Russian, German, and French, in addition to Yiddish. He also knew Latin. Dobbe was astonished that such an educated man should live in an attic room on Market Street. But what amazed her most of all was that although he had the title "Doctor," he couldn't write prescriptions. "Why don't you become a real doctor?" she would ask him. "I am a doctor," he would answer. "I'm just not a physician." "What kind of a doctor?" "A doctor of philosophy." Although she had no idea of what this meant, she felt it must be very important. "Oh my blessed mother," she would say, "where did you get such a brain?"

Then one evening after Dobbe had given him his crackers and his glass of tea with milk, he began questioning her about where she came from, who her parents were, and why she had not married. Dobbe was surprised. No one had ever asked her such questions. She told him her story in a quiet voice and stayed until eleven o'clock. Her father had been a porter at the kosher butcher shops. Her mother had plucked chickens in the slaughterhouse. The family had lived in a cellar at No. 19 Market Street. When she had been ten, she had become a maid. The man she had worked for had been a fence who bought stolen goods from thieves on the square. Dobbe had had a brother who had gone into the Russian army and had never returned. Her sister had married a coachman in Praga and had died in childbirth. Dobbe told of the battles between the underworld and the revolutionaries in 1905, of blind Itche and his gang and how they collected protection money from the stores, of the thugs who attacked young boys and girls out on Saturday afternoon strolls if they were not paid money for security. She also spoke of the pimps who drove about in carriages and abducted women to be sold in Buenos Aires. Dobbe swore that some men had even sought to inveigle her into a brothel, but that she had run away. She complained of a thousand evils done to her. She had been robbed; her boy friend had been stolen; a competitor had once poured a pint of kerosene into her basket of bagels; her own cousin, the shoemaker, had cheated her out of a hundred rubles before he had left for America. Dr. Fischelson listened to her attentively. He asked her questions, shook his head, and grunted.

"Well, do you believe in God?" he finally asked her.

"I don't know," she answered. "Do you?"

"Yes, I believe."

"Then why don't you go to synagogue?" she asked.

"God is everywhere," he replied. "In the synagogue. In the marketplace. In this very room. We ourselves are parts of God."

"Don't say such things," Dobbe said. "You frighten me."

She left the room and Dr. Fischelson was certain she had gone to bed. But he wondered why she had not said "good night." "I probably drove her away with my philosophy," he thought. The very next moment he heard her footsteps. She came in carrying a pile of clothing like a peddler.

"I wanted to show you these," she said. "They're my trousseau." And she began to spread out, on the chair, dresses—woolen, silk, velvet. Taking each dress up in turn, she held it to her body. She gave him an account of every item in her trousseau—underwear, shoes, stockings.

"I'm not wasteful," she said. "I'm a saver. I have enough money to go to America."

Then she was silent and her face turned brick-red. She looked at Dr. Fischelson out of the corner of her eyes, timidly, inquisitively. Dr. Fischelson's body suddenly began to shake as if he had the chills. He said, "Very nice, beautiful things." His brow furrowed and he pulled at his beard with two fingers. A sad smile appeared on his toothless mouth and his large fluttering eyes, gazing into the distance through the attic window, also smiled sadly.

VII

The day that Black Dobbe came to the rabbi's chambers and announced that she was to marry Dr. Fischelson, the rabbi's wife thought she had gone mad. But the news had already reached Leizer the Tailor, and had spread to the bakery, as well as to other shops. There were those who thought that the "old maid" was very lucky; the doctor, they said, had a vast hoard of money. But there were others who took the view that he was a run-down degenerate who would give her syphilis. Although Dr. Fischelson had insisted that the wedding be a small, quiet one, a host of guests assembled in the rabbi's rooms. The baker's apprentices who generally went about barefoot, and in their underwear, with paper bags on the tops of their heads, now put on light-colored suits, straw hats, yellow shoes, gaudy ties, and they brought with them huge cakes and pans filled with cookies. They had even managed to find a bottle of vodka although liquor was forbidden in wartime. When the bride and groom entered the rabbi's chamber, a murmur arose from the crowd. The women could not believe their eyes. The woman that they saw was not the one they had known. Dobbe wore a wide-brimmed hat which was amply adorned with cherries, grapes, and plumes, and the dress that she had on was of white silk and was equipped with a train; on her feet were high-heeled shoes, gold in color, and from her thin neck hung a string of imitation pearls. Nor was this all: her fingers sparkled with rings and glittering stones. Her face was veiled. She looked almost like one of those rich brides who were married in the Vienna Hall. The bakers' apprentices whistled mockingly. As for Dr. Fischelson, he was wearing his black coat and broad-toed shoes. He was scarcely able to walk; he was leaning on Dobbe. When he saw the crowd from the doorway, he became frightened and began to retreat, but Dobbe's former employer approached him saying, "Come in, come in, bridegroom. Don't be bashful. We are all brethren now."

The ceremony proceeded according to the law. The rabbi, in a worn satin gabardine, wrote the marriage contract and then had the bride and groom touch his handkerchief as a token of agreement; the rabbi wiped the point of the pen on his skullcap. Several porters who had been called from the street to make up the quorum supported the canopy. Dr. Fischelson put on a white robe as a reminder of the day of his death and Dobbe walked around him seven times as custom required. The light from the braided candles flickered on the walls. The shadows wavered. Having poured wine into a goblet, the rabbi chanted the benedictions in a sad melody. Dobbie uttered only a single cry. As for the other women, they took out their lace handkerchiefs and stood with them in their hands, grimacing. When the baker's boys began to whisper wisecracks to each other, the rabbi put a finger to his lips and murmured, *"Eh nu oh,"* as a sign that talking was forbidden. The moment came to slip the wedding ring on the bride's finger, but the bridegroom's hand started to tremble and he had trouble locating Dobbe's index finger. The next thing, according to custom, was the smashing of the glass, but though Dr. Fischelson kicked the goblet several times, it remained unbroken. The girls lowered their heads, pinched each other gleefully, and giggled. Finally one of the apprentices struck the goblet with his heel and it shattered. Even the rabbi could not restrain a smile. After the ceremony the guests drank vodka and ate cookies. Dobbe's former employer came up to Dr. Fischelson and said, *"Mazel tov,* bridegroom. Your luck should be as good as your wife." "Thank you, thank you," Dr. Fischelson murmured, "but I don't look forward to any luck." He was anxious to return as quickly as possible to his attic room. He felt a pressure in his stomach and his chest ached. His face had become greenish. Dobbe had suddenly become angry. She pulled back her veil and called out to the crowd, "What are you laughing at? This isn't a show." And without picking up the cushion-cover in which the gifts were wrapped, she returned with her husband to their rooms on the fifth floor.

Dr. Fischelson lay down on the freshly made bed in his room and began reading the *Ethics.* Dobbe had gone back to her own room. The doctor had explained to her that he was an old man, that he was sick and without strength. He had promised her nothing. Nevertheless she returned wearing a silk nightgown, slippers with pompoms, and with her hair hanging down over her shoulders. There was a smile on her face, and she was bashful and hesitant. Dr. Fishelson trembled and the *Ethics* dropped from his hands. The candle went out. Dobbe groped for Dr. Fischelson in the dark and kissed his mouth. "My dear husband," she whispered to him, *"Mazel tov."*

What happened that night could be called a miracle. If Dr. Fischelson hadn't been convinced that every occurrence is in accordance with the laws of nature, he would have thought that Black Dobbe had bewitched him. Powers long dormant awakened in him. Although he had had only a sip of the benediction wine, he was as if intoxicated. He kissed Dobbe and spoke to her of love. Long forgotten quotations from Klopfstock, Lessing, Goethe, rose to his lips. The pressures and aches stopped. He

Mazel tov: good luck.

embraced Dobbe, pressed her to himself, was again a man as in his youth. Dobbe was faint with delight; crying, she murmured things to him in a Warsaw slang which he did not understand. Later, Dr. Fischelson slipped off into the deep sleep young men know. He dreamed that he was in Switzerland and that he was climbing mountains—running, falling, flying. At dawn he opened his eyes; it seemed to him that someone had blown into his ears. Dobbe was snoring. Dr. Fischelson quietly got out of bed. In his long nightshirt he approached the window, walked up the steps and looked out in wonder. Market Street was asleep, breathing with a deep stillness. The gas lamps were flickering. The black shutters on the stores were fastened with iron bars. A cool breeze was blowing. Dr. Fischelson looked up at the sky. The black arch was thickly sown with stars—there were green, red, yellow, blue stars; there were large ones and small ones, winking and steady ones. There were those that were clustered in dense groups and those that were alone. In the higher sphere, apparently, little notice was taken of the fact that a certain Dr. Fischelson had in his declining days married someone called Black Dobbe. Seen from above even the Great War was nothing but a temporary play of the modes. The myriads of fixed stars continued to travel their destined courses in unbounded space. The comets, planets, satellites, asteroids kept circling these shining centers. Worlds were born and died in cosmic upheavals. In the chaos of nebulae, primeval matter was being formed. Now and again a star tore loose, and swept across the sky, leaving behind it a fiery streak. It was the month of August when there are showers of meteors. Yes, the divine substance was extended and had neither beginning nor end; it was absolute, indivisible, eternal, without duration, infinite in its attributes. Its waves and bubbles danced in the universal cauldron, seething with change, following the unbroken chain of causes and effects, and he, Dr. Fischelson, with his unavoidable fate, was part of this. The doctor closed his eyelids and allowed the breeze to cool the sweat on his forehead and stir the hair of his beard. He breathed deeply of the midnight air, supported his shaky hands on the window still and murmured, "Divine Spinoza, forgive me. I have become a fool."

TELL ME A RIDDLE
Tillie Olsen

1

For forty-seven years they had been married. How deep back the stubborn, gnarled roots of the quarrel reached, no one could say—but only now, when tending to the needs of others no longer shackled them together, the roots swelled up visible, split the earth between them, and the tearing shook even to the children, long since grown.

Why now, why now? wailed Hannah.

As if when we grew up weren't enough, said Paul.

Poor Ma. Poor Dad. It hurts so for both of them, said Vivi. They never had very much; at least in old age they should be happy.

Knock their heads together, insisted Sammy; tell 'em: you're too old for this kind of thing; no reason not to get along now.

Lennie wrote to Clara: They've lived over so much together; what could possibly tear them apart?

Something tangible enough.

Arthritic hands, and such work as he got, occasional. Poverty all his life, and there was little breath left for running. He could not, could not turn away from this desire: to have the troubling of responsibility, the fretting with money, over and done with; to be free, to be *care*free where success was not measured by accumulation, and there was use for the vitality still in him.

There was a way. They could sell the house, and with the money join his lodge's Haven, cooperative for the aged. Happy communal life, and was he not already an official; had he not helped organize it, raise funds, served as a trustee?

But she—would not consider it.

"What do we need all this for?" he would ask loudly, for her hearing aid was turned down and the vacuum was shrilling. "Five rooms" (pushing the sofa so she could get into the corner) "furniture" (smoothing down

the rug) "floors and surfaces to make work. Tell me, why do we need it?"
And he was glad he could ask in a scream.

"Because I'm use't."

"Because you're use't. This is a reason, Mrs. Word Miser? Used to can get unused!"

"Enough unused I have to get used to already. . . . Not enough words?" turning off the vacuum a moment to hear herself answer. "Because soon enough we'll need only a little closet, no windows, no furniture, nothing to make work, but for worms. Because now I want room. . . . Screech and blow like you're doing, you'll need that closet even sooner. . . . Ha, again!" for the vacuum bag wailed, puffed half up, hung stubbornly limp. "This time fix it so it stays; quick before the phone rings and you get too important-busy."

But while he struggled with the motor, it seethed in him. Why fix it? Why have to bother? And if it can't be fixed, have to wring the mind with how to pay the repair? At the Haven they come in with their own machines to clean your room or your cottage; you fish, or play cards, or make jokes in the sun, not with knotty fingers fight to mend vacuums.

Over the dishes, coaxingly: "For once in your life, to be free, to have everything done for you, like a queen."

"I never liked queens."

"No dishes, no garbage, no towel to sop, no worry what to buy, what to eat."

"And what else would I do with my empty hands? Better to eat at my own table when I want, and to cook and eat how I want."

"In the cottages they buy what you ask, and cook it how you like. *You* are the one who always used to say: better mankind born without mouths and stomachs than always to worry for money to buy, to shop, to fix, to cook, to wash, to clean."

"How cleverly you hid that you heard. I said it then because eighteen hours a day I ran. And you never scraped a carrot or knew a dish towel sops. Now—for you and me—who cares? A herring out of a jar is enough. But when *I* want, and nobody to bother." And she turned off her ear button, so she would not have to hear.

But as *he* had no peace, juggling and rejuggling the money to figure: how will I pay for this now?; prying out the storm windows (there they take care of this); jolting in the streetcar on errands (there I would not have to ride to take care of this or that); fending the patronizing relatives just back from Florida (at the Haven it matters what one is, not what one can afford), he gave *her* no peace.

"Look! In their bulletin. A reading circle. Twice a week it meets."

"Haumm," her answer of not listening.

"A reading circle. Chekhov they read that you like, and Peretz. Cultured people at the Haven that you would enjoy."

"Enjoy!" She tasted the word. "Now, when it pleases you, you find a reading circle for me. And forty years ago when the children were morsels and there was a Circle did you stay home with them once so I could go? Even once? You trained me well. I do not need others to enjoy. Others!" Her voice trembled. "Because *you* want to be there with others. Already it makes me sick to think of you always around others. Clown, grimacer, floormat, yesman, entertainer, whatever they want of you."

And now it was he who turned on the television loud so he need not hear.

Old scar tissue ruptured and the wounds festered anew. Chekhov indeed. She thought without softness of that young wife, who in the deep night hours while she nursed the current baby, and perhaps held another in her lap, would try to stay awake for the only time there was to read. She would feel again the weather of the outside on his cheek when, coming late from a meeting, he would find her so, and stimulated and ardent, sniffing her skin, coax: "I'll put the baby to bed, and you—put the book away, don't read, don't read."

That had been the most beguiling of all the "don't read, put your book away" her life had been. Chekhov indeed!

"Money?" She shrugged him off. "Could we get poorer than once we were? And in America, who starves?"

But as still he pressed:

"Let me alone about money. Was there ever enough? Seven little ones —for every penny I had to ask—and sometimes, remember, there was nothing. But always *I* had to manage. Now *you* manage. Rub your nose in it good."

But from those years she had had to manage, old humiliations and terrors rose up, lived again, and forced her to relive them. The children's needings; that grocer's face or this merchant's wife she had had to beg credit from when credit was a disgrace; the scenery of the long blocks walked around when she could not pay; school coming, and the desperate going over the old to see what could yet be remade; the soups of meat bones begged "for-the-dog" one winter. . . .

Enough. Now they had no children. Let *him* wrack his head for how they would live. She would not exchange her solitude for anything. *Never again to be forced to move to the rhythms of others.*

For in this solitude she had won to a reconciled peace.

Tranquillity from having the empty house no longer an enemy, for it stayed clean—not as in the days when it was her family, the life in it, that had seemed the enemy: tracking, smudging, littering, dirtying, engaging her in endless defeating battle—and on whom her endless defeat had been spewed.

The few old books, memorized from rereading; the pictures to ponder (the magnifying glass superimposed on her heavy eyeglasses). Or if she wishes, when he is gone, the phonograph, that if she turns up very loud and strains, she can hear: the ordered sounds and the struggling.

Out in the garden, growing things to nurture. Birds to be kept out of the pear tree, and when the pears are heavy and ripe, the old fury of work, for all must be canned, nothing wasted.

And her one social duty (for she will not go to luncheons or meetings) the boxes of old clothes left with her, as with a life-practised eye for finding what is still wearable within the worn (again the magnifying glass superimposed on the heavy glasses) she scans and sorts—this for rag or rummage, that for mending and cleaning, and this for sending away.

Being able at last to live within, and not move to the rhythms of others, as life had helped her to: denying; removing; isolating; taking the children one by one; then deafening, half-blinding—and at last, presenting her solitude.

And in it she had won to a reconciled peace.

Now he was violating it with his constant campaigning: *Sell the house and move to the Haven.* (You sit, you sit—there too you could sit like a stone.) He was making of her a battleground where old grievances tore. (Turn on your ear button—I am talking.) And stubbornly she resisted—so that from wheedling, reasoning manipulation, it was bitterness he now started with.

And it came to where every happening lashed up a quarrel.

"I will sell the house anyway," he flung at her one night. "I am putting it up for sale. There will be a way to make you sign."

The television blared, as always it did on the evenings he stayed home, and as always it reached her only as noise. She did not know if the tumult was in her or outside. Snap! she turned the sound off. "Shadows," she whispered to him, pointing to the screen, "look, it is only shadows." And in a scream: "Did you say that you will sell the house? Look at me, not at that. I am no shadow. You cannot sell without me."

"Leave on the television. I am watching."

"Like Paulie, like Jenny, a four-year-old. Staring at shadows. *You cannot sell the house.*"

"I will. We are going to the Haven. There you would not hear the television when you do not want it. I could sit in the social room and watch. You could lock yourself up to smell your unpleasantness in a room by yourself—for who would want to come near you?"

"No, no selling." A whisper now.

"The television is shadows. Mrs. Enlightened! Mrs. Cultured! A world comes into your house—and it is shadows. People you would never meet in a thousand lifetimes. Wonders. When you were four years old, yes, like Paulie, like Jenny, did you know of Indian dances, alligators, how they use bamboo in Malaya? No, you scratched in your dirt with the chickens and thought Olshana was the world. Yes, Mrs. Unpleasant, I will sell the house, for there better can we be rid of each other than here."

She did not know if the tumult was outside, or in her. Always a ravening inside, a pull to the bed, to lie down, to succumb.

"Have you thought maybe Ma should let a doctor have a look at her?" asked their son Paul after Sunday dinner, regarding his mother crumpled on the couch, instead of, as was her custom, busying herself in Nancy's kitchen.

"Why not the President too?"

"Seriously, Dad. This is the third Sunday she's lain down like that after dinner. Is she that way at home?"

"A regular love affair with the bed. Every time I start to talk to her."

Good protective reaction, observed Nancy to herself. The workings of hos-til-ity.

"Nancy could take her. I just don't like how she looks. Let's have Nancy arrange an appointment."

"You think she'll go?" regarding his wife gloomily. "All right, we have to have doctor bills, we have to have doctor bills." Loudly: "Something hurts you?"

She startled, looked to his lips. He repeated: "Mrs. Take It Easy, something hurts?"

"Nothing. . . . Only you."

"A woman of honey. That's why you're lying down?"

"Soon I'll get up to do the dishes, Nancy."

"Leave them, Mother, I like it better this way."

"Mrs. Take It Easy, Paul says you should start ballet. You should go to see a doctor and ask: how soon can you start ballet?"

"A doctor?" she begged. "Ballet?"

"We were talking, Ma," explained Paul, "you don't seem any too well. It would be a good idea for you to see a doctor for a checkup."

"I get up now to do the kitchen. Doctors are bills and foolishness, my son. I need no doctors."

"At the Haven," he could not resist pointing out, "a doctor is *not* bills. He lives beside you. You start to sneeze, he is there before you open up a Kleenex. You can be sick there for free, all you want."

"Diarrhea of the mouth, is there a doctor to make you dumb?"

"Ma. Promise me you'll go. Nancy will arrange it."

"It's all of a piece when you think of it," said Nancy, "the way she attacks my kitchen, scrubbing under every cup hook, doing the inside of the oven so I can't enjoy Sunday dinner, knowing that half-blind or not, she's going to find every speck of dirt. . . ."

"Don't, Nancy, I've told you—it's the only way she knows to be useful. What did the *doctor* say?"

"A real fatherly lecture. Sixty-nine is young these days. Go out, enjoy life, find interests. Get a new hearing aid, this one is antiquated. Old age is sickness only if one makes it so. Geriatrics, Inc."

"So there was nothing physical."

"Of course there was. How can you live to yourself like she does without there being? Evidence of a kidney disorder, and her blood count is low. He gave her a diet, and she's to come back for follow-up and lab work. ...But he was clear enough: Number One prescription—start living like a human being.... When I think of your dad, who could really play the invalid with that arthritis of his, as active as a teenager, and twice as much fun...."

"You didn't tell me the doctor says your sickness is in you, how you live." He pushed his advantage. "Life and enjoyments you need better than medicine. And this diet, how can you keep it? To weigh each morsel and scrape away each bit of fat, to make this soup, that pudding. There, at the Haven, they have a dietician, they would do it for you."

She is silent.

"You would feel better there, I know it," he says gently. "There there is life and enjoyments all around."

"When is the matter, Mr. Importantbusy, you have no card game or meeting you can go to?"—turning her face to the pillow.

For a while he cut his meetings and going out, fussed over her diet, tried to wheedle her into leaving the house, brought in visitors:

"I should come to a fashion tea. I should sit and look at pretty babies in clothes I cannot buy. This is pleasure?"
"Always you are better than everyone else. The doctor said you should go out. Mrs. Brem comes to you with goodness and you turn her away."
"Because *you* asked her to, she asked me."

"They won't come back. People you need, the doctor said. Your own cousins I asked; they were willing to come and make peace as if nothing had happened...."
"No more crushers of people, pushers, hypocrites, around me. No more in *my* house. You go to them if you like."

"Kind he is to visit. And you, like ice."
"A babbler. All my life around babblers. Enough!"

"She's even worse, Dad? Then let her stew a while," advised Nancy.

"You can't let it destroy you; it's a psychological thing, maybe too far gone for any of us to help."

So he let her stew. More and more she lay silent in bed, and sometimes did not even get up to make the meals. No longer was the tongue-lashing inevitable if he left the coffee cup where it did not belong, or forgot to take out the garbage or mislaid the broom. The birds grew bold that summer and for once pocked the pears, undisturbed.

A bellyful of bitterness and every day the same quarrel in a new way and a different old grievance the quarrel forced her to enter and relive. And the new torment: I am not really sick, the doctor said it, then why do I feel so sick?

One night she asked him: "You have a meeting tonight? Do not go. Stay...with me."

He had planned to watch "This Is Your Life," but half sick himself from the heavy heat, and sickening therefore the more after the brooks and woods of the Haven, with satisfaction he grated:

"Hah, Mrs. Live Alone And Like It wants company all of a sudden. It doesn't seem so good the time of solitary when she was a girl exile in Siberia. 'Do not go. Stay with me.' A new song for Mrs. Free As A Bird. Yes, I am going out, and while I am gone chew this aloneness good, and think how you keep us both from where if you want people, you do not need to be alone."

"Go, go. All your life you have gone without me."

After him she sobbed curses he had not heard in years, old-country curses from their childhood: Grow, oh shall you grow like an onion, with your head in the ground. Like the hide of a drum shall you be, beaten in life, beaten in death. Oh shall you be like a chandelier, to hang, and to burn. . . .

She was not in their bed when he came back. She lay on the cot on the sun porch. All week she did not speak or come near him; nor did he try to make peace or care for her.

He slept badly, so used to her next to him. After all the years, old harmonies and dependencies deep in their bodies; she curled to him, or he coiled to her, each warmed, warming, turning as the other turned, the nights a long embrace.

It was not the empty bed or the storm that woke him, but a faint singing. *She* was singing. Shaking off the drops of rain, the lightning riving her lifted face, he saw her so; the cot covers on the floor.

"This is a private concert?" he asked. "Come in, you are wet."

"I can breathe now," she answered; "my lungs are rich." Though indeed the sound was hardly a breath.

"Come in, come in." Loosing the bamboo shades. "Look how wet you are." Half helping, half carrying her, still faint-breathing her song.

A Russian love song of fifty years ago.

He had found a buyer, but before he told her, he called together those children who were close enough to come. Paul, of course, Sammy from New Jersey, Hannah from Connecticut, Vivi from Ohio.

With a kindling of energy for her beloved visitors, she arrayed the house, cooked and baked. She was not prepared for the solemn after-dinner conclave, they too probing in and tearing. Her frightened eyes watched from mouth to mouth as each spoke.

His stories were eloquent and funny of her refusal to go back to the doctor; of the scorned invitations; of her stubborn silence or the bile "like a Niagara"; of her contrariness: "If I clean it's no good how I cleaned; if I don't clean, I'm still a master who thinks he has a slave."

(Vinegar he poured on me all his life; I am well marinated; how can I be honey now?)

Deftly he marched in the rightness for moving to the Haven; their money from social security free for visiting the children, not sucked into daily needs and into the house; the activities in the Haven for him; but mostly the Haven for *her:* her health, her need of care, distraction, amusement, friends who shared her interests.

"This does offer an outlet for Dad," said Paul; "he's always been an active person. And economic peace of mind isn't to be sneezed at, either. I could use a little of that myself."

But when they asked: "And you, Ma, how do you feel about it?" could only whisper:

"For him it is good. It is not for me. I can no longer live between people."

"You lived all your life *for* people," Vivi cried.

"Not with." Suffering doubly for the unhappiness on her children's faces.

"You have to find some compromise," Sammy insisted. "Maybe sell the house and buy a trailer. After forty-seven years there's surely some way you can find to live in peace."

"There is no help, my children. Different things we need."

"Then live alone!" He could control himself no longer. "I have a buyer for the house. Half the money for you, half for me. Either alone or with me to the Haven. You think I can live any longer as we are doing now?"

"Ma doesn't have to make a decision this minute, however you feel, Dad," Paul said quickly, "and you wouldn't want her to. Let's let it lay a few months, and then talk some more."

"I think I can work it out to take Mother home with me for a while," Hannah said. "You both look terrible, but especially you, Mother. I'm going to ask Phil to have a look at you."

"Sure," cracked Sammy. "What's the use of a doctor husband if you can't get free service out of him once in a while for the family? And absence might make the heart...you know."

"There was something after all," Paul told Nancy in a colorless voice. "That was Hannah's Phil calling. Her gall bladder.... Surgery."

"Her *gall* bladder. If that isn't classic. 'Bitter as gall'—talk of psychosom——"

He stepped closer, put his hand over her mouth, and said in the same colorless, plodding voice. "We have to get Dad. They operated at once. The cancer was everywhere, surrounding the liver, everywhere. They did what they could...at best she has a year. Dad...we have to tell him."

2

Honest in his weakness when they told him, and that she was not to know. "I'm not an actor. She'll know right away by how I am. Oh that poor woman. I am old too, it will break me into pieces. Oh that poor woman. She will spit on me: 'So my sickness was how I live.' Oh Paulie, how she will be, that poor woman. Only she should not suffer.... I can't stand sickness, Paulie, I can't go with you."

But went. And play-acted.

"A grand opening and you did not even wait for me.... A good thing Hannah took you with her."

"Fashion teas I needed. They cut out what tore in me; just in my throat something hurts yet.... Look! so many flowers, like a funeral. Vivi called, did Hannah tell you? And Lennie from San Francisco, and Clara; and Sammy is coming." Her gnome's face pressed happily into the flowers.

It is impossible to predict in these cases, but once over the immediate effects of the operation, she should have several months of comparative well-being.

The money, where will come the money?

Travel with her, Dad. Don't take her home to the old associations. The other children will want to see her.

The money, where will I wring the money?

Whatever happens, she is not to know. No, you can't ask her to sign papers to sell the house; nothing to upset her. Borrow instead, then after....

I had wanted to leave you each a few dollars to make life easier, as other fathers do. There will be nothing left now. (Failure! you and your "business is exploitation." Why didn't you make it when it could be made? —Is that what you're thinking, Sammy?)

Sure she's unreasonable, Dad—but you have to stay with her; if there's to be any happiness in what's left of her life, it depends on you.

Prop me up, children, think of me, too. Shuffled, chained with her, bitter woman. No Haven, and the little money going.... How happy she looks, poor creature.

The look of excitement. The straining to hear everything (the new hearing aid turned full). Why are you so happy, dying woman?

How the petals are, fold on fold, and the gladioli color. The autumn air.

Stranger grandsons, tall above the little gnome grandmother, the little spry grandfather. Paul in a frenzy of picture-taking before going.

She, wandering the great house. Feeling the books; laughing at the maple shoemaker's bench of a hundred years ago used as a table. The ear turned to music.

"Let us go home. See how good I walk now." "One step from the hospital," he answers, "and she wants to fly. Wait till Doctor Phil says."

"Look—the birds too are flying home. Very good Phil is and will not show it, but he is sick of sickness by the time he comes home."

"Mrs. Telepathy, to read minds," he answers; "read mine what it says: when the trunks of medicines become a suitcase, then we will go."

The grandboys, they do not know what to say to us. . . . Hannah, she runs around here there, when is there time for herself?

Let us go home. Let us go home.

Musing; gentleness—*but for the incidents of the rabbi in the hospital, and of the candles of benediction.*

Of the rabbi in the hospital:

Now tell me what happened, Mother..

From the sleep I awoke, Hannah's Phil, and he stands there like a devil in a dream and calls me by name. I cannot hear. I think he prays. Go away, please, I tell him, I am not a believer. Still he stands, while my heart knocks with fright.

You scared *him*, Mother. He thought you were delirious.

Who sent him? Why did he come to me?

It is a custom. The men of God come to visit those of their religion they might help. The hospital makes up the list for them—race, religion —and you are on the Jewish list.

Not for rabbis. At once go and make them change. Tell them to write: Race, human; Religion, none.

And of the candles of benediction:

Look how you have upset yourself, Mrs. Excited Over Nothing. Pleasant memories you should leave.

Go in, go back to Hannah and the lights. Two weeks I saw candles and said nothing. But she asked me.

So what was so terrible? She forgets you never did, she asks you to light the Friday candles and say the benediction like Phil's mother when she visits. If the candles give her pleasure, why shouldn't she have the pleasure?

Not for pleasure she does it. For emptiness. Because his family does. Because all around her do.

That is not a good reason too? But you did not hear her. For heritage, she told you. For the boys, from the past they should have tradition.

Superstition! From the savages, afraid of the dark, of themselves: mumbo words and magic lights to scare away ghosts.

She told you: how it started does not take away the goodness. For centuries, peace in the house it means.

Swindler! does she look back on the dark centuries? Candles bought instead of bread and stuck into a potato for a candlestick? Religion that stifled and said: in Paradise, woman, you will be the footstool of your husband, and in life—poor chosen Jew—ground under, despised, trembling in cellars. And cremated. And cremated.

This is religion's fault? You think you are still an orator of the 1905 revolution? Where are the pills for quieting? Which are they?

Heritage. How have we come from the savages, how no longer to be savages — this to teach. To look back and learn what humanizes — this to teach. To smash all ghettos that divide us—not to go back, not to go back—this to teach. Learned books in the house, will humankind live or die, and she gives to her boys—superstition.

Hannah that is so good to you. Take your pill, Mrs. Excited For Nothing, swallow.

Heritage! But when did I have time to teach? Of Hannah I asked only hands to help.

Swallow.

Otherwise—musing; gentleness.

Not to travel. To go home.

The children want to see you. We have to show them you are as thorny a flower as ever.

Not to travel.

Vivi wants you should see her new baby. She sent the tickets—airplane tickets—a Mrs. Roosevelt she wants to make of you. To Vivi's we have to go.

A new baby. How many warm, seductive babies. She holds him stiffly, *away* from her, so that he wails. And a long shudder begins, and the sweat beads on her forehead.

"Hush, shush," croons the grandfather, lifting him back. "You should forgive your grandmamma, little prince, she has never held a baby before, only seen them in glass cases. Hush, shush."

"You're tired, Ma," says Vivi. "The travel and the noisy dinner. I'll take you to lie down."

(*A long travel from, to, what the feel of a baby evokes.*)

In the airplane, cunningly designed to encase from motion (no wind, no feel of flight), she had sat severely and still, her face turned to the sky through which they cleaved and left no scar.

So this was how it looked the determining, the crucial sky, and this was how man moved through it, remote above the dwindled earth, the concealed human life. Vulnerable life, that could scar.

There was a steerage ship of memory that shook across a great, circular sea: clustered, ill human beings; and through the thick-stained air, tiny fretting waters in a window round like the airplane's—sun round, moon round. (The round thatched roofs of Olshana.) Eye round—like the smaller window that framed distance the solitary year of exile when only her eyes could travel, and no voice spoke. And the polar winds hurled themselves across snows trackless and endless and white—like the clouds which had closed together below and hidden the earth.

Now they put a baby in her lap. Do not ask me, she would have liked to beg. Enough the worn face of Vivi, the remembered grandchildren. I cannot, cannot. . . .

Cannot what? Unnatural grandmother, not able to make herself embrace a baby.

She lay there in the bed of the two little girls, her new hearing aid turned full, listening to the sound of the children going to sleep, the baby's fretful crying and hushing, the clatter of dishes being washed and put away. They thought she slept. Still she rode on.

It was not that she had not loved her babies, her children. The love— the passion of tending—had risen with the need like a torrent; and like a torrent drowned and immolated all else. But when the need was done— oh the power that was lost in the painful damming back and drying up of what still surged, but had nowhere to go. Only the thin pulsing left that could not quiet, suffering over lives one felt, but could no longer hold nor help.

On that torrent she had borne them to their own lives, and the riverbed was desert long years now. Not there would she dwell, a memoried wraith. Surely that was not all, surely there was more. Still the springs, the springs were in her seeking. Somewhere an older power that beat for life. Somewhere coherence, transport, meaning. If they would but leave her in the air now stilled of clamor, in the reconciled solitude, to journey to her self.

And they put a baby in her lap. Immediacy to embrace, and the breath of *that* past: warm flesh like this that had claims and nuzzled away all else and with lovely mouths devoured; hot-living like an animal— intensely and now; the turning maze; the long drunkenness; the drowning into needing and being needed. Severely she looked back—and the shudder seized her again, and the sweat. Not that way. Not there, not now could she, not yet. . . .

And all that visit, she could not touch the baby.

"Daddy, is it the. . .sickness she's like that?" asked Vivi. "I was so glad to be having the baby—for her. I told Tim, it'll give her more happiness than anything, being around a baby again. And she hasn't played with him once."

He was not listening, "Aahh little seed of life, little charmer," he crooned, "Hollywood should see you. A heart of ice you would melt. Kick, kick. The future you'll have for a ball. In 2050 still kick. Kick for your grandaddy then."

Attentive with the older children; sat through their performances (command performance; we command you to be the audience); helped Ann sort autumn leaves to find the best for a school program; listened gravely to Richard tell about his rock collection, while her lips mutely formed the words to remember: *igneous, sedimentary, metamorphic;* looked for missing socks, books, and bus tickets; watched the children whoop after their grandfather who knew how to tickle, chuck, lift, toss, do tricks, tell secrets, make jokes, match riddle for riddle. (Tell me a riddle, Grammy. I know no riddles, child.) Scrubbed sills and woodwork and furniture in every room; folded the laundry; straightened drawers; emptied the heaped baskets waiting for ironing (while he or Vivi or Tim nagged: You're supposed to rest here, you've been sick) but to none tended or gave food —and could not touch the baby.

After a week she said: "Let us go home. Today call about the tickets."

"You have important business, Mrs. Inahurry? The President waits to consult with you?" He shouted, for the fear of the future raced in him. "The clothes are still warm from the suitcase, your children cannot show enough how glad they are to see you, and you want home. There is plenty of time for home. We cannot be with the children at home."

"Blind to around you as always: the little ones sleep four in a room because we take their bed. We are two more people in a house with a new baby, and no help."

"Vivi is happy so. The children should have their grandparents a while, she told to me. I should have my mommy and daddy. . . ."

"Babbler and blind. Do you look at her so tired? How she starts to talk and she cries? I am not strong enough yet to help. Let us go home."

(To reconciled solitude.)

For it seemed to her the crowded noisy house was listening to her, listening for her. She could feel it like a great ear pressed under her heart. And everything knocked: quick constant raps: let me in, let me in.

How was it that soft reaching tendrils also became blows that knocked?

C'mon, Grandma, I want to show you. . . .

Tell me a riddle, Grandma. (*I know no riddles.*)

Look, Grammy, he's so dumb he can't even find his hands. (Dody and the baby on a blanket over the fermenting autumn mould.)

I made them—for you. (Ann) (Flat paper dolls with aprons that lifted on scalloped skirts that lifted on flowered pants; hair of yarn and great ringed questioning eyes.)

Watch me, Grandma. (Richard snaking up the tree, hanging exultant, free, with one hand at the top. Below Dody hunching over in pretend-cooking.) (*Climb too, Dody, climb and look.*)

Be my nap bed, Grammy.(The "No!" too late.) Morty's abandoned heaviness, while his fingers ladder up and down her hearing-air cord to his drowsy chant: eentsiebeentsiespider. *Children trust.*

It's to start off your own rock collection, Grandma. That's a trilobite fossil, 200 million years old (millionsof years on a boy's mouth) and that one's obsidian, black glass.

Knocked and knocked.

Mother, I *told* you the teacher said we had to bring it back all filled out this morning. Didn't you even ask Daddy? Then tell *me* which plan and I'll check it: evacuate or stay in the city or wait for you to come and take me away. (Seeing the look of straining to hear.) It's for Disaster, Grandma. (*Children trust.*)

Vivi in the maze of the long, the lovely drunkenness. The old old noises: baby sounds; screaming of a mother flayed to exasperation; children quarreling; children playing; singing; laughter.

And Vivi's tears and memories, spilling so fast, half the words not understood.

She had started remembering out loud deliberately, so her mother would know the past was cherished, still lived in her.

Nursing the baby: My friends marvel, and I tell them, oh it's easy to be such a cow. I remember how beautiful my mother seemed nursing my brother, and the milk just flows. . . . Was that Davy? It must have been Davy. . . .

Lowering a hem: How did you ever. . .when I think how you made everything we wore. . .Tim, just think, seven kids and Mommy sewed everything. . .do I remember you sang while you sewed? That white dress with the red apples on the skirt you fixed over for me, was it Hannah's or Clara's before it was mine?

Washing sweaters: Ma, I'll never forget, one of those days so nice you washed clothes outside; one of the first spring days it must have been. The bubbles just danced while you scrubbed, and we chased after, and you stopped to show us how to blow our own bubbles with green onion stalks. . .you always. . . .

"Strong onion, to still make you cry after so many years," her father said, to turn the tears into laughter.

While Richard bent over his homework: Where is it now, do we still have it, the Book of the Martyrs? It always seemed so, well—exalted, when you'd put it on the round table and we'd all look at it together; there was even a halo from the lamp. The lamp with the beaded fringe you could move up and down; they're in style again, pulley lamps like that, but without the fringe. You know the book I'm talking about, Daddy, the Book of the Martyrs, the first picture was a bust of Socrates? I wish there was something like that for the children, Mommy, to give them what you.... (And the tears splashed again.)

(What I intended and did not? Stop it, daughter, stop it, leave that time. And he, the hypocrite, sitting there with tears in his eyes—it was nothing to you then, nothing.)

...The time you came to school and I almost died of shame because of your accent and because I knew you knew I was ashamed; how could I?...Sammy's harmonica and you danced to it once, yes you did, you and Davy squealing in your arms.... That time you bundled us up and walked us down to the railway station to stay the night 'cause it was heated and we didn't have any coal, that winter of the strike, you didn't think I remembered that, did you, Mommy?...How you'd call us out to see the sunsets....

Day after day, the spilling memories. Worse now, questions, too. Even the grandchildren: Grandma, in the olden days, when you were little....

It was the afternoons that saved.

While they thought she napped, she would leave the mosaic on the wall (of children's drawings, maps, calendars, pictures, Ann's cardboard dolls with their great ringed questioning eyes) and hunch in the girls' cupboard, on the low shelf where the shoes stood, and the girls' dresses covered.

For that while she would painfully sheathe against the listening house, the tendrils and noises that knocked, and Vivi's spilling memories. Sometimes it helped to braid and unbraid the sashes that dangled, or to trace the pattern on the hoop slips.

Today she had jacks and children under jet trails to forget. Last night, Ann and Dody silhouetted in the window against a sunset of flaming man-made clouds of jet trail, their jacks ball accenting the peaceful noise of dinner being made. Had she told them, yes she had told them of how they played jacks in her village though there was no ball, no jacks. Six stones, round and flat, toss them out, the seventh on the back of the hand, toss, catch and swoop up as many as possible, toss again....

Of stones (repeating Richard) there are three kinds: earth's fire jetting; rock of layered centuries; crucibled new out of the old (*igneous, sedimentary, metamorphic*). But there was that other—frozen to black glass, never to transform or hold the fossil memory...(let not my seed fall on stone). There was an ancient man who fought to heights a great rock that crashed back down eternally—eternal labor, freedom, labor...(stone will perish, but the word remain). And you, David, who with a stone slew, screaming: Lord, take my heart of stone and give me flesh.

Who was screaming? Why was she back in the common room of the prison, the sun motes dancing in the shafts of light, and the informer being brought in, a prisoner now, like themselves. And Lisa leaping, yes, Lisa, the gentle and tender, biting at the betrayer's jugular. Screaming and screaming.

No, it is the children screaming. Another of Paul and Sammy's terrible fights?

In Vivi's house. Severely: you are in Vivi's house.

Blows, screams, a call: "Grandma!" For her? Oh please not for her. Hide, hunch behind the dresses deeper. But a trembling little body hurls itself beside her—surprised, smothered laughter arms surround her neck, tears rub dry on her cheek, and words too soft to understand whisper into her ear (Is this where you hide too, Grammy? It's my secret place, we have a secret now).

And the sweat beads, and the long shudder seizes.

It seemed the great ear pressed inside now, and the knocking. "We have to go home," she told him, "I grow ill here."

"It's your own fault, Mrs. Bodybusy, you do not rest, you do too much." He raged, but the fear was in his eyes. "It was a serious operation, they told you to take care.... All right, we will go to where you can rest."

But where? Not home to death, not yet. He had thought to Lennie's, to Clara's; beautiful visits with each of the children. She would have to rest first, be stronger. If they could but go to Florida—it glittered before him, the never-realized promise of Florida. California: of course. (The money, the money, dwindling!) Los Angeles first for sun and rest, then to Lennie's in San Francisco.

He told her the next day. "You saw what Nancy wrote: snow and wind back home, a terrible winter. And look at you—all bones and a swollen belly. I called Phil: he said: 'A prescription, Los Angeles sun and rest.' "

She watched the words on his lips. "You have sold the house," she cried, "that is why we do not go home. That is why you talk no more of the Haven, why there is money for travel. After the children you will drag me to the Haven."

"The Haven! Who thinks of the Haven any more? Tell her, Vivi, tell Mrs. Suspicious: a prescription, sun and rest, to make you healthy.... And how could I sell the house without *you?*"

At the place of farewells and greetings, of winds of coming and winds of going, they say their good-byes.

They look back at her with the eyes of others before them: Richard with her own blue blaze; Ann with the nordic eyes of Tim; Morty's dreaming brown of a great-grandmother he will never know; Dody with the laughing eyes of him who had been her springtide love (who stands beside her now); Vivi's, all tears.

The baby's eyes are closed in sleep.

Good-bye, my children.

3

It is to the back of the great city he brought her, to the dwelling places of the cast-off old. Bounded by two lines of amusement piers to the north and to the south, and between a long straight paving rimmed with black benches facing the sand—sands so wide the ocean is only a far fluting.

In the brief vacation season, some of the boarded stores fronting the sands open, and families, young people and children, may be seen. A little tasselled tram shuttles between the piers, and the lights of roller coasters prink and tweak over those who come to have sensation made in them.

The rest of the year it is abandoned to the old, all else boarded up and still; seemingly empty, except the occasional days and hours when the sun, like a tide, sucks them out of the low rooming houses, casts them onto the benches and sandy rim of the walk—and sweeps them into decaying enclosures once again.

A few newer apartments glint among the low bleached squares. It is in one of these Lennie's Jeannie has arranged their rooms. "Only a few miles north and south people pay hundreds of dollars a month for just this gorgeous air, Grandaddy, just this ocean closeness."

She had been ill on the plane, lay ill for days in the unfamiliar room. Several times the doctor came by—left medicine she would not take. Several times Jeannie drove in the twenty miles from work, still in her Visiting Nurse uniform, the lightness and brightness of her like a healing.

"Who can believe it is winter?" he asked one morning. "Beautiful it is outside like an ad. Come, Mrs. Invalid, come to taste it. You are well enough to sit in here, you are well enough to sit outside. The doctor said it too."

But the benches were encrusted with people, and the sands at the sidewalk's edge. Besides, she had seen the far ruffle of the sea: "there take me," and though she leaned against him, it was she who led.

Plodding and plodding, sitting often to rest, he grumbling. Patting the sand so warm. Once she scooped up a handful, cradling it close to her better eye; peered, and flung it back. And as they came almost to the brink and she could see the glistening wet, she sat down, pulled off her shoes and stockings, left him and began to run. "You'll catch cold," he screamed, but the sand in his shoes weighed him down—he who had always been the agile one—and already the white spray creamed her feet.

He pulled her back, took a handkerchief to wipe off the wet and the sand. "Oh no," she said, "the sun will dry," seized the square and smoothed it flat, dropped on it a mound of sand, knotted the kerchief corners and tied it to a bag—"to look at with the strong glass" (for the first time in years explaining an action of hers)—and lay down with the little bag against her cheek, looking toward the shore that nurtured life as it first crawled toward consciousness the millions of years ago.

He took her one Sunday in the evil-smelling bus, past flat miles of blister houses, to the home of relatives. Oh what is this? she cried as the light began to smoke and the houses to dim and recede. Smog, he said, everyone knows but you. . . . Outside he kept his arms about her, but she walked with hands pushing the heavy air as if to open it, whispered: who has done this? sat down suddenly to vomit at the curb and for a long while refused to rise.

One's age as seen on the altered face of those known in youth. Is this they he has come to visit? This Max and Rose, smooth and pleasant, introducing them to polite children, disinterested grandchildren, "the whole family, once a month on Sundays. And why not? We have the room, the help, the food."

Talk of cars, of houses, of success: this son that, that daughter this. And *your* children? Hastily skimped over, the intermarriages, the obscure work—"my doctor son-in-law, Phil"—all he has to offer. She silent in a corner. (Car-sick like a baby, he explains.) Years since he has taken her to visit anyone but the children, and old apprehensions prickle: "no incidents," he silently begs, "no incidents." He itched to tell them. "A very sick woman," significantly, indicating her with his eyes, "a very sick woman." Their restricted faces did not react. "Have you thought maybe she'd do better at Palm Springs?" Rose asked. "Or at least a nicer section of the beach, nicer people, a pool." Not to have to say "money" he said instead: "would she have sand to look at through a magnifying glass" and went on, detail after detail, the old habit betraying of parading the queer-ness of her for laughter.

After dinner—the others into the living room in men- or women-clusters, or into the den to watch TV—the four of them alone. She sat close to him, and did not speak. Jokes, stories, people they had known, beginning of reminiscence, Russia fifty–sixty years ago. Strange words across the Duncan Phyfe table: *hunger; secret meetings; human rights; spies; betrayals; prison; escape*—interrupted by one of the grandchildren: "Commercial's on; any Coke left? Gee, you're missing a real hair-raiser." And then a granddaughter (Max proudly: "look at her, an American queen") drove them home on her way back to U.C.L.A. No incident—except that there had been no incidents.

The first few mornings she had taken with her the magnifying glass, but he would sit only on the benches, so she rested at the foot, where slatted bench shadows fell, and unless she turned her hearing aid down, other voices invaded.

Now on the days when the sun shone and she felt well enough, he took her on the tram to where the benches ranged in oblongs, some with tables for checkers or cards. Again the blanket on the sand in the striped shadows, but she no longer brought the magnifying glass. He played cards, and she lay in the sun and looked towards the waters; or they walked— two blocks down to the scaling hotel, two blocks back—past chili-hamburger stands, open-doored bars. Next to New and Perpetual Rummage Sale stores.

Once, out of the aimless walkers, slow and shuffling like themselves, someone ran unevenly towards them, embraced, kissed, wept: "dear friends, old friends." A friend of *hers,* not his: Mrs. Mays who had lived next door to them in Denver when the children were small.

Thirty years are compressed into a dozen sentences; and the present, not even in three. All is told: the children scattered; the husband dead; she lives in a room two blocks up from the sing hall—and points to the domed auditorium jutting before the pier. The leg? phlebitis; the heavy breathing? that, one does not ask. She, too, comes to the benches each day to sit. And tomorrow, tomorrow, are they going to the community sing? Of course he would have heard of it, everybody goes—the big doings they wait for all week. They have never been? She will come to them for dinner tomorrow and they will all go together.

So it is that she sits in the wind of the singing, among the thousand various faces of age.

She had turned off her hearing aid at once they came into the auditorium —as she would have wished to turn off sight.

One by one they streamed by and imprinted on her—and though the savage zest of their singing came voicelessly soft and distant, the faces still roared—the faces densened the air—chorded into

children-chants, mother-croons, singing of the chained
love serenades, Beethoven storms, mad Lucia's scream
drunken joy-songs, keens for the dead, work-singing

while from floor to balcony to dome a bare-footed sore-covered little girl threaded the sound-thronged tumult, danced her ecstasy of grimace to flutes that scratched at a cross-roads village wedding

Yes, faces became sound, and the sound became faces; and faces and sound became weight—pushed, pressed

"Air"—her hands claw his.

"Whenever I enjoy myself. . . ." Then he saw the gray sweat on her face. "Here. Up. Help me, Mrs. Mays," and they support her out to where she can gulp the air in sob after sob.

"A doctor, we should get for her a doctor."

"Tch, it's nothing," says Ellen Mays, "I get it all the time. You've missed the tram; come to my place. Fix your hearing aid, honey...close ...tea. My view. See, she *wants* to come. Steady now, that's how." Adding mysteriously: "Remember your advice, easy to keep your head above water, empty things float. Float."

The singing a fading march for them, tall woman with a swollen leg, weaving little man, and the swollen thinness they help between.

The stench in the hall: mildew? decay? "We sit and rest then climb. My gorgeous view. We help each other and here   we   are."

The stench along into the slab of room. A washstand for a sink, a box with oilcloth tacked around for a cupboard, a three-burner gas plate. Artificial flowers, colorless with dust. Everywhere pictures foaming: wedding, baby, party, vacation, graduation, family pictures. From the narrow couch under a slit of window, sure enough the view: lurching rooftops and a scallop of ocean heaving, preening, twitching under the moon.

"While the water heats. Excuse me...down the hall." Ellen Mays has gone.

"You'll live?" he asked mechanically, sat down to feel his fright; tried to pull her alongside.

She pushed him away. "For air," she said; stood clinging to the dresser. Then, in a terrible voice:

After a lifetime of room. Of many rooms.

Shhh.

You remember how she lived. Eight children. And now one room like a coffin.

She pays rent!

Shrinking the life of her   into one room   like a coffin   Rooms and rooms like this   I lie on the quilt and hear them talk

Please, Mrs. Orator-without-Breath.

Once you went for coffee   I walked   I saw   A Balzac   a Chekhov to write it   Rummage   Alone   On scraps

Better old here than in the old country!

On scraps   Yet they sang like   like   Wondrous! *Humankind   one has to believe*   So strong   for what? To rot   not grow?

Your poor lungs beg you. They sob between each word.

Singing.   Unused   the life in them. She   in this poor room   with her   pictures   Max   You   The children   Everywhere   unused   the life   And who has meaning?   Century after century   still all in us not   to   grow?

Coffins, rummage, plants: sick woman. Oh lay down. We will get for you the doctor.

"And when will it end. Oh, *the end.*" *That* nightmare thought, and this time she writhed, crumpled against him, seized his hand (for a moment again the weight, the soft distant roaring of humanity) and on the strangled-for breath, begged: "Man...we'll destroy ourselves?"

And looking for answer—in the helpless pity and fear for her (for *her*) that distorted his face—she understood the last months, and knew that she was dying.

4

"Let us go home," she said after several days.

"You are in training for a cross-country trip? That is why you do not even walk across the room? Here, like a prescription Phil said, till you are stronger from the operation. You want to break doctor's orders?"

She saw the fiction was necessary to him, was silent; then: "At home I will get better. If the doctor here says?"

"And winter? And the visits to Lennie and to Clara? All right," for he saw the tears in her eyes, "I will write Phil, and talk to the doctor."

Days passed. He reported nothing. Jeannie came and took her out for air, past the boarded concessions, the hooded and tented amusement rides, to the end of the pier. They watched the spent waves feeding the new, the gulls in the clouded sky; even up where they sat, the wind-blown sand stung.

She did not ask to go down the crooked steps to the sea.

Back in her bed, while he was gone to the store, she said: "Jeannie, this doctor, he is not one I can ask questions. Ask him for me, can I go home?"

Jeannie looked at her, said quickly: "Of course, poor Granny. You want your own things around you, don't you? I'll call him tonight. . . . Look, I've something to show you," and from her purse unwrapped a large cookie, intricately shaped like a little girl. "Look at the curls—can you hear me well, Granny?—and the darling eyelashes. I just came from a house where they were baking them."

"The dimples, there in the knees," she marveled, holding it to the better light, turning, studying, "like art. Each singly they cut, or a mold?"

"Singly," said Jeannie, "and if it is a child only the mother can make them. Oh Granny, it's the likeness of a real little girl who died yesterday —Rosita. She was three years old. *Pan del Muerto,* the Bread of the Dead. It was the custom in the part of Mexico they came from."

Still she turned and inspected. "Look, the hollow in the throat, the little cross necklace. . . . I think for the mother it is a good thing to be busy with such bread. You know the family?"

Jeannie nodded. "On my rounds. I nursed. . . . Oh Granny, it is like a party; they play songs she liked to dance to. The coffin is lined with pink velvet and she wears a white dress. There are candles. . . ."

"In the house?" Surprised, "They keep her in the house?"

"Yes," said Jeannie, "and it is against the health law. I think she is. . . prepared there. The father said it will be sad to bury her in this country; in Oaxaca they have a feast night with candles each year; everyone picnics on the graves of those they loved until dawn."

"Yes, Jeannie, the living must comfort themselves." And closed her eyes.

"You want to sleep, Granny?"

"Yes, tired from the pleasure of you. I may keep the Rosita? There stand it, on the dresser, where I can see; something of my own around me."

In the kitchenette, helping her grandfather unpack the groceries, Jeannie said in her light voice:

"I'm resigning my job, Grandaddy."

"Ah, the lucky young man. Which one is he?"

"Too late. You're spoken for." She made a pyramid of cans, unstacked, and built again.

"Something is wrong with the job?"

"With me. I can't be"—she searched for the word—"What they call professional enough. I let myself feel things. And tomorrow I have to re-port a family. . . ." The cans clicked again. "It's not that, either. I just don't know what I want to do, maybe go back to school, maybe go to art school. I thought if you went to San Francisco I'd come along and talk it over with Momma and Daddy. But I don't see how you can go. She wants to go home. She asked me to ask the doctor."

The doctor told her himself. "Next week you may travel, when you are a little stronger." But next week there was the fever of an infection, and by the time that was over, she could not leave the bed—a rented hospital bed that stood beside the double bed he slept in alone now.

Outwardly the days repeated themselves. Every other afternoon and evening he went out to his newfound cronies, to talk and play cards. Twice a week, Mrs. Mays came. And the rest of the time, Jeannie was there.

By the sickbed stood Jeannie's FM radio. Often into the room the shapes of music came. She would lie curled on her side, her knees drawn up, intense in listening (Jeannie sketched her so, coiled, convoluted like an ear), then thresh her hand out and abruptly snap the radio mute—still to lie in her attitude of listening, concealing tears.

Once Jeannie brought in a young Marine to visit, a friend from high-school days she had found wandering near the empty pier. Because Jeannie asked him to, gravely, without self-consciousness, he sat himself cross-legged on the floor and performed for them a dance of his native Samoa.

Long after they left, a tiny thrumming sound could be heard where, in her bed, she strove to repeat the beckon, flight, surrender of his hands, the fluttering footbeats, and his low plaintive calls.

Hannah and Phil sent flowers. To deepen her pleasure, he placed one in her hair. "Like a girl," he said, and brought the hand mirror so she could see. She looked at the pulsing red flower, the yellow skull face; a desolate, excited laugh shuddered from her, and she pushed the mirror away—but let the flower burn.

The week Lennie and Helen came, the fever returned. With it the excited laugh, and incessant words. She, who in her life had spoken but seldom and then only when necessary (never having learned the easy, social uses of words), now in dying, spoke incessantly.

In a half-whisper: "Like Lisa she is, your Jeannie. Have I told you of Lisa who taught me to read? Of the highborn she was, but noble in herself. I was sixteen; they beat me; my father beat me so I would not go to her. It was forbidden, she was a Tolstoyan. At night, past dogs that howled, terrible dogs, my son, in the snows of winter to the road, I to ride in her carriage like a lady, to books. To her, life was holy, knowledge was holy, and she taught me to read. They hung her. Everything that happens one must try to understand why. She killed one who betrayed many. Because of betrayal, betrayed all she lived and believed. In one minute she killed, before my eyes (there is so much blood in a human being, my son), in prison with me. All that happens, one must try to understand.

"The name?" Her lips would work. "The name that was their pole star; the doors of the death houses fixed to open on it; I read of it my year of penal servitude. Thuban!" very excited, "Thuban, in ancient Egypt the pole star. Can you see, look out to see it, Jeannie, if it swings around *our* pole star that seems to *us* not to move.

"Yes, Jeannie, at your age my mother and grandmother had already buried children...yes, Jeannie, it is more than oceans between Olshana and you...yes, Jeannie, they danced, and for all the bodies they had they might as well be chickens, and indeed, they scratched and flapped their arms and hopped.

"And Andrei Yefimitch, who for twenty years had never known of it and never wanted to know, said as if he wanted to cry: but why my dear friend this malicious laughter?" Telling to herself half-memorized phrases from her few books. "Pain I answer with tears and cries, baseness with indignation, meanness with repulsion...for life may be hated or wearied of, but never despised.'"

Delirious: "Tell me, my neighbor, Mrs. Mays, the pictures never lived, but what of the flowers? Tell them who ask: no rabbis, no ministers, no priests, no speeches, no ceremonies: ah, false—let the living comfort themselves. Tell Sammy's boy, he who flies, tell him to go to Stuttgart and see where Davy has no grave. And what?" A conspirator's laugh. "And what? where millions have no graves—save air."

In delirium or not, wanting the radio on; not seeming to listen, the words still jetting, wanting the music on. Once, silencing it abruptly as of old, she began to cry, unconcealed tears this time. "You have pain, Granny?" Jeannie asked.

"The music," she said, "still it is there and we do not hear; knocks, and our poor human ears too weak. What else, what else we do not hear?"

Once she knocked his hand aside as he gave her a pill, swept the bottles from her bedside table: "no pills, let me feel what I feel," and laughed as on his hands and knees he groped to pick them up.

Nighttimes her hand reached across the bed to hold his.

A constant retching began. Her breath was too faint for sustained speech now, but still the lips moved:

> *When no longer necessary to injure others*
> *Pick pick pick Blind chicken*
> *As a human being responsibility*

"David!" imperious, "Basin!" and she would vomit, rinse her mouth, the wasted throat working to swallow, and begin the chant again.

She will be better off in the hospital now, the doctor said.

He sent the telegrams to the children, was packing her suitcase, when her hoarse voice startled. She had roused, was pulling herself to sitting.

"Where now?" she asked. "Where now do you drag me?"

"You do not even have to have a baby to go this time," he soothed, looking for the brush to pack. "Remember, after Davy you told me—worthy to have a baby for the pleasure of the rest in the hospital?"

"Where now? Not home yet?" Her voice mourned. "Where *is* my home?"

He rose to ease her back. "The doctor, the hospital," he started to explain, but deftly, like a snake, she had slithered out of bed and stood swaying, propped behind the night table.

"Coward," she hissed, "runner."

"You stand,' he said senselessly.

"To take me there and run. Afraid of a little vomit."

He reached her as she fell. She struggled against him, half slipped from his arms, pulled herself up again.

"Weakling," she taunted, "to leave me there and run. Betrayer. All your life you have run."

He sobbed, telling Jeannie. "A Marilyn Monroe to run for her virtue. Fifty-nine pounds she weighs, the doctor said, and she beats at me like a Dempsey. Betrayer, she cries, and I running like a dog when she calls; day and night, running to her, her vomit, the bedpan. . . ."

"She needs you, Grandaddy," said Jeannie. "Isn't that what they call love? I'll see if she sleeps, and if she does, poor worn-out darling, we'll have a party, you and I: I brought us rum babas."

They did not move her. By her bed now stood the tall hooked pillar that held the solutions—blood and dextrose—to feed her veins. Jeannie moved down the hall to take over the sickroom, her face so radiant, her grandfather asked her once: "you are in love?" (Shameful the joy, the pure overwhelming joy from being with her grandmother; the peace, the serenity that breathed.) "My darling escape," she answered incoherently, "my darling Granny"—as if that explained.

Now one by one the children came, those that were able. Hannah, Paul, Sammy. Too late to ask: and what did you learn with your living, Mother, and what do we need to know?

Clara, the eldest, clenched:

Pay me back, Mother, pay me back for all you took from me. Those others you crowded into your heart. The hands I needed to be for you, the heaviness, the responsibility.

It this she? Noises the dying make, the crablike hands crawling over the covers. The ethereal singing.

She hears that music, that singing from childhood; forgotten sound— not heard since, since.... And the hardness breaks like a cry: Where did we lose each other, first mother, singing mother?

Annulled: the quarrels, the gibing, the harshness between; the fall into silence and the withdrawal.

I do not know you, Mother. Mother, I never knew you.

Lennie, suffering not alone for her who was dying, but for that in her which never lived (for that which in him might never live). From him too, unspoken words: *good-bye Mother who taught me to mother myself.*

Not Vivi, who must stay with her children; not Davy, but he is already here, having to die again with *her* this time, for the living take their dead with them when they die.

Light she grew, like a bird, and, like a bird, sound bubbled in her throat while the body fluttered in agony. Night and day, asleep or awake (though indeed there was no difference now) the songs and the phrases leaping.

And he, who had once dreaded a long dying (from fear of himself, from horror of the dwindling money) now desired her quick death profoundly, for *her* sake. He no longer went out, except when Jeannie forced him; no longer laughed, except when in the bright kitchenette, Jeannie coaxed his laughter (and she who seemed to hear nothing else, would laugh too, conspiratorial wisps of laughter).

Light, like a bird, the fluttering body, the little claw hands, the beaked shadow on her face; and the throat, bubbling, straining.

He tried not to listen, as he tried not to look on the face in which only the forehead remained familiar, but trapped with her the long nights in that little room, the sounds worked themselves into his consciousness, with their punctuation of death swallows, whimpers, gurglings.

Even in reality (swallow)   *life's lack of it*
Slaveships   deathtrains   clubs   eeenough
The bell   summon what ennobles
78,000 in one minute (whisper of a scream) *78,000 human beings*
we'll destroy ourselves?

"Aah, Mrs. Miserable," he said, as if she could hear, "all your life working, and now in bed you lie, servants to tend, you do not even need to call to be tended, and still you work. Such hard work it is to die? Such hard work?"

The body threshed, her hand clung in his. A melody, ghost-thin, hovered on her lips, and like a guilty ghost, the vision of her bent in listening to it, silencing the record instantly he was near. Now, heedless of his presence, she floated the melody on and on.

"Hid it from me," he complained, "how many times you listened to remember it so?" And tried to think when she had first played it, or first begun to silence her few records when he came near—but could reconstruct nothing. There was only this room with its tall hooked pillar and its swarm of sounds.

No man one   except through others
Strong   with the not yet   in the now
Dogma dead   war dead   one country

"It helps, Mrs. Philosopher, words from books? It helps?" And it seemed to him that for seventy years she had hidden a tape recorder, infinitely microscopic, within her, that it had coiled infinite mile on mile, trapping every song, every melody, every word read, heard, and spoken—and that maliciously she was playing back only what said nothing of him, of the children, of their intimate life together.

"Left us indeed, Mrs. Babbler," he reproached, "you who called others babbler and cunningly saved your words. A lifetime you tended and loved, and now not a word of us, for us. Left us indeed? Left me."

And he took out his solitaire deck, shuffled the cards loudly, slapped them down.

Lift high banner of reason (tatter of an orator's voice) *justice freedom*
light
Humankind   life worthy   capacities
Seeks (blur of shudder) *belong   human being*

"Words, words," he accused, "and what human beings did *you* seek around you, Mrs. Live Alone, and what humankind think worthy?"

Though even as he spoke, he remembered she had not always been isolated, had not always wanted to be alone (as he knew there had been a voice before this gossamer one; before the hoarse voice that broke from silence to lash, make incidents, shame him—a girl's voice of eloquence that spoke their holiest dreams). But again he could reconstruct, image, nothing of what had been before, or when, or how, it had changed.

Ace, queen, jack. The pillar shadow fell, so, in two tracks; in the mirror depths glistened a moonlike blob, the empty solution bottle. And it worked in him: *of reason and justice and freedom...Dogma dead:* he remembered the full quotation, laughed bitterly. "Hah, good you do not know what you say; good Victor Hugo died and did not see it, his twentieth century."

Deuce, ten, five. Dauntlessly she began a song of their youth of belief:

These things shall be, a loftier race
than e'er the world hath known shall rise
with flame of freedom in their souls
and light of knowledge in their eyes

King, four, jack. "In the twentieth century, hah!"

They shall be gentle, brave and strong
to spill no drop of blood, but dare
all .. that may.
on earth and fire and sea and air

"To spill no drop of blood, hah! So, cadaver, and you too, cadaver Hugo, 'in the twentieth century ignorance will be dead, dogma will be dead, war will be dead, and for all mankind one country—of fulfilment?' Hah!"

And every life (long strangling cough) *shall be a song*

The cards fell from his fingers. Without warning, the bereavement and betrayal he had sheltered—compounded through the years—hidden even from himself—revealed itself,
    uncoiled,
    released,
    sprung

and with it the monstrous shapes of what had actually happened in the century.

A ravening hunger or thirst seized him. He groped into the kitchenette, switched on all three lights, piled a tray—"you have finished your night snack, Mrs. Cadaver, now I will have mine." And he was shocked at the tears that splashed on the tray.

"Salt tears. For free. I forgot to shake on salt?"

Whispered: "Lost, how much I lost."

Escaped to the grandchildren whose childhoods were childish, who had never hungered, who lived unravaged by disease in warm houses of many rooms, had all the school for which they cared, could walk on any street, stood a head taller than their grandparents, towered above—beautiful skins, straight backs, clear straightforward eyes. "Yes, you in Olshana," he said to the town of sixty years ago, "they would be nobility to you."

And was this not the dream then, come true in ways undreamed? he asked.

And are there no other children in the world? he answered, as if in her harsh voice.

And the flame of freedom, the light of knowledge?
And the drop, to spill no drop of blood?

And he thought that at six Jeannie would get up and it would be his turn to go to her room and sleep, that he could press the buzzer and she would come now; that in the afternoon Ellen Mays was coming, and this time they would play cards and he could marvel at how rouge can stand half an inch on the cheek; that in the evening the doctor would come, and he could beg him to be merciful, to stop the feeding solutions, to let her die.

To let her die, and with her their youth of belief out of which her bright, betrayed words foamed; stained words, that on her working lips came stainless.

Hours yet before Jeannie's turn. He could press the buzzer and wake her to come now; he could take a pill, and with it sleep; he could pour more brandy into his milk glass, though what he had poured was not yet touched.

Instead he went back, checked her pulse, gently tended with his knotty fingers as Jeannie had taught.

She was whimpering; her hand crawled across the covers for his. Compassionately he enfolded it, and with his free hand gathered up the cards again. Still was there thirst or hunger ravening in him.

That world of their youth—dark, ignorant, terrible with hate and disease —how was it that living in it, in the midst of corruption, filth, treachery, degradation, they had not mistrusted man nor themselves; had believed so beautifully, so...falsely?

"Aaah, children," he said out loud, "how we believed, how we belonged." And he yearned to package for each of the children, the grandchildren, for everyone, *that joyous certainty, that sense of mattering, of moving and being moved, of being one and indivisible with the great of the past, with all that freed, ennobled man.* Package it, stand on corners, in front of stadiums and on crowded beaches, knock on doors, give it as a fabled gift.

"And why not in cereal boxes, in soap packages?" he mocked himself. "Aah. You have taken my senses, cadaver."

Words foamed, died unsounded. Her body writhed; she made kissing motions with her mouth. (Her lips moving as she read, poring over the

Book of the Martyrs, the magnifying glass superimposed over the heavy eyeglasses.) *Still she believed?* "Eva!" he whispered. "Still you believed? You lived by it? These Things Shall Be?"

"Once pound soup meat," she answered distinctly, "one soup bone."

"My ears heard you. Ellen Mays was witness: 'Humankind...one has to believe.' " Imploringly: "Eva!"

"Bread, day-old." She was mumbling. "Please, in a wooden box...for kindling. The thread, hah, the thread breaks. Cheap thread"—and a gurgling, enormously loud, began in her throat.

"I ask for stone; she gives me bread—day-old." He pulled his hand away, shouted: "Who wanted questions? Everything you have to wake?" Then dully, "Ah, let me help you turn, poor creature."

Words jumbled, cleared. In a voice of crowded terror:

"Paul, Sammy, don't fight.

"Hannah, have I ten hands?

"How can I give it, Clara, how can I give it if I don't have?"

"You lie," he said sturdily, "there was joy too." Bitterly: "Ah how cheap you speak of us at the last."

As if to rebuke him, as if her voice had no relationship with her flailing body, she sang clearly, beautifully, a school song the children had taught her when they were little; begged:

"Not look my hair where they cut...."

(The crown of braids shorn.) And instantly he left the mute old woman poring over the Book of the Martyrs; went past the mother treadling at the sewing machine, singing with the children; past the girl in her wrinkled prison dress, hiding her hair with scarred hands, lifting to him her awkward, shamed, imploring eyes of love; and took her in his arms, dear, personal, fleshed, in all the heavy passion he had loved to rouse from her.

"Eva!"

Her little claw hand beat the covers. How much, how much can a man stand? He took up the cards, put them down, circled the beds, walked to the dresser, opened, shut drawers, brushed his hair, moved his hand bit by bit over the mirror to see what of the reflection he could blot out with each move, and felt that at any moment he would die of what was unendurable. Went to press the buzzer to wake Jeannie, looked down, saw on Jeannie's sketch pad the hospital bed, with *her;* the double bed alongside, with him; the tall pillar feeding into her veins, and their hands, his and hers, clasped, feeding each other. And as if he had been instructed he went to his bed, lay down, holding the sketch (as if it could shield against the monstrous shapes of loss, of betrayal, of death) and with his free hand took hers back into his.

So Jeannie found them in the morning.

That last day the agony was perpetual. Time after time it lifted her almost off the bed, so they had to fight to hold her down. He could not endure and left the room; wept as if there never would be tears enough.

Jeannie came to comfort him. In her light voice she said: Grandaddy, Grandaddy don't cry. She is not there, she promised me. On the last day, she said she would go back to when she first heard music, a little girl on the road of the village where she was born. She promised me. It is a wedding and they dance, while the flutes so joyous and vibrant tremble in the air. Leave her there, Grandaddy, it is all right. She promised me. Come back, come back and help her poor body to die.

For two of that generation
Seevya and Genya

Death deepens the wonder

KING OF THE BINGO GAME
Ralph Ellison

The woman in front of him was eating roasted peanuts that smelled so good that he could barely contain his hunger. He could not even sleep and wished they'd hurry and begin the bingo game. There, on his right, two fellows were drinking wine out of a bottle wrapped in a paper bag, and he could hear soft gurgling in the dark. His stomach gave a low, gnawing growl. "If this was down South," he thought, "all I'd have to do is lean over and say, 'Lady, gimme a few of those peanuts, please ma'm,' and she'd pass me the bag and never think nothing of it." Or he could ask the fellows for a drink in the same way. Folks down South stuck together that way; they didn't even have to know you. But up here it was different. Ask somebody for something, and they'd think you were crazy. Well, I ain't crazy. I'm just broke, 'cause I got no birth certificate to get a job, and Laura 'bout to die 'cause we got no money for a doctor. But I ain't crazy. And yet a pinpoint of doubt was focused in his mind as he glanced toward the screen and saw the hero stealthily entering a dark room and sending the beam of a flashlight along a wall of bookcases. This is where he finds the trapdoor, he remembered. The man would pass abruptly through the wall and find the girl tied to a bed, her legs and arms spread wide, and her clothing torn to rags. He laughed softly to himself. He had seen the picture three times, and this was one of the best scenes.

On his right the fellow whispered wide-eyed to his companion, "Man, look a-yonder!"

"Damn!"

"Wouldn't I like to have her tied up like that..."

"Hey! That fool's letting her loose!"

"Aw, man, he loves her."

"Love or no love!"

The man moved impatiently beside him, and he tried to involve himself in the scene. But Laura was on his mind. Tiring quickly of watching the picture he looked back to where the white beam filtered from the projection room above the balcony. It started small and grew large; specks of dust dancing in its whiteness as it reached the screen. It was strange how the beam always landed right on the screen and didn't mess up and fall somewhere else. But they had it all fixed. Everything was fixed. Now suppose when they showed that girl with her dress torn the girl started taking off the rest of her clothes, and when the guy came in he didn't untie her but kept her there and went to taking off his own clothes? *That* would be something to see. If a picture got out of hand like that those guys up there would go nuts. Yeah, and there'd be so many folks in here you couldn't find a seat for nine months! A strange sensation played over his skin. He shuddered. Yesterday he'd seen a bedbug on a woman's neck as they walked out into the bright street. But exploring his thigh through a hole in his pocket he found only goose pimples and old scars.

The bottle gurgled again. He closed his eyes. Now a dreamy music was accompanying the film and train whistles were sounding in the distance, and he was a boy again walking along a railroad trestle down South, and seeing the train coming, and running back as fast as he could go, and hearing the whistle blowing, and getting off the trestle to solid ground just in time, with the earth trembling beneath his feet, and feeling relieved as he ran down the cinder-strewn embankment onto the highway, and looking back and seeing with terror that the train had left the track and was following him right down the middle of the street, and all the white people laughing as he ran screaming...

"Wake up there, buddy! What the hell do you mean hollering like that? Can't you see we trying to enjoy this here picture?"

He stared at the man with gratitude.

"I'm sorry, old man," he said. "I musta been dreaming."

"Well, here, have a drink. And don't be making no noise like that, damn!"

His hands trembled as he tilted his head. It was not wine, but whiskey. Cold rye whiskey. He took a deep swoller, decided it was better not to take another, and handed the bottle back to its owner.

"Thanks, old man," he said.

Now he felt the cold whiskey breaking a warm path straight through the middle of him, growing hotter and sharper as it moved. He had not eaten all day, and it made him light-headed. The smell of the peanuts stabbed him like a knife, and he got up and found a seat in the middle aisle. But no sooner did he sit than he saw a row of intense-faced young girls, and got up again, thinking, "You chicks musta been Lindy-hopping somewhere." He found a seat several rows ahead as the lights came on, and he saw the screen disappear behind a heavy red and gold curtain; then the curtain rising, and the man with the microphone and a uniformed attendant coming on the stage.

He felt for his bingo cards, smiling. The guy at the door wouldn't like it if he knew about his having *five* cards. Well, not everyone played the bingo game; and even with five cards he didn't have much of a chance.

For Laura, though, he had to have faith. He studied the cards, each with its different numerals, punching the free center hole in each and spreading them neatly across his lap; and when the lights faded he sat slouched in his seat so that he could look from his cards to the bingo wheel with but a quick shifting of his eyes.

Ahead, at the end of the darkness, the man with the microphone was pressing a button attached to a long cord and spinning the bingo wheel and calling out the number each time the wheel came to rest. And each time the voice rang out his finger raced over the cards for the number. With five cards he had to move fast. He became nervous; there were too many cards, and the man went too fast with his grating voice. Perhaps he should just select one and throw the others away. But he was afraid. He became warm. Wonder how much Laura's doctor would cost? Damn that, watch the cards! And with despair he heard the man call three in a row which he missed on all five cards. This way he'd never win...

When he saw the row of holes punched across the third card, he sat paralyzed and heard the man call three more numbers before he stumbled forward, screaming,

"Bingo! Bingo!"

"Let that fool up there," someone called.

"Get up there, man!"

He stumbled down the aisle and up the steps to the stage into a light so sharp and bright that for a moment it blinded him, and he felt that he had moved into the spell of some strange, mysterious power. Yet it was as familiar as the sun, and he knew it was the perfectly familiar bingo.

The man with the microphone was saying something to the audience as he held out his card. A cold light flashed from the man's finger as the card left his hand. His knees trembled. The man stepped closer, checking the card against the numbers chalked on the board. Suppose he had made a mistake? The pomade on the man's hair made him feel faint, and he backed away. But the man was checking the card over the microphone now, and he had to stay. He stood tense, listening.

"Under the O, forty-four," the man chanted. "Under the I, seven. Under the G, three. Under the B, ninety-six. Under the N, thirteen!"

His breath came easier as the man smiled at the audience.

"Yessir, ladies and gentlemen, he's one of the chosen people!"

The audience rippled with laughter and applause.

"Step right up to the front of the stage."

He moved slowly forward, wishing that the light was not so bright.

"To win tonight's jackpot of $36.90 the wheel must stop betweeen the double zero, understand?"

He nodded, knowing the ritual from the many days and nights he had watched the winners march across the stage to press the button that controlled the spinning wheel and receive the prizes. And now he followed the instructions as though he'd crossed the slippery stage a million prize-winning times.

The man was making some kind of a joke, and he nodded vacantly. So tense had he become that he felt a sudden desire to cry and shook it away. He felt vaguely that his whole life was determined by the bingo wheel; not only that which would happen now that he was at last before it, but all that had gone before, since his birth, and his mother's birth and the birth of his father. It had always been there, even though he had not been aware of it, handing out the unlucky cards and numbers of his days. The feeling persisted, and he started quickly away. I better get down from here before I make a fool of myself, he thought.

"Here, boy," the man called. "You haven't started yet."

Someone laughed as he went hesitantly back.

"Are you all reet?"

He grinned at the man's jive talk, but no words would come, and he knew it was not a convincing grin. For suddenly he knew that he stood on the slippery brink of some terrible embarrassment.

"Where are you from, boy?" the man asked.

"Down South."

"He's from down South, ladies and gentlemen," the man said. "Where from? Speak right into the mike."

"Rocky Mont," he said. "Rock' Mont, North Car'lina."

"So you decided to come down off that mountain to the U.S.," the man laughed. He felt that the man was making a fool of him, but then something cold was placed in his hand, and the lights were no longer behind him.

Standing before the wheel he felt alone, but that was somehow right, and he remembered his plan. He would give the wheel a short quick twirl. Just a touch of the button. He had watched it many times, and always it came close to double zero when it was short and quick. He steeled himself; the fear had left, and he felt a profound sense of promise, as though he were about to be repaid for all the things he'd suffered all his life. Trembling, he pressed the button. There was a whirl of lights, and in a second he realized with finality that though he wanted to, he could not stop. It was as though he held a high-powered line in his naked hand. His nerves tightened. As the wheel increased its speed it seemed to draw him more and more into his power, as though it held his fate; and with it came a deep need to submit, to whirl, to lose himself in its swirl of color. He could not stop it now, he knew. So let it be.

The button rested snuggly in his palm where the man had placed it. And now he became aware of the man beside him, advising him through the microphone, while behind the shadowy audience hummed with noisy voices. He shifted his feet. There was still that feeling of helplessness within him, making part of him desire to turn back, even now that the jackpot was right in his hand. He squeezed the button until his fist ached. Then, like the sudden shriek of a subway whistle, a doubt tore through his head. Suppose he did not spin the wheel long enough? What could he do, and how could he tell? And then he knew, even as he wondered, that as long as he pressed the button, he could control the jackpot. He and only he could determine whether or not it was to be his. Not even the man with the microphone could do anything about it now. He felt drunk. Then, as though he had come down from a high hill into a valley of people, he heard the audience yelling.

"Come down from there, you jerk!"

"Let somebody else have a chance..."

"Ole Jack thinks he done found the end of the rainbow..."

The last voice was not unfriendly, and he turned and smiled dreamily into the yelling mouths. Then he turned his back squarely on them.

"Don't take too long, boy," a voice said.

He nodded. They were yelling behind him. Those folks did not understand what had happened to him. They had been playing the bingo game day in and night out for years, trying to win rent money or hamburger change. But not one of those wise guys had discovered this wonderful thing. He watched the wheel whirling past the numbers and experienced a burst of exhaltation: This is God! This is the really truly God! He said it aloud, "This is God!"

He said it with such absolute conviction that he feared he would fall fainting into the footlights. But the crowd yelled so loud that they could not hear. Those fools, he thought. I'm here trying to tell them the most wonderful secret in the world, and they're yelling like they gone crazy. A hand fell upon his shoulder.

"You'll have to make a choice now, boy. You've taken too long."

He brushed the hand violently away.

"Leave me alone, man. I know what I'm doing!"

The man looked surprised and held on to the microphone for support. And because he did not wish to hurt the man's feelings he smiled, realizing with a sudden pang that there was no way of explaining to the man just why he had to stand there pressing the button forever.

"Come here," he called tiredly.

The man approached, rolling the heavy microphone across the stage.

"Anybody can play this bingo game, right?" he said.

"Sure, but..."

He smiled, feeling inclined to be patient with this slick looking white man with his blue sport shirt and his sharp gabardine suit.

"That's what I thought," he said. "Anybody can win the jackpot as long as they get the lucky number, right?"

"That's the rule, but after all..."

"That's what I thought," he said. "And the big prize goes to the man who knows how to win it?"

The man nodded speechlessly.

"Well then, go on over there and watch me win like I want to. I ain't going to hurt nobody," he said, "and I'll show you how to win. I mean to show the whole world how it's got to be done."

And because he understood, he smiled again to let the man know that he held nothing against him for being white and impatient. Then he refused to see the man any longer and stood pressing the button, the voices of the crowd reaching him like sounds in distant streets. Let them yell. All the Negroes down there were just ashamed because he was black like them. He smiled inwardly, knowing how it was. Most of the time he was ashamed of what Negroes did himself. Well, let them be ashamed for something this time. Like him. He was like a long thin black wire that was being stretched and wound upon the bingo wheel; wound until he wanted to scream; wound, but this time himself controlling the winding and the sadness and the shame, and because he did, Laura would be all right. Suddenly the lights flickered. He staggered backwards. Had something gone wrong? All this noise. Didn't they know that although he controlled the wheel, it also controlled him, and unless he pressed the button forever and forever and ever it would stop, leaving him high and dry, dry and high on this hard high slippery hill and Laura dead? There was only one chance; he had to do whatever the wheel demanded. And gripping the button in despair, he discovered with surprize that it imparted a nervous energy. His spine tingled. He felt a certain power.

Now he faced the raging crowd with defiance, its screams penetrating his eardrums like trumpets shrieking from a juke-box. The vague faces glowing in the bingo lights gave him a sense of himself that he had never known before. He was running the show, by God! They had to react to him, for he was their luck. This is *me,* he thought. Let the bastards yell. Then someone was laughing inside him, and he realized that somehow he had forgotten his own name. It was a sad, lost feeling to lose your name, and a crazy thing to do. That name had been given him by the white man who had owned his grandfather a long lost time ago down South. But maybe those wise guys knew his name.

"Who am I?" he screamed.

"Hurry up and bingo, you jerk!"

They didn't know either, he thought sadly. They didn't even know their own names, they were all poor nameless bastards. Well, he didn't need that old name; he was reborn. For as long as he pressed the button he was The-man-who-pressed-the-button-who-held-the-prize-who-was-the-King-of-Bingo. That was the way it was, and he'd have to press the button even if nobody understood, even though Laura did not understand.

"Live!" he shouted.

The audience quieted like the dying of a huge fan.

"Live, Laura, baby. I got holt of it now, sugar. Live!"

He screamed it, tears streaming down his face. "I got nobody but YOU!"

The screams tore from his very guts. He felt as though the rush of blood to his head would burst out in baseball seams of small red droplets, like a head beaten by police clubs. Bending over he saw a trickle of blood splashing the toe of his shoe. With his free hand he searched his head. It was his nose. God, suppose something has gone wrong? He felt that the whole audience had somehow entered him and was stamping its feet in his stomach and he was unable to throw them out. They wanted the prize, that was it. They wanted the secret for themselves. But they'd never get it; he would keep the bingo wheel whirling forever, and Laura would be safe in the wheel. But would she? It had to be, because if she were not safe the wheel would cease to turn; it could not go on. He had to get away, *vomit* all, and his mind formed an image of himself running with Laura in his arms down the tracks of the subway just ahead of an A train, running desperately *vomit* with people screaming for him to come out but knowing no way of leaving the tracks because to stop would bring the train crushing down upon him and to attempt to leave across the other tracks would mean to run into a hot third rail as high as his waist which threw blue sparks that blinded his eyes until he could hardly see.

He heard singing and the audience was clapping its hands.

Shoot the liquor to him, Jim, boy!
Clap-clap-clap
Well a-calla the cop
He's blowing his top!
Shoot the liquor to him, Jim, boy!

Bitter anger grew within him at the singing. They think I'm crazy. Well let 'em laugh. I'll do what I got to do.

He was standing in an attitude of intense listening when he saw that they were watching something on the stage behind him. He felt weak. But when he turned he saw no one. If only his thumb did not ache so. Now they were applauding. And for a moment he thought that the wheel had stopped. But that was impossible, his thumb still pressed the button. Then he saw them. Two men in uniform beckoned from the end of the stage. They were coming toward him, walking in step, slowly, like a tap-dance team returning for a third encore. But their shoulders shot forward, and he backed away, looking wildly about. There was nothing to fight them with. He had only the long black cord which led to a plug somewhere back stage, and he couldn't use that because it operated the bingo wheel. He backed slowly, fixing the men with his eyes as his lips stretched over his teeth in a tight, fixed grin; moved toward the end of the stage and realizing that he couldn't go much further, for suddenly the cord became taut and he couldn't afford to break the cord. But he had to do something. The audience was howling. Suddenly he stopped dead, seeing the men halt, their legs lifted as in an interrupted step of a slow-motion dance. There was nothing to do but run in the other direction and he dashed forward, slipping and sliding. The men fell back, surprised. He struck out violently going past.

"Grab him!"

He ran, but all too quickly the cord tightened, resistingly, and he turned and ran back again. This time he slipped them, and discovered by running in a circle before the wheel he could keep the cord from tightening. But this way he had to flail his arms to keep the men away. Why couldn't they leave a man alone? He ran, circling.

"Ring down the curtain," someone yelled. But they couldn't do that. If they did the wheel flashing from the projection room would be cut off. But they had him before he could tell them so, trying to pry open his fist, and he was wrestling and trying to bring his knees into the fight and holding on to the button, for it was his life. And now he was down, seeing a foot coming down, crushing his wrist cruelly, down, as he saw the wheel whirling serenely above.

"I can't give it up," he screamed. Then quietly, in a confidential tone, "Boys, I really can't give it up."

It landed hard against his head. And in the blank moment they had it away from him, completely now. He fought them trying to pull him up from the stage as he watched the wheel spin slowly to a stop. Without surprise he saw it rest as double-zero.

"You see," he pointed bitterly.

"Sure, boy, sure, it's O. K.," one of the men said smiling.

And seeing the man bow his head to someone he could not see, he felt very, very happy; he would receive what all the winner's received.

But as he warmed in the justice of the man's tight smile he did not see the man's slow wink, nor see the bow-legged man behind him step clear of the swiftly descending curtain and set himself for a blow. He only felt the dull pain exploding in his skull, and he knew even as it slipped out of him that his luck had run out on the stage.

THE WATCHERS
Florence Engel Randall

From the moment Althea awoke that morning, she knew their building had been chosen. She knew it even before she saw the excitement in her husband's eyes as he handed her the official notice that had been put under their door.

"Well," he said, smiling at her while she read it, "what do you think of that?"

"I had a feeling, George," she said, "even before I opened my eyes, I had a feeling that this would happen today."

"We were due to be next," George said. "The setup here is about perfect for it."

"Will you be home early?" She watched him while he sipped his coffee.

"It won't start until late," he said. "It won't start until it gets dark. You know how these things are."

"Just the same," she said, "I couldn't bear it just sitting around and waiting for you. We have so much to do. We have to have dinner first and then change our clothes and find seats. We want to have good seats," she reminded him. "They won't reserve any for us, you know."

"Don't worry about it." He touched her cheek lightly with the back of his hand. "I'll be home in plenty of time."

"Do you have everything? I was never so scared in my life yesterday when I found your gun on the top of the dresser. I just couldn't believe my eyes. I wanted to run after you but I didn't know which route you had taken."

"I always carry a spare," he said. "You know that. I always keep a spare in my coat pocket. Why don't you trust me?"

"I know I'm being foolish," Althea said, kissing him goodbye. "Just be careful, that's all. I don't want you to be so sure of yourself that you'll get careless."

"You be careful," he said. "Do you have to go out today?"

She frowned. "I have to go marketing, and then I thought I'd go downtown and buy a new dress for tonight. All the women will be dressed up and I don't want to go looking like a frump."

"Watch out for the department stores," he reminded her. "They can be dangerous. Don't take any crowded elevators and check the dressing room before you try anything on."

She locked and double-locked the door after him, then fastened the chain before she had her own breakfast. Standing at the window while she drank her coffee, she thought how ridiculous it was the way they went through the same routine each morning as if the very fact that they had to take precautions was making them nervous. When they were first married two years ago, it would never have occurred to either of them that there was any reason for worry.

It must be because we're so much in love, she told herself, stacking the dishes in the washer. Love breeds its own vulnerability, its own fear.

When the signal flashed on the wall, Althea had just finished dressing. She watched it for a moment. It was their code, all right. Three lights in a row, the flickering pause, and then the slow, deliberate hold. She pressed the button that buzzed downstairs.

"Who is it?" she said, her mouth against the intercom.

"It's all right," said a woman's voice, clear and high and a bit too shrill. "I've already shown my identification to your doorman. I'm Sally Milford— Cary Milford's wife. My husband works in your husband's office."

"What do you want?" said Althea cautiously. "I'm much too busy to see anyone this morning. Besides, I'm on my way out." She bit her lip. George would be right if he scolded her for being careless. Why had she told this woman she was going out?

"I'll only take a moment of your time. It's important."

"Can't you tell me what it is over the intercom?"

"If I wanted to talk this way, I could have called you on the phone. I must see you. Please."

"All right," said Althea, reluctantly, knowing she was being foolish, "you can come up."

She checked her own gun even though she knew it was loaded and she palmed the small dagger—the one her mother had given her as a wedding present—the one with the jeweled handle.

"Things are so different now," her mother had said, sighing. She had lifted the dagger from the tissue paper and had studied it for a moment before she handed it to Althea. "In my day we could walk the streets without this sort of thing."

"That's not true," Althea reminded her. "You told me you used to wear stilt-like heels and you always carried a whistle in your purse."

"But that's not the same. It still wasn't like this," said her mother. "Did you know we weren't allowed to carry weapons?"

"You weren't?" said Althea, startled.

"That was before everyone realized that our laws were lagging behind our customs and public opinion. That was before the Citizen's Defense Act was passed."

"There is only one crime," Althea said firmly, "and that is to be a victim. Nothing makes sense otherwise."

"I suppose not." Her mother shook her head. "I guess I'm just being sentimental," she added wistfully. Sometimes I miss the policemen we used to have. They would wear blue uniforms and they would drive around with sirens blaring and lights flashing. It seems a shame they became obsolete. Why I can even remember the time when we could take a walk in the park."

"In the park?" said Althea, incredulous. "You could actually do that?"

Now Althea bit her lip. There was no point in daydreaming. She stationed herself at the one-way peephole. The woman who now came within her range of vision was thin of face and well-dressed. She blinked her eyes nervously and hesitated before she knocked.

"Just a moment," said Althea. She unfastened the chain and the two locks, and then stepped back so that when the door opened she would be behind it. "Come in," she said.

"Where are you?"

"Right behind you," said Althea, her hand on her gun. "You're not very smart to walk right in like that, are you?"

"But I know who you are," said Sally Milford, her eyes wide with fright. "My husband and your husband are good friends."

"The first thing you have to learn," said Althea, "is not to trust anyone." She kicked the door shut. "Hold up your hands." She found a small acid gun in Sally's purse and a knife in the pocket of her jacket. "Just put them on the table," Althea directed, "and then sit down. Would you like some coffee?"

Sally shook her head. "Look," she said, her mouth trembling, "I wouldn't trouble you like this—I wouldn't have come at all if I didn't, in a way, know you. You see that, don't you?"

"No," said Althea firmly, "I don't see anything. Suppose you tell me what you want."

Sally clasped her hands on the edge of the table. "I have a brother-in-law who knows someone on the Board of Commissioners," she said, leaning forward in her eagerness, "and we heard that your apartment house has been chosen."

"These things are supposed to be a secret," Althea said sharply. "No one except the people involved is supposed to know. Don't you realize what can happen to you if they find out? And what can happen to me?"

"I'm sorry but I just couldn't help it. When I heard about it—all I could think was that I simply had to go. I have never been to a performance and, the way things look, I'll never have a chance."

"Where do you live?" Althea asked, putting the gun away.

"On the East Side. You know how safe it's getting to be over there. We haven't had an incident in months."

"That doesn't mean they won't choose your building eventually."

"Do you really think they will?"

"Why not?" said Althea.

"Then, in that case, why can't you make believe that we're visiting you or something? They do have special passes for visitors and then, when we're finally chosen, we could reciprocate. Cary and I could invite you and George. That way we could each see two performances."

"It wouldn't work," said Althea. "In the first place, we have the perfect setting for this sort of thing. That's why we picked this particular apartment building. We could have had a much better place to live but both George and I agreed that our best chance was being here. We had to wait two years for this day, and if they ever suspect that this was a put-up thing, you know what would happen to us."

"I suppose I was foolish to even hope." Sally stood up. "I thought it would work out."

"It won't," said Althea, feeling a sudden pity for her. "Believe me, Sally, it won't. I happen to know that Mrs. Tremont, who lives on the third floor, has her sister-in-law staying with her; that, of course, makes it possible for her sister-in-law to go tonight, but if she had just arrived today someone would be sure to report it and Mrs. Tremont would get into trouble."

"You said you were going out," said Sally. "Do you want a ride with me?"

"I'm going downtown," said Althea. "I thought I'd buy a new dress for tonight."

"I haven't been shopping in ages," said Sally. "Cary won't let me go without him and he's been much too busy on Saturdays. We could shop together and maybe have lunch."

"Just remember one thing," Althea warned as she reached for her coat and hat. "No matter what you say, I won't change my mind. You can spend the whole day with me if you like but I still won't change my mind."

"I know you're right," said Sally as they pressed the button for the elevator. "It's just that I'm glad to have some company on the subway."

"Are you still taking the subway?" Althea stared at her, amazed. "George insists that I take the bus. Not taxis—they're not too reliable anymore but a bus is still fine."

"It takes too long," said Sally. "The subway is much quicker. I have my own system. I never wait on a platform if I'm alone and I usually ride in the first car where the motorman is and, just in case anyone is following me, I change at every other stop."

"Now," said Althea, watching as the elevator stopped at their floor, "run!"

They pounded through the corridor and down one flight of steps. Then they rang for the elevator again. When it arrived, it was empty and they rode it the rest of the way down.

It turned out to be, Althea told George later, a rather pleasant day. With the two of them together, the shopping proved much easier. Sally stood watch while Althea tried on dresses and Althea stood guard while Sally shopped. When they finally parted, it was after four.

Althea took a bus uptown again and got off three blocks before her destination. She glanced behind to make sure she wasn't being followed; then she bought a steak at the meat market. Steak would be the quickest thing to cook for dinner and she didn't want to load her arms with too many packages. It was difficult enough carrying the dress, although she had insisted that the clerk put it in a shopping bag instead of a box. With a shopping bag she would feel less clumsy and have one hand free.

The doorman beamed at her when she entered the lobby.

"This is a great day for us," he said.

Althea nodded. "I bought a new dress," she told him happily, "a black sheath."

"I'll ride the elevator with you if you like," he offered generously. "Most of the tenants are home by now."

"You're not supposed to leave your post," Althea reminded him. "Anyone could come in while you were away. You know what happened to the last doorman we had?"

"You're right," he admitted. "For a moment I forgot."

"By the way," she whispered, "do you know who will be giving the performance?"

He shook his head. "No one knows," he said. "I've been asking but no one knows for sure. I think it's a young one. They usually are."

"You'd think those kids could learn," said Althea, ringing for the elevator. "My parents were pretty strict with me—I can tell you that."

"That's the best way," the doorman said. "You have to be firm with them. I always say that from the time they can walk, they can be taught. Now, you take that kid of Mrs. Hammond. You know the Hammonds on the fifth floor? He got his first slash today and was sent home from school in disgrace."

"Oh, no," said Althea, in horror. "He's only eleven. He's only allowed two more mistakes."

"The way Mrs. Hammond spanked him, he'll learn," the doorman said. "That'll never happen to him again, I can tell you that."

"Who was the other boy?"

"It was a girl," said the doorman. "A pretty little thing, I understand. Well, she'll get her first gold star for that."

"I got a gold star when I was twelve," said Althea, stepping into the elevator.

She rode it to the fourth floor and got out. She took the stairs the rest of the way, then stood before her own front door for a moment, listening. When she was positive it was safe, she inserted her key in the lock.

At precisely six o'clock George came home and, by seven thirty, they had finished dinner and were dressed.

"I'd like to go now," said Althea, impatiently.

"It won't get dark until eight," George said. "You know how it is this time of year. Even then, we'll have to wait a while."

"I can see the stands from here," said Althea, craning her neck as she peered out of the window. "People are beginning to arrive now. Please, darling, let's go."

"You're like a child," he said, hugging her. "Just an anxious little kid."

"I can't help it," she said. "I'm excited. Aren't you thrilled, George?"

"Come on," he said, indulgently. He looked at her, chic and lovely in her new black sheath. "No pockets," he said, shaking his head. "What made you buy a dress without any pockets? I didn't know they made them that way anymore."

"I'll only wear it when I'm with you," she said. "Besides, I have a knife in my purse."

"Just see that you keep it handy." He held the door for her. "I'm glad you used your head this morning."

"For a moment I was tempted," Althea confessed. "Sally seems like a sweet person and it might be fun if we could go there sometimes, but then I realized we'd be taking a chance."

"It doesn't pay to take chances," said George. "Otherwise you can end up giving the performance instead of watching it."

"The doorman told me it was a young one. Probably a girl."

"It usually is," said George.

"Do you know what she did?" Althea asked as they walked through the back of the lobby and out into the courtyard. "No one seems to know what she did."

"Probably something stupid," said George, looking around and waving to their neighbors. "You know, honey, you were right. The stands are filling up."

The stands had been placed next to their building. They were permanent, sturdily built of brick and stone, and erected when the building itself had been new. Optimistically every building had its stands ready for the day when it would be chosen, and Althea looked around proudly as she and George found seats in the second row.

Mr. and Mrs. Hammond were there and seated between them was their son, Timmy. Timmy's right arm was bandaged and he huddled close to his mother.

"I heard about it," said Althea, with sympathy. "I'm sure Timmy will never let it happen again."

"Because she was pretty. Because it was a girl," said Mrs. Hammond bitterly. "She called to him and he ran right over, leaving his knife in his pocket as if a knife ever did anybody any good in a pocket. Just because it was a little girl, he trusted her. But he's learned his lesson, haven't you, Timmy?" she said, slapping him across the face.

"No more," Timmy wept, putting his bandaged arm across his eyes. "Please, Mommy, don't hit me anymore."

He'll never amount to anything, Althea thought, staring at him in dismay. Only three chances and he's used up one already. He's too soft. When I have a child—

She thought about it for a moment, longing for a child but the apartment they were in was too small and they hadn't wanted to move until they had a chance at a performance. Maybe now—maybe now that they were finally spectators—perhaps now that the longed-for, dreamed-about moment had finally arrived, they could move to a larger place and she would have a child.

"You have to train them from the beginning," she whispered to George.

"Sure," he said, knowing what she meant. "It won't happen to us."

"It won't happen to us," she agreed, seeing the way George, even now, even at this moment of pleasure and relaxation, kept his hand in his pocket; George's hand curled over the bulge of his gun.

Althea leaned back. She had known, of course, what the stage setting would be but, just the same, sitting there, part of the expectant, eager audience, she had to admire its reality.

It represented a street scene. It could have been Althea's own street with its middle-class, red-brick buildings, the old-fashioned canopies extending from the wide entrances to the edge of the curb. Behind the lighted windows of the buildings, Althea could see the people, all the families together, having dinner, watching television, reading, talking, laughing—all the people of the city settling down for the night.

In the center of the stage was a street lamp, still unlit although it was twilight now; on the far right, there was a fire hydrant. The first floor of the center building was occupied by a shop. The sign said, "ANTIQUES," and Althea could see the lovely things in the window—the paintings in the carved, ornate frames, the delicate crystal goblets, a curved brass bowl. Suddenly the street light went on, dominating the center of the stage with its soft, gentle glow.

The curtain is rising, thought Althea, taking a deep breath. She always loved that moment in the theater, that magic moment when all the murmuring and the movement and the whispering stopped, the hush and wonder when the curtain rose and the stage lay there before them, the play ready to begin.

Someone somewhere in the back coughed and Althea drew a deep, sighing gasp of impatience.

The stage became alive. From the center building a man emerged, a nondescript man walking his dog at night. The dog tugged and the man whistled softly between his teeth as the two of them walked down the street. The stage became empty again and Althea clasped her hands in her lap, amazed to discover that they were shaking.

At the far right two shadows blurred, moved, took form. Now a girl and a boy strolled down the street. His arm was flung around her shoulders and, from the way she smiled at him, Althea knew they were in love. They moved slowly across the stage. They stopped before the antique shop and the girl pointed to the brass bowl and the boy nodded and gestured expansively, showing her there was nothing in the world he wouldn't get for her. They disappeared on the far left and the stage was empty again.

Althea unclasped her hands and, because her palms were wet, she rubbed them furtively together. Beside her she could hear the sound of George's breathing, slow, heavy, as if each breath were an effort.

Onstage, in the lighted backdrop, in the center building, some of the windows began to darken as if the occupants were retiring for the night.

It's getting late, thought Althea, watching. The lights are dimming all over the city. People are yawning and stretching and getting into bed and even the sounds of the distant traffic seem muted as if someone had muffled all the rolling wheels.

A shadow, part of the shadow of the building, almost part of the square shape of the center building, took on form, and Althea saw that it was a man, a man who had been there all the time, hiding there without her being conscious of his presence.

From the far right she could hear the clicking of high heels on the pavement. Someone else, she thought, will walk down this street this night.

There was a rustle and a stir in the stands.

"Please, Mommy," Timmy whispered. "I don't want to stay here."

"Oh, you'll stay all right," said Mrs. Hammond grimly. "You just open your eyes wide. You watch everything, Timmy Hammond, if you know what's good for you."

"Be quiet down there," someone hissed. "Do you want to spoil everything?"

Althea gripped George's arm.

The footsteps grew louder and a girl came into view, entering downstage from the right. The shadow that was the man moved, and then became very still, waiting.

The girl moved across the stage. She paused under the street light. She touched the lamppost as if the feel of it under her fingers gave her some sort of reassurance. She hesitated, reluctant to leave the light.

Althea could see her clearly now. She was very young. She could be no more than nineteen—perhaps twenty. She wore a red suit and a little red beret with a feather stuck jauntily in it and her handbag was tucked under her arm. Her hair was blond and it tumbled loose over her shoulders.

Althea watched absorbed as the second figure moved again, the man crouching and then straightening as he ran toward the light, toward the girl in the red suit. At the clear view of his black-jacketed, black-clad figure, there was a sudden roar of applause. Althea clapped until her hands ached.

Out of the dark, into the light, he moved. The girl had her back toward him, not seeing him as the watchers saw him—sinuous, beautiful in his grace, tall, broad of shoulder, his hair allowed to grow long in back and his black cap set on the back of his head. The knife in his hand caught the light and sparkled.

He ran and then stopped. Deliberately, he stalked her. Professional that he was, he began to move slowly, coming down light on the balls of his feet.

The girl whirled around and, at the sight of him, she made a little whimpering sound in her throat. Her back now to the audience, she darted to the left and, as if they were part of a rigid dance pattern, the man stepped after her. She turned and ran to the right, her heels clicking frantically but he was there before her.

"Please," said the girl in the red suit. She darted back to the lamppost, back where the light was the brightest, where she could be seen most clearly. She turned and faced the backdrop, faced the buildings, the windows where the people were. Her right hand still clutched her purse, her left was now at her throat.

"Oh, please." Her voice rose to a keening wail of terror and anguish.

"Please," she screamed, her voice begging, her body begging. Then blindly she turned again and ran.

This cry in the night had awakened the sleepers. It had roused the dreamers. The darkened windows in the backdrop were illuminated again. Figures moved; there were silhouettes framed in the windows. The sleepers were awake. The dreamers had stopped dreaming and the city was alert and watching.

"Help me."

The city held its breath and listened.

"Please, help me."

But, Althea saw, she couldn't run far enough. She couldn't run fast enough. The man had her pinned against the wall now, pinned against the lighted, listening backdrop of the building and her handbag fell to the ground.

"I beg you." She was almost hidden by the man's bulk as he bent over her. "Won't someone help me?"

The man in the black jacket raised his arm and the knife flashed. The girl screamed in agony, her cheek now as crimson as her suit. Dodging under his arm, she ran again, the slowing rhythm of her clicking heels the only sound to be heard.

The man watched her for a moment. The quiet, lighted windows watched and the filled stands watched. The man stood very still as if he were resting and then, gracefully, quickly, easily, he caught her again.

That does it, thought Althea, her heart pounding; that does it.

The knife gleamed and Althea held her breath. The arm lifted. The black-draped arm lifted and fell, lifted and fell. The red suit crumpled, falling as if it were empty, the red suit only a splotch now on the pavement. Then the man moved toward the hushed, absorbed watchers.

And there he stood, bowing and smiling, the knife dripping red at his side. Over and over again he took his bow while they all gave him the ultimate, the supreme tribute of their silence.

THE GREAT WALL OF CHINA
Franz Kafka

translated by willa and edwin muir

The Great Wall of China was finished off at its northernmost corner. From the south-east and the south-west it came up in two sections that finally converged there. This principle of piecemeal construction was also applied on a smaller scale by both of the two great armies of labor, the eastern and the western. It was done in this way: gangs of some twenty workers were formed who had to accomplish a length, say, of five hundred yards of wall, while a similar gang built another stretch of the same length to meet the first. But after the junction had been made the construction of the wall was not carried on from the point, let us say, where this thousand yards ended; instead the two groups of workers were transferred to begin building again in quite different neighborhoods. Naturally in this way many great gaps were left, which were only filled in gradually and bit by bit, some, indeed, not till after the official announcement that the wall was finished. In fact it is said that there are gaps which have never been filled in at all, an assertion, however, which is probably merely one of the many legends to which the building of the wall gave rise, and which cannot be verified, at least by any single man with his own eyes and judgment, on account of the extent of the structure.

Now on first thoughts one might conceive that it would have been more advantageous in every way to build the wall continuously, or at least continuously within the two main divisions. After all the wall was intended, as was universally proclaimed and known, to be a protection against the peoples of the north. But how can a wall protect if it is not a continuous structure? Not only cannot such a wall protect, but what there is of it is in perpetual danger. These blocks of wall left standing in deserted regions could be easily pulled down again and again by the nomads, especially as these tribes, rendered apprehensive by the building operations, keep changing their encampments with incredible rapidity, like locusts, and so perhaps had a better general view of the progress of the wall than we, the builders. Nevertheless the task of construction probably could not have been carried out in any other way. To understand this we must take into account the following: The wall was to be a protection for centuries: accordingly the most scrupulous care in the building, the application of the architectural wisdom of all known ages and peoples, an unremitting sense of personal responsibility in the builders, were indispensable prerequisites for the work. True, for the more purely manual tasks ignorant day laborers from the populace, men, women and children who offered their services for good money, could be employed; but for the supervision even of every four day laborers an expert versed in the art of building was required, a man who was capable of entering into and feeling with all his heart what was involved. And the higher the task, the greater the responsibility. And such men were actually to be had, if not indeed so abundantly as the work of construction could have absorbed, yet in great numbers.

For the work had not been undertaken without thought. Fifty years before the first stone was laid the art of architecture, and especially that of masonry, had been proclaimed as the most important branch of knowledge throughout the whole area of a China that was to be walled round, and all other arts gained recognition only in so far as they had reference to it. I can still remember quite well us standing as small children, scarcely sure on our feet, in our teacher's garden, and being ordered to build a sort of wall out of pebbles; and then the teacher, girding up his robe, ran full tilt against the wall, of course knocking it down, and scolded us so terribly for the shoddiness of our work that we ran weeping in all directions to our parents. A trivial incident, but significant of the spirit of the time.

I was lucky inasmuch as the building of the wall was just beginning when, at twenty, I had passed the last examination of the lowest grade school. I say lucky, for many who before my time had achieved the highest degree of culture available to them could find nothing year after year to do with their knowledge, and drifted uselessly about with the most splendid architectural plans in their heads, and sank by thousands into hopelessness. But those who finally came to be employed in the work as supervisors, even though it might be of the lowest rank, were truly worthy of their task. They were masons who had reflected much, and did not cease to reflect, on the building of the wall, men who with the first stone which they sank in the ground felt themselves a part of the wall. Masons of that kind, of course, had not only a desire to perform their work in the most thorough manner, but were also impatient to see the wall finished in its complete perfection. Day laborers have not this impatience, for they look only to their wages, and the higher supervisors, indeed even the supervisors of middle rank, could see enough of the manifold growth of the construction to keep their spirits confident and high. But to encourage the subordinate supervisors, intellectually so vastly superior to their apparently petty tasks, other measures must be taken. One could not, for instance, expect them to lay one stone on another for months or even years on end, in an uninhabited mountainous region, hundreds of miles from their homes; the hopelessness of such hard toil, which yet could not reach completion even in the longest lifetime, would have cast them into despair and above all made them less capable for the work. It was for this reason that the system of piecemeal building was decided on. Five hundred yards could be accomplished in about five years; by that time, however, the supervisors were as a rule quite exhausted and had lost all faith in themselves, in the wall, in the world. Accordingly, while they were still exalted by the jubilant celebrations marking the completion of the thousand yards of wall, they were sent far, far away, saw on their journey finished sections of the wall rising here and there, came past the quarters of the high command and were presented with badges of honor, heard the rejoicings of new armies of labor streaming past from the depths of the land, saw forests being cut down to become supports for the wall, saw mountains being hewn into stones for the wall, heard at the holy shrines hymns rising in which the pious prayed for the completion of the wall. All this assuaged their impatience. The quiet life of their homes, where they rested some time, strengthened them; the humble credulity with which their reports were listened to, the confidence with which the simple and peaceful burgher believed in the eventual completion of the wall, all this tightened up again the cords of the soul. Like eternally hopeful children they then said farewell to their homes; the desire once more to labor on the wall of the nation became irresistible. They set off earlier than they needed; half the village accompanied them for long distances. Groups of people with banners and scarfs waving were on all the roads; never before had they seen how great and rich and beautiful and worthy of love their country was. Every fellow-countryman was a brother for whom one was building a wall of protection, and who would return lifelong thanks for it with all he had and did. Unity! Unity! Shoulder to shoulder, a ring of brothers, a current of blood no longer confined within the narrow circulation of one body, but sweetly rolling and yet ever returning throughout the endless leagues of China.

Thus, then, the system of piecemeal construction becomes comprehensible; but there were still other reasons for it as well. Nor is there anything odd in my pausing over this question for so long; it is one of the crucial problems in the whole building of the wall, unimportant as it may appear at first glance. If I am to convey and make understandable the ideas and feelings of that time I cannot go deeply enough into this very question.

First, then, it must be said that in those days things were achieved scarcely inferior to the construction of the Tower of Babel, although as regards divine approval, at least according to human reckoning, strongly at variance with that work. I say this because during the early days of building a scholar wrote a book in which he drew the comparison in the most exhaustive way. In it he tried to prove that the Tower of Babel failed to reach its goal, not because of the reasons universally advanced, or at least that among those recognized reasons the most important of all was not to be found. His proofs were drawn not merely from written documents and reports; he also claimed to have made enquiries on the spot, and to have discovered that the tower failed and was bound to fail because of the weakness of the foundation. In this respect at any rate our age was vastly superior to that ancient one. Almost every educated man of our time was a mason by profession and infallible in the matter of laying foundations. That, however, was not what our scholar was concerned to prove; for he maintained that the Great Wall alone would provide for the first time in the history of mankind a secure foundation for a new Tower of Babel. First the wall, therefore, and then the tower. His book was in everybody's hands at that time, but I admit that even today I cannot quite make out how he conceived this tower. How could the wall, which did not form even a circle, but only a sort of quarter or half-circle, provide the foundation for a tower? That could obviously be meant only in a spiritual sense. But in that case why build the actual wall, which after all was something concrete, the results of the lifelong labor of multitudes of people? And why were there in the book plans, somewhat nebulous plans, it must be admitted, of the tower, and proposals worked out in detail for mobilizing the people's energies for the stupendous new work?

There were many wild ideas in people's heads at that time—this scholar's book is only one example—perhaps simply because so many were trying to join forces as far as they could for the achievement of a single aim. Human nature, essentially changeable, unstable as the dust, can endure no restraint; if it binds itself it soon begins to tear madly at its bonds, until it rends everything asunder, the wall, the bonds and its very self.

It is possible that these very considerations, which militated against the building of the wall at all, were not left out of account by the high command when the system of piecemeal construction was decided on. We—and here I speak in the name of many people—did not really know ourselves until we had carefully scrutinized the decrees of the high command, when we discovered that without the high command neither our book learning nor our human understanding would have sufficed for the humble tasks which we performed in the great whole. In the office of the command—where it was and who sat there no one whom I have asked knew then or knows now—in that office one may be certain that all human thoughts and desires were revolved, and counter to them all human aims and fulfilments. And through the window the reflected splendors of divine worlds fell on the hands of the leaders as they traced their plans.

And for that reason the incorruptible observer must hold that the command, if it had seriously desired it, could also have overcome those difficulties which prevented a system of continuous construction. There remains, therefore, nothing but the conclusion that the command deliberately chose the system of piecemeal construction. But the piecemeal construction was only a makeshift and therefore inexpedient. Remains the conclusion that the command willed something inexpedient.—Strange conclusion!—True, and yet in one respect it has much to be said for it. One can perhaps safely discuss it now. In those days many people, and among them the best, had a secret maxim which ran: Try with all your might to comprehend the decrees of the high command, but only up to a certain point; then avoid further meditation. A very wise maxim, which moreover was elaborated in a parable that was later often quoted: Avoid further meditation, but not because it might be harmful; it is not at all certain that it would be harmful. What is harmful or not harmful has nothing to do with the question. Consider rather the river in spring. It rises until it grows mightier and nourishes more richly the soil on the long stretch of its banks, still maintaining its own course until it reaches the sea, where it is all the more welcome because it is a worthier ally.—Thus far may you urge your meditations on the decrees of the high command.—But after that the river overflows its banks, loses outline and shape, slows down the speed of its current, tries to ignore its destiny by forming little seas in the interior of the land, damages the fields, and yet cannot maintain itself for long in its new expanse, but must run back between its banks again, must even dry up wretchedly in the hot season that presently follows.—Thus far may you not urge your meditations on the decrees of the high command.

Now though this parable may have had extraordinary point and force during the building of the wall, it has at most only a restricted relevance for my present essay. My enquiry is purely historical; no lightning flashes any longer from the long since vanished thunderclouds, and so I may venture to seek for an explanation of the system of piecemeal construction which goes farther than the one that contented people then. The limits which my capacity for thought imposes upon me are narrow enough, but the province to be traversed here is infinite. Against whom was the Great Wall to serve as a protection? Against the people of the north. Now, I come from the south-east of China. No northern people can menace us there. We read of them in the books of the ancients; the cruelties which they commit in accordance with their nature make us sigh beneath our peaceful trees. The faithful representations of the artist show us these faces of the damned, their gaping mouths, their jaws furnished with great pointed teeth, their half-shut eyes that already seem to be seeking out the victim which their jaws will rend and devour. When our children are unruly we show them these pictures, and at once they fly weeping into our arms. But nothing more than that do we know about these northerners. We have not seen them, and if we remain in our villages we shall never see them, even if on their wild horses they should ride as hard as they can straight towards us— the land is too vast and would not let them reach us, they would end their course in the empty air.

Why, then, since that is so, did we leave our homes, the stream with its bridges, our mothers and fathers, our weeping wives, our children who needed our care, and depart for the distant city to be trained there, while our thoughts journeyed still farther away to the wall in the north? Why? A question for the high command. Our leaders know us. They, absorbed in gigantic anxieties, know of us, know our petty pursuits, see us sitting together in our humble huts, and approve or disapprove the evening prayer which the father of the house recites in the midst of his family. And if I may be allowed to express such ideas about the high command, then I must say that in my opinion the high command has existed from old time, and was not assembled, say, like a gathering of mandarins summoned hastily to discuss somebody's fine dream in a conference as hastily terminated, so that that very evening the people are drummed out of their beds to carry out what has been decided, even if it should be nothing but an illumination in honor of a god who may have shown great favor to their masters the day before, only to drive them into some dark corner with cudgel blows tomorrow, almost before the illuminations have died down. Far rather do I believe that the high command has existed from all eternity, and the decision to build the wall likewise. Unwitting peoples of the north, who imagined they were the cause of it! Honest, unwitting Emperor, who imagined he decreed it! We builders of the wall know that it was not so and hold our tongues.

*   *   *

During the building of the wall and ever since to this very day I have occupied myself almost exclusively with the comparative history of races— there are certain questions which one can probe to the marrow, as it were, only by this method—and I have discovered that we Chinese possess certain folk and political institutions that are unique in their clarity, others again unique in their obscurity. The desire to trace the causes of these phenomena, especially the latter, has always teased me and teases me still, and the building of the wall is itself essentially involved with these problems.

Now one of the most obscure of our institutions is that of the empire itself. In Pekin, naturally, at the imperial court, there is some clarity to be found on this subject, though even that is more illusive than real. Also the teachers of political law and history in the high schools claim to be exactly informed on these matters, and to be capable of passing on their knowledge to their students. The further one descends among the lower schools the more, naturally enough, does one find teachers' and pupils' doubts of their own knowledge vanishing, and superficial culture mounting sky-high round a few precepts that have been drilled into people's minds for centuries, precepts which, though they have lost nothing of their eternal truth, remain eternally invisible in this fog of confusion.

But it is precisely this question of the empire which in my opinion the common people should be asked to answer, since after all they are the empire's final support. Here, I must confess, I can only speak once more for my native place. Except for the nature gods and their ritual, which fills the whole year in such beautiful and rich alternation, we think only about the Emperor. But not about the present one; or rather we would think about the present one if we knew who he was or knew anything definite about him. True—and it is the sole curiosity that fills us—we are always trying to get information on this subject, but, strange as it may sound, it is almost impossible to discover anything, either from pilgrims, though they have wandered through many lands, or from near or distant villages, or from sailors, though they have navigated not only our little stream, but also the sacred rivers. One hears a great many things, true, but can gather nothing definite.

So vast is our land that no fable could do justice to its vastness, the heavens can scarcely span it—and Pekin is only a dot in it, and the imperial palace less than a dot. The Emperor as such, on the other hand, is mighty throughout all the hierarchies of the world: admitted. But the existent Emperor, a man like us, lies much like us on a couch which is of generous proportions, perhaps, and yet very possibly may be quite narrow and short. Like us he sometimes stretches himself and when he is very tired yawns with his delicately cut mouth. But how should we know anything about that—thousands of miles away in the South—almost on the borders of the Tibetan Highlands? And besides, any tidings, even if they did reach us, would arrive far too late, would have become obsolete long before they reached us. The Emperor is always surrounded by a brilliant and yet ambiguous throng of nobles and courtiers—malice and enmity in the guise of servants and friends—who form a counter-weight to the Imperial power and perpetually labor to unseat the ruler from his place with poisoned arrows. The Empire is immortal, but the Emperor himself totters and falls from his throne, yes, whole dynasties sink in the end and breathe their last in one death-rattle. Of these struggles and sufferings the people will never know; like tardy arrivals, like strangers in a city, they stand at the end of some densely thronged side street peacefully munching the food they have brought with them, while far away in front, in the market square at the heart of the city, the execution of their ruler is proceeding.

There is a parable that describes this situation very well: The Emperor, so it runs, has sent a message to you, the humble subject, the insignificant shadow cowering in the remotest distance before the imperial sun; the Emperor from his death-bed has sent a message to you alone. He has commanded the messenger to kneel down by the bed, and has whispered the message to him; so much store did he lay on it that he ordered the messenger to whisper it back into his ear again. Then by a nod of the head he has confirmed that it is right. Yes, before the assembled spectators of his death—all the obstructing walls have been broken down, and on the spacious and loftily mounting open staircases stand in a ring the great princes of the Empire—before all these he has delivered his message. The messenger immediately sets out on his journey; a powerful, an indefatigable man, now pushing with his right arm, now with his left, he cleaves a way for himself through the throng; if he encounters resistance he points to his breast, where the symbol of the sun glitters; the way, too, is made easier for him than it would be for any other man. But the multitudes are so vast; their numbers have no end. If he could reach the open fields, how fast he would fly, and soon doubtless you would hear the welcome hammering of his fists on your door. But instead how vainly does he wear out his strength; still he is only making his way through the chambers of the innermost palace; never will he get to the end of them; and if he succeeded in that nothing would be gained; he must fight his way next down the stair; and if he succeeded in that nothing would be gained; the courts would still have to be crossed; and after the courts the second outer palace; and once more stairs and courts; and once more another palace; and so on for thousands of years; and if at last he should burst through the outermost gate—but never, never can that happen—the imperial capital would lie before him, the center of the world, crammed to bursting with its own refuse. Nobody could fight his way through here even with a message from a dead man.—But you sit at your window when evening falls and dream it to yourself.

Just so, as hopelessly and as hopefully, do our people regard the Emperor. They do not know what emperor is reigning, and there exist doubts regarding even the name of the dynasty. In school a great deal is taught about the dynasties with the dates of succession, but the universal uncertainty in this matter is so great that even the best scholars are drawn into it. Long-dead emperors are set on the throne in our villages, and one that only lives in song recently had a proclamation of his read out by the priest before the altar. Battles that are old history are new to us, and one's neighbor rushes in with a jubilant face to tell the news. The wives of the emperors, pampered and overweening, seduced from noble custom by wily courtiers, swelling with ambition, vehement in their greed, uncontrollable in their lust, practise their abominations ever anew. The more deeply they are buried in time the more glaring are the colors in which their deeds are painted, and with a loud cry of woe our village eventually hears how an Empress drank her husband's blood in long draughts thousands of years ago.

Thus, then, do our people deal with departed emperors, but the living ruler they confuse among the dead. If once, only once in a man's lifetime, an imperial official on his tour of the provinces should arrive by chance at our village, make certain announcements in the name of the government, scrutinize the tax lists, examine the school children, enquire of the priest regarding our doings and affairs, and then, before he steps into his litter, should sum up his impressions in verbose admonitions to the assembled commune—then a smile flits over every face, each man throws a stolen glance at his neighbor, and bends over his children so as not to be observed by the official. Why, they think to themselves, he's speaking of a dead man as if he were alive, this Emperor of his died long ago, the dynasty is blotted out, the good official is having his joke with us, but we will behave as if we did not notice it, so as not to offend him. But we shall obey in earnest no one but our present ruler, for not to do so would be a crime. And behind the departing litter of the official there rises in might as ruler of the village some figure fortuitously exalted from an urn already crumbled to dust.

Similarly our people are but little affected by revolutions in the state or contemporary wars. I recall an incident in my youth. A revolt had broken out in a neighboring, but yet quite distant, province. What caused it I can no longer remember, nor is it of any importance now; occasions for revolt can be found there any day; the people are an excitable people. Well, one day a leaflet published by the rebels was brought to my father's house by a beggar who had crossed that province. It happened to be a feast day, our rooms were filled with guests, the priest sat in the chief place and studied the sheet. Suddenly everybody started to laugh; in the confusion the sheet was torn; the beggar, who however had already received abundant alms, was driven out of the room with blows, the guests dispersed to enjoy the beautiful day. Why? The dialect of this neighboring province differs in some essential respects from ours, and this difference occurs also in certain turns of the written speech, which for us have an archaic character. Hardly had the priest read out two lines before we had already come to our decision. Ancient history told long ago, old sorrows long since healed. And though—so it seems to me in recollection—the gruesomeness of the living present was irrefutably conveyed by the beggar's words, we laughed and shook our heads and refused to listen any longer. So eager are our people to obliterate the present.

If from such appearances any one should draw the conclusion that in reality we have no Emperor, he would not be far from the truth. Over and over again it must be repeated: There is perhaps no people more faithful to the Emperor than ours in the south, but the Emperor derives no advantage from our fidelity. True, the sacred dragon stands on the little column at the end of our village, and ever since the beginning of human memory it has breathed out its fiery breath in the direction of Pekin in token of homage—but Pekin itself is far stranger to the people in our village than the next world. Can there really be a village where the houses stand side by side, covering all the fields for a greater distance than one can see from our hills, and can there be dense crowds of people packed between these houses day and night? We find it more difficult to picture such a city than to believe that Pekin and its Emperor are one, a cloud, say, peacefully voyaging beneath the sun in the course of the ages.

Now the result of holding such opinions is a life on the whole free and unconstrained. By no means immoral, however; hardly ever have I found in my travels such pure morals as in my native village. But yet a life that is subject to no contemporary law, and attends only to the exhortations and warnings which come to us from olden times.

I guard against large generalizations, and do not assert that in all the countless villages in my province it is so, far less in all the five hundred provinces of China. Yet perhaps I may venture to assert on the basis of the many writings on this subject which I have read, as well as from my own observation—the building of the wall in particular, with its abundance of human material, provided a man of sensibility with the opportunity of traversing the souls of almost all the provinces—on the basis of all this, then, perhaps I may venture to assert that the prevailing attitude to the Emperor shows persistently and universally something fundamentally in common with that of our village. Now I have no wish whatever to represent this attitude as a virtue; on the contrary. True, the essential responsibility for it lies with the government, which in the most ancient empire in the world has not yet succeeded in developing, or has neglected to develop, the institution of the empire to such precision that its workings extend directly and unceasingly to the farthest frontiers of the land. On the other hand, however, there is also involved a certain feebleness of faith and imaginative power on the part of the people that prevents them from raising the empire out of its stagnation in Pekin and clasping it in all its palpable living reality to their own breasts, which yet desire nothing better than but once to feel that touch and then to die.

This attitude then is certainly no virtue. All the more remarkable is it that this very weakness should seem to be one of the greatest unifying influences among our people; indeed, if one may dare to use the expression, the very ground on which we live. To set about establishing a fundamental defect here would mean undermining not only our consciences, but, what is far worse, our feet. And for that reason I shall not proceed any further at this stage with my enquiry into these questions.

TALE OF THE LAUGHING FISH
Anonymous

translated by leon surmelian

Once upon a time a fisherman caught a fish that was so pretty and unlike any fish he ever saw that he put it in a clay bowl and took it to the king in Baghdad, hoping to receive a reward for it. The king looked at the fish with amazement and delight and had it placed in a fine silver bowl. The fisherman received his reward and departed. The king showed this fish to all his courtiers and said to his vizier: 'Take it to my wife. She likes fish.'

When the vizier took the silver bowl to the queen's quarters she asked suspiciously: 'Is this a male or female fish?'

The fish leapt out of the bowl and shook with loud laughter. It did a few flip-flops and jumped back into the water. The queen and the vizier were astonished, and she cried: 'Take it away. I can't keep it in my room, it may be a male fish for all I know, and I couldn't even think of eating a male fish.'

The vizier told the king what happened, and the king was incredulous. He wondered 'What did the fish mean by laughing?' It worried him no end, and he felt offended too. A laughing fish was an unheard of thing.

Some time later the queen took to bed and the court hakims could not cure her. The king sent for Lokhman, who lived in Aleppo and was the greatest hakim in the world. As the vizier prepared for his journey to Aleppo, the queen told him: 'Find out on your way if people are talking about me, where my name is mentioned, and where it's not.'

The vizier mounted his horse and set out for Aleppo accompanied by two palace guards. On his way he made inquiries to see if people talked about the queen, and stopped at a village to rest for a while before continuing his journey. An old ploughman was tilling his field and his seven-year-old son said: 'Father, do you see these three horsemen? They are coming to ask you some questions. One is the king's vizier. You can answer them any way you like, but don't get angry with me if I talk out of turn, and speak the truth.'

'Why should the king's vizier want to talk to a poor ploughman like me? I told you a thousand times not to talk nonsense. You do say the craziest things.'

The horseman rode up to them and the vizier said: 'Greetings, pappy. How's your health? How have you been? And what's the news around here?'

He got the ploughman talking about himself and other villagers to find out what they knew or said about the queen. 'I want to know how our people are getting along and I like to listen to their complaints,' said the vizier.

The boy gathered enough courage to break in at this moment and say: 'May the king's vizier live long, you are wasting your time. No matter where you go you will hear the queen's name mentioned. People do talk about her. You might as well save yourself all this trouble.'

The vizier was taken aback. How did this little fellow know what the queen told him? He mounted his horse.

'Where to?' the boy asked.

'The queen has been ill for some months and we are going to Aleppo to fetch Lokhman. Maybe he can cure her,' said the king's vizier.

'Lokhman isn't in Aleppo, he is in Damascus,' the boy said.

'We were told he is in Aleppo.'

'Not now. He went to Damascus.'

'How do you know?'

'Never mind how I happen to know it. You listen to me and save yourself the trouble of going all the way to Aleppo when he is in Damascus.'

And sure enough, they found Lokhman to be in Damascus.

'Who told you I wasn't in Aleppo?' the famous hakim asked the king's vizier on their way to Baghdad.

'A ploughman's son, a seven-year-old boy we met on our way,' replied the vizier. 'Somehow that little boy knew it.'

This worried Lokhman. 'If he knows so much about me at seven, what will become of me when he grows up?' he thought to himself. 'I shall lose my practice, that's sure. This boy can ruin my reputation.'

When Lokhman reached Baghdad and examined the queen, he prescribed for her the heart and blood of a healthy peasant boy, and the boy of his choice—and the queen's—was the ploughman's son. But the vizier had taken a fancy to the lad and fooled them both. The blood the queen drank and found so refreshing was that of a slaughtered lamb. The queen was just pretending to be sick, and she got well after this treatment. Lokhman received a large reward from the king and left with the assurance he was rid of the ploughman's son.

The king kept brooding over the loud laughter of the fish and questioned all the wise men in his kingdom in his desire to get to the bottom of it, but no one could give him a reason that made sense.

'May the king live long.' said the vizier, 'I know a small village lad who seems to know everything. The boy is a mind reader. Let's ask him.'

The king gave the vizier a bag of gold and told him to bring that boy immediately to Baghdad. The chamberlain rode back to the ploughman's village, glad he had saved the boy's life, and hoping the little fellow could solve this riddle that baffled everybody in the palace.

'Greetings, pappy,' he said to the ploughman.

'Greetings, and a thousand blessings to you, king's vizier.'

'I came to take your boy to the king.'

The ploughman was thunderstruck. 'Why should you take him to the king? We are poor people, and he is just a little boy. Why should the king be interested in a little boy?'

'He is a very wise little boy, that's why. Here is a bag of gold for you as a present from the king.'

The old ploughman feared kings and courts and thought his son might not come back if he let him go. But the lad knew what he was wanted for and urged his father to take the money. 'God is merciful,' he said. 'I will come back safe and sound, don't worry.'

The ploughman brightened at these words of his son, thanked the vizier for the king's present, and let his son go with him. The vizier lifted the boy onto his horse and rode back to Baghdad.

He presented his charge to the king in fine new clothes. The boy bowed seven times, on the eighth kissed the hem of the king's robe, and stood before him with folded hands. He listened carefully to what the king told him, and said:

'May the king live long. I know why the fish laughed, but I cannot tell you.'

'Tell me!'

'May the king live long, you will be sorry if I do.'

'Take him to jail,' the king said to the vizier, just to frighten the little fellow.

That night the boy stayed in jail. The next morning the king, the vizier, and all the courtiers tried hard to make him talk, but all he would say was, 'I know why the fish laughed, but I cannot tell.' The king lost his patience and ordered his executioners to chop off the boy's head.

'Allow me, O king, to tell you a story before you chop off my head,' the boy said, 'and if you still want to kill me, you can, my life is in your hands.'

'Go ahead, I am listening,' said the king.

'May the king live long,' said the boy, 'once upon a time a king was hunting in the desert and asked for water, but no water was to be had. His men scurried around looking for a spring and at last found some water in a hole. They filled a cup and gave it to the king. As he raised the cup to his parched lips his little dog jumped on him from a rock and knocked the cup out of his hand, and it broke into a thousand pieces. This annoyed the king so much that he drew his sword and slashed the dog in two.

'There were some wise men with the king, who said: 'Why did you kill this poor dog? Maybe it wanted to warn you of something. Let's have one of our horses drink this water before you drink it yourself. It may be poisoned.'

'A horse drank from the hole, swelled up and died on the spot. The king was sorry. "Ah, I killed my dog for nothing," he sighed.

'Before you kill me, O king, be sure you too will not regret it and say, "I killed a poor ploughman's son for nothing." '

The king relented, but kept the boy in jail. The next morning the boy kept repeating: 'I know why the fish laughed, but I cannot tell it, you will be sorry if I do.'

When the boy saw the executioners coming back, he said: 'May the king live long, allow me to tell you about another dog before they chop off my head.'

The king was willing to listen.

'One day a king dined in the house of his vizier, and after dinner they amused themselves with a playful monkey. The king called the queen to come watch the monkey's tricks, and she left her baby in the cradle and joined the king and his courtiers in the banquet hall. The king's dog stayed with the baby, as was its habit. A huge deadly snake crawled out of a crack in the wall and coiled around the cradle, but before it could strangle the baby, the dog sprang on the monstrous snake and tore it to bits after a savage struggle.

'Servants saw the dog licking its bloody paws and thought it had killed and eaten the baby. During the ensuing clamour and commotion the dog, spattered all over with the serpent's blood, was slain by his master. The king ran into the room and found the baby unharmed. The cradle was tipped over to one side, and the child lay sleeping peacefully in it. The king was very sorry, and sighed, "Ah, I killed my faithful dog for nothing."

'And now, O king, watch out that you do not say, "I killed a poor ploughman's son for nothing." '

The boy spent another night in jail. The next morning the king ordered that the ploughman's son be brought before him. The boy's answer was the same to all the threats and promises of the king. 'I know why the fish laughed, but I cannot tell you, you will be sorry if I do.' He was a stubborn lad and would not budge. The king was so exasperated now that the boy sensed this was his last chance. He had to tell another story to save his life. He threw himself at the king's feet and begged him not to turn him over to the executioners until he heard this story also.

'A king who had no children was very fond of his parrot. He liked to take his parrot on his knee and talk to it, play with it. One day the parrot was very sad and downcast, and the king said: "What's the matter? Don't you feel well? Or don't you get enough to eat?"

' "May the king live long," said the parrot in a human voice, "I didn't come out of a hole in the wall, you know. I have a father, a mother, my own kith and kin to think of, and I miss them. But you never let me go home."

' "May God bless your sweet father's soul, why didn't you tell me before? You can fly home any time you like, and be sure to give my regards to your parents, but come back, I will miss you very much if you don't."

'The king opened his window and let the parrot fly home. After two weeks of loving and cooing the parrot was ready to come back, and said to its parents: "The king is waiting for me, and I want to take him a present when I go back." "Give him these two apple seeds," the parents said, and wrapped them up in a piece of paper. The parrot flew back with this paper in its beak and dropped it on the king's knee. The king opened the paper, showed the seeds to his courtiers, and gave them to his gardener to plant them in a secluded spot in his pleasure garden. "Let's see what will come out of these seeds," he said.

'In two or three years two apple-trees, the like of which the king had never seen before, grew out of these seeds, and each bore a single apple. One day as one of these apples grew ripe it fell to the ground, and the gardener picked it up and took it to the king, expecting a reward. The king was delighted with the apple. He admired its size, colour and fragrance, and showed it to his courtiers.

' "Let's see what it tastes like," the king said. He took out his diamond-handled pocket knife and peeled the apple. Just as he was putting a slice of it in his mouth the parrot brushed up against him and with a mighty sweep of its wing knocked the apple out of his hand. This made the king so angry that he seized the parrot and tore it in two. "You brought the seeds yourself but you won't let me eat this apple," he said.

'The king's courtiers were shocked. "May the king live long, perhaps your parrot had a reason for doing what it did. Let's feed a slice of this apple to a lamb and see what happens," they said.

'One slice was enough to kill the lamb. The king was sorry, but he couldn't bring his parrot back to life. He thought his gardener tried to poison him, and the man went home with bowed head, knowing his hours were numbered.

' "The king will chop off our heads tomorrow," he said to his wife. "These are poisonous apples."

' "Then we had better eat the other apple before the executioners get here," said his wife.

'The gardener plucked the apple from the other tree, sliced it in two, ate one half and gave the other half to his wife. And lo and behold, instead of dying they recovered the bloom of their early youth so that they could hardly recognize each other.

'When the executioners knocked on their door the next morning and walked in with their swords, what did they see? The gardener and his wife had become a couple of fifteen-year-olds...The king questioned them and learned they ate the other apple and didn't die.

' "May the king live long," said the gardener, "both were apples of immortality, but the one I brought you had fallen to the ground and I suppose was poisoned by a snake. I didn't pluck it from the tree. That's why the lamb died. But look at us...." The king pardoned them, and was glad to have the two apple trees of immortality in his garden.

'I have finished my tale, O king, and now you can do with me what you like, but before you order my execution be sure you won't regret it later and say: "Why did I kill the ploughman's son when he meant well and wished me no harm?" '

The king softened and spoke to the boy in a friendly voice. 'Now tell me, son, why the fish laughed, so that I can have some peace of mind, and I will pardon you and give you anything you want.'

'Do you really want me to tell you? You will be sorry if I do,' the boy said again.

'Yes, you must tell me why the fish laughed. I cannot rest until I know the reason.'

'Very well then, I will tell you. But you must let me be king for three hours.'

The king stepped down from the throne and had the little boy sit in his place. 'You are king for three hours.' The boy ordered the vizier and all the courtiers to gather before him. They did. Then he ordered the queen to appear before him with her forty maids-of-honour, and they too came and stood before him. The king stood beside the throne.

'Do you remember the fish I sent you in a silver bowl?' the king asked his wife.

'Yes, I remember. I didn't want to keep it in my room, thinking it might be a male fish. As for eating it, without knowing its sex, heaven forbid! You know how I feel about such things.'

The boy-king ordered that one of the queen's maids-of-honour take off her clothes. He pointed her out and said, 'The one in the green dress, standing next to the queen.'

'Why, this is preposterous!' the queen protested. 'Whoever heard of a maid-of-honour, and one so young and attractive, and so very modest, undressing before men? What kind of nonsense is this? She is the daughter of the King of the East. And the son of the King of the West, the son of the King of the South, the son of the King of the North, all want to marry her. She gets ten proposals a day, and now you expect her to stand naked before men? For shame! She will do nothing of the sort.'

'Then I will not tell you why the fish laughed,' said the boy, speaking from the king's throne.

'Take off her clothes!' the king commanded in an angry voice. 'This boy is king for three hours and I expect all of you to obey him instantly.'

The vizier dragged the maid-of-honour to the centre of the throne-room and stripped her of her clothing, and oho, no daughter of Eve was she, but a virile son of Adam.

'Take off your clothes, all of you!' the king roared. And as all the maids-of-honour undressed they turned out to be boys, all forty of them. The king and the vizier stared at them and at the queen and at each other with unbelieving eyes, and the blood froze in their veins.

'May the king live long,' said the little boy seated on the throne, 'now you see it with your own eyes, now you know why the fish laughed and I could not tell you.'

'Executioners!' called the king.

The executioners came in and bowed.

'Chop off the heads of all these men! And the queen's too.'

Forty-one heads flew off under their heavy swords.

The king kissed the wise little boy on the forehead and made him his heir and successor. The boy sent for his father and mother, and they came to Baghdad to live with him. And after the king passed away the ploughman's son ruled as king.

Three apples fell from heaven; one for the teller of this tale, one for the listener, and one for him who heeds the teller's words.

Biographies
of the Authors

Machado de Assis (1839–1908)

A giant of nineteenth-century Brazilian literature, Machado de Assis is only beginning to acquire an international reputation in the 1970's. Of humble mulatto origins, he received little formal education; yet the pervasive knowledge of ancient and contemporary literature exhibited in his works indicates a self-education that was both extensive and enthusiastic. Enthusiasm was an integral part of Machado's personality: his collected works at the comparatively youthful age of thirty filled ten volumes. While writing he supported himself variously as editor, typesetter, clerk and proofreader, and still found time to build a brilliant social reputation.

Now known primarily for his novels, his first one, *Resurrection,* was not published until 1872. Contrasting with the naturalism then dominant in the literary world, his novels exhibit rich symbolism, increasing technical experimentation, and subtle use of point of view. Running throughout is a highly sophisticated comic element combined with increasingly insightful psychology. Among the most interesting works available in English (translated by Helen Caldwell) are *Esau and Jacob* (1965), *Don Casmurro* (1966), and *The Psychiatrist and Other Stories* (1963) from which "The Request" is taken.

Jorge Luis Borges (1899–   )

One of the most respected South American authors, Borges was born and lives in Buenos Aires. Producing essays, poems, and short stories, he combines native Spanish-American themes with highly sophisticated universal concerns. His early work was mainly poetic in a loose and experimental style, with an emphasis on striking metaphors. Two collections of this period, *Fervor of Buenos Aires* (1923) and *The Moon Across the Street* (1925), Borges now believes were too affected and dogmatic. Later he concentrated on short fiction, particularly his "ficciones," complex tales of speculation and fantasy masquerading as popular literature. His international reputation became established with the publication of *Ficciones* (1944) and *El Aleph* (1949). A complementary volume of essays, *Other Inquisitions 1937–1952,* appeared in 1952. Borges treats the failure of men to order and complete their knowledge of the universe; the ambiguities of human existence give rise to images of complexity and paradox, hence the title of Borges' interesting recent work, *Labyrinths* (1962) where the story included in this volume appeared, and the method behind *Dreamtigers* (1964).

Since 1955, Borges has served as Director of the Argentine National Library and is Professor of English and American Literature at the University of Buenos Aires. In 1961 he lectured at the University of Texas and then traveled extensively in the United States in 1962. He returned in 1967–68 to give the Norton Poetry Lectures at Harvard and to tour and lecture throughout the country.

Ray Bradbury (1920–   )

The most admired American science fiction writer, Bradbury combines an elegant style with a deeply held moral concern for the quality of man's existence. Born in Waukegan, Illinois, he published his first short story when he was twenty-one years old and since then has been prolific. Bradbury works in many media, including television, radio, film, and theatre. His fiction is represented in *Best American Short Stories* of 1946, 1948 and 1952. Among his most famous novels and story collections are *The Martian Chronicles* (1950), *Dandelion Wine* (1957), *R Is for Rocket* (1962), *The Illustrated Man* (1951) and *Fahrenheit 451* (1953). The last two were made into films.

Willa Cather (1873–1947)

Born in Virginia, Miss Cather moved with her family to Red Cloud, Nebraska, in 1883. She graduated from the University of Nebraska in 1895, and for some years taught school and worked for small publications in Pittsburgh. The publication of a book of verse, *April Twilights* (1903), and a volume of short stories, *The Troll Garden* (1905), won her an editorship at *McClure's Magazine*, a prominent muckraking journal of the era which first published "The Sculptor's Funeral." After the publication of *Alexander's Bridge* (1912), she retired to devote herself exclusively to writing.

Although her first novel deals with the city, Miss Cather's fame rests primarily on her portrayal of the American West. Her tales are sophisticated examples of the American success story, in which the hero overcomes material obstacles through force of will. Her best known works are *My Antonia* (1918), *Death Comes for the Archbishop* (1927), and the Pulitzer Prize-winning *One of Ours* (1922).

Anton Chekhov (1860–1904)

A physician by profession, Chekhov used his literary talent to put himself through medical school. His first pieces were sketches for Moscow comic papers, and it was not until he had begun his medical practice that he scored his first literary success with *Particolored Stories* (1886), which won him an editorship of a literary supplement and eventually freed him from his physician's duties. By 1889 the author's mature style had developed: "A Dreary Story," published that year, is typically Chekhovian in its sombreness, for the working of large social forces upon the characters makes communication between them impossible. The plays upon which Chekhov's reputation rests were produced late in life.

The Seagull (1896) was a popular failure but a literary success, and secured the author's reputation in the new field. *The Three Sisters* and *Uncle Vanya* followed in 1901 and 1899 respectively; Chekhov was tricked into appearing on stage during the first performance of *The Cherry Orchard* shortly before his death in 1904.

Feodor Dostoevsky (1821-1881)

Nineteenth-century Russia produced many great writers, but none greater than Dostoevsky. Born and raised in Moscow, his life was filled with the kind of terrible events associated with fiction: for instance, while he was a boy, his father was murdered by his own serfs. Later, after serving in the army, Dostoevsky himself was arrested for political conspiracy and sentenced to death. As he faced the firing squad, a last-minute reprieve arrived from the Czar, who apparently never intended to have the execution carried out. The death sentence was commuted to five years' imprisonment at hard labor. The years in the Siberian prison became the basis for *The House of the Dead* (1862), the collection of prison stories and reminiscences from which "Akulka's Husband" is taken.

Dostoevsky's literary success began with his first novel, *Poor Folk* (1846). When he tried to resume his interrupted career after prison, however, the reviews he edited or contributed to failed. Finding himself sinking deeper and deeper into poverty, he nevertheless managed to write two long novels, *The Idiot* (1869) and *The Possessed* (1871). In an attempt to write his way out of debt, he produced at incredible speed *Crime and Punishment* (1866), one of the finest of all detective novels; *Notes from Underground* (1866), an unusual monologue; and *The Gambler* (1867), a study of a compulsive gambler, which was partly autobiographical. During his last years he returned to political favor, edited a conservative magazine and published several novels. The best of these, one of the world's great novels, is *The Brothers Karamazov* (1880), a searching examination of human character, personality and motivation.

Ralph Ellison (1914–   )

Born in Oklahoma City, Ellison early developed his musical talent and attended Tuskegee Institute, intending to become a composer. While on a visit to New York, he received encouragement from Richard Wright to become a writer. Since 1939, Ellison has written numerous short stories, essays and reviews. His excellent novel, *Invisible Man,* won the National Book Award for 1952 and continues to receive high critical praise. The novel recounts the odyssey of a black man's search for identity in race, politics, culture, religion and family. Beginning in the rural South and moving to the urban North, the novel presents a great variety of incident and character and is remarkable for the range and flexibility of its language. Undergirding the novel is Ellison's faith in the principles of freedom upon which the country was founded.

In 1964 Ellison collected many of his essays and reviews in *Shadow and Act,* but so far has not collected his several short stories. A popular lecturer, he has also held appointments at several American colleges and universities, such as Yale, Rutgers, Bennington and New York University.

William Faulkner (1897–1962)

One of the finest American novelists of the twentieth century, Faulkner was born and spent his life in central Mississippi. Leaving both high school and college before graduating, he served in the Royal Canadian Air Force during World War I. He began writing poetry and published *The Marble Faun*, a volume of poems, in 1924. A first novel, *Soldier's Pay,* appeared in 1926. His greatness as a writer rests on a series of novels and short stories that delve into the history of his imaginary Yoknapatawpha County and chronicle the elemental passions and conflicts of its people. In accepting the Nobel Prize in 1949, Faulkner said that he thought the subject of literature is "the human heart in conflict with itself." The best books in the series illustrate this conflict: *The Sound and the Fury* (1929), *As I Lay Dying* (1930), *Light in August* (1932), and *Absalom, Absalom!* (1936). Each of these works also demonstrates Faulkner's technical proficiency, often virtuosity. In 1954 his novel, *A Fable,* received the Pulitzer Prize.

Carlos Fuentes (1928–   )

One of Mexico's most exciting contemporary novelists, Fuentes is intimately involved with the cultural affairs of his country. He worked on cultural dissemination programs with the University of Mexico and the Mexican Ministry of Foreign Affairs. A critic as well as an author, he is an outstanding theorist of style and form in Latin American literature. In *La nueva novela hispanoamericana* (1969) he discusses the ideal style, which is a combination of detail and psychology. Among his fictional works are the short story collection *Cantar de ciego* (1964) and several novels. Among those translated into English are *Where the Air Is Clear* (1960), *The Death of Artemio Cruz* (1964), and *A Change of Skin* (1968).

John Hawkes (1925–   )

Hawkes's writing career dates from his undergraduate days at Harvard, a time when his memory was filled with the experience of being a World War II ambulance driver. His first novel, *The Cannibal* (1949), portrays a postwar Germany gripped by social and moral havoc, a havoc that becomes part of a vision of universal chaos afflicting, in subsequent works, Italy, England and America. All the works exhibit fragmentation, grotesque imagery, and an underlying sense of terror. These features give them a curiously modern Gothic flavor.

Later novels include *The Beetle Leg* (1951), *The Lime Twig* (1960), *Second Skin* (1964), and *The Blood Oranges* (1971). Hawkes has also written many stories and several plays. "Death of an Airman" is taken from the story and short novel collection, *Lunar Landscapes* (1963, 1969). Currently he teaches at Brown University.

Nathaniel Hawthorne (1804–1864)

Hawthorne grew up in Salem, Massachusetts, a once-proud town, but by the early nineteenth century of diminished economic and political importance. After graduating from Bowdoin College in Maine, he undertook a lonely, twelve-year, self-imposed apprenticeship in writing. The results of that period are to be seen in *Twice-Told Tales* (1837). In 1839 he worked for a year in the Boston Customs House, then moved to the experimental commune, Brook Farm. After leaving the community he married and settled in Concord, where he wrote *Mosses from an Old Manse* (1846). He then accepted a three-year appointment to the Salem Custom House and after that wrote *The Scarlet Letter* (1850), *The House of the Seven Gables* (1851), and *The Blithedale Romance* (1852). A college friend, President Franklin Pierce, appointed him to the American Consulate in Liverpool, thus enabling him to travel in Europe. While there, he wrote *The Marble Faun* (1860).

The finest craftman of the nineteenth-century New England writers, Hawthorne was surprised and delighted by the popular success of *The Scarlet Letter*. In a very short time he went from being "the obscurist man of letter in America" to being one of the most prominent. Many of his concerns for the moral nature of man so evident in stories and novels appear almost modern, and his employment of symbols and allegories continues to fascinate readers.

Ernest Hemingway (1899–1961)

The son of a doctor, Hemingway grew up in a fashionable Chicago suburb. After high school he joined the staff of the *Kansas City Star* and planned to become a journalist until World War I interrupted his career. He served as an ambulance driver in Italy, was wounded, and later joined the Italian army. When the war ended he became Paris correspondent for the Hearst newspapers. Again his career was interrupted as he became more and more involved with Gertrude Stein's Parisian circle of expatriate writers and artists. Soon he left reporting to devote full time to his literary career.

His early works, preoccupied as they are with violence, sterility and death, reflect many of his wartime experiences. The short story collection, *In Our Time* (1924), and the novel, *The Sun Also Rises* (1926), are known, in part, for their skillful portrayal of the atmosphere of post-World War I Europe. Later books include short story collections and several novels, *A Farewell to Arms* (1929), *For Whom the Bell Tolls* (1940) and the Pulitzer Prize-winning *The Old Man and the Sea* (1952). By the time Hemingway received the 1954 Nobel Prize in Literature, he was a legend; the spare, balanced style he created has had many imitators and has become an integral part of modern prose technique.

Aldous Huxley (1894–1963)

Born into a perennially distinguished British family, and given a traditional education at Eton and Oxford, Aldous Huxley was one of the twentieth century's most incisive social satirists. Pessimistic of the future, he criticized the scientific, social and political institutions that were incapable of dealing with contemporary human problems. In his youth Huxley served on the editorial staffs of various British periodicals but soon quit to write full time. During a long, full career he published poetry and drama, almost twenty collections of essays, several volumes of stories—including *Limbo* (1920), *Mortal Coils* (1922), which includes "Nuns at Luncheon," and *Young Archimedes* (1924)—and numerous novels among which are *Antic Hay* (1923), *Point Counter Point* (1928) and *Brave New World* (1932).

Huxley travelled throughout his life and lived for extended periods in France,

Mexico and the United States. In his later years he became interested in Eastern mysticism and drug-induced religious vision. *The Doors of Perception* (1954) and *Heaven and Hell* (1956) study the effects of mescaline. His last novel, *Island* (1962), combines these interests with the social concern of his early years, thus ending his writing career on a new, optimistic note.

Shirley Jackson (1919–1965)

Raised in California and New York, Miss Jackson attended Syracuse University. Her first literary success was "The Lottery" (1946), a highly sophisticated horror story. A strong interest in the occult dominates her work, contrasting sharply with a warm, lighthearted, comic strain. Her novels include *The Road Through the Wall* (1948), *Life Among the Savages* (1953), *We Have Always Lived in the Castle* (1962), and *The Haunting of Hill House* (1959), which was made into a film. Many of her early stories, including "After You, My Dear Alphonse," were collected in *Adventures of the Demon Lover* (1949).

James Joyce (1882–1941)

Joyce left Ireland in his early twenties and spent the rest of his life in the continental cities of Trieste, Rome, Paris and Zurich. He was an accomplished musician and linguist and was able to earn his living by giving language lessons and by translating. As his eyesight failed and a series of painful operations did not restore it, his writing became more and more aural.

The subject of his work was Ireland, specifically its capital city. Dublin provides the setting for *A Portrait of the Artist as a Young Man* (1914), is always in the foreground of *Ulysses* (1922), figures prominently in *Finnegans Wake* (1939) and is the focus for *Dubliners* (1914), the collection of short stories which includes "Araby." Joyce became aware early in his career of the possibilities Dublin held for his fiction. In 1905 he wrote his publisher, "I do not think that any writer has yet presented Dublin to the world." By the time he died he had presented the city and in the process helped shape modern literature.

It is difficult to overestimate the importance of Joyce for modern fiction. Many later writers are heavily in his debt. In his fiction Joyce combines an intense interest in specific, local incident, character and setting with an awareness of the power of artistic devices such as symbols, allusions, puns and parodies. In *Ulysses* he uses a different narrative technique and a different narrator for each chapter, and in his final work, *Finnegans Wake,* he recreates the history of the Western world through multilingual puns.

Franz Kafka (1883–1924)

Kafka's life was short, sad and inauspicious. He was born, lived and died in Prague, Czechoslovakia, where he studied law and worked in an accident insurance office. He wrote at night in his spare time and liked to share his fiction with a few friends. Publishing little during his life, he left instructions that after his death his manuscripts were to be destroyed. Fortunately, his literary executor disobeyed the instructions, and Kafka's work appeared posthumously over several years. A wide range of readers responded to the bizarre, neurotic, often wildly comic, qualities of Kafka's stories and novels.

Kaka's major works were not translated into English until several—in some cases many—years after he wrote them, and none appeared while he was alive. *The Castle* was translated in 1930, *The Trial* in 1937, *Amerika* in 1938, and *A Franz Kafka Miscellany* in 1940. The last includes many of his most famous sketches, paradoxes and stories. It is therefore important to recognize his startling prophetic originality for his descriptions of a world run by an inescapable and inaccessible bureaucracy often appear more contemporary than they actually were.

D. H. Lawrence (1885–1930)

The son of a coal miner from the industrial English Midlands, Lawrence captures the scenes and conflicts of his boyhood in several early works, most notably *Sons and Lovers* (1913). One of his prominent concerns is the volatile relationship between men and women, a theme he combines with a historical analysis of a typical Midlands family in *The Rainbow* (1915) and *Women in Love* (1920).

Lawrence graduated from Nottingham University and in 1914 married the daughter of a German baron, Frieda von Richthofen Weekley. Together they travelled the world, searching out the mystic and primitive. The importance of harmony between man and the forces of nature is explored in several essays and in the late novels, *The Plumed Serpent* (1926), *The Man Who Died* (1931) and *Lady Chatterley's Lover* (1928). One of the most prolific modern authors, Lawrence published poetry, stories, drama, travel books and essays in addition to his well-known novels.

John Lennon (1940–   )

A native of Liverpool, Lennon attended local schools, among them Liverpool Art College. Most famous as the oldest Beatle, he also acts, writes and makes films. He published two volumes of short fiction: *In His Own Write* (1964) in which "No Flies on Frank" appeared, and *A Spaniard in the Works* (1965); material from the first has been made into a one-act play.

Tom Mac Intyre (1930–   )

Poet, translator, novelist, storyteller, journalist and critic: these are some of the ways in which Tom Mac Intyre exercises his literary talent. A fine speaker of verse and prose, he has made several visits to lecture and teach in the United States. In the 1960's he gave up a secure teaching position for the less certain life of a writer. Among his books are a novel, *The Charollais* (1969), a collection of stories including "Stallions" entitled *Dance the Dance* (1969), an account of gun-running in Ireland, *Through the Bridewell Gate* (1971), translations from Gaelic poetry, *Blood Relations* (1972) and a play, *Eye-Winker, Tom-Tinker* (1972). There is a fine comic sense and an evident love of language in almost all of his writing.

Herman Melville (1819–1891)

Melville gleaned most of the material for his writing from the years he worked as a sailor. Born into genteel poverty, he ran away to sea at eighteen, signing on as cabin boy for a merchantman bound for Liverpool. From 1841–44 he served on a whaler and once spent several weeks living among the Tahitians. Out of his experience in Tahiti he wrote an immensely popular book, *Typee: A Real Romance of the South Seas* (1846). His subsequent novels and stories were less popular and became increasingly complex and metaphysical. After the loss of an audience, Melville lapsed into obscurity, ending his life as a customs inspector on the New York docks. Ironically, a hundred years after publication, *Moby Dick* (1851) and *The Confidence Man* (1857)—two novels rejected during Melville's lifetime—are widely read and viewed as highwater marks in American literature.

Joyce Carol Oates (1938–   )

Born and raised near Lockport, New York, Miss Oates graduated from Syracuse University in 1960. After graduate work at the University of Wisconsin, she taught at several American universities and is presently Associate Professor of English at the University of Windsor, Ontario, Canada. Recognition of Miss Oates's talent was rapid and extensive. Her stories appear with amazing regularity in *Best American Short Stories* of 1963, 1964, 1965, 1967, 1969 and 1970, and placed in the O. Henry Awards in 1963, 1964, 1965 and 1967. "Upon the Sweeping Flood" appeared in a collection of the same name, published in 1966. Other short story collections are *The Wheel of Love* (1970) and *Marriages and Infidelities* (1972). A prolific writer, her novel, *Them,* set in Detroit, won the National Book Award for 1970. Other novels include *With Shuddering Fall* (1964), *A Garden of Earthly Delights* (1967), *Expensive People* (1968) and *Wonderland* (1971). She also publishes collections of poetry and criticism.

Frank O'Conner (1903–1966)

"Frank O'Connor" is the pen name of Michael O'Donovan. Born in Cork, Ireland—a city which figures prominently in most of his writing—O'Connor was educated at Dublin University. Like many Irish writers he became involved in the nationalist movement which was trying to gain Ireland's independence. He also wrote and directed several plays for the Abbey Theatre in Dublin. His short stories were compared to those of Chekhov, and several prominent older writers encouraged his writing. In addition to the stories now collected in three volumes, O'Connor wrote numerous travel books, a few plays, translations of Gaelic poetry, *Kings, Lords, and Commons* (1959), personal reminiscences, *Mirror in the Roadway* (1956), a critical book on Shakespeare, *Shakespeare's Progress* (1960), and another, *The Lonely Voice* (1963) on the short story. In 1952 he moved to New York, where he spent the last years of his life. His autobiography, *An Only Child,* was published in 1961.

Tillie Olsen (1931–   )

Miss Olsen was born in Nebraska and moved with her family to San Francisco before she was two years old. She began writing in her late twenties after a varied career as waitress, factory worker, secretary and transcriber. Her short stories have been widely published and were chosen for inclusion in *Best American Short Stories* in 1957, 1964 and 1971. She has been Resident Scholar at Radcliffe Institute for Independent Studies and Creative Writing Fellow at Stanford University. In 1959 she received a Ford Foundation Fellowship, and in 1961 "Tell Me a Riddle" won the O'Henry Award as best story of the year. A collection of her stories, *Tell Me a Riddle,* was reissued in 1971. Miss Olsen lives and writes in San Francisco.

Caius Petronius (A.D. First Century)

Little is known about the life and personality of Petronius except for a brief sketch in the *Annals* of the Roman historian Tacitus. There Petronius is described as passing his days in sleep and his nights in the business and pleasures of life. His reputation as an arbiter of taste rested upon his refined sense of luxury. Nero employed him as chief of his revels, and for a time the emperor would not indulge in any excess or go to any entertainment unless Petronius approved. Petronius distinguished himself as proconsul and consul of Bithynia, where he successfully conducted government and business affairs. According to Tacitus, a political rival, jealous of Petronius' "expertise in the science of pleasure," denounced him to Nero, who sentenced him to death. Before he could be executed, however, Petronius took his own life in a leisurely fashion, spending his last hours chatting with friends, listening to light, comic verse and watching entertainments. The two literary works attributed to him are the *Satyricon* and a group of poems. The *Satyricon* is notable for its comedy, satire and characterization. Several episodes, such as "Dinner with Trimalchio" and "The Widow of Ephesus," may be viewed as independent stories embedded in the loose narrative line.

Edgar Allan Poe (1809-1849)

Poe's life was a dreary one of poverty, pathos and hard work. The orphaned son of a professional actor and actress, he was raised and educated in the home of a wealthy Richmond merchant which he left after an argument over gambling debts. Enlisting in the army at eighteen, he later entered West Point, but quickly changed his mind and withdrew. During these turbulent years his first volume of poems, *Tamerlane,* was published (1827) and further editions were issued in 1829 and 1831. Poe's short stories were collected and published during his lifetime as *Tales of the Grotesque and Arabesque* (1840). But it was not until the publication of *The Raven and Other Poems* (1945) that he received any genuine recognition. In the interim he supported himself through editorships and general literary hack work; many of his influential comments on prose technique originally appeared in book reviews and editorials. When he was only forty years old, Poe died in Baltimore under sordid circumstances having been trapped into drinking too much alcohol.

Florence Engel Randall (1929-   )

After a successful career as a short story writer for magazines such as *Harper's, Redbook* and *Ladies' Home Journal,* Mrs. Randall began writing novels. *Hedgerow* appeared in 1967, followed by *The Place of Sapphires* (1969) and *The Almost Year* (1971). Several of her articles on writing have been published by *The Writer.*

Saki (Hector Hugh Munro, 1870-1916)

Born in Burma, the son of a police official, Munro returned to his native Britain for his education. In 1908 he settled in London after serving several years as a foreign correspondent in Russia, the Balkans, and Paris. Out of this experience he wrote *The Rise of the Russian Empire* (1916), a serious historical work. Munro's fiction is in quite another vein, however. Filled with comedy, satire and fantasy, the primary aim of most of his stories is to burlesque pretension and stupidity, yet often a note of horror and cruelty creeps in. Besides his numerous stories, collected posthumously as *The Short Stories of Saki* (1930), he published a novel, *The Unbearable Bassington* (1914). He was killed in France during World War I.

Issac Bashevis Singer (1904–   )

Singer, the son and grandson of rabbis, received an orthodox Jewish rabbinical education in his native Poland. Writing first in Hebrew, he later changed to Yiddish. His first novel, *Satan in Goray*, was published in 1935, the same year in which he emigrated to the United States, where he joined the staff of the *Jewish Daily Forward. Gimpel the Fool*, a volume of short stories, appeared in 1957, followed by *The Spinoza of Market Street* (1961) and *Short Friday* (1969). In addition to these collections of short fiction, Singer has published several novels, the most noted of which are *The Family Muskat* (1949), *The Magician of Lublin* (1960), *The Slave* (1962), *and Enemies: A Love Story* (1972).

Dylan Thomas (1914–1953)

One of the most popular modern poets and public readers of poetry, Thomas, the son of a schoolteacher, was born in Swansea, Wales. Although he gained a wide audience in Great Britain through his BBC radio programs and in the United States from his unusually successful reading tours, he always returned to Wales as the source of his artistic inspiration and personal pleasure. After working in film, radio and journalism he settled permanently in Laugharne, a tiny Welsh fishing village. There, in a small storage shed converted into a workroom, he wrote his poems and stories. A meticulous craftsman, Thomas would sometimes revise a poem a hundred times before being satisfied that it was what he wanted. The Welsh atmosphere which permeates his poetry is equally important in his fiction. Besides *The Collected Poems of Dylan Thomas*, published the year of his death, there is the fictional autobiography, *Portrait of the Artist as a Young Dog* (1940); a collection of radio broadcasts later expanded to include essays and stories, such as "A Story," *Quite Early One Morning* (1954); what may well be the finest modern radio play, *Under Milk Wood* (1954); the two film scripts, *Twenty-Years A-Growing* and *The Doctor and the Devils* (1953); a volume of letters; a collection of short stories, *Adventures in the Skin Trade* (1955); and a miscellany of fiction and prose writings, *A Prospect of the Sea* (1955). Several recordings of Thomas reading poetry and prose are available.

Eudora Welty (1909–   )

A Mississippian by birth and inclination, Miss Welty is rooted in the life of the Deep South. Like Faulkner, she works with local characters and situations, but unlike him she shows little concern for larger social and historical forces; her work emanates from a deeply personal human response to her environment.

She attended Mississippi State College for Women, the University of Wisconsin, and Columbia University. For a time she worked in an advertising agency, but soon left to devote full time to her writing. In 1943 she placed first in the annual O. Henry Awards, and that same year received a Guggenheim Fellowship. Since then she has continuously produced stories and novels. Among the novels are *Delta Wedding* (1946), *The Golden Apples* (1949), *The Ponder Heart* (1954), *Losing Battles* (1971), which was subsequently dramatized for the theatre, and *The Optimist's Daughter* (1972). Miss Welty lives now in her birthplace, Jackson, Mississippi.

John A. Williams (1925–   )

Born in Jackson, Mississippi, Williams grew up in Syracuse, New York, where he did undergraduate and graduate work at the university there. From 1960 to 1970 he wrote or edited ten books, including five novels: *The Angry Ones* (1960), *Night Song* (1961), *Sissie* (1963), *The Man Who Cried I Am* (1967) and *Sons of Darkness, Sons of Light* (1969). He also edited the influential anthology, *The Angry Black* (1962), which four years later he revised as *Beyond the Angry Black* (1966). A former Director of Information for the American Committee on Africa, he travelled throughout much of Africa reporting for *Newsweek* in 1964 and gathering material for a 1965 television production. Some of his later books include *The King God Didn't Save* (1970), *This Is My Country Too* (1965) and a novel, *Captain Blackman* (1972).

Giovanni Verga (1840–1922)

Verga began writing popular novels but later introduced a terse psychological style that brought a lessening of popularity but wide critical acclaim. A Sicilian, his best novels and stories portray accurately and sympathetically his island peasant population. His affinity for the simple and primitive so attracted D. H. Lawrence that Lawrence translated several Verga volumes, including *Maestro-Don Gesualdo* (1923), *Little Novels of Sicily* (1925), and *Cavalleria Rusticana and Other Stories* (1928). Two excellent recent translations of important Verga works are *The House by the Medlar Tree (I Malavoglia)*, published in 1964, and *The She-Wolf and Other Stories* (1958).